**Two couples brought together
by baby bonds
in...**

The Baby
ConneCtion

A child can unite a family in unexpected ways!

GW00362191

Next month, don't miss

The Baby Connection: Twins!

featuring

My Husband, My Babies by Debra Salonen

Unexpected Babies by Anna Adams

The Baby Connection

PEGGY NICHOLSON

MARISA CARROLL

*M&B™ and M&B™ with the Rose Device
are trademarks of the publisher.
Harlequin Mills & Boon Limited, Eton House,
18-24 Paradise Road, Richmond, Surrey TW9 1SR*

THE BABY CONNECTION © by Harlequin Books S.A. 2008

The Baby Bargain © Peggy Nicholson 2000
Little Girl Lost © Carol I Wagner and Marian L Franz 2003

ISBN: 978 0 263 86593 6

024-0308

*Harlequin Mills & Boon policy is to use papers that are
natural, renewable and recyclable products and made from
wood grown in sustainable forests. The logging and
manufacturing processes conform to the legal environmental
regulations of the country of origin.*

*Printed and bound in Spain
by Litografia Rosés S.A., Barcelona*

The Baby Bargain

PEGGY NICHOLSON

This book is for my dad, Erwin Grimes of Kerrville, Texas, who gave me my wings.

And as always, Ron. Thank you.

CHAPTER ONE

A YEAR AGO TODAY, St. Patrick's Day, he and his dad had sat here in this booth, eating bacon cheeseburgers. Guys' Night Out, his dad had called it, and he'd ordered the jumbo basket of onion rings, then winked at Sean, both of them knowing that if they'd brought Dana along, she would have fussed about too much grease and cholesterol.

That was the last meal they'd ever shared. Sean had slept over in town that night with the Wilsons, though he'd protested that he was old enough to stay by himself out at the Ribbon R for a three-day weekend. "Or you could take me with you," he'd pleaded, not for the first time. "It's not like missing one crummy Friday is going to hurt my grades." He'd been a straight-A student last year in ninth grade, when things like that mattered. Seemed to matter.

If you'd taken me along... He'd never have let it happen. Somehow Sean felt that if he'd been with them, he'd have known not to cross that hillside. Or if it had happened—the avalanche—he'd never have quit—never, ever, *never*—till he found his dad and dug him free. Not like Dana, who hadn't dug deep enough, fast enough, long enough. Stupid, gutless Dana, who quit and skiied off for the help that came too late.

Quitter. Anger felt like a lump of smoldering charcoal in his stomach, gray-white dust over a ruby center. He picked up his glass of soda and took a tiny sip—had to make it last—then jumped as Judy, the night waitress at Moe's Truckstop, loomed up behind him.

"Here, you're done with that, kiddo." She reached for his plate, which still held a curl of limp lettuce and a slice of tomato.

"Am not!" He caught hold of it and glared up at her. He didn't have enough money to order anything else, but he was darned if he'd leave yet. The Ribbon R was nothing but an aching and an emptiness. Nobody but Dana and her loudmouth baby waiting there for him.

"Suit yourself." Judy shrugged and turned to welcome the group coming through the arch from the front room—the convenience store Moe ran—of the truck stop. "Sit anywhere you like," she called, and headed toward the counter where she kept the menus.

Kids from school, Sean realized, watching them as they chose the big circular booth on the far side of the café. Seniors. They didn't spare him a glance. The biggest guy, a football jock, maneuvered his date with a possessive hand at the small of her slender back.

The skin on Sean's palm tingled as if it slid across silk. He curled his fingers hard around the feeling, making a fist, as the jock's date smiled up at him and edged into the booth. She wore a long, slinky yellow dress, with a dyed green carnation pinned between her breasts. Sean swallowed with an audible gulp, wondering if she had let the jock pin it on her—the lucky stiff—then jumped as the three boys at the table swung their heads to fix him with cold, unblinking stares.

Caught me looking. Wishing. He turned back to his plate and hunched his shoulders. With the girls' giggles sounding like sleigh bells behind him, he felt his face grow hot, then hotter. Frantically he grabbed his drink and rubbed the misty glass across his cheek. Oh, no, was the back of his neck turning red?

"California," one of the guys jeered, not bothering to lower his voice.

Almost a curse word, Sean had learned since he'd moved here from San Diego two years ago. Coloradans thought Californians were buying up every last acre of their lousy state that the Texans hadn't already grabbed. Though who in his right mind would want it? *If I had my way, I'd go back to San Diego in a heartbeat.* He would, too, any day now, as soon as his mother felt well enough to take him. A wave of emotion swept through him, like a black hole yawning wide; greasy slopes led down into his own private darkness. He closed his eyes tight and waited for the feeling to pass.

"Sean?" Judy patted his shoulder. "Your mama's on the phone." She nodded toward the corridor that led to the rest rooms and the pay phone.

"My—" Hope flew up like a startled bird—then fell as he realized. "My stepmother, you mean."

"That nice, nice lady named Dana, who your daddy liked enough to marry—yep, that one. She wants you."

"Tell her I'm not here," he blurted desperately.

"Ha! I'm not your press secretary, Mr. President. Tell her yourself."

He kept his eyes on his sneakers as he casually crossed the room, but he stole a glance over his shoulder as he reached the hallway.

The three girls in the booth were all primped up, wearing fancy dresses in bright colors. The St. Patrick's Day dance was tonight, he remembered. Another reason he'd felt blue today. *I wonder if I'll ever have a date.* The few friends he'd made in his first year at the high school he'd lost, because he just couldn't make himself care. The only girl he really talked to was Zoe, but she was a senior and his boss on the yearbook. The head editor. Nobody a sopho-more could ever date.

The receiver of the wall-mounted pay phone dangled at knee level. He sighed and picked it up. "'Lo."

"Sean?" Dana's low voice hummed with tension.

"Yeah." He should have just hung up on her. He sighed again and swung around to slouch against the rough plaster.

"You...didn't come home."

Yeah, no fooling, Sherlock. He didn't say anything.

"Did you miss your bus?"

I gave it a miss, right. If there was one day of the year he couldn't stand the sight of Dana...that he needed to spend by himself, this was it. Crappy St. Patrick's Day. "Looks like it, doesn't it."

He heard her sigh down the telephone line. "I can't pick you up, Sean. We have guests tonight—for the whole week—skiers. I'm just about to put supper on the table."

"Doesn't matter." In San Diego he could have taken a cab home, the way his mother always did when she'd partied too much. In Trueheart, Colorado, it'd be easier to catch a coyote and ride it home. Or hitch. "I'll manage."

"Judy gets off work at ten. She said she'd be happy to give you a ride."

No way. He'd rather walk ten miles in the snow and slush than listen to one of Judy's pull-up-your-socks pep talks. "Don't worry about it. I'll manage."

"Sean, honey, *please.* Come home. I know what you're—"

"No. You don't." He replaced the receiver on its hook with stony deliberation—it was that or smash it against the phone, then keep on smashing till he held nothing but splinters. *No, you don't.* He was standing, staring at his fingers curled around the black plastic, when an icy draft brushed his cheek.

Someone coming through the fire exit at the end of the hallway, he saw from the corner of his eye. She slammed the door behind her and stood panting, one hand pressed to her throat—long, tall Zoe Montana, reminding him of a

Christmas tree with her shiny green dress and her carrot-red hair. He felt better already, just looking at her.

"Oh, *rats!*" she said. Her fine, goldy-red eyebrows drew into a scowl. "You didn't see me."

"I didn't?" She was hard to miss. She was taller than his five foot six-and-a-half inches by several more, though he was all muscle while she was all freckly skin and bones—most of that leg, like one of those big wading birds. *A stork on fire*, the captain of the football team had called her once in the cafeteria, and everybody had laughed.

She let out a long-suffering sigh, the way she did when one of the airheads on the yearbook staff failed to meet a section deadline, and hooked a thumb at the door to the ladies'. "Is anybody in there?"

"Uh, don't think so."

"Thank *God*." She slipped around the door and vanished.

Sean crossed his arms, leaned back against the wall and waited. Zoe Montana was maybe the only person in Trueheart worth talking to.

She came out a few minutes later, looking less wild eyed. More like the yearbook editor about to give her most junior photographer a shooting assignment. But then, Zoe's assignments were always interesting. She was the smartest girl—the smartest *person*—in their whole regional high school, and that probably included the teachers.

"What are you doing here?" he asked. And in a long, silky dress. She always wore slacks or jeans to school, with bulky sweaters and funky lace-up knee boots. Or clunky Steve Maddens, which raised her height to over six feet, when she was in a mood to kick butt. Idly he lifted his fingers, shaping a square to frame her, and wished he had his camera. It was the first time he'd ever realized Zoe was more than funny looking. *Snckk.* He took a mental photograph.

"Is there anybody out there?" Zoe nodded toward the café. "Anybody from school, I mean?"

"Some jocks and jock-bunnies, eating supper before the dance." The dance that Zoe must be going to, also, Sean realized with quickening interest. He didn't know she had a boyfriend. Who would be sharp enough to keep up with her?

"Shoot. I'm dying for a cup of coffee." She sagged back against the opposite wall.

"Then come have one with me." He was astonished at his own daring—then his heart sank as he remembered. *Crap!* He had less than a dollar left.

"Thanks, but..." She shook her head. "I'm not in the mood for company." Her eyes sharpened on his face. "I mean the kind of company in there." She crossed her forefingers between them. "No clowns tonight. Not one more."

"Oh." He had clowning down to an art form, but he didn't think she meant him. Still, Sean felt like a bozo, with nothing more to say. "I guess you're going to the dance?" He threw out the question at random.

"I guess I'm *not*."

"But you're all..." He waved his hand, taking in her finery. She even had boobs, he realized, stealing a peek at the gap between the long lapels of the coat that matched her party dress. Not honkers, but somehow right for Zoe. Her clothes had always disguised them before.

"The creep stood me up—okay?" she said between clenched teeth.

"Or maybe he had car trouble," Sean suggested, wanting to wipe that look of angry humiliation off her face. She didn't deserve to be stood up just because she was too tall and too smart for her own good.

"No, I finally called his house. His little brother told me he had a date with Amanda Clayton and that he'd already left.'' Zoe stared blankly down at the toes of her green high heels.

Amanda Clayton? A babe, if Sean had ever seen one. Little and brunette and cuddly. *And dumb as a post.* Her longtime steady had rolled his car after a party last weekend, Sean had heard, and was in the hospital down in Durango with both legs in casts. High school dances were like a game of musical chairs, he'd always thought, and this time poor Zoe was left standing. Stork ablaze. "So why didn't you just…'' *Call me?* He'd have been happy to help her out.

"Stay home? Right, and tell my dad why? He'd have stomped down to the gym and dragged Bobbie out by his ear. Or maybe shot him. I have enough to live down without that, thank you. So I—'' Zoe shrugged and turned toward the fire exit. "I've got to go.'' She spun back again, tottered on her heels, and braced one long arm out against the wall. "Oh, and Sean, do me a favor? You never saw me.''

She must be just riding around, he realized, killing time till it was safe to go home. "Then how about a favor for a favor?'' Her embarrassment made him feel bolder. "Could you give me a ride out to the ranch? There's no hurry,'' he added, as she opened her mouth. "You could drop me at my turnoff out on the highway—any time tonight at all.''

She closed her soft pink lips and cocked her head, studying him. Being Zoe, he knew, she saw more than he wanted to show. He shrugged and held her blue-eyed gaze with an effort.

"Yeah, I could do that,'' she said thoughtfully, her eyes turning inward in that look that usually ended in another crazy assignment for him—like the time she'd hidden him in the ceiling above the teachers' lounge to take candid photos. "I'd be happy to.''

Two hours of cruising around in Zoe's baby-blue antique Mustang. Sean had held his breath when they drove past the small sign out on the highway that said Ribbon River Dude Ranch, 4 miles, Guests Welcome, but Zoe had given him a sideways smile and had kept on driving. All the way to Cortez, where they bought hamburgers and French fries—Zoe's treat—at the drive-through window in the McDonald's. They ate in the parking lot while they punched the buttons on her car radio, ceaselessly scanning the airwaves for anything but country music. Sean preferred hard rock, golden oldies, songs that reminded him of the West Coast; Zoe liked anything with a Latin sound. Her mother had been Hispanic, Sean remembered her telling him once while they developed film in the school dark-room. That was another thing they shared, besides their impatience with small-town life: they'd both lost a parent; though Zoe's mom had died ages ago, when she was six.

Driving back, they passed the Ribbon R again. "You don't want to go home yet," Zoe said, and it wasn't quite a question. She drove almost halfway to town, then flipped on her blinker as they neared the turnoff to the private airport that lay a few miles to the south. Sean felt his stomach jump, then swarm with butterflies. Surely she couldn't mean to—

But she did. Zoe chose the left-hand fork in the road, which wound around the back side of the airport, and stopped at the far end of the north-south runway, where the road skirted the edge of a bluff. She parked facing the drop-off, with the far-off lights of Trueheart twinkling in the thin mountain air like diamonds scattered in the snow. Two other cars were parked at discreet intervals along the over-look. Sean stole a glance at the one on his right, but its windows were too steamed up for him to see anything.

"I come here in summer to watch the planes take off," Zoe said, ignoring their neighbors. "Did you ever do that?

They zoom right overhead. It feels like they're going to snap off your antenna they fly so low—then *whoosh*—they're out there beyond you and gone.''

"Wow." His throat was too dry, and his mind a blank. What did she want from him?

"I'm going to fly away like that one of these days. Soon. I just got admitted to Harvard—early admission. Did I tell you that?''

She hadn't, but he'd heard. The whole school had been abuzz with the news last week. Nobody from their school had ever been admitted to Harvard. And Zoe Montana was the baby of her class, a year younger than the next youngest senior—not even seventeen yet, since she'd skipped a grade of school back in elementary.

"That'll be neat.'' For her. For him it meant he'd have zero friends next year, instead of one. "I wish I could fly away.'' His mother's last letter from the health spa had said he should be patient, finish the tenth grade in Colorado. But after that, surely she'd agree that he belonged with her. If he belonged anywhere.

"Yeah,'' Zoe murmured without conviction, then said it again, louder and brighter. "Yeah! Boston...Harvard... Everything's going to be different then. Better.''

He glanced at her, surprised. What was wrong with her life now? She had an overdose of brains. A grudging respect in the school, if not popularity. A rich rancher daddy who loved her—he must love her to have given her this wonderful car. And she was escaping Southwest Colorado, going off to the real world where exciting things happened. She was practically grown up, practically free, while he—he was trapped here in Nowhere City. Trapped by his own age—couldn't drive, couldn't drink, couldn't vote, couldn't hold a real job. Couldn't choose with whom he wanted to live. His dad had appointed Dana his guardian, and had never once asked Sean what he thought about that.

"Oh, rats, rats, *rats!*" Zoe started the Mustang, reversed it hastily onto the road, then popped it into forward gear. The tires slipped on an icy rut, then caught, and they zoomed off around the perimeter road.

"Hey, your headlights!" Sean reached for the switch, and she batted his hand aside.

"Uh-uh! Look behind you."

Sean turned—to see that a car had stopped behind the first car back at the bluff. A spotlight switched on, illuminating the luckless couple twined together in the backseat. "The sheriff!"

"Nosy Noonan. And he's a friend of my dad's." Zoe passed the first hangar and hung a hard right, driving along the far side of the building toward the airfield, then tucked her Mustang in neatly ahead of a pickup truck set up as a snowplow.

The giant curved blade blocked Sean's view of the road entirely, provided perfect cover. "Whew!" She was clever.

"Get down, get *down!*" she cried in a giggling frenzy. "If he shines his light…!" She leaned sideways toward him over the gearshift, her frizzy hair brushing his knees. Sean laughed and hunched down over her, his chest pressed against her quivering shoulder. He stayed there that way, in a state of total bliss, long after the sheriff's car had cruised past. Her shampoo smelled of lemon and a spice Dana used sometimes in her cooking; rosemary, that was it. Something soft was touching his thigh, and he thought— hoped—prayed—it was her breast.

"Is it safe to come out?" she asked finally in a muffled voice.

"I think…" Except he wasn't. He was absorbed totally in feeling all the wonderful sensations of a warm girl sprawled across his lap. Zoe. Her giggles made her seem younger, more his own age than an impossible two years older.

She jabbed an elbow gently into his ribs, and he had to sit up. Curling one hand around his thigh just above his knee, she pushed herself upright—then slowly turned her head to look at him over her right shoulder. Their lips were only inches apart.

Every muscle in his legs tensed and hardened. Heat pooled in his lap. *Oh, Zoe!*

She pulled completely away from him and sat, clutching her steering wheel, staring out through the windshield.

He counted his own heartbeats, dizzy from the lack of blood in his head. *What do you want from me, Zoe Montana?* Anything, anything at all that she wanted, he'd give—and give gladly.

"Want to see a special place?" she said finally, not looking at him, her voice sounding funny. "My special place?"

TEN MINUTES LATER they sat in the cockpit of a wrecked Cessna, which was parked on the far side of the hangar. Zoe had claimed the pilot's seat, which to Sean seemed only fitting. She could take him anywhere she wanted tonight.

They even had supplies for their journey. Zoe had pulled two down sleeping bags, and a sack that contained water and granola bars, from the trunk of her car—part of a safety kit her father made her carry in winter, in case she ever was caught out in a blizzard.

"I found this last fall." Zoe stroked the Cessna's steering yoke. "Some elk hunter flipped it coming in for a landing. He walked away and swore he'd never fly again. Something's twisted in the frame. Luke, the mechanic here, bought it cheap from the insurance company. Said he's going to fix it one of these days. But meanwhile she just sits here, all lonely."

"Cool." In every sense of the word. Huddled in his ski

jacket, Sean was starting to shiver, partly from the cold, partly from excitement.

"I'm going to be a pilot someday," Zoe said dreamily. "Dad promised he'd pay for my flying lessons when I graduate from college."

And *his* dad had promised that when Sean graduated from high school, he'd give Sean a motorcycle, an old Harley he could fix up himself. That they'd ride together all the way up to Alaska, then back again, the summer after his senior year. Dreams...so fragile that a mound of moving snow could crush them. The snowbound runway beyond the windshield shimmered, then blurred, and Sean blinked frantically. "So tell me about college, what that'll be like."

"College..." She tipped back her head and stared up at the dented ceiling. "It's going to be...different. Very, *very*...different."

"Different how?"

She turned to fix him with her wide, light eyes, and was quiet so long that he wondered if he'd said something really stupid. "I'm freezing," she said at last. "Want to get into the bags?"

They zipped themselves into the puffy down bags and sat shoulder to shoulder in the wide, flat space in the rear that once must have held passenger seats.

"Much better," Zoe murmured, leaning against him. She sighed contentedly. "Mmm...how will college be different? Well, for starters, nobody's going to call me a brain, or a grind or a teacher's pet at Harvard. I won't be a freak. I'll be normal."

Just as he had been a normal kid, back in San Diego, before Dana married his dad and lured them off to Colorado. "That's good."

"Yeah...and maybe I'll throw all my clothes away and start over. No more thumbing my nose at the cowgirls and the cheerleaders. I want a whole new image—sleek, elegant, sophisticated. I'm going to scout the campus for a day or two when I get there. Before I check in. See what everybody's wearing…''

He was so used to Zoe's rebel tomboy looks that it was hard picturing her dressing to blend in, but Sean knew what she meant. You got tired of fighting, but what else could you do? Once they had you pigeonholed, they'd laugh at you even harder if you tried to change. If he broke down and bought a Stetson and boots like the cow-patty crowd wore, that wouldn't get him accepted now. They'd brand him as a phony—and a coward.

''And maybe I'll switch to using my middle name. Elena.'' She gave it the Spanish pronunciation, making it sound rich and exotic.

I'd miss "Zoe." But he nodded gravely. A fresh start; it was what he wanted, too. ''Elena—it's pretty.''

''And…'' She tipped her head down to rest it against his shoulder. ''Promise you won't tell anyone?''

''I swear.'' He drew a shaky breath and, holding it, put his arm around the soft, puffy expanse of her waist. When she didn't stiffen, didn't pull away—actually seemed to settle a little closer against him—he felt as if the Cessna had taken off. He was floating, flying… ''I swear I won't.''

''I'm thinking of dyeing my hair. Black. Or maybe an auburn so dark it's practically black.''

He loved her crazy red hair, loved the fact that, in her own way, she was a freak like him, a fish in the wrong pond. Even holding her, he felt a wave of loneliness wash over him. She was soaring away, off to somewhere she'd fit in, while he—

''You think that's crazy?'' Zoe demanded in a tiny, dubious voice.

While he—he was her friend. Here to back her up, even when she was crazy—and dyeing her fire-engine-red curls was the worst kind of crazy crime. "No... No, I don't think so. I think you'd look wonderful with black hair," he lied. "Or maybe...um...auburn? That might be an even better idea." At least, less of a crime.

"Good!" she laughed delightedly. "I'm *so* glad you think so!" Somehow she'd slipped down to half-lie across his lap—the nylon bags were slippery. She squirmed around to rest her head across his thighs, smiling up at him. "And that brings me to one last little thing I mean to change."

He stared down at her, helplessly, hopelessly enthralled. "W-what?"

"I thought maybe you could help me with this..." She stared up at him, smiling no longer, then reached up to finger the collar of his jacket. "You see...the problem is...I'm still a virgin."

CHAPTER TWO

WHEN MITZY BARLOW invited him over for Saturday supper, the first week in June, Rafe Montana had gone gladly, anticipating an evening of hot, no-holds-barred sex.

Instead she'd served pot roast.

She'd served it up with such a hopeful, fluttery smile—fussing over the homey details like candles on the table, bran rolls she'd baked herself, glazed carrots just like the ones he'd enjoyed in the restaurant last week when he took her out on their first date—that Rafe realized immediately, with a sinking heart, that this wasn't to be a simple night of fun between two healthy, sensible adults who knew precisely what they wanted.

Oh, no, this was an audition. Along with the peas, pot roast and carrots, Mitzy was dishing out all the unspoken reasons she'd make a good—no, a perfect—wife. *His* perfect wife.

How could a man so misread a woman's intentions? Rafe wondered, scowling through the windshield as his headlights fled before him up the valley. He would have sworn from the way she talked last week—hell, from the way she came on to him—that they were in complete agreement. After dinner they'd danced, and you couldn't have wedged an ace of hearts between them, the way she'd melted into his arms. And later, when he'd walked her to her door, Mitzy had made it crystal clear what she wanted. While he kissed her good-night, she'd drawn the hand he'd placed lightly on her shoulder down to her breast—then held it there while she moaned and squirmed against him. He'd felt plain apologetic, when he came up for air, explaining that he couldn't stay. That since he hadn't presumed to make arrangements for someone to sleep over with his daughter out at Suntop Ranch, he had to go home to Zoe.

Mitzy had caught him off guard on their first date. But this Saturday, when she'd insisted in a husky voice that it was *her* turn to entertain *him,* he'd come prepared. At his pointed suggestion, Zoe was sleeping over in Trueheart tonight with her best friend, Lisa Harding. And yesterday he'd stopped by the barber's for a trim, a week before his usual cut. Plus he'd shaved for the second time today, just before setting out. And along with a thirty-dollar bottle of French wine, he'd brought a wallet full of condoms.

But then Mitzy served pot roast—her great-grandmother Barlow's recipe. Rafe had sat there at the table with his expectant grin fading on his face, wondering if he should tell her how he felt before the meal. Or after.

Like all men, he was a coward when it came to hurting a woman, so he'd opted for after, praying with each bite of overdone beef that he was wrong. That Mitzy just liked to cook. Or that maybe she was building up his strength for the evening's entertainment.

No such luck. Along with the strawberry shortcake, their limping conversation had taken a turn for the worse. Mitzy had started quizzing him on Zoe. How had he ever *managed,* raising a small daughter alone out on a ranch miles from anywhere, without even a neighbor's wife to give him advice?

She'd shaken her head and smiled knowingly when he'd insisted they'd managed just fine. Seeing that smirk, he'd felt his temper rise. No one had better hint to *him* that he hadn't done his best for Zoe. He'd shaped his whole life around her from the very start.

And he hadn't been fool enough to try to raise her alone,

though he owed Mitzy no explanation and so had given none. He'd recruited Mrs. Higgins to be their live-in house-keeper after Pilar's death, and that arrangement had worked out fine.

At least it had up until last year, when Mrs. Higgins had fallen head over heels for the new county agent and, after thirty years a widow, remarried. Since then, she could only come three days a week to cook and clean, but neither Zoe nor he would have dreamed of trying to replace her. After all these years, she was family. Besides, by this time Zoe hardly needed constant supervision.

"But if it wasn't so bad before," insisted Mitzy, "what about now, now that she's...um...a young lady?" Didn't Rafe find himself at a loss dealing with sex and the other issues a young woman faced?

"When it comes to the birds and the bees, ranch kids learn most of the answers before town kids think up the questions," Rafe had observed dryly. As to other issues— things a teenage daughter wouldn't care to discuss with her own father—she could take those to Mrs. Higgins.

Besides, though this was nothing he'd share with Mitzy, Zoe was maturing late. That date earlier this spring, for the St. Patrick's Day dance, had been her first real night out. And apparently nothing had come of it. The kid—what had his name been—Bobbie?—must not have measured up. Which hardly surprised Zoe's father. She had been chosen valedictorian of her class this spring, just as he'd predicted. He'd been so puffed up with pride, watching her give the graduation address last week, he'd thought he might burst. But where was a girl like that going to find someone to match her in a small town like Trueheart? It was one more reason he'd pushed her to apply to Harvard.

"But now that she's interested in boys, don't you think she needs advice on how to dress, how to behave...how to flirt?" Mitzy demanded.

"She's not interested. Not yet," he said to close off this line of inquisition. He felt his teeth come together with a *click* when Mitzy burst out laughing.

"At sixteen? Of course she is, Rafe! And if you think she isn't, that just shows how out of touch you really are."

He kept the edge out of his voice with an effort. "She's been pushing herself hard in school these past four years, Mitzy. Really hard. She has won national awards four years running in the science fairs. And then with her extracurricular work—the yearbook and choir. And volunteering down at the hospital in Durango—"

"But I suppose Zoe knows you'd disapprove of her choice," Mitzy mused, ignoring him entirely. "I imagine any young man who dared to date *your* daughter would have to pass a pretty fierce inspection at the door."

She had that double-damn right, at least. But that was beside the point. As yet, there were no randy young studs sniffing after Zoe for him to check out. Zoe was too busy being a tomboy and a scholar. "That doesn't leave much time for boys," he finished, and smacked down his coffee cup. End of subject.

"Oh, there's *always* time for boys," Mitzy purred, rising from the table. She came up behind him, and, resting one hand possessively on his shoulder, reached around him for the dessert he'd barely touched. Her forearm drew across his chest, and her breast brushed the back of his arm.

Rafe felt himself stiffen all over. He went too long between women. Managing a spread the size of Suntop Ranch, he had little time or energy left to go courting in town, where the available women were. And bringing a lover back to the ranch, with his daughter living there, had never been an acceptable solution. At least that would be changing soon, when Zoe went off to college.

"Let's have our brandy in front of the fire, shall we?" Mitzy said from the counter, lifting two balloon glasses.

Rafe sighed and followed her to her big couch in the living room, which he'd noted with approval only an hour ago when he first arrived. One reason he went a long time between lovers was that he refused to play the games that some men played. He couldn't stomach stringing a woman along, pretending to agree with her dreams when he was after something else entirely.

Still, though he believed in straight talk, he hesitated. Telling another person that you knew what she wanted, before she'd declared herself, felt downright rude. On the other hand, maybe these tippy-toe hints were as close to a declaration as Mitzy could come.

She handed him his brandy, then clinked her glass against his. *"To us,"* she said softly, and held his gaze over the rim as she drank. She licked her upper lip, then smiled a slow invitation.

But Rafe was stuck back on "us." There was no "us" yet, as far as he was concerned. "Us" sounded like a matched pair in harness trotting down the long, long road together. *No, thanks, Mitzy.* She was moving way too fast. "To good times," he said firmly.

"What about you?" Mitzy murmured, snuggling back into the hollow of his shoulder. "With your chick leaving the nest in September, won't you be terribly...lonely?"

"No." He finished half his glass in a gulp, and straightened the arm she was leaning against along the top of the sofa, making himself into a hard, unbending corner. "I won't be." At least, he thought not. "You've got to understand, Mitzy. I've been sitting on that...nest for almost seventeen years." Hatching his one fabulous, freckled egg for the past ten years all by himself, except for Mrs. Higgins. "I was nineteen when Zoe was born."

"That must have been *so* hard," she said softly. "But I suppose the good side of it is, now you're still a young

man. Why, you even have time to start a second family, if
you feel like it.''

"What I feel like, after all this time of being a responsible, hard-working daddy, is taking a break,'' he said
bluntly. "Being footloose and fancy free. Free to come and
go as I choose, when I choose.'' To chase one woman or
twenty, or none at all.

She was right; he was still a young man. But he'd missed
most of the good times that a young man enjoyed. Those
wild and crazy times that made the best memories, that a
man could look back on with rueful pleasure when he
reached his settle-down years. So far, Rafe had had to live
his life backward, and though he didn't regret it—look what
he had to show for his hard work—still... If this wasn't
his time now, when would it ever be?

"Oh,'' Mitzy said in a small voice.

Good, she was getting his message.

"Do you mean to...travel much?'' She tipped her head
to gaze up at him.

"Some,'' he allowed cautiously. As manager and part
owner of one of the region's largest ranches, he'd never be
able to travel far or long. But he'd finally found himself a
good foreman, and he paid the man well enough to keep
him. Anse could take up the slack if Rafe wanted a week
or two away in the off-seasons.

Though it wasn't as if Rafe had any particular plans. He
wasn't one of those middle-aged idiots desperately trying
to recapture the lost years and live them now. At thirty-
five, he was too old, too stiff, to hit the rodeo trail, although
that had been his intention before he and Pilar had made a
baby.

And he was too wise to chase the girls he'd missed out
on seventeen years ago—the pretty rodeo queens, the
spunky barrel racers, the sassy waitresses. Somewhere
along the line his tastes had changed. To him, those girls

all looked like slightly older sisters of Zoe, staying up way past their curfews. No, nowadays when he wanted company, he wanted a warm and knowing woman in his bed, not some giggling child.

The warm woman leaning against him stirred. "I've always wanted to travel, too. I've been thinking about flying down to Cancún, sometime this month. Laze around the beach, drink too many margaritas, take a lo-o-ong siesta every afternoon." She arched her back and smiled up at him then, and hooking an arm around his neck, leaned backward. "Want to come with me?"

If there hadn't been so many strings attached... Rafe had shaken his head regretfully, resisting the urge of both gravity and nature to follow her down on the cushions. "June is branding month, moving the cows up from the home pastures..." And he was a full-time father for one last summer, before he could cut loose.

She pouted prettily. "What if I waited till July?"

"I don't think you should wait for me," he'd said in all truth. Any woman who dreamed of starting a second family with *him* would have a long, long wait, indeed.

He'd made his excuses and left soon after that, though it had been a hard-won retreat. Sensing his cooling, Mitzy had redoubled her efforts to fan his flames. But knowing she wouldn't thank him tomorrow if he took what she was offering tonight, he'd politely declined—and gained no gratitude for his self-control. He winced, remembering her final tearful reply as he stood shuffling on her doorstep, hat in his hands.

"Thanks? Thanks for *nothing,* cowboy!"

"Well, damnation, what was I supposed to do?" he now asked the night and the mountains. His truck was mounting the last rise of the county road that twisted up the valley past Suntop.

He'd given nothing tonight, taken nothing. Felt nothing

now but shame and frustration and emptiness. A man felt nothing but small when he failed to give a woman what she needed, wanted. And as for his own wants— He thought of that handful of condoms in his wallet and groaned aloud with embarrassment. If he hadn't needed both hands for steering, he would have yanked them out and tossed them to the winds!

He reached the main gate to the ranch, and, as his truck turned under the big name board that arched overhead and rumbled across the cattle guard and onto his own land, Rafe heaved a sigh of relief. At least here on Suntop, everything was simple.

As he drove the last half-mile up to the manager's house, his eyes automatically swept the pastures to either side, his mind cataloguing the state of the grass—greening up nicely since they'd moved the yearlings last week. The condition of the fences—a post on the right looked wobbly, tell Anse tomorrow. He braked as a whitetail deer soared over the right fence, touched once, twice on the roadway, then flew away over the left into darkness. He brought the truck to a halt and waited, and sure enough here came a second, then a third, fourth and fifth. A fawn raced frantically along the barbed wire, calling, and one of the does leaped back the way she'd come to meet it.

Rafe drove on—then let out a grunt of surprise as he topped the last rise and saw Zoe's Mustang.

Must have just arrived, he realized as he parked beside it, outside the back door. She'd yet to shut off her headlights, and the passenger door swung wide. Great. Much as he loved his daughter, she wasn't the sort of company he'd had in mind tonight. And given his mood, he'd sooner get over his frustration alone, with a cold beer and a good book by the fire, than be forced to sit in the kitchen, eating a bowl of ice cream, while Zoe quizzed him in cheerful detail about his big night out.

"Daddy!" Zoe leaped down the porch steps to the yard, with the dogs, Woofle and Trey, bounding at her heels. "What are you doing back?"

"Called it an early night," he said, walking around to her door to close it. As he leaned in to turn off her lights, he saw the bags of groceries crowding the seat and the floorboards. He scooped up the nearest four and straightened. "You're supposed to be over at Lisa's," he noted.

"She, um…got sick. Flu, I guess. It seemed smarter to not stay over. So I swung by the grocery store, then came back." Zoe reached for one of his bags. "Here—give me that one."

"I've got it."

She tugged it out of his arms. "This one's got the eggs. There's a *really* heavy one with lots of cans. If you'd get that…"

"Sure." He followed her up the steps to the porch, the dogs surging delightedly around their feet, celebrating this reunion as if he and Zoe had been gone a month instead of hours. "Woof, sit."

The Airedale dropped on the stoop, stub tail wagging, while the jealous Border collie, hearing a command, spun on her furry length and shoved out the kitchen door for her own—just as Zoe stepped up over the threshold from the mudroom.

"*Watch* it!" Arms full, Rafe lunged helplessly toward her, then stopped short as she tripped over the dog and went sprawling headlong. "Zoe!" He set his bags down. "Baby, are you—"

"I'm fine." She pushed herself to her elbows, laughing, as the collie bathed her face with apologetic kisses. "Stop, Trey! Back off!" She curled her long legs under her and sat, as Rafe dropped on his boot heels beside her. Then her smile vanished, and her mouth rounded to an "Oh" of dismay.

"You're hurt! Where?" He ran his hands down her slender arms. She'd broken her wrist years before in just such a fall. Not yet grown into her legs, she was always tripping, still clumsy as a foal.

"N-no, I..." She was staring beyond him at the cans and boxes that had scattered across the floor. Her eyes switched to his face and she gave him a shaky smile. "I'm fine, Daddy, really. Perfectly fine." She started to rise. "If you'd go get the rest of the groceries, I'll—"

"You'll sit till you catch your breath." Rafe glanced around for a chair, stood to get it. He scanned the spilled groceries, seeking the carton of eggs she'd mentioned. A blue box had tumbled nearly to the stove. As the words on its label registered in the back of his mind, his gaze stopped. Swung back. And locked on.

"Um, Daddy?" she said in a tiny quaver as he crossed the room.

He could hear the blood thumping in his ears. Those words *couldn't* say what he thought they'd said.

What they really said.

Impossible. He straightened, holding a pregnancy test kit.

"What's this for?" he asked in a voice that didn't sound remotely like his own.

THE DUDES in Aspen Cabin and Cottonwood Cabin, who had driven over to the Indian cliff houses at Mesa Verde National Park for the day, had returned, tired, sunburned and happy—and an hour and a half later than they'd promised.

By that time Dana had assumed they'd stopped to eat in town. Recklessly switching her menu at the last minute, she'd decided that Sunday would be Barbecue Night, instead—you really needed a crowd out on the deck to make it a festive occasion. She'd told Sean to scatter the coals and let the fire die out in the outdoor grill, while she'd whipped up a tomato-and-onion quiche with a spinach salad for her remaining guests, the two sisters from Boston. They were perpetually fussing about calories, anyway, so let them eat light for once.

But no sooner had Dana pulled the quiche from the oven than the truants had trooped in, appetites raging, consciences shameless, innocently expecting a hot, home-cooked meal to materialize out of thin air.

"They're brats," she confided to Petra in the privacy of her kitchen. "Could even teach you a thing or two, sweetie, but don't you listen."

No fear there. Utterly absorbed in a game of Follow the Leader with Zorro, the cat, Petra scuttled across the linoleum, rump high, diaper askew. "Ca, ca, ca, *ca!*" she declared, reaching for Zorro's tail, as he leaped up to the safety of a chair tucked under the kitchen table. Zorro whisked the endangered prize out of sight, then stepped serenely onto the next chair and sat to lick a paw.

"*Cat,* that's right," Dana crooned absently while she sliced the quiche into cocktail-size bites and arranged them on a platter. This, two bottles of wine and a bowl full of cherries, should keep her guests amused for the next twenty minutes or so.

But what then? *Think, Dana.*

She was too tired to think, and the pressure of ten healthy appetites demanding satisfaction in her living room sent her thoughts whirling like clothes in the dryer. Oh, drat, she hadn't moved the load from the washer an hour ago, had she?

Focus, she commanded herself as she tucked the bottles of wine under her elbow, then hoisted the platter and bumped her hip against the swinging door that led into the dining room. As she passed the long mahogany table, she realized she'd told Sean to set it for four. She'd need another eight settings now.

But first food, she reminded herself. "Cocktail hour!" she announced with a smile and a flourish, handing the platter to Caroline Simmons and nodding at the coffee table. "And Leo, would you play bartender?" He was the one member of the latecomers who'd had the grace to look embarrassed. She placed the bottles of chardonnay on the sideboard, where he'd find glasses and a corkscrew.

"Could you use any help in the kitchen?" he asked, smiling down at her.

"Oh, thanks, not at all! Just sit down and put your feet up. You've had a long day." She threaded her way through the rest of her milling guests, with a smile and a word for each, then went up the front stairs, consciously imitating Zorro's unruffled serenity. Once she'd turned at the newel post on the landing and was out of sight, she took the last steps three at a time. *Help? Oh, no, not me!*

Arriving at Sean's door—closed as always—she paused and drew a breath, steeling herself. Then knocked. "Sean?"

No answer, though she could hear music turned down low, beyond his barricade. "Sean, please." He hated it if she opened his door without permission, but then, the other rule of his game was that he never seemed to hear her. "Sean!" She gritted her teeth and opened the door. "Sean, honey—"

"I *told* you, you're supposed to knock!" he growled, glaring back at her from over his shoulder. He lay sprawled on his stomach on the bed, a book propped on his pillow.

"I need help," she said, voice quivering with the effort to keep it level. She didn't sound far from tears, she realized. Wasn't. *Oh, do I need help.* This job had never been intended for one. That wasn't the way she and Peter had planned it.

But now all she had was Peter's son, glaring at her with Peter's brown eyes. And none of Peter's tenderness.

"Please, Sean? I need eight more places set at the table, then some help in the kitchen."

"Uh."

She resisted the urge to demand if that meant yes or no. *Hope for the best.* "Thank you." She shut the door gently.

Go ahead with the original barbecue? she asked herself as she hurried downstairs. No, the coals would take forever to reach grilling heat. But she couldn't see cooking tomorrow's steaks indoors tonight—what a waste. And Monday's chicken was still frozen solid. Pasta, she decided, topped with peas, bacon and roasted red peppers. Garlic bread and salad. She shoved through the kitchen door.

Petra sat on the floor, face screwed to a tiny red knot of woe, beating on the linoleum with a wooden spoon in time to her hiccuping sobs. "Oh, *sweetheart,* did you miss me?" Dana scooped the baby up, kissed the top of her downy head, then settled her onto one hip and set to cooking one-handed. *Peter, Peter, oh, Peter, if you could see us now...*

CHAPTER THREE

LATE AS IT WAS, supper had been a success, Dana told herself as she paraded a steaming apple tart straight from the oven to the table. Sean followed glumly, carrying a bowl piled high with round scoops of vanilla ice cream. "So who wants pie?" she asked gaily amid the groans of delight and "oohs" of admiration.

Beyond the kitchen door, the phone rang. Dana glanced over her shoulder, her brows drawing together. It was well past nine, late for anyone to be calling. The phone rang again, and she bit her lip—Petra was sleeping in there in her playpen!

"I'll get it," Sean muttered, thumping his bowl down beside her.

By the time she'd served out dessert, he'd still not returned. So either the call was some tourist inquiring about vacancies at the Ribbon R, and for once Sean was handling it, or the caller had wanted her stepson in the first place.

Much as they needed to fill all the gaps in their summer schedule, Dana found herself hoping the call had been for Sean. At fourteen, he didn't seem to get enough phone calls—didn't seem to have any friends to speak of. Although, he confided in her so little, she supposed she'd be the last to know if he did. Still, a schoolmate calling Sean nights—she pictured a giggling thirteen-year-old charmer with a terrible crush and twice Sean's social skills—now, that would be a welcome development. Dana ached for his loneliness, but so far she'd found no way to cure it. *Peter would have known how—*

Stop, she told herself firmly. After fourteen months, it was time she stopped calling on Peter.

Fourteen months or fourteen years or fourteen lifetimes, how could she not? She sat, smiling at her guests around the table, glad for the candlelight that turned tears in the eyes to sparkles.

WHEN ALL HER DUDES had left the table to wander sleepily from the main house and off up the hill to their cabins, Dana set to clearing away. A very long day, she mused as she entered the kitchen, arms loaded. "Sean?" she murmured to warn him, in case he was still engaged in conversation.

No Sean.

Dana frowned, staring at the phone on the wall beside the back door. Its receiver had been dropped on the counter. And— Her frown deepened. He'd left the door ajar.

Hand at her throat, she spun to the playpen—then breathed again at the sight of the small, blanket-draped lump in its center. At least the baby was still covered. The draft of cool mountain air would have done her no harm. Still… *Does he ever think?* She lifted the receiver to her ear, heard the dial tone, let out a *tckk* of irritation and hung it up.

What had caused him to bolt like that? The worst of it was, if she went after Sean and asked what was wrong, she knew exactly what he'd say. "Nothing," she murmured, and grimaced.

Okay. So leave him alone, then. He'd be up in the loft of the barn, one of his hideouts when he wanted to escape her. Or else mooching along the Ribbon River—the snow-melt stream that stairstepped down the mountain, chuckling past the cabins, then the house, to spread out into glistening trout pools when it reached the valley meadows.

Dana turned back to her daughter. *If I can't help Sean, at least your wants are simple, my love.* Gathering the sleeper into her arms, she buried her nose against Petra's warm neck and, with eyes closed, simply breathed in her scent for a moment. Then she carried the baby softly up to bed.

HALF AN HOUR LATER she was rinsing the last pots and pans. Sean had yet to make an appearance, though a few moments ago she'd half thought she heard him thump through the front door. Had he returned that way to avoid her? But if that wasn't him... Dana frowned out the window into the darkness. Go find him and coax him home? Or leave him be?

Something moved in the glass. She blinked, and then realized—a reflection from the room behind her; the dining room door swinging open. Sean stood in the doorway, one arm bracing the door wide, as silently he watched her.

The skin along her spine contracted in a rippling shudder. *Not Sean, but someone much taller, wider, darker.* Standing with the stillness of a predator.

Why didn't I lock the door?

She hadn't for the same reason she never did. Guests trooped in and out all day; Sean came and went; and this wasn't Vermont, where she'd been raised, where everyone locked up. Out here in the West, you depended on distance to protect you. The guest ranch was four miles down a private road from the highway. No one came here by chance.

Behind her, the stranger moved at last, letting the door go and striding on into the kitchen. The blood thrummed in her ears. Dana chose her longest carving knife from the drainage rack, examined it for imaginary food specks, rinsed it, then, still holding it, let her right hand casually droop below the rinse water. She shut off the faucet and half turned.

"Oh!" She'd meant the word to deceive, but her shock was real. He was closer than she'd expected. Bigger.

And angrier—black, level brows drawn down over deep-set eyes.

"Wh-wh-what do you—" She stuttered to a stop. Did she really want to know what he wanted?

"Sean Kershaw. Where is he?" A low, gravelly voice, its steadiness somehow more deadly than any shout. No drama to this rage, but pure, cold intention.

"Sean?" Whatever this invasion was, it wasn't what she'd thought. Still, it was bad—trouble. *Teacher?* she asked herself, and rejected the hope immediately. This was no indoor man. His face was tanned to the color of buck-skin. The lines fanning out from the corners of his blue eyes spoke of years squinting in the harsh sun. "Wh-why do you want Sean?"

"That's between him and me."

The intruder turned a slow circle on his heels, scanning the kitchen as if Sean might be cowering in a corner. He wore boots, Dana realized, which was why he seemed so enormous. Though even in his socks he'd still top her five-three by nearly a foot.

Nevertheless, she let go of her weapon. She could no more imagine herself stopping this man with a knife than she could imagine stopping a train. "I'm afraid it isn't," she said coolly—to his back. He was striding back the way he'd come.

Hey! She goggled after him, then felt rage awaken as he retreated. "It's considered polite to knock, you know!" she cried, hurrying to catch up.

"I knocked. You didn't hear me." He was already past the dining room, heading for the front door.

Good riddance, whoever he was! But no—her mouth dropped as he turned toward the stairs.

"He's up there?"

"Don't you *dare*—"

"Good." He took the stairs two at a time without a backward glance.

Her baby! The hair bristled on her arms, at her nape. Dana flew up the steps, a primal humming sound in her throat. *You stay away from my baby!*

The door to Petra's room stood wide. Dana flung herself through it and slammed into his back—"Ooof!"

"Huh?" he muttered absently. He'd stopped short just inside the room to flick on the light. She grabbed his elbows from behind and, with a little growl of despair—might as well try to uproot the oak banister!—she attempted to wheel him around and out. He glanced over his shoulder with a startled frown, then simply shrugged, breaking her hold. "Who's this?" He nodded at the sleeping child.

"Mine," Dana said flatly. She caught a fistful of the back of his shirt and tugged, and, lucky for him, he allowed himself to be towed backward out of the room. He hit the light switch as he passed it, then pulled the door quietly shut.

Dana let him go and swung around to put herself between him and Petra's door. Chin up, she stared at him breathing hard. "Get out of my house this...minute."

Startling white against the tan, a reluctant smile flickered across his hard face. "Good for you," he said simply, then turned away...

To open the next door down the hall—Sean's room! Dana pressed a hand to her throat, swallowed, then charged after him. But—*thank you, God*—Sean hadn't returned.

The stranger stood in the center of Sean's bedroom, surveying the posters pinned to the wall—surly rock groups and a surfer shooting a blue-green pipeline at Maui. The desk piled high with books and camera accessories. Discarded shirts and jeans draped over the chair and the top of the closet door.

"Get *out*." Dana bared her teeth. She supposed she could run uphill and ask her wrangler, Tim, for help, if by any miracle he was home on a Saturday night. Or run downstairs and phone the sheriff. But no way would she leave Petra to do either.

"You're his sister, I reckon?" the man murmured, without turning.

"His stepmother."

His dark head snapped around, and the blue eyes reassessed her, a quick head-to-toe appraisal. She crossed her arms over her breasts and glared back at him. *Why the surprise?* "And who the hell are you?"

"Rafe Montana." He brushed past her and stalked out the door, headed for her bedroom.

"He's not *here*," she hissed, bracing her hands against the doorjamb and leaning after him. "Can't you see?"

He stood there, looking down at the big brass bed that she'd shared with no man for fourteen months and thirteen days. The soft, rumpled down comforter that was no substitute for Peter's living warmth.

"So where is he?" Montana turned to take in the rest of her room.

She felt his eyes touch the books stacked on her bedside table, testimony to all the nights she could not sleep; the vase of blue columbines on the wide windowsill; the bottles of perfume on her dresser, which she hadn't uncapped for more than a year—and she felt as if he'd run his hands across her body. *You trespasser.* She stamped her foot to reclaim his attention. "I'm not *about* to tell you, when I don't know what you want. When you barge in here like a—a maniac!"

"That's about how I feel," he said, swinging to face her.

Two long strides and he towered above her. "I'm Zoe's father."

"Who's Zoe?"

"Who—" His eyes narrowed with rage. "You don't *know?*"

She shook her head wordlessly. His daughter. He was no longer a maniac, but an outraged...father. *And he wants Sean.* Her hand rose of its own accord to her lips. *My Sean?*

"Uh-huh," Montana said dryly, as if she'd spoken her thought aloud. "And where's *his* father?"

"He's...not here, either." Montana might seem somewhat more human, claiming a daughter, but still, no way was Dana admitting she didn't have a man to back her. "He should be home any minute."

"Sooner the better." Montana walked out of her bedroom, glanced through the open door to the empty bathroom, then headed back down the hall.

Hands clenched, Dana tagged at his heels. "If you would just tell me what this is about—"

"He's around here someplace, isn't he?" Montana growled, descending the stairs. "You thought he was in his room. So..." He walked through to the kitchen again, then out the back door.

She caught up with him on the deck. He stood with big hands on his lean hips, staring up the slope toward the corral and the barn. A light shone through the cottonwoods from one of the cabins along the creek. "Where is he, Mrs. Kershaw? In the barn? Or—what's that house beyond—the bunkhouse?"

"One of the guest cabins. But if you barge in on my dudes, I'll call the sheriff and have you arrested, so help me God. Now, *tell* me—" She stopped with a gulp as a thought hit her. "*Oh...*" She drifted past him, down the two steps to the gravel where her old pickup should have been parked. Turned a slow circle of bewilderment.

Montana joined her, glanced down at the ruts made by the tires, and swore. "Where's he gone?"

"I...don't know." At fourteen, Sean had no license yet. Peter had allowed him to drive the truck on their property, and though Dana didn't entirely approve, she hadn't dared revoke that privilege after Peter was gone. Sean had extended his range without asking, she'd noticed this last six months, to include the private road out as far as the highway. But he wouldn't dare— "Did you pass an old pickup on your way in from the public road?"

"I passed nobody."

Which meant, she supposed, that Sean had already departed. Or fled, she realized, staring up at Montana. *He knew you were coming!* That phone call during supper.

"Where would he be on a Saturday night, Mrs. Kershaw? Down in Trueheart at one of the bars?"

"Sean?" She laughed incredulously. "Of course not!"

He stepped closer, till they stood almost toe to toe. "You haven't a clue where your punk is, do you, lady? I guess I should have expected that. Running wild..."

Insults on top of invasion, and the truth in his charge only made it sting more. She tipped up her chin. "And I suppose you know *precisely* where your daughter is this minute, huh?" What was she supposed to do? Keep a fourteen-year-old boy who outweighed her by twenty pounds— who barely could stand the sight of her—on a leash? She was doing the best she could!

"You better believe I do," Montana said coolly. "Zoe's locked in her bedroom without even a phone for company. And that's where she'll stay till I thrash this out."

A tyrant, on top of all else! Dana paired two fingers and jabbed them directly into his second shirt button—it was like prodding warm stone. "Thrash *what* out?" *Please, not what I'm thinking.* This had to be some sort of ridiculous mistake. Perhaps he had the wrong Sean.

They both jumped as, inside the kitchen, the phone rang. Montana caught her arms and moved her aside with a gentleness that belied his temper. She stood for a moment, blinking, strangely undone by the sensation of a man's hands upon her—it had been so long—then spun and went after him. She saw him lift her phone to his ear. "Don't you *dare!*"

"She's right here," Montana said in response to the caller's question, then handed her the receiver with ironic courtesy.

"Mrs. Kershaw?" inquired a male voice. "This is Colorado State Trooper Michael Morris calling, ma'am. Do you have a son named Sean?"

"Oh, *God!*" Not Sean, too! Slowly she sagged against the counter. *No, no, oh, no.* She was dimly aware that Montana had set one broad hand on her shoulder, steadying her, and that he'd tipped his head down close enough to hear the trooper's voice. His temple brushed her hair.

"Oh, no, ma'am, nothing like that—not an accident! Sorry to scare you. But I've got a Sean Kershaw stopped here on Route 160, and it appears he isn't licensed to drive. We've checked the plates, and you're the owner of record of this vehicle. Did you give him permission to drive, ma'am?"

"I…" She drew in a shaking breath. Sean was all right! He wouldn't be once she got hold of him, but for now… *Thank you, thank you, oh, thank you!* "No, Officer, I did not." She straightened, and Montana's hand fell away from her shoulder, though he still hovered within hearing range. She met his eyes and smiled her relief, and, wonder of wonders, his mouth quirked with warmth and wry humor. A very nice mouth indeed, she noticed, when it wasn't hardened by temper.

"Well, that's good," said the trooper. "I'm afraid, though, we've got a situation here, ma'am. I ought to take

him in and book him, but we've had a tractor trailer tip
over, down by Durango. Took out a few cars with it. All
the tow trucks are out on the job, and I should be over
there, too. If you and another licensed driver could get
down here in a hurry, I'd release the car and your son into
your custody. Saves me a trip to the station.''

"Tell him yes," Montana said in a whispered growl, his
eyes lighting.

No way was she taking *him* along. "I'll...yes. Of
course." She'd ask Leo Simmons, the dude in Cottonwood
Cabin, to help her out. "Tell me again where you're lo-
cated?"

The trooper told her quickly, then added, "I've got a
second kid here, too, ma'am, in case you could contact her
parents for me. She won't be charged, since she wasn't
driving, but..."

"Who?" Dana asked with a sinking heart. Somehow she
knew already.

"She refuses to say, ma'am. A tall, redheaded, mouthy
kid."

The shock dawning in Rafe Montana's eyes was almost
laughable. He shook his head, shook it again as if he were
slinging water out of his eyes, and snatched the phone from
her grasp.

"Ask her if her name's Zoe Montana," he rasped.
"Never mind who I am! *Ask* her."

There came a long pause. Montana stood as still as a
rock, teeth clenched, as he glared into the distance, utterly
oblivious of Dana's wide-eyed scrutiny. Then, as the
trooper spoke again, Montana swore under his breath and
said, "You tell her for me, Officer, that her father's on his
way."

"Know *just* where your daughter is, do you?" Dana
couldn't resist murmuring.

CHAPTER FOUR

STRAPPED INTO her car seat on the rear bench of Rafe Montana's long-cab pickup truck, Petra whined and fretted till they reached the smoother highway. As the big truck settled into a mile-eating drone, her long lashes drooped on her fat rosy cheeks and she slept.

"Never fails," Montana murmured, glancing in the rearview mirror.

The voice of experience, Dana realized, studying his hard-edged profile. Perhaps he had other, younger children aside from Zoe. And for that matter— "Where's Zoe's mother?"

Five fence posts whipped into the headlights, then passed, their barbed wire swooping and falling, before he spoke. "She died in a car wreck when Zoe was six."

"Oh. I'm sorry." She watched his mouth curve wryly. Yes, she supposed it was a bit late to be offering sympathy. For that matter, he might well have replaced Zoe's mother years ago. With his darkly smoldering good looks, that intense vitality, he'd find plenty of volunteers for the job.

The taillights of a car appeared as the pickup topped a rise. The country was flattening out into sagebrush-covered slopes, the dryer land to the west falling away toward state border. The truck closed on the car in a rush—slipped out, passed it by and roared on.

"What about your husband?" Montana asked without taking his eyes off the road. "You didn't leave him a message."

She didn't answer the question behind that statement.
"No, I…didn't." To confess would be to admit he'd scared
her. Scared her still in some way she could not fathom. But
her instinct was to raise any and every barrier against him
she could find.

At the same time, though, necessity demanded that she
understand his outrage before they reached Sean, that she
defuse it if she could. "Why did you want my stepson, Mr.
Montana?"

"If I'm going to drive you halfway to Utah, Mrs. Kershaw, you can call me Rafe." A tractor trailer thundered
past, shaking the truck, and he flicked on his high beams.

She would have preferred the formality of last names,
but he'd maneuvered her neatly. Now she'd look ungra-
cious not to reciprocate. "Then it's Dana." She straightened her shoulders. "But what about Sean?"

"My daughter's pregnant." He glanced at her, as she
shook her head. "Oh, yes. I caught her sneaking a pregnancy test kit into the house this evening."

"Not Sean!" Dana said emphatically. "That's not possible."

"You're saying my Zoe's a liar?"

His voice grew softer and more level with rage, she was
learning. "No, I…" Wouldn't dare, but still… She thought
of three ways to ask the same essential question—*Is she
sure Sean is the father?* But no matter how she phrased it,
she might as well set a match to a stick of dynamite.
"There must be some mistake," she said, instead. "Is she
sure she's pregnant?"

"She told me she's missed two months, almost three.
What do you think?"

The worst, quite likely. Dana bit her lip. But still…
"Sean isn't even dating." How could he? She gave him an
allowance, but it was woefully meager. Peter had cashed in
his main life insurance policy to buy the ranch. His little

term policy had paid off enough to create a trust fund that someday would cover Sean's and Petra's college tuitions. But the family's day-to-day finances were cut to the bone. Sean had no money for dating, and no transportation aside from his beloved mountain bike. "Where have they been, um, meeting?"

"Didn't get to the bottom of that. She clammed up on me, so I locked her in her room to think about it."

"For all the good that did you." Dana couldn't resist the jab, and noticed it made the muscles in his jaw jump and his knuckles tighten on the wheel. To her mind, a girl who was old enough to make a baby was too old to be locked up like a rebellious ten-year-old.

"You're doing a better job? Your kid's running wild and unsupervised, stealing your car when he wants it. Speeding...knocking up girls."

"*Girl.* If he did that at all. I still don't believe it."

"I'll ask him when I meet him, how's that?" Rafe suggested darkly. "Your sonny boy and I are going to have a *long,* earnest talk, believe me."

Withdrawn, unconfident Sean pitted against this full-grown, outraged male in his prime? "No, I don't think so. Not tonight. Not till I talk to him myself." Peter would never have allowed his son to be bullied, and now she stood in Peter's place. "Tomorrow..." Once she'd gotten Sean's version. Once Rafe Montana had cooled down. Perhaps after she'd consulted a lawyer. *God, where would I find the money?*

"We'll see about that," Rafe said with dangerous calm.

Indeed they would. Dana clenched her hands. Sean's refusal to forgive her might wound her daily, but still, she was all he had. No way would she throw him to this wolf. She changed the subject. "How much farther?"

"Another twenty miles. Almost to Four Corners."

"Where could they have been going?" California? Sean

missed San Diego, somehow seemed to believe that if he could go back there, life would be as it was. As if Peter waited there on the front lawn of the suburban house that he and Sean had shared when Dana first met them. If only it were that easy.

"They were headed for Arizona, I imagine. Zoe's great-aunt lives in Phoenix. She's Catholic, like all Pilar's folks. I suppose Zoe figured she'd take her side."

"Side on what?"

"Zoe is all set to go away to college in three months," Rafe said obliquely.

"College?" Dana had been picturing a ninth or tenth grader! Sean with a senior? Sean, who had all the social sophistication of a golden retriever pup? Now she *knew* there was some mistake!

"Harvard, just like her—" Rafe paused. "Harvard. She's...bright."

As in *very bright,* Dana interpreted the pride echoing behind that western understatement.

"She's been working all her life for this. Aims to be a doctor, a surgeon—though the school counselor tells me she could shoot higher than that if she wants. Sky's the limit. But Harvard's the start...the door she has to walk through to get where she's going. Where she deserves to go. Her life's just blossoming, just starting to happen—" He slammed the wheel with a fist. "And now this? I don't think so. Now that your kid has messed her up, there's only one way out."

"Abortion, you mean," Dana murmured. She suppressed a sudden urge to look back at Petra. To grab the baby and pull her over the seat and into her arms. "Does Zoe agree?" Zoe, who'd broken out of her room somehow and tried to flee the state?

"She... Neither of us was making much sense back

there,'' Rafe growled. "We're not used to banging heads. But once she's calmed down and thought it through…''

I wonder. "There's always adoption," Dana observed, her voice carefully neutral.

"Zoe starts college in *three months.*" Montana's words might have been carved from Rocky Mountain granite.

THEY DROVE THE REST of the way in silence. But angry as he was, Rafe found he couldn't focus all his thoughts on the coming confrontation. Sitting only two feet to his right, she tugged at his awareness. *Dana Kershaw.* Small and dark, she should have looked boyish with her short, silky brown hair falling into her big slate-green eyes, yet she was anything but. She had a softness and a warmth about her that were feminine to the core. Reminded him of the little half-Siamese cat Zoe had owned for years, all silky fur to the touch, daintily elegant—and absolute hell on dogs five times her size, if they looked sideways at her kittens. His lips twitched as he remembered the way she'd faced him down at her baby's door. Not a woman to be crossed.

Kershaw's a lucky man, he found himself thinking. You could tell the good 'uns at a glance, just like he could size up a corral full of horses and choose the best mount. He grimaced, realizing where this thought was heading—it was just a leftover from his earlier frustration. God, was it only three hours ago that he'd been sitting across a table from Mitzy Barlow? It seemed another lifetime.

What he'd learned about Zoe—like a knife stroke cutting that happy life from this strange present, him speeding through the night with a gentle, fierce woman, her eyes reflecting like fathomless pools in the windshield whenever a car passed them by. And Zoe, turned from his loving, loyal daughter into a defiant stranger! One stumble across the kitchen floor and he'd picked up someone he'd never met before—a young woman who'd loved a man, made a baby by him, cast her father's wisdom aside to fly to her mate. To flee as if he were some kind of ogre, not the father who'd turned his own world upside down to make a good life for his own baby... How could everything change this fast?

Nothing's changed, he told himself savagely, and wished he could believe it. *Not really.* There'd be a week or two of hurt feelings and ugly necessities, a week or two of sorrow after that, then they'd get back on track. *She's worked too hard. I won't let this ruin her life.*

His headlights picked out a creek bending in from the darkness to edge the highway, then a state police car parked on the shoulder above it; ahead of that, a pickup. Two pale faces stared back through the truck's rear window, as Rafe swung in behind the patrol car and parked. "We settle with the Statie first, Dana. He'll want to hear that we're taking this seriously."

"Believe me, I am." She checked her child, who was still sleeping, then hurried after Rafe as he strode to meet the state trooper, now unfolding from his car.

She handled it well, Rafe had to admit, as Officer Morris assured them that he could arrest Sean for everything from car theft to speeding. Dana didn't try to excuse or defend her son, but simply promised that he would be punished, that such a grievous misjudgment would never be repeated. Clearly of a mind to be satisfied, the trooper finally nodded, marched off to his car, got in and carved a swift U-turn, then headed off toward the truck crash near Durango.

"You were lucky," Rafe observed, hearing the distant engine shift into overdrive. He turned. And now, for someone who'd run flat out of luck...

Both doors of the shabby pickup opened as he stalked toward it. "Daddy?" Zoe called fearfully from the far side.

But Rafe had another target in his sights. The greedy, undisciplined spoiler who'd led them all to this disaster. "I want a word with you, punk,'' he said quietly, barely aware that Dana Kershaw plucked at his elbow. He shrugged her off.

Head high, the boy paused beside his open door and let him come. Rafe's strides slowed and he drew in a harsh breath. This was his enemy? Half a head shorter than him, with the gangly limbs, the too-big feet and hands of a boy? He'd pictured an eighteen-year-old, at least! ''*You're* Sean Kershaw?'' He glanced toward the cab in spite of himself, as if the kid's older brother might burst forth.

''My stepson,'' Dana declared, swinging around to stand shoulder to shoulder with the kid.

Rage and frustration had been building inside Rafe all night. He'd contained himself—barely—but had promised himself a full and glorious venting when he found its deserving target. But now? You could stomp a man, but this—this unshaved brat? He caught the kid's collar between thumb and forefinger. ''How the hell old *are* you?'' he demanded, ignoring both Dana's and Zoe's yelps of protest.

''Old enough and get your hands off me!'' The boy chopped up a forearm, breaking his grip.

''Old enough for what, you little runt? To wreck my daughter's life?''

''He's fourteen, and you leave him alone,'' Dana cried, stepping between them. ''I said we'd talk *tomorrow*,'' she added in an urgent undertone.

''Fourteen!'' Rafe shook his head. What the hell?

''Daddy!'' Zoe pleaded.

Zoe had betrayed him for this—this puppy? ''Get in the truck,'' he snapped without glancing aside.

''Don't,'' countered the kid. ''He can't make you do anything you don't want.''

''Oh, can't I?'' He prodded the boy's shoulder. ''Mind your own business, sonny.''

The boy batted his hand aside. "This *is* my business."

"Sean, be quiet! Rafe, *please*." Dana caught his upper arm with both her hands.

Even through the mists of rage, he could feel each separate small fingertip digging into his muscles. *She's married,* he reminded himself, and felt his rage kick up a notch. He swung his arm back, pushing her away from the fray. "Yeah, you've made it your business, big shot. You've made a baby nobody wants or needs. A baby the grown-ups will have to deal with now. Good going!"

"Nobody's asking you to deal with anything—" The boy's voice cracked on the last word and jumped half a squeaking octave.

Rafe threw back his head and laughed. The situation was so absurd, it was that or weep.

Sean shoved him hard with both hands. "Zoe doesn't *want* an abortion, and if she doesn't want one, I don't want one!"

Rafe rocked back on his heels, then rocked forward, looming over the kid. *How do you like that?* Sixty pounds lighter, yet the kid was going toe to toe with him. Guts. Still, "Easy for you to say, twerp. You won't be around to pick up the pieces."

"I will! If Zoe needs me, I'll be there. I'll get a job and take care of her. I'll— I'll—"

"At fourteen?" Rafe jeered incredulously, shaking his head—and saw the blow coming from the corner of his eye, a roundhouse swing. His head tipped reflexively to the right, and the blow whistled past his ear. *"Hey!"*

Sean growled wordlessly and took another shot. Rafe caught it on his palm and swept it aside. "Back off!"

They circled, Rafe with open hands up and out, dimly aware of the women shrieking from outside the whirlwind of Sean's flailing fists. *Duck in and put a shoulder into his stomach,* Rafe told himself. He could toss the kid up over his shoulder, trundle him down to the stream that gurgled beyond the truck. Dump him in to cool off.

Another blow sailed in, and he took it on his raised forearm as he stepped to one side. Somebody should have taught this kid to hit. Anyone really wanting to hurt him could have done so with ease.

"Rafe, *please,* he's just a child!" Dana cried, and that decided him. Sean was a child—acting as a man. And standing by his woman, as foolishly touching as that might seem to an adult. And though apparently Dana didn't understand, the masculine code required that you honor your opponent's courage, no matter how incompetently displayed. *So don't demean him. Treat him as I would a man.* Sean had earned that courtesy with his spunk. The kid came in grunting and slugging. Rafe sighed inwardly, chose his shot and, pulling his punch to the limit of credibility, hit the kid as lightly as he could.

Sean wobbled two steps backward and sat—and Rafe found himself nose to nose with Dana Kershaw. "You…big…*bully!*" She smacked her hands against his chest. "*Stop* it!"

Just what he'd been trying to do.

She smacked him again. "What kind of a man picks on a child?"

"Be quiet, Dana." He'd been showing his respect, man to man. Now she was ruining his gesture—would humiliate the kid, if she didn't hush up. "He'll be fine." Learning to take his knocks—that was how a boy became a man. And the kid wasn't sniveling, Rafe noted with approval, glancing over her head. He was staggering to his feet with Zoe's help…brushing her aside. Crap, was he coming for more?

Fearful the kid might wade in all over again, Rafe allowed Dana to back him down the road. "Take it easy," he warned her, as she shoved him again. He caught her slender wrists and pinned her hands against his heart, scowling down at her. "Ea-sy!" Her pulse leaped beneath his fingertips, and he felt his own surge to meet it. He threw her hands hastily aside and retreated.

"*Me,* easy?" she cried, and turned up her palms in an appeal to the heavens.

Behind her, Zoe had caught the kid in a bear hug and was holding him back. Tears streaming, she glared over his shoulder. "I'm so ashamed of you, Daddy!"

Ashamed of me?! Now that punch landed—knocked him speechless. All those years of being his daughter's hero, to be shattered like this? Rafe felt the first stab of pain, then rage overwhelmed it like a breaking black wave. Rage felt *much* better. "Get in the truck! *Now!*"

If he'd lost her affection, still she had a sixteen-year habit of obedience. She murmured something in Sean's ear, then let him go.

"Zoe!" he called hoarsely after her. But head down, she marched off to Rafe's truck, scrambled in and slammed the door mightily.

A moment later, a baby's startled wail split the night.

"Petra!" Dana homed in on the sound, then brushed past Rafe without a glance.

The sobs gained volume and heartache, mixed with the crooning cries of two sympathetic women.

Damn it all to hell and back again! All he'd wanted to-night was to get laid. Rafe turned heavily to glare at Sean Kershaw. "Nice sound, huh? They do that for the first twelve months without a break to draw breath, except when they're puking or pooping. Think about it."

Halfway to his truck, he met Dana returning, arms full of the child and her bulky car seat. He opened his mouth to offer help, then shut it, knowing her answer already. Their eyes locked, held as they neared. She tipped up her chin and swept proudly past him, her baby's hiccuping sobs trailing back on the cold night air.

Rafe sighed, then stood beside his truck till she'd started hers, completed her turn and headed for home. He followed at a wary distance.

CHAPTER FIVE

DANA WOULD HAVE LOVED to pull a pillow over her head and sleep in the next morning—she'd tossed and turned most of the night, worrying about Sean. But the demands of a dude ranch, on top of the more strident demands of a baby who rose with the sun, had her stumbling from her bed at the usual hour.

In spite of her worries, morning flew by in a rush—diapering, nursing and dressing Petra, then rushing downstairs to cook a hearty breakfast for Tim, the dude wrangler. His customary Sunday hangover had rendered him even surlier and more silent than usual, she noted with despair. This time he hadn't bothered to shave. And he was scheduled to take all her dudes into the high country for an all-day trail ride, leaving at ten. So much for the cheerful, dashing trail boss of her guests' fantasies—a Disneyland cowpoke on a rearing steed, who'd spin thrilling yarns, dispense homespun cowboy wisdom, whisk them off on the Wild West adventure of a lifetime. Dana supposed the larger, sleeker, full-service guest ranches could afford to employ such entertainers, but the Ribbon R was a minimalist outfit, at minimalist prices. Her dudes would have to make do with a shambling, groaning, tobacco-chewing misanthrope, who at least wouldn't lose them in the back hills. She hoped.

Packing box lunches for the ride, at last she had a moment to think about Sean. When she'd come downstairs, a dirty plate on the counter and a tumbler with a puddle of milk in its bottom told her he'd preceded her.

He'd yet to return.

Gone off on his mountain bike? She hoped not. She hadn't had the heart, last night, to mete out a punishment for his driving escapade. It would have seemed one blow too many, after Zoe's announcement and Rafe Montana's brutality. So she'd told him they would discuss his behavior—discuss everything—this morning.

Sean-fashion, he'd given her his silent answer. *Oh, yeah? Catch me first.*

Sean, Sean, what am I going to do with you? He had been so unhappy before—and now this? Every time she thought things were as hard as they could be, they got a little harder. She bit down on her lip and finished wrapping the sandwiches, while Petra pulled at her pants leg and whined.

Once she'd seen Tim and his dudes on their way up through the home pasture, she prepped for the evening barbecue—got the steaks marinating, the baked beans simmering, the potato salad made. While Petra dragged out the contents of her special kitchen cabinet—the only one without a baby-proof latch—and sat fitting lids onto aluminum pots with scowling concentration, then lifting them off again with shrieks of glee, Dana made bread. Enough dough for this week's evening meals, plus enough to freeze for the next. Kneading it, she leaned into each stroke, her head drooping tiredly.

Sean still had not returned. Hanging out in the barn, or perhaps gone hiking up into the mountains? He rarely rode, though Peter had given him a surefooted, spunky little paint named Guapo when they'd first arrived. They'd all ridden that first fall, the three of them, laughing and awed by the beauty of their new home. Sean had liked her back then.

They'd been able to talk about anything and everything. But now...

We'll have to. This couldn't be shoved under the rug, as Sean preferred to do. This had to be faced. Responsibility acknowledged.

And then?

That depended on what Zoe decided to do, she supposed. *What Rafe Montana decides,* she corrected herself, grimacing. The bully. But there was no way to deny that he was the dominant personality here, the one who would call the shots. He would shape his daughter's future, and therefore Sean's. *Should I find a lawyer?* Someone to advise her stepson on his paternal rights and responsibilities? The money made her hesitate. She'd decided this morning that she'd wait to see what Montana did next, but she wasn't certain this was the wise approach.

Petra dropped a pot lid with a *clang* that made Dana jump. "Petra, what a noisy girl! You're going to be a drummer someday?" Please, anything but!

"Ga," the baby chortled, then smile gave way to frown. She rolled over onto all fours and crawled purposefully toward her mother.

"About that time, is it?" Dana wiped a forearm over her brow, brushing back her hair. "Can you wait a minute, sweetheart?" She patted the dough into balls, placed them in greased ceramic bowls. "Yes, sweetie, I know. Just a minute more. Be patient." After covering each bowl with a clean cloth, she set the dough to rise on the warming shelf above the stove. "There." She scooped up her tearful daughter and blew into her neck till Petra giggled. "See, silly girl? I didn't forget you."

She checked her diaper, then carried her out to the back deck and their favorite spot: a porch swing that hung under an arbor of climbing pink roses and honeysuckle. Sinking into one cushioned corner, she kicked off her shoes, dragged a pillow onto her lap, propped one arm and her baby against one bent knee while she left the other foot on the ground to rock them. "Lunchtime," she agreed, as Petra patted her blouse. And no one around for miles, she assured herself, looking uphill as she unbuttoned. Just birdsong, the fragrance of sun-warmed roses, a precious moment of peace...the delicious tingle as the milk let down in her breasts...the rhythmic suck of warm lips drawing her down into sleepy pleasure.

Sometime later, a ripple of consciousness disturbed her waking dream. Dana's eyes drifted half open, focused drowsily on a long pair of jeans-clad legs. Idly she rode them upward, up past lean hips, a flat stomach, a wide chest in a snap-front western shirt that flared to wider shoulders...up a strong brown throat to the startled face of Rafe Montana. His lips had parted in surprise; his eyes were narrowed slits of sapphire in his suntanned face. She felt her own face turning a color to rival the roses.

"Pardon me, ma'am!" He wheeled and walked back down the steps to the ground, then stopped there, facing away. "Didn't meant to intrude like that. I..."

The liquid pleasure of the moment seemed to flow over his form like honey, taking him in, making him a part of the mountains, the sunshine, the fragrance, her love for her daughter. He had all the power and grace of a bull elk who had suddenly walked into her world. It took an effort to remember that she disliked him—that he'd hit Sean last night, something she'd never forgive. "Of course." She supposed he'd tried the front door, and receiving no answer to his knock, this time hadn't barged through, but had walked around to the back.

"If you could wait a minute?" Gently she detached Petra and moved her to her other breast.

"Sure." He glanced awkwardly down at his boots, then

he stepped backward and sat on the top step of the deck, careful not to look behind.

She felt oddly powerful and more than a little smug at being able to abash a man like this with a simple, earthy act. Women's magic.

Sleepy, swirling magic, which bound all it touched, enchantress as well as enchanted. Petra's lips suckled at her nipple and the enchantment spread—a golden wire drawn from her breasts to her womb, then drawn tighter in soft, rhythmic tugs that her hips yearned to answer. The sensation spooled out to include the man, as if he were the cause, the one who held the gilded wire, the one who tugged, instead of an unknowing bystander. Dana closed her eyes and shuddered. She'd been dead to her own body for so long—just a mother, a widow. How odd for it to awaken just now.

Means nothing, she told herself. *I don't even like him. He hurt Sean.*

He was overwhelmingly male and perhaps "like" had nothing to do with instinct. Simply by being, he reminded her she was female. A woman without a mate—not a reminder for which she was grateful.

Montana spoke without turning. "I asked Zoe about Sean's father."

As if he could read her mind! Dana tipped back her head to stare at a pendant blossom. Blown, its vibrant rosiness fading to drab violet, the first petals fallen. "Yes?"

"I…meant to talk with him. But Zoe tells me I can't."

I talk to him all the time. But he never answers, not in words. "That's right," she said bleakly. She reached to pluck a petal, rubbed it across her lips.

"I'm…sorry. If you'd told me…"

"Mmm," she hummed wordlessly. *Who owed you an explanation?*

"I reckon I scared you, stomping in like that. And I wanted to say I'm sorry."

"Oh." It was handsomely done, no self-justifications, no excuses. But Dana wasn't in a forgiving mood. Not because of the intrusion, but because of Sean. "Thank you," she said coldly.

"Hmmph." He pulled his Stetson off, inspected it, whacked a denim-clad calf with it.

Clearly he had more to say. She waited, and when it didn't come, she asked, "How's Zoe?"

"She threw up this morning." He whacked his leg again. "Not the first time, she tells me."

"She needs to see a doctor. Forget that test kit. Let a gynecologist examine her. She should be on vitamins, eating right—"

He let out a huff of bitter amusement. "I'm known around these parts, Dana, for being a devil on nutrition. Pound for pound, my cattle are the best fed in the state. You think I'd neglect my daughter? But she'll be eating for one, not two."

A rancher. She should have known it, with his boots and his outdoor tan. A man used to giving orders, not taking them. King of his own small kingdom. "That's what Zoe wants?"

"What she will want, once she sees sense."

So he'd yet to bully her into submission. In spite of the complications Zoe's stand might mean for the Kershaws, Dana felt a flash of admiration. It would take courage to cross this man.

"In the meantime, she should see a doctor."

He grunted assent. "Another reason I wanted to see you. She has a pediatrician, of course, but now... Is there anybody you'd recommend?"

Had he no other female in his life to advise him? A sister, a lover, a friend? Despite his high-handed arrogance, his explosive temper, Rafe Montana was one of the most attractive men she'd ever laid eyes on, so surely he had a woman. Petra had fallen asleep while they spoke, and now her mouth slipped away from the breast. Dana buttoned her blouse one handed while she considered. Ought to stay out of this. The fewer ties between the Kershaws and the Montanas, the better, to her mind. But a good doctor was essential. "Yes, I go to a woman obstetrician in Durango. Cassandra Hancock. She's gentle and extremely competent."

"Does she do abortions?" he asked bluntly.

Dana winced, worked the top button through its hole, and reached for the hand towel she'd brought from the kitchen. "I wouldn't know. But I'm sure if she doesn't, she could advise *Zoe*. Tell her the best place to go." She laid the towel over her shoulder, moved Petra to burping position and stood. Patting the baby's back, she walked slowly back and forth. Rafe shifted to watch, and she felt herself drawn irresistibly closer with each turn, till she stood above him, staring out over her land. She glanced down, and their eyes linked. His were the dark, high-altitude blue of the mountaintop skies, direct as a bolt of summer lightning. Her heart bumped in her breast half a dozen times before his eyes released her and shifted to her baby.

The straight line of his mouth softened. "But I suppose you don't believe in abortions."

"I believe in choice, Mr. Montana."

"Rafe."

"But choice cuts both ways, doesn't it…Rafe? What does Zoe choose? It's her life, her body, her baby."

All restless energy, he surged to his feet. "She's in no emotional shape to choose wisely!" He took all the steps in a stride and stopped on the last one, which put them on a level—too close. So close Dana could see the pale line of a scar drawn across the carved fullness of his bottom lip.

She rocked back on her heels, but held her ground. "Whether she is or not, you can't take that choice from her." *Or can you?* He was so clearly used to having his way.

The muscles along his angular jaw fluttered and stilled. "Someone should have taken that choice from Zoe's mother."

Dana blinked. Blunt words, indeed. "Oh?"

"Pilar was eighteen when we…found out. And—" His jaw clenched again and his gaze swung off to the east, to the mountain that walled off that side of the valley. "And it ruined her life."

But she got you. He had a profile like the head on a Roman coin—harsh, emphatic, all jutting lines and angles, with not a softening curve except for that bottom lip. Zoe's mother had gotten herself a harsh and beautiful man. *Was that the choice that wrecked her life?* Eyes wide, Dana rested her cheek against Petra's dark curls and waited.

"It's like…" His shoulders jerked, then squared and went taut. "Like history repeating itself. Some kind of enormous, ugly joke. Pilar had already been accepted into Harvard when we… Full scholarship—she was from a poor family. Would have been the first of her family ever to go to college. She was brilliant—that's where Zoe gets her brains. Meant to be a doctor, too. Instead she—" He shook his head. "It was a criminal waste."

"Or maybe she…chose what she wanted."

One bark of savage laughter—it was instantly stifled. "You think so? No, it was a waste of her talents, her hard work, her dreams, her family's hopes. Just when Pilar's life was about to open out, to expand—she'd never even been out of Colorado before—we made one stupid mistake. I made one. And her life contracted to a crummy one-room trailer, a baby with colic, a nineteen-year-old husband who could barely keep himself in boot leather, much less support a family. Yeah, she made one hell of a choice.''

''I see...''

''I hope to God you do.'' Rafe shrugged, setting aside any personal connection to the picture he'd just painted. ''So, a wise man learns from his mistakes. And if he loves his daughter, he damn sure stops her from making the same mistakes.''

Do we ever get to shield the ones we love from their mistakes? She'd tried to stop Peter from crossing that south-facing slope, nervously citing what she'd read about alpine snow conditions, but he'd teased her about learning cross-country skiing from a book and had pushed on. They'd both been cold and tired at the end of the day, eager to reach their lodge... *Wouldn't have needed to cross that hill at all if I hadn't read the map wrong, taken us down the wrong fork in the trail.* She hadn't even been able to shield Peter from *her* mistakes, much less his own.

''Hey.'' A warm, rough hand cupped her cheek. ''Are you okay?''

''I...'' She blinked back the tears, took a step backward. Slipped a hand down to Petra's bottom. ''Oops!'' She managed a trembly smile. ''Flood tide. If you'd excuse us a minute?''

SHE TOOK CLOSER TO TWENTY, stopping to wash her face after she'd put Petra down in her crib. *What's gotten into you?* she scolded the damp face with its shadowy eyes, which gazed back at her from her mirror. After months of gray, steely calm, suddenly she felt raw and ragged, her emotions swinging wildly from elation to despair. Like a compass needle following a prowling magnet.

Not enough sleep, she answered herself, heading down-

stairs. *Forgot lunch.* She pushed through the dining room
door—and stopped short. *Rafe Montana in my kitchen.*

Peeking under the towel that covered a bowl of her rising
dough. He whipped around, as guilty as a boy caught
scooping a fingerful of icing off a cake. "You were so long,
I wondered if something was wrong."

I'm fine. Dana didn't want to acknowledge his concern.
"She took a while falling back to sleep."

He grimaced. "At least she sleeps. Zoe worked a double
shift from the word go. Started climbing out of her crib at
nine months. I'd wake up at 3:00 a.m. and she'd be bumping around the trailer like a raccoon on the hunt, turning
out cupboards. Pulled the phone down on her head one
night—Lord, what a racket."

"A handful." She could imagine him at nineteen, working a man's job all day, still needing the sleep of a boy at
night. *It must have been desperately hard for you and Pilar,
both.* But watching his face, she could see his memories of
Zoe's baby years were rueful, not grudging.

His expression hardened. "A handful still. Which brings
me back to my problem…"

"Yes?" But problems or not, she had an evening meal
to prepare. She dusted flour over her marble pastry slab and
turned out the first ball of risen dough. Dug the heel of her
right hand into its spongy softness, folded its far edge back
toward the center, turned the dough, then shoved again,
settling into her rhythm—knead, fold, rotate a quarter turn.
Knead again…

Rafe drifted closer and stared down at her hands.
"You've got to help me, Dana."

An order, not a request, she noted wryly. Knead, fold,
turn, knead… She sprinkled more flour on the marble.
"Help you how?"

"Zoe got her brains from Pilar, but she got her stub-
bornness from me." He gripped the edge of the table and

leaned closer. "I'm not getting through to her, what a disaster this baby would be. I thought maybe a woman... somebody who's gone through it recently and who's going it alone..."

She looked up at him with something like hatred. "You'd use me—me and my baby—as an object lesson? How handy that my husband died. It makes us seem more pathetic!"

He jerked upright. "I didn't mean it like—"

"Oh, I'm sure you didn't think at all." She brushed the hair away from her eyes with the back of her hand.

"I didn't think of it like that, dammit. You're anything but pathetic." His scowl softened. The corner of his mouth slowly tilted. "Though, with flour all over your face..."

I look like a clown? So much for indignation. She swiped the back of a hand across her nose, and he burst into laughter.

"Here—" He tucked three fingers under her chin to support it.

If her hands hadn't been full of dough, she would have edged out of reach. Instead, she stood paralyzed, her lashes falling to shut him out—to shut out this fragile, disturbing moment—while he cleaned her off, his fingers brushing across the bridge of her nose, the tops of her cheeks, her shivering lashes.

"Better," he observed huskily.

Was it? Was it really? A wave of black dismay—of echoing loss—washed over her. "Thanks," she whispered, staring down at her dough. After a moment her hands moved again—knead, fold, turn...

"*Will* you help me persuade her, Dana?"

Give a little to get what you wanted, she thought, loss turning to disgust. He thought he could buy her cooperation that easily, with one gesture of tossed-off tenderness? "No, Rafe, I won't. Zoe doesn't need some stranger telling her

what to do.'' Nor, for that matter, a parent trying to shape
her life according to his own lights. ''What about getting
her some professional counseling? I'm sure that Dr. Hancock—''

''*I'm* the only counselor Zoe needs, dammit! A baby will
wreck her life!''

''Then if you're all she needs,'' Dana said coolly, ''she
doesn't need me.''

''But, dammit—'' He saw her chin tip up in warning and
he shut his mouth with an effort, locked his jaw over his
words. Stood rocking on his boot heels and scowling, while
she patted the first ball of dough into a loaf, settled it into
its greased pan and placed it on the warming shelf. She
turned out another ball of risen dough, pressed out the
yeasty gas, commenced kneading.

''All right,'' he said grimly, ''then look at it this way.
You owe me this help.''

Her hands paused as she looked up. ''Excuse me?''

''Your son knocked up my daughter. If you'd ridden
herd on him, hadn't let him run wild, had taught him a
proper respect for girls—''

Dana threw up a floury hand. ''Now, wait a minute. Your
daughter is—what—two years older than Sean? And everyone knows girls are *years* more mature than boys. So just
who seduced *whom?* And *who* should have known better?''

''At fourteen, he's old enough to know right from
wrong! Or at least, old enough to know how not to get
caught. Didn't you tell him about condoms?''

''Didn't you tell your brilliant daughter?'' she shot back.

''She knew,'' he said with dangerous calm.

''Then—''

''Condoms do fail.'' His gaze turned distant and bleak.

''Is that what—''

He shrugged and spun on his heel, surveyed her kitchen,
swung back again. ''She's not giving me any of the gory

details, and frankly—'' His shrug was more of a shudder. ''Frankly, I don't want to know. Every time I think about it, I get this urge to hammer your kid into the ground like a cedar fence post.''

Dana dusted her hands and came carefully around the table. ''If you ever lay so much as a *finger* on Sean again—'' She prodded his chest with a fingertip ''—I'll have you in jail for assault, Rafe Montana. See if I don't!''

''Assault?'' He caught her wrist, trapping her hand in that gesture of threat, forefinger touching his breast. ''Last night, he swung on *me*.''

''Yes, but who finished it?'' She yanked backward, but he held her easily.

''That was a lesson he needed to learn. You don't take on someone you can't handle.''

''I'll thank you not to give my son lessons!''

''Then who will?'' He brought her hand down to his side, then drew it slightly behind him, a subtle tug that swayed her closer. She flattened her other hand on his chest to catch her balance—could feel his heart thudding against her palm. ''*You'll* teach him how to grow up a man? Not your strong point, I'd say.'' His eyes roved down her face to her mouth. He smiled slowly and shook his head. ''Not your strong point at all, thank God.''

She shoved his chest hard, and he let her go. ''Nobody asked you for lessons, and I'm telling you again, don't you *dare*—'' She cut herself short as the screen door to the deck creaked.

Sean stood there, gaping at them both.

CHAPTER SIX

THE BOY'S LOOK OF SHOCK turned to a thunderous scowl and he stepped backward—spun away. Rafe Montana lunged after him before the door banged shut. "You! Come here!"

So much for her warning! Dana yelped a protest and followed. She flung out onto the deck to find them faced off like a couple of dogs, hackles risen and weight on the balls of their feet. She caught Montana's collar and gave a warning tug. "I said don't!"

"And I heard you," he told her evenly, his eyes locked on Sean.

Which was hardly a promise to obey, she realized. Retaining her grip, Dana glared at Sean. "Sean, if you'd please go in the—" The bruise on his jaw registered—blue-green and glorious. "Oh, Sean!" She let go of Montana and flew to her stepson, caught his chin in her hand.

Sean jerked out of her grasp and edged away. "It's nothing."

"Oh, no, it isn't!" She touched his shoulder, but he stepped aside. "Sean, please…"

"Shut up, Dana." Sean didn't spare her a glance.

"*What* did you say?" Rafe demanded in a voice of quiet thunder.

"I—I s-said…" The boy stopped as Rafe shook his head.

"Don't," he said with ominous calm. "Not ever. Not around me."

"Rafe, I can handle this, thank you," Dana insisted.

"Some job you're doing." His eyes switched to Sean. "You and I have to talk."

Sean clenched his hands. "I've only got one thing to say to you, Mr. Montana. Where's Zoe?"

Montana seemed to grow a foot. "You went looking for my daughter? You went on my *land?*"

Sean gulped and shook his head, but he didn't back down. "Uh-uh. Zoe was supposed to meet me where—" His hand flew toward his mouth—a touchingly childish gesture—and stopped midair. Fisted again. "She didn't meet me," he finished sullenly. "What'd you do to her?"

"Zoe is grounded. She doesn't set foot off Suntop till I give the word, and when she does, believe me, it won't be to meet you."

"No!" Sean shook his head wildly as his voice cracked. "I've got to see her!"

"Get this straight," Rafe said softly. "You won't be seeing my daughter again—ever. You've done your damage, and now you're finished. It's over."

"It isn't!" Sean cried raggedly. "Dana?"

"Oh, Sean…" He never asked her for anything, and now that he had, she'd give all she held precious to help. But he might as well ask her to move a mountain.

"You come sneaking on my land, and I'll have you arrested for trespassing," Rafe continued. "And I promise you, sonny boy, this charge will stick. You got that?"

"Try and stop me, asshole!" Sean spun, jumped three steps to ground level and took off running.

Rafe took two strides after him, but Dana blocked his path. "Don't."

"So help me God, Dana, if he comes sniffing after her onto my land, I'll hog-tie the brat and haul him home to you in my truck!"

"I've heard enough threats for one day." Dana swiped the hair from her eyes, retreated to her swing and sat.

"How long have you been raising him alone? He's out of control."

"And I've had enough criticism about my child-rearing techniques, thank you. Want me to start in on yours?" Crossing her arms to wall him out, she closed her eyes, tipped her head back. Willed him to disappear in a puff of smoke.

No such luck. He growled something wordless, and the swing tilted as he sat down beside her. Their thighs brushed, and she shied away. After a moment, the swing rocked backward on its chains, glided forward. Dana heaved a sigh up from around her toes, lifted her heels up to the cushion, clasped her ankles. The swing arced gently through her self-imposed darkness, through the fragrance of roses. How odd to be rocked; she'd grown so used to doing for herself.

"Well, what now?" he asked finally.

"Now? I suppose I take the steaks out to warm up. I start the coals, bake the bread, make cookies for dessert tonight..." A distant, sleepy wail drifted through an upstairs window. "I comfort my daughter..."

"And what do I do about mine?"

"Try listening instead of ranting?" she suggested.

Warm fingers closed around her arm, just above her elbow. "Help me persuade her. Please?"

She bet he didn't beg for help often. Still, she sighed and shook her head. "Can't do it, Rafe. Zoe needs to find *her* way, not be shoved into somebody else's plan for her life."

"It's the best plan," he insisted. "The only plan right for her."

"Then maybe she'll come to see that in time. But it's not for me to say." *Nor you.*

The swing lurched as he stood. She squeezed her eyes

tighter shut, then waited, willing him gone. At least her life had been peaceful before he stormed into it. If he left now... Was it too late to go back to that?

"Thanks," he said bitterly.

"You're welcome, Rafe." Eyes closed, Dana waited till the crunch of his steps across the gravel had faded. Till she could hear nothing but the Ribbon River, chuckling down the mountainside. She sighed again, opened her eyes and went into her kitchen.

Who was she kidding? From now on, nothing would be the same.

"HERE COMES YOUR DADDY," drawled Anse Kirby from his higher vantage point. He'd been lounging sideways, one arm braced back on the rump of his red roan, Tiger, watching Zoe wrestle with the top wire of the fence. Now he straightened in the saddle and gathered his reins.

"Oh?" Zoe levered her pliers around the curve of the cedar post, tightening the wire, then hammered the loosened staple home. She pulled a second staple from the carpenter's apron she wore over her jeans and whacked that in, downstream of the first. "What should I do? Turn cartwheels?"

"Smile might go a long ways." Anse apparently addressed the lowering sun.

"Yeah, go ahead. Take his side." As her father's top hand, he could hardly do else, Zoe supposed, but she was in no mood to be fair.

"Just a general observation. Woofle's outgrinned you 'bout twelve to one, today."

"Well, he had a banner day—found something dead to roll in. Me, I've done nothing but ride fence." A chore she usually loved in the summertime. But not today. Not when she'd been given into Anse's care like a five-year-old pest, with the implicit order, *Keep her occupied.* "I'm sorry, I know I've been a grump."

"We all get a mood on, from time to time." He made no visible move, but, responsive to a tensing of Anse's thighs, Tiger swung to face the oncoming rider and set off at a lazy jog. Ignoring the horsemen, Zoe slogged off to the next post. Out on her flank, Woofle rose from the grass and trotted on a parallel course, careful to preserve the twenty-foot margin she'd ordained.

She'd completed that post, when the shadow of a horse and rider blocked the sun. "Anse will finish up here, Zoe. Let's go."

She shrugged and hung her hammer over the wire, untied her apron and draped it over the post. Anse had already dismounted and collected Miel, her little palomino, who'd been standing ground-hitched, placidly grazing. He passed her the reins with a wink. "Thanks for the help, Zoe."

Like he needed it. She gave him a reluctant smile. "Sure. Anytime." Probably every day this summer, if her father had his way. *But he won't.* She cast Rafe a mutinous glance as her leg swung over the saddle and she found her stirrups.

Under the brim of his Stetson, his eyes were expressionless. He jerked his chin uphill. "Suntop?"

It was their favorite ride. A rift in the mountains to the west allowed the setting sun to shine through, gilding that hilltop long after the rest of their valley was plunged in to purple shadows. The ranch took its name from the peak. But today? She shrugged, and when he turned Tobasco, his big half Arab, half quarterhorse gelding up the slope, she went with him. But not knee to knee as they usually rode, with her on his left so that his roping hand was unobstructed. Tensing her inside leg, she forced Miel five feet to the left of their normal position. The palomino lashed her silver tail, but accepted the command, ears disapproving. Zoe pulled her Stetson low over her forehead, giving her father nothing but the top of her hat.

They rode in silence, just the *jingle* of a bit, the soft *swish* as the horses breasted the waist-high wildflowers, the lush grass. June was always her favorite month, but this year? Everything had changed—such a stupid jerk, *she'd* changed everything. *And now I get to live with it.*

Her eyes lit on a blue columbine, robin's egg blue, with a central streak of white in its throat. A keeper. "Don't wait," she called, twisting around in her saddle. She chose one of the whippy bamboo poles from the bundle she always carried behind her, reached for the orange surveyor's ribbon in her saddlebag. Dismounted and set up her flag so she could find the plant tomorrow. She'd been hybridizing wild columbine since she was twelve, combining colors and petal markings in search of bluer blues, bigger blossoms, odd new patterns. She had some stunners by now.

He waited for her, of course, and this time their eyes met as she mounted. "That's just what I mean, Zoe. You won't have time to think about things like that if you keep your baby. You know a lot, but there'll be professors at Harvard who could take you to the next level, then the next, and the next. Show you things you've never dreamed about."

Or that I have. But she couldn't let it matter. "Do you remember that time back in ninth grade when Mrs. Pollock tried to make me dissect that frog?"

His lips curved up, then abruptly down. "That's different."

"Sure is. That was just a poor dorky frog." A frog she'd ransomed, with a month of detentions and a twenty-page essay for her refusal. "But this is a baby."

Tobasco danced sideways to some inner turmoil of his rider, then snorted and swerved back into line. "I brought you up to face the hard choices. Do you remember the time I shot Nacho?"

She would never forget it. They'd been up in the high country, moving the cattle to their summer range, a day's ride from the nearest vet, and a vet couldn't have healed that break, anyhow. Nacho had been Rafe's friend, his partner, the smartest, funniest horse she'd ever known. If her father could have cut off his arm to save that old gelding, he'd have done so. "I remember. But you had no choice, Daddy. I have."

"It's the wrong choice. It'll wreck your life. Wreck everything you've worked for."

"It'll *change* my life."

"For the worst!"

"Is that what it did to yours—what I did?"

His eyes swerved away. "I was thinking about your mother."

"I wrecked *her* life," Zoe said flatly. But she'd known that from the time she could toddle. For the first three years after her mother's death, there had been no one to keep her, while her father cowboyed from ranch to ranch, except her mother's parents—Zoe's *abuelo* and *abuelita,* Paco and Inéz Cavazos. She'd understood their language long before she spoke it, and the house had been filled with it, her presence constantly invoking words of regretful, soft Spanish. Long, meandering tales recounting Pilar's scholastic triumphs, her shining talents, her grace, her beauty, her ultimate tragedy. Nobody's fault, *niña,* but *¡qué lástima!*— what a pity and what a waste! A waste that she'd been ransoming all her life, just as she'd paid for the frog, report card after dazzling report card.

But now that obligation collided with this. Couldn't he see?

"You didn't wreck anybody's life. You were Pilar's pride and joy."

Was I? But then, where was Pilar going the day she slammed out of the house, weeping and raging, and drove off—never to return? Zoe couldn't recall the words of that last fight; it merged into too many before it. But she could remember the bitterness, the rifle-crack retorts flying back and forth, while she peeked through her bedroom door. *If I was her pride and joy, then why did she leave me? Why wasn't I in the car with her when it hit the abutment?*

She'd never dared ask. Without Pilar, she and her dad had simply closed ranks and soldiered on.

"You're *my* pride and joy," her father continued huskily. "I want only the very, very best for you. And a baby at seventeen, sweetheart. That isn't it."

"You always taught me to make the best of things."

"The best of this is to own up to your mistake. To look an ugly but necessary choice in the eye and to take it, like I did with Nacho."

"But this time I'm not deciding just for me, Daddy. What's best for my—"

"No!" he cried harshly. "Don't think like that. It's a possibility, not a person. Just a fork in your road. You take one fork and your life will be a trap—a cage with you looking out through the bars, wishing for what might have been. You take the other fork, Zoe, and you—" He turned up his free hand to the blue above. "You fly...you fly as high and far as your wings will take you. *Trust* me on this. I'm right. I know I'm right."

There was a lump in her throat the size of an ice cube. His love was so much harder to resist than his rage. But still... "It's not just a fork. It's a teeny bit of Sean and me, dividing and growing by the hour."

"Sean!" Tobasco threw up his blood-bay head, then snapped it down and pranced in place, a drumbeat of frustration; speed denied. "If I was choosing a sire for my grandchild—"

"*Daddy!*" He was hopeless—a hundred years out of date—and she knew she was turning as red as a stoplight.

"Nothing but an insolent little—"

"He's a good kid!" *An absolute hunk in the making,* but she knew better than to say that.

"That's all you were shooting for—good? You deserve the best—in another five years or so."

"He is the best. You're underestimating him."

"Whatever he is, he's out of this. This is between you and me. Someday you'll know I was right."

She shook her head. *Don't say it, don't say it!* Once he'd said something he never backed down.

"You're getting an abortion as fast as I can arrange it," he said. "Tomorrow I'll—"

"No!" she yelled, yanking off her hat and slamming it to the ground. Miel shied violently, and Zoe spun her back around, half rearing. "No, I am *not,* and you can't make me!" They were back to where they'd deadlocked last night.

"Zoe…"

She'd heard that tone before, like gravel sliding down a chute—that time he'd fired a hand for beating a horse, the time he'd thrown that party of drunken hunters off the ranch. Heard it only once or twice in her life aimed *her* way. She shook her head, helpless to stop him or back down.

"You take my advice on this one…or you get out of my house. Off my land."

"F-f-fine," she cried through trembling lips. "Then I'll do that!" She touched her spurs to Miel's flanks and shot off down the mountain.

"Zoe!" he yelled after her. But even had it been safe to take her eyes off the slope ahead, the grass blurring with the horse's speed and her tears, she wouldn't have looked back. She swerved Miel to the right, choosing a gentler grade before they fell head over heels. Woofle shot off to

the left, ears flying, tongue flapping, taking the direct dow
hill line, racing her home.

Her home no longer. *You want me, you come stop me,*
she thought, gritting her teeth against the threatening sobs.
Please, take it back. Tobasco could catch her mare any day.
But she heard no thundering hoofbeats behind—only Miel,
huffing like a little steam engine through the high grass.

She'd thrown half a dozen shirts, a few pairs of jeans
into the open suitcase on her bed, when he filled her doorway. She yanked open her lingerie drawer and seized a
handful of underthings. Dumped those on the growing pile.
"You'll have to keep Miel for me," she muttered without
turning her head. "Till I can…" Her eyes filled with tears.
There was no way she could afford to keep a horse on her
own. She'd be lucky to keep herself. *And my baby.*

He stalked across to the bed, lifted her stacks of clothes
out and set them on the spread, closed the suitcase and
tucked it under one arm. "Forget what I said, Zoe. I didn't
mean it."

"Oh." She spun away, hugging herself to contain the
sobs. "Oh, Daddy, I…"

He came up behind her, hovering, unable to touch her.
"You're my daughter, right or wrong, baby. But this is
wrong."

"I can't do it. I won't!"

"Whoa! *Hush.* Don't be so quick to decide. We've both
been shooting our mouths off way too much. I'd like you
to consider it, just for a day or two. Would you do that for
me? Please?"

She stood, face averted, tears dripping, torn between
pleasing him and speaking her heart. "If I—" She stopped
and knuckled her nose. "If I do that, Daddy, will you do
something for me?"

"Whatever you need, sweetheart."

"I need to see Sean."

CHAPTER SEVEN

"THEY'RE COMING!" Sean yelled as he loped up from the meadows, waving his fishing rod. For the past hour he'd kept vigil on the low concrete bridge that spanned the Ribbon River, a quarter mile below the house.

Ever since Dana had informed him of the Montanas' request for a Monday-afternoon interview with the Kershaws, Sean had affected a sullen nonchalance, but the details betrayed his true emotion. He'd taken a second shower after lunch—an unheard-of event—then changed from his father's old Grateful Dead T-shirt to a blue cotton dress shirt, tucked into a fresh pair of jeans.

"It's them!" he panted, stumbling to a halt where she knelt at the foot of the stairs to the front porch.

In the distance, Rafe Montana's shiny black pickup raised a trail of dust as it approached the bridge. Dana glanced down at the window boxes she'd been planting—her own form of nervous make-work. "Sean, would you run grab the pitcher of lemonade from the fridge and that platter of cookies on the counter?"

Might as well do the thing handsomely, she'd decided. High tea and civilized conversation on the porch. Petra had done her own small part to make the affair a success by nursing earlier than usual, then allowing herself to be put down for an afternoon nap. "Sleep on, sweetie," Dana murmured as she pulled off her gardening gloves and brushed her bangs from her eyes. She glanced down at her jeans, swept them free of peat moss, then tucked the tails of her red sleeveless shirt. She'd had a strange impulse to wear a sundress for this occasion and had rejected the notion. Who was she trying to impress—Zoe? Though she *had* clipped on a pair of opal ear studs that she hadn't worn in more than a year.

She touched one lobe nervously, then turned as Sean banged out the front door. "On the table, thank you." The view from the front porch out over the lower valley was one of the ranch's finest—soothing, serene, conducive to calm discussion. *Now, if Rafe and Sean will just keep their tempers...*

"Welcome," Sean muttered, rattling down the stairs. He clutched half a dozen of her shortbread cookies bundled in a paper napkin.

"I thought we'd eat those here on the porch," she called after him, but if he heard, he didn't respond. He brought up short beside Rafe's pickup and yanked open Zoe's door.

For one dreadful moment Dana feared he'd lift her down from the truck and kiss her. She could see Rafe scowling already through the windshield. Then Zoe tumbled out, all impossibly long legs, raucous red hair and brilliant smile. She turned to wave up at Dana. "Good afternoon, Mrs. Kershaw!"

"Hello, Zoe." So finally, she'd formally meet the girl. There had been no time, the other night. Or no, apparently not. Because Zoe had already spun away to grab Sean's arm and drag him toward the river.

"Half an hour and not a minute more," Rafe called after them. "And stay in sight." He crossed his arms. *"Zo-e?"*

This time she glanced back impatiently. *"Yes,* Daddy, we will!"

Rafe sauntered up the lawn to Dana, shaking his head. "Not quite what I'd planned. I meant to introduce you two."

"Bound to happen one of these days." She stood irresolute before him for a moment. Shake his hand? No, that didn't feel right, but some gesture seemed necessary....

She tipped her head toward the porch. "Well, there's lemonade for the chaperones. Come on up."

Rafe accepted a glass and a cookie, then prowled her porch, staring down toward the river. Finally he settled on a chair that gave him a clear view of the proceedings. Dana followed his gaze and saw Zoe perched on a water-smoothed boulder on the far side of the creek; Sean sat cross-legged before her, leaning forward intently, courtier at the feet of his queen.

"I told her if they so much as held hands, I'd call a halt," Rafe growled. "So far, so good."

"What exactly did you have in mind?" Dana pulled up a chair beside him. She'd assumed some sort of family council, perhaps a discussion of Sean's, and therefore her, responsibilities.

Eyes fixed on the distant pair, he heaved a sigh. "Being the hard guy has gotten me nowhere. So now I'm trying the soft approach. I asked her not to knee-jerk rule out abortion—to consider it for a day or two. And in return, she asked to see your boy. I'm praying that maybe what she has in the back of her mind is asking his approval to terminate." He turned to skewer her with his gaze, twin spears of blue. "Do you think he'd give it, if that's what she's asking?"

"I think Sean wants only one thing in the world—whatever's best for Zoe."

"If that were true, he'd never have gotten her in trouble."

"You never made a mistake?"

He growled something wordless and gulped lemonade. "What burns me up," he muttered after a moment, "is how unfair it is! His life will roll merrily on, exactly as before. While Zoe? Her whole life has been derailed."

"Only if she chooses for that to be so." And it was Zoe who had messed with the track switch, Dana was sure, watching the girl's animated gestures.

Rafe grimaced. "She may not feel she has a choice, at this point. Zoe has her principles. Always has. She's been a vegetarian since she was eight, when it hit her what happens to the cattle after we ship 'em out."

One more reason to get her to a doctor—and soon, Dana worried. She'd need to take extra care with her diet if she ate no meat.

"One more reason she has to go away to college, find a career," Rafe said, echoing her thoughts grimly. "She loves the outdoors, but she'll never make a rancher or a rancher's wife."

"She's your only child?" Dana already knew his answer. He looked like an eagle, guarding his one fledgling from the top of a pine tree.

Eyes fixed on the girl, he nodded.

Which meant he'd carved himself a kingdom—and what a struggle that must have been, the way land prices were rising in Colorado—and now he had no one to cherish and inherit his achievement. *Does that hurt, I wonder?* How could it not? And it showed the man's basic generosity— Rafe was looking to his daughter's good at the cost of his own. *He'll never force her into an abortion,* Dana realized with a rush of relief. If he wouldn't demand that Zoe follow in his footsteps with the ranch, then he wouldn't insist on this, despite how deeply he felt it.

He turned the full weight of his gaze upon her. "What about Sean? You're his stepmother. I suppose that means his mother's dead, too?"

"No. His mother's in San Diego." She found that it was easier to speculate about Rafe's past than to reveal her own, but his eyes dragged the story from her. "When she and Peter divorced—a year before I ever met Peter…" Though

Margot still saw her as the thief, the home wrecker. Somehow she must have thought that someday, someway, she'd win Peter back. "She gave him full custody."

"That's odd."

"Not, apparently, if you knew her. She has…problems."

Rafe dropped a hand on the back of her chair and leaned closer. "The sort of problems that Sean might pass on to his child?"

"N-no." This had never occurred to her. She bit her lip and turned to look down at Peter's son. He'd been depressed this past year, but that was entirely understandable, normal…

Two fingertips hooked around her chin and reclaimed her gaze. "What are we talking, here, Dana? Mental illness?"

"Oh, no. Not unless you want to call extreme self-involvement an illness. She just sees the world as circling around her own problems."

"*What* problems?"

"She…drinks too much. And takes pills—downers, uppers, whatever her mood requires. Not illegal drugs, just too many drugs from too many obliging doctors."

"Wonderful!" His hand dropped away. "My grandchild's likely to be an alcoholic—or an addict. Well, that settles it!"

"Don't think that way!" she pleaded. "It's just a rotten upbringing, that's all. Her mother was an actress—B movies and such. And apparently the father bailed out early—sent money, but no love or attention when she needed it. Margot was dragged up, a typical Hollywood child, alternately spoiled and neglected. How can you blame her?"

"Hey, that's the beauty of it nowadays. Nobody's ever to blame. So she gave her kid away like a pair of worn-out shoes?"

"Maybe it was the one truly unselfish thing she's ever done. She was going into a clinic to dry out at that point.

Peter was a rock, obviously the one who could best care for Sean. So she gave him up.''

''But after his father died? How long had you two been married?''

''Only a year.'' The skiing weekend had been their anniversary gift to each other.

''She didn't want to change her mind after that?''

Dana shrugged. ''She toyed with the idea, I think. But Peter had appointed me guardian. He made me promise that I'd never let Margot have Sean. He was convinced she'd ruin him, just as she'd been ruined. So if she'd insisted, I would have fought her.''

''Though you'd only had the kid for a year?''

She met his eyes point-blank. ''Sean was the person Peter loved most in all the world. And I promised.''

She felt as if no one had looked at her—really *seen* her—for fourteen long months. Now his blue eyes moved through her like sunshine through clear water. As his gaze roved down to her lips, she turned away, but saw nothing, felt only the drumming of her heart, the play of his gaze upon her stirring flesh.

''So she didn't insist,'' he murmured finally.

''What? Oh, no, she didn't. At the time Peter died, she'd just entered another clinic, her third or fourth attempt to dry out. Some sort of health–exercise–clean-living community. No room for children, apparently. She wrote Sean once or twice, maybe made some promises she didn't keep—that's precisely her style. And that's the last we've heard of her, thank God.''

''Wish to God she'd taken him!'' he muttered.

So much for their moment of connection. ''Well, she didn't.''

Restless, he stood and paced behind her, looking down at their children. Sean and Zoe had taken off their shoes and were now wading downstream toward the bridge, arms outstretched for balance, still talking nonstop. "Whatever else they are, they're friends," she murmured, as he paused behind her.

"So?"

"So I'm glad. To my mind, at the very least, babies should be made in friendship."

He snorted. "Babies shouldn't be made by accident—period!"

But now that they've made one, what do we do? And Sean—she'd worried that he had no friends, while all along—for the past few months, anyway—he'd had Zoe. However they solved this problem, Rafe wouldn't allow their friendship to continue, she was sure. *Sean, I'm so sorry....*

Rafe stopped to lean out over the balustrade, and she went to join him.

"Nice land," he murmured, peering out over her valley. "Great water, wonderful grazing—and you're wasting it on dudes."

"I'm afraid I know a lot more about people and cooking than I do about cows."

He made a wry sort of sound, something between a grunt and a laugh. "I tried to buy this spread, 'bout three years back. A nice old girl owned it then, a widow lady. She was running it as a dude ranch, too, though it seemed like she had more cats around the place than tourists."

"Peter's Aunt Harriet. She decided that she and the cats had had enough of snow country, that they were moving to Florida. So she offered the place to Peter—she wanted it to stay in the family. We bought it summer before last." Dana swallowed painfully, and turned her empty glass round and round on the railing. "I was the one who really wanted it. Who pushed Peter into buying. He was happy enough teaching high school in San Diego. If..." *If I'd let well enough alone...* The vista below blurred to a rainy watercolor.

"Ifs will break your heart if you let them, Dana."

He was right. She'd made a resolution, months ago, that it was time to stop grieving, for Petra's sake if not her own. Above all else, Peter would have wanted her to raise his daughter in happiness. A child's first perceptions were crucial and they should be of a joyful world—a world of butterflies and skyrockets and laughter—not a world of sorrow. *But sometimes it's so hard, Peter!*

"So it's just you running this outfit?" he asked after a moment. Moving them back to a safe topic.

"No, there's also Tim, my dude wrangler, such as he is."

"Meaning?"

"Meaning he wrangles with the dudes, he wrangles with me, he'd kick the dog if we had one. I guess you'd call him a cowboy curmudgeon." And a lazy, hard-drinking bum. But for the money she could pay, Tim was probably as good as she could get. At least he showed up for work most days, since his cabin was part of his salary.

Rafe frowned. "That can't be good for business, can it?"

"It's not the best." One of her guest families last week had demanded a discount at the end of their stay. Tim was supposed to have given them daily riding lessons, but he'd failed to appear for three of the seven days. If they'd complained earlier, she might have corrected the situation, but they hadn't. After their refund, she'd barely recouped her expenses on that one. "I try to sell him as local color."

He opened his mouth to disagree, and she hurried on. "And Sean helps out." When he felt like it. "He owns a fourth of the ranch, by Peter's will."

"Does he," Rafe muttered, turning around to study the clapboards with which the house was sheathed. "So how come he isn't painting his inheritance? If he lets this go another year... And I noticed your corral around back, when I was here yesterday. Some of those rails need replacing. Then there's your truck. If he owns a piece of that, too—''

"Rafe, he's not even fifteen."

"If he's old enough to make a baby, he's damn sure old enough to take care of what he owns. Old enough not to be dogging it, while you're working yourself to a frazzle."

"Thank you, but I'm on top of the situation."

"Are you?"

High-handed. She'd had him pegged right the first time he barged into her kitchen. "You could mind your own business, you know." Maybe he could.

"That's just what I'm doing. You think I wouldn't look into the character of a young man who seduced my daughter?"

"Rafe." She jabbed him with a forefinger and leaned into it. "Your precious Zoe is a *cradle robber!* She's the one who should have known better. A fourteen-year-old boy is a slave to his—"

"Hush!" He shoved her fingers aside. "Here they come."

She glanced aside guiltily, to see Zoe and Sean walking up the lawn with their arms wrapped around each other's waists, presenting a united front, Sean's face glowing with a pride of possession that made Dana blink. Her stepson's feelings ran deeper than friendship, she was beginning to fear.

"Daddy?" Coming to a halt on the lawn below, Zoe tipped back her head.

She wasn't a pretty child, but someday she would be a striking woman, Dana thought, when she grew into her body. Right now, Zoe was too thin, too awkward and too pale—her clouds of freckles stood out against her pallor.

Her eyes were Rafe's own—dark blue, direct and, at the moment, very anxious. ''We've decided,'' she announced.

Beside her, Sean squared his shoulders and nodded.

''What?'' Rafe said tensely, moving to lean out over the railing.

''You brought me up to make the hard choices...'' Zoe gulped and continued, her eyes suddenly sparkling with tears. ''So I— So we're—making it.''

''Good girl,'' Rafe murmured.

''We're keeping our baby,'' she blurted defiantly.

CHAPTER EIGHT

"THE HELL YOU SAY!" Rafe started for the stairs. "You
spent half an hour deciding that? Playing patty-cakes with
Romeo there? Right. We're out of here."

"Rafe!" Dana caught at the back of his shirt, then let
go and scurried after. "Rafe, wait!" As Rafe stalked toward his daughter, Sean pulled away from Zoe and moved
to block him, chin up, hands fisting.

"No!" Dana cried, dashing between them, arms raised.
"Now everybody…just…calm *down!*" She flattened either
hand on a heaving male chest. "Zoe, dear, it looks like you
want what's good for your baby," she said, speaking very
fast. "And of course, your father—" she patted his chest—
exhibit A "—only wants what's best for you." Her audience was nodding reluctantly. She caught a breath and
forged on. "So, in that case, since we're all agreed on that,
perhaps there's another possibility you ought to consider.
Have you thought about adoption?"

"Um, not really," Zoe admitted. "I—"

"I think you should, then—we should be exploring *every*
option. So if you and Sean would sit down and drink a
glass of lemonade, and think *very* carefully about that, consider the pros and the cons, your father and I are going to
take a walk." She clamped onto his forearm and swept him
downhill.

"Wait a minute!" he protested, though she'd gotten him
moving. "Adoption? I don't think—"

"*Don't* think, please, not yet. Just walk with me, Rafe."

She transferred her clasp to his inner elbow, and reluctantly he came along. "The first rule of negotiations is to keep talking, right? If you grab Zoe and stomp off now, you're ending any chance that we can work this out."

"Adoption isn't a satisfactory ending, dammit! She's off to Harvard in September."

"You know, you might have to compromise." The slope steepened to a rocky path as they neared the river.

"Compromise, hell!"

"She isn't one of your silly cows you can just shove down a chute. She's your—*oops!*" The rock she'd stepped on rolled out from under her.

He spun around, his free arm whipping around her waist to clamp her against him. "Easy!"

She dangled for a startled moment in his arms, then he lowered her toes to the ground. "Easy there." His voice had dropped to an intimate growl. They stood molded together from breast to thigh. "You've got to watch where you're going."

In this electric moment, all she could watch was the pulse hammering in the hollow of his throat…his smiling mouth when she made herself look higher. Blue eyes to drown in. She could drown in this sensation of infinite strength, hers for the asking.

She couldn't ask. She squirmed, then he let her go, except for her hand. "Take it slow," he advised, following her down the path.

Resentment flared as she heard the amusement in his voice—an insufferably masculine smugness that he could make her aware of him, make her body respond to his. *I suppose he thinks I'm the starved little widow.* But if she hungered, it was for something much deeper and more essential than a superb male body.

"As I was saying," she said determinedly, "you may have to compromise. You probably could bully Zoe into having an abortion, but at what cost?'' Reaching the river, she stopped on a boulder and kicked off her huaraches. ''Do you think she'd ever forgive you if you did that?''

''Maybe not right away, but eventually.'' Rafe watched as she rolled up her jeans. Sitting on a nearby rock, he pulled off his boots. ''But maybe that's my role here, Dana. I'm the guy who has to make the tough decisions. The ones nobody thanks you for, but that are right in the end.''

''Maybe.'' Arms outstretched, she stepped delicately into the ankle-deep, icy water and grimaced. ''Or maybe you're the tough guy whose daughter never speaks to him again. What if, ten years from now, Zoe decides to start a family and finds out, for some reason, that she can't? That you'd forced her to abort her one chance ever.''

''That's not likely to happen,'' he protested, joining her as she waded downstream.

''No,'' Dana admitted. ''But if it did?''

He scowled unhappily.

''Or maybe Zoe never forgives you for stealing a choice away that should have been hers to make. A choice that would have shaped her growing up.''

''It's too early for her to grow up! Too rough a way to grow up. I wanted something better for her than Pilar—'' He shook his head helplessly. ''Dammit!''

He was so frustrated that she wanted to laugh aloud. He probably hadn't met a problem in years that he couldn't fix, handle or demolish—and now this, presented to him by the person he loved most in the world. Not an enemy to be overwhelmed by superior force or wit, but his own fragile daughter.

''If you let *Zoe* make the choice, whatever choice she makes, I think you stand the best chance that she won't regret it one day. That she won't blame you. Won't blame herself.'' They'd reached the midpoint of the river, and Dana halted, with water the color and clarity of aquamarines rushing around her calves. ''That's worth a compromise, surely?''

They waded on till the chill in the water drove them out, then she led him to the smoother boulders on the far bank. Stretching out and closing her eyes, she let the delicious heat of the rocks soak through her body. Rafe sat beside her, looking moodily back at the porch, where Zoe and Sean talked intently on the top step.

BAD ENOUGH TO BE WORRIED about Zoe, without this distraction. Rafe glanced down at the woman beside him, wishing she were teasing him, reluctantly certain she was not. He'd seen the tears in her big gray-green eyes whenever she spoke of her husband. *She's not ready for a lover yet.* But tell that to his hormones, which stood to attention and saluted every time he laid eyes on her.

With her off in a daydream, he could feast his eyes, and he did so now, turning to rest one hand on the rock beside her head. That motion had its own momentum—he could see himself turning all the way over and settling down upon her...lacing his fingers into her shiny hair...tasting those ripe-berry lips for the first time, while she sighed and molded her softness to his urgent hardness.

Down, boy. He glanced toward the house, hauling his thoughts back to reality with a major effort of will. Zoe and Sean paced the lawn, talking, talking, talking. Nothing resolved there yet.

Rafe's head swung back to Dana the way a sunflower follows the sun. His attraction was much more than physical. She had warmth, wit, a sense of humour. And she was a keeper of promises. *If I'd found you any other time...*

But not now. This was a woman in no mood to be chased, and even if she were, bedding her should be the last thing on his mind, what with Zoe's disaster.

She stirred beside him, and guiltily he turned toward the

house, where the kids were—surprise, surprise—still talking.

"What's wrong with adoption?" she murmured drowsily.

"Turns my stomach." He glanced down and found she hadn't opened her eyes. "To think of my own blood out in the world where I can't protect it? Blown off to God knows where like a bit of dandelion fluff? Always wondering if it lit on hard rock or fertile ground? That isn't right. If you make a child, then you care for it—all the way through. Better her child was never born than that."

"The child might not agree."

"You're thinking of a happy, well-cared-for baby like your Petra. But once she's out of your hands, who knows what happens to her?"

Dana opened her eyes and gave him a gentle smile. "A lot of good people out there are desperate for a baby. An adoption agency—"

He scowled and shook his head. "Even assuming that, good people divorce, grow ill, go bankrupt…die. So there's your baby, given off to fate, and you not knowing. Not ever able to step in and fix things if they need fixing. Doesn't strike me as much of a solution."

She turned over abruptly and sat up, facing away from him. "But it may be the best solution you can hope for, in this case."

"Maybe." He could feel a muscle ticking in his jaw. "But I don't feel it. It's not right for the child, and it's damn sure not right for Zoe. I want her to walk away from this with no damage, no regrets, no looking back. If she gives away her child, she'll always be wondering where her baby is. Is the kid happy, healthy, loved? It would be an anchor she'd drag behind her all her life, when I want her to fly."

"Rafe, no matter what she decides, there's going to be some heartache in this one."

"I'm here to minimize it."

"If you can." Dana drew up her knees, crossed her forearms on top to support her chin. "It's not as if I'm thrilled with the idea, either. That's Peter's grandchild she'd be giving up. He told me once that grandchildren are the pay-off for all the grief your children give you. He wanted lots of grandkids. Imagined them coming here, summering with us, riding, playing in this river... So to give away his first grandchild—who knows?—possibly the only one there'll ever be—"

"If Sean keeps scoring like this, believe me, there'll be more."

Her back stiffened. Regretting the dig, he yearned to rub a knuckle up her spine, apology and exploration all in one—but he didn't.

His eyes shifted to a movement on the lawn. Zoe waving at them. "Uh-oh, here we go."

WHEN THEY REACHED the house, Dana tried to persuade everyone to sit up on the porch, but Zoe wasn't having it. She stood, arms crossed low over her flat middle, her chin tucked, Sean at her side. "We've thought about it," she said dully, "and I guess we could do that—give our baby up for adoption." She clamped her teeth onto her lip and stared at the ground. Sean rubbed her shoulder blades, and Rafe shot him a warning glare, which the kid blandly ignored. "But we have some conditions," Zoe continued with soft determination.

Rafe opened his mouth to state that she and Sean were in no position to make conditions, but Dana nudged him and spoke. "Like what, Zoe?"

"We couldn't just give her—him?—away and never know what happened. If our baby was happy. Treated right.

So first, if we give her up, whoever adopts her has to be somebody we like and trust. And it's got to be somebody local, so we can keep an eye on her. And I want visitation rights.''

Dana blew out an audible breath. ''I can see why you'd want that, Zoe. But a lot of people who adopt wouldn't—''

''Most wouldn't,'' Rafe amended, gripping her arm to stop her. ''But wait—what about this?'' The answer had come to him all at once, fully formed, almost laughable in its simplicity and its rightness. ''Let Dana adopt your baby.'' He felt her body jolt, and she swung to stare at him, but he kept his gaze fixed on Zoe, *willing* her to see the rightness of this. Why hadn't he thought of this sooner?

''Dana would make a wonderful mother—you can see that, the way she is with her own. She raises your child, and I pay for it—schooling, medical, college, whatever—I handle every penny of the cost. And, of course, since I live just the other side of the mountain, I can drop in from time to time, see how your kid is doing and let you know. And then Sean will be right here to keep an eye on things.'' And change the diapers. He shot the kid a malicious grin. *Thought you'd play and not pay, sonny?* ''How about that?''

''Umm…'' Zoe's narrowed eyes moved from his face to Dana's. She pursed her lips and frowned. ''I don't know if—''

''It would work—work beautifully. What do you think, Dana?'' Rafe turned to meet her eyes—and flinched. The sensation was akin to staring down the bore of a double-barreled shotgun, with a shaky finger on its trigger. Her pupils had expanded to two black circles of shock, her brows were arched in disbelief, her face had gone greeny-white.

From a second-floor window, a plaintive wail sounded—

Dana's own baby. Dana blinked rapidly, as if coming awake from a trance, then murmured with brittle calm, "If everyone will excuse me?" She backed away a step. "Come with me, Rafe."

Once they'd passed through the front door, she closed it—and flew at him. "How *dare* you?"

"Whoa! It's a good idea." She'd caught a fistful of his shirt, but clearly her intentions weren't to undress him.

"It's a rotten, stupid, *despicable* idea! You dump your troubles in my lap and go your merry way? And how could you toss it out like that, without asking me first?"

"I just thought it that minute." He peeled her fingers from his collar and held them.

"Well, *un*think it!" She glanced toward the ceiling. Petra's wails were gaining in volume and conviction. "I'm almost overwhelmed as it is! I can barely take care of my own. And you want to double my load?"

"No, I don't. You weren't listening. If you needed child care, a nanny or whatever they call 'em, I'd—"

"You need your head examined, Rafe Montana. That's what you need!" She snatched her hand from his grasp and turned toward the stairs.

"Think about it," he urged her, as she started up. "It's the perfect solution."

"For you, maybe!"

THAT NIGHT AT SUNTOP, they had a fire burning in the den. Rafe sat watching the evening news, while Zoe was curled in an easy chair across the room, tapping away on her laptop computer. When the phone rang, they glanced at each other warily. Rafe used the telephone for business, rarely for pleasure. Zoe normally kept in touch with a couple of girlfriends, but not this week, not since Rafe had grounded her. Car and phone privileges had been revoked till further notice.

"Shall I—" Zoe began, then stopped as Rafe shook his head.

She sat, glowering, while Rafe punched mute on the TV control and went to his adjoining office to answer. "Hello?"

"Rafe, it's Dana Kershaw."

An odd little jolt of pleasure shot through him. "Dana." He shut the door to the den, meeting Zoe's inquiring gaze as he did so. "What can I do for you?" He glanced toward the door that led to the kitchen—his office had been a pantry before he remodeled the house—but decided against closing that one.

"Actually, it's what I can do for you," she said briskly.

Still hadn't forgiven him for dropping his brainstorm on her like that. He'd thought to give her a little time to consider it, then push it again. "Oh?"

"I called my obstetrician, Dr. Hancock in Durango, and made an appointment for Zoe, this Friday at four p.m."

His smile faded. A doctor made the baby less of an abstraction, more a bitter reality. "You shouldn't have."

"Yes, but *you* should have, Rafe, and since you haven't…" She went on to request that if he and Zoe decided on some other doctor, would he please be sure to cancel this appointment. "And that's all I called about," she added, sounding less sure of herself in the face of his icy silence. "Oh, except I meant to ask, is Zoe taking a good multivitamin every day?"

"I set out mineral blocks in the pastures for my cattle to lick. You think I'd forget my daughter?"

"I'm sorry. It's just that…" She sighed, a soft sound that tautened the muscles in his thighs, as if she'd breathed upon him. "I'm sorry. But as long as I'm minding your business for you, here's one more thought. If you'd like me to, or if Zoe would be more comfortable, I'd be happy to drive her to the doctor. Accompany her into the office if she liked, or wait outside in the parking lot or whatever.''

Rafe didn't know about Zoe, but it certainly eased his discomfort. Women's business was best left to women. ''I'll ask her and get back to you.''

''Well, good. Then…''

Suddenly he didn't want her to cut their connection. ''You see that you're proving me right, don't you?''

''About?'' she asked on a note of caution.

''You've got just what it takes. You're organized, caring…'' Her house smelled of baking cookies. ''If I was choosing a mother for Zoe's baby—'' *My grandchild,* he realized with a grimace. He was too young for this nonsense!

''Rafe, you can forget it. Now, if that's all you—''

''But why?'' he blurted. ''I promise you, we could make this work. I've got more than enough money to smooth your way.''

''It's not a matter of money. I just—no! No, absolutely not. Forget it.''

''Hard to, when it's the obvious answer staring us in the face. And since you won't back me on arguing for an abortion, don't you think you should put your money where your mouth is?''

''No, actually I was thinking what a splendid father *you* are, Rafe. You've clearly done a fabulous job on Zoe. Me, I'm a rank beginner—Petra's less than a year old. But you've got sixteen-plus years of on-the-job training. I think *you* should adopt.''

Sixteen years was enough for a lifetime. *It's my turn to play, dammit! My turn to be free.* ''Thanks, but as I've made plain from the start, I'm not in favor of perpetuating the problem, much less diapering it.''

''Ah, but you could leave that to your nanny,'' Dana

observed with wicked innocence. ''With all that money to smooth your way…''

When it came to verbal encounters, women were cutting horses, men were calves. Whichever way he turned, she was there ahead of him, blocking his path. ''Besides,'' he said, giving up and going for a knock-out punch. ''I'm seriously seeing a woman right now—'' He'd dated Mitzy Barlow only last Saturday, though that seemed a lifetime ago, and she, at least, had been way too serious. ''And I doubt that she'd want to adopt someone else's child.''

''Oh,'' Dana said blankly.

There was an odd resonating silence between them, which Rafe suddenly wanted to fill with retractions or, at least, qualifications. But elaborating on a lie was the last thing he should do. *Quit while you're ahead.* And now, at least, they were even. She had a ghost for a husband, and he had an imaginary lover.

''Oh,'' said Dana again. Then her voice gained confidence. ''Well, in that case, you'd better start working on Zoe. Convince her that insisting on visitation rights, once she gives up her baby for adoption, may not be practical.''

''Right,'' he said gruffly. Though if he worked on anyone, it would be Dana. He still thought she was the perfect solution. But he needed a lever to move her, some argument she couldn't counter or ignore.

''So will you and Zoe decide about Dr. Hancock, and whether you want me to chauffeur?''

He'd ask his daughter, Rafe assured her. As Dana said goodbye, some instinct made him turn—in time to see Zoe fading back from the kitchen door. He hung up and sauntered after her.

She was neck deep inside the freezer, rummaging through its contents. ''Pizza or chicken potpies?'' she muttered.

''Eavesdropper,'' he said mildly.

"Well, you were talking about *me*." She yanked out a pizza, then slammed the door and turned to glare at him, unrepentant.

"Among other things."

"Yeah—like who are you seeing seriously? You mean that woman, Mitzy What's-her-name? You've only been out with her twice, Daddy!"

Swearing to himself, he did his best to look like the cat that has been into the cream. "Sometimes it happens that way." Her eyes glinted, and as she opened her mouth with the obvious retort, he aimed a finger. "But *not* to minors."

From: RedColumbine@Westbest.com
To: SanDiegan@Pipeline.net
9:30 P.M. Me again. Dad thinks I'm updating my journal. Wonder how long till he catches on that I'm plugging into the phone jack, not the electrical socket? But meantime, I just found out—he has a serious babe-friend!!! Mitzy Barlow, a real estate agent down in Durango. And I wanted to know: have you had a chance to ask Dana yet? I thought she looked pretty weirded out when Daddy popped his suggestion. But if she did like the idea...and you did. (Do you?) Tell me soon as you find out? 'Night, now, and I kiss you in the place that always gives you goose bumps.
Zzzzoe

P.S. Dana didn't seem at all like I imagined she'd be. Seemed sort of nice. Is it all an act or what?

CHAPTER NINE

THE FEINSTEINS had checked out of Aspen Cabin that morning. So after lunch Dana and Petra went up to ready it for the next set of guests, due sometime that evening. Dana spread a blanket on the bedroom floor and left the baby there, while she cleaned the bathroom and kitchenette.

Before starting on the living room, she checked and found that Petra had discovered the lowest drawer on the bureau and was working it open with fierce determination. Dana admired her discovery, drew the drawer out another inch to be sure nothing temptingly mouth-size awaited within, then hurried off to sweep the living room and plump the couch pillows.

Shrieks of glee from the bedroom announced that the drawer had been conquered, and Dana went to applaud. "You got it open, you clever girl!" She presented the tennis ball she'd brought along in her cleaning kit by dropping it into the drawer. "There. See? It's a place to put treasures."

Petra giggled uproariously, snatched up the toy and did her best to cram it into her mouth. When that didn't work, she offered it to her mother with a brow-crinkling frown.

"Thank you, sweetie. It's a beautiful ball. Why don't we put it in here and *close* the drawer." Dana left it open a crack so the baby could see the prize, and went to the bed. She whipped off the sheets, bundled them and turned—to find Sean slouched in the bedroom doorway. "Why, hello," she said. "Did you need something?"

"Nope. Just wondered what you and the monster were doing." He sauntered over to the dresser and squatted beside it. "What ya got, cupcake?"

His latest nickname for his sister, from an epic encounter she'd had with a chocolate cupcake last month. Sometimes Dana wished she hadn't named Petra after her father. The tribute apparently pained his firstborn. *One more time I blew it.* And Sean had been keeping score ever since the avalanche. *I wish you'd been there, too, Sean. To see how hard I tried.*

"Whoa—a ball!" he exclaimed, suitably impressed by Petra's revelation. "Check this out." He sent it careering off the inner walls of the drawer, while Petra stared in stupefaction. She flapped her hands with excitement and reached for it, eager to try the new trick.

Sean stood, as Dana snapped the first sheet out over the mattress. "Here." He crossed to the far side of the bed and pulled the fitted corner into place.

"Thanks," Dana said casually, careful to hide her shock. They finished that sheet, and she wafted the top one into position.

"What Mr. Montana said yesterday," Sean mumbled, tucking in the bottom corner. "About you adopting the— Zoe's— Um, our…"

She'd thought it was too good to be true. Not spontaneous forgiveness, but need. "Your baby, yes." She smoothed out the sheet and reached for the blanket. Still, she shouldn't knock it. They were talking; that was something. "What of it?"

His face was very pink. "I just wondered if you'd— What you thought about…that."

"Well…" *Is this where I fail you again, Sean? I'm doomed forever to be the wicked stepmother who won't come through for you?* But even to win his forgiveness, she couldn't see it. *There's only so much of me to go around.* "Well, I thought it was...interesting. What did you think?"

She shouldn't jump to the conclusion that he'd necessarily second Rafe's motion. At fourteen, Sean was more likely to be wishing this dilemma would simply go away, leaving him a footloose teenager with no more than a normal teenager's worries or burdens. *Never mind me. For Sean's sake, I shouldn't do it.* It would mean the end of his childhood. She tossed him a pillowcase, and shook her own pillow into its cotton sleeve. *Oh, Peter, should I give up your grandchild to save your son?*

"I, uh...guess it could work. Petra would have somebody to play with." He went to his half sister, who was emitting little grunts and whimpers of frustration—the drawer had jammed halfway out. "That better?" He eased it open a trifle.

So he did want her to adopt. She couldn't win with him. "We could make it work, if we had to," she agreed, sitting down on the bed. "But you and Zoe want what's best for your baby." He nodded solemnly, and she saw for the first time the resemblance between him and Petra—something about the eyebrows, the shape of their foreheads. "And what a baby needs most of all, Sean, is *two* loving parents."

"Petra doesn't have that," he muttered, reaching for her ball. He sent it flying up toward the cabin ceiling and caught it, then challenged Dana with a look.

"That's right," she agreed, willing the tears not to come, but they came anyway, blurring his face. "And I would do anything in the world for that not to be so, Sean. But it is so."

Petra let out a yelp and patted Sean's arm, reaching for her toy. He handed it over, but held on, so they grasped it together.

"Petra's fine right now," Dana continued, "but her life would be so much richer if she had a daddy to tickle and cuddle her.'' To show her the safety and strength of a man's arms. The wonderful comfort of a man's deep, loving voice. *I miss it, but she doesn't even know what she's missing. And do you ever find it in a lover if you never knew it first in a father?* ''I try to be her world, but I'm only half a world.''

The baby started to complain, and Sean released the ball. ''I play with her. Sometimes.''

They both knew it wasn't often. He seemed to shun his sister, though when he was trapped into interacting, he did it with sensitivity and humor. He was Peter's son; she would have expected no less.

''Yes, you give her a glimpse of what a daddy could be,'' Dana agreed.

''So I could do that for Zoe's and my baby, too. I can tickle and hug, can't I, cupcake?'' He caught the baby around her fat middle and lifted her overhead. ''Huh, how's that? You like that, huh? Huh?'' He brought the chortling child down to his lap, wrapped his arms around her and blew into her hair. ''That's not so hard.'' He looked up at her mother expectantly.

''Yes. You do a good job. But in four years, you'll probably be going away—off to college or some such.''

His gaze dropped to the baby's downy head. ''If not before.''

So he still dreamed of escaping Colorado—her—the heartache life had handed him. *But escaping to where, Sean?* A mother who never grew up? Who seemed to want a parent more than she did a son? Dana wasn't going to argue that one now. ''Yes, well… So, about the time your baby really started needing a father, you'd be gone.'' *Leaving me holding the bag.* Rafe and he both were thinking like men. *I should be surprised?*

''Um, yeah, I guess so.''

''And what if your baby turns out to be a son? A little

girl learns to be a woman by watching her mother, copying what she does—dolls, dress-up, makeup. But it's best for a boy if he has a man to tag along after, to show him how to walk like a man, think like a man.''

"Yeah…" Sean whispered. "I had that once."

And if I could give that back to you—give it back to me…

He sat there, thinking, while she smoothed the bedspread, then abruptly he set Petra aside and stood. "Well, thanks."

A retort born of guilt leaped to her lips, but she smothered it stillborn. That hadn't really sounded like sarcasm. "You're welcome," she said quietly, as he walked out the door.

From: SanDiegan@Pipeline.net
To: RedColumbine@Westbest.com
Hiya, Gorgeous! I asked Dana about adopting, and she said NO WAY. But I'm not sure she was being selfish (this time). Her reasons why not sort of seemed to make sense. I never thought about a baby needing two parents before, but— Oops, here she comes! HATE this computer in the kitchen. I'll write you tonight, after she goes upstairs. MegaKISS, your Sean

ON WEDNESDAY, Rafe gave Zoe two assignments. One, start halter-breaking the foals born this spring, and, two, make up her mind about adoption, if she still wouldn't take his advice. "We'll talk this evening," he warned her, as he set off with two of the hands to inspect the irrigation ditches.

He rode in again an hour before supper, as she was working with the third foal of the day—a fine husky colt that was as stubborn as he was intelligent. Willy, the oldest hand at Suntop, had helped her halter the fuzzy black baby, then shackle him by a short lead to the fence post planted in the center of the training corral. Zoe stood before the post with one hand on the lead, so the foal thought that she held him, while Willy led his dam to the far side of the corral and tied her there.

After an hour of plunging and squealing and fighting the lead, the exhausted foal was about to give in. Rafe reined Tobasco to a halt outside the pen and sat, watching. Ignoring him, Zoe kept up her nonstop flow of soothing words. "*Ah, caballito, no seas tonto.* Some things you gotta accept, you muleheaded little fuzzy black beauty. It's okay, 'sokay, *guapacito,* there's nothing to fear. *Ninguna cosita…*"

The colt reared one last time—and surrendered, plunging toward her, clearly feeling the wonderful slackening of the hateful pressure behind his ears as his resistance to the halter ended. "*Good* baby. Yes, that's the way. You see, there's *ninguna cosita* to fear." Zoe reeled him in, and he came haltingly, to stand at last trembling before her. She praised him with her hands and her words, then unclipped him from the post. "And now I lead you to mama. That's not so bad, is it?" The colt walked by her side, his eyes fixed on his dam, who nickered a placid welcome.

Zoe stopped him halfway there, and he snorted, but obeyed the halter's pull. "*Such* a smart one." She brought the foal up on the mare's right side, preventing him from going straight to the comforting udder. The mare nuzzled her child's stubbly mane, as Zoe untied her and led them both across the corral to Rafe. "I thought he'd never quit!"

"The smart ones know when to give in."

She bristled, but he was looking off toward a scrap of flaming cloud in the west, with Venus setting below it. Perhaps that remark had not been aimed her way. *The smart ones learn what to ignore.*

He opened the gate, and she led mare and foal to the gate of the home pasture, where the other mares and foals grazed. She unclipped the colt, stroked him one last time, then sent him hurrying after his mother. He was already nursing greedily as she turned away.

By the time Rafe had tended to his mount, she'd washed up and was messing around the kitchen. They'd have one of the frozen casseroles that Mrs. Higgins had left them. Zoe set out a slab of cheddar, some bread and fruit to round out their meal, then collapsed on the sofa till her father came downstairs again, hair wet from his shower.

While they ate, they talked of ranch matters, her success with the foals today, a story Willy had told her at lunchtime about a rattlesnake and a rooster. Zoe picked chunks of chicken from her portion and passed them by turns to Woofle and Trey, who crouched under the table to either side of her chair, the only two guys at Suntop Ranch who didn't disapprove of her vegetarian stance.

At last Rafe set his plate aside and looked up.

Here it comes. To forestall him, Zoe said, ''Mrs. Kershaw called at lunch.''

''Did she?'' The grim line of his mouth eased for a moment.

''I told her I'd be happy if she'd drive me to the doctor,'' Zoe reported dutifully. ''Though really, Daddy, if you'd let me drive myself—''

''We've already been through that.''

''But this is *so* embarrassing. If you'd just—''

''But I won't, and that is *that*.''

''Fine!'' She clashed the utensils on her plate, stood and slammed it into the sink. ''Whatever.''

''Did you give some thought to what I asked? If you're dead set on the adoption route, then we have to start looking for an agency, or possibly a lawyer. Maybe the doctor will...'' Rafe trailed off, as Zoe crossed her arms and leaned back against the counter.

''I have thought about it. I've thought about it a lot. And, of course, it's still adoption. But I have one more condition,

Daddy, besides what Sean and I said yesterday, about visitation rights and all.''

How the devil had she done it—reversed their positions so she was the one dictating conditions and he the one scrambling to fulfill them? A muscle fluttered somewhere below Rafe's eye, but he said with outward calm, ''Oh?''

''I've been thinking—and Mrs. Kershaw completely agrees with us—with this. She says it's absolutely critical that a baby have *two* parents, not just a mother. So if Sean and I are going to give our baby up, it's got to be to a couple—not to a single mom or a single anybody. And, of course, the couple needs to be happily married, I guess— or at least happy. That's maybe the most important of—''

''Mrs. Kershaw put this notion into your head?'' Rafe threw his napkin down on the table and stood. Damn the woman—she was crossing him at every turn! How the blue blazes was he supposed to produce not just one, but *two* loving adoptive parents who'd be thrilled and delighted to have the real mother wandering in and out of their lives at will? ''You're asking for the moon, Zoe.''

She shook her head, reminding him of the colt fighting the halter. ''I'm asking for what my baby needs. If that's impossible to arrange, then I guess I'll just have to raise her myself. Sean says he'll stick it out with me—help me whenever he can right now, then marry me when he's eighteen.''

''You're...just...*kids!*'' Rafe exploded. ''There's no way you can do that! No way I want you to try to do that—''

''But—''

''No buts! Not another damn but, not one word.'' He stomped into his office, snatched up the phone and dialed.

''Hello?'' Dana sounded breathless and harried. The hiccuping sobs of a baby sounded in the background.

Just what she deserved. ''Did you tell my daughter that

a baby needs two parents? That she shouldn't give up her child if it's not to a couple?''

"*What?* Oh…well, not precisely, but I suppose I did—''

"You did a truckload of damage is what you did, and I'll thank you to keep your opinions to yourself from now on! What gives *you* the—''

"Rafe, I've got eight hungry dudes in my dining room, I'm in the midst of a Chinese stir-fry, Petra seems to be teething. This is *not* a good time to talk.''

"I'm not talking. I'm telling you—''

"Then tell me later!'' *Click!*

He snatched the phone away from his ear, swore at it, smashed it down onto its base—and it rang under his hand. He drew in a shaking breath, blew it out, lifted it and said evenly, "We have to talk about this.''

"Rafe? That's got to be ESP!'' a woman cried happily.

Not Dana Kershaw with her velvety alto. A higher, chirpier voice—*oh, no!* "Mitzy?'' he said stupidly.

"Who else? You were just picking up the phone to call me?''

CHAPTER TEN

"I'M SO GLAD you gave us a second chance!" Beaming at Rafe above the candle flame, Mitzy Barlow impulsively stretched a hand across the restaurant table.

Rafe swallowed and took it reluctantly. *Us.* That was the same song she'd sung on their last date. "It's you giving me a second chance," he said gallantly and all too truthfully.

She squeezed his fingers and widened her eyes at him. "But Rafe, it was all such a silly misunderstanding! I guess I came on like Suzy Homemaker, inviting you over to my place, but really, that was just so we could be more…comfortable. That's all it was, truly." Her fingers stroked his palm with soft insistence. "Why, when it comes to independence, I bet I treasure mine more than you do yours! A girl just wants to have fun, know what I mean?"

If he hadn't, she was more than willing to show him. Rafe sighed inwardly and nodded toward the dance floor, where several couples drifted to the slow music of the house's Friday-night band. "Dance?" Conversation was exhausting him.

"I'd love to."

She melted into his arms the way she had the last time they'd danced—had that been only two weeks ago? But though her body was as warm and willing as before, its effect on him wasn't the same. When she pressed her breasts to his chest, he felt a reflexive stirring, but that was all it was. Reflex. He might have left his heart back at the table along with his hat. *This isn't the one.* The words rose up unbidden, as if someone spoke from the bottom of a well. He frowned and pulled her closer.

She was the only one going. He'd thought, when Mitzy phoned him on Wednesday, that it must be Fate nudging him toward the obvious solution. If Dana Kershaw wouldn't take Zoe's baby at any price, and with Zoe insisting anyway that she'd give up her baby only to a two-parent family—a family that would grant her unlimited visitation rights!—then it was up to Rafe to find such an openminded, generous couple. *Local family,* he reminded himself ironically. Or if he couldn't find one—

Mitzy tipped back her head and wriggled against him, as he guided her in a slow turn. "What are you thinking?"

About babies. If he said that, she'd probably jump him here on the floor. "Thinking that lead guitar man has some nice moves." She smiled wickedly and bumped her hip against him, and he added, "But then, so do you." Which made her giggle.

I can't do this. That same voice, his but not his, welled up in his mind again. She was a fine-looking woman, but she came on too strong, or too eager, or just plain wrong for him. She smiled too much, showing too many teeth, and she laughed in all the wrong places. Always would.

Face it, he'd seen someone who *would* do, too recently, and the contrast was brutal. *But she's not available.*

And this one was too available. A man wanted to hunt his woman, as he would an elk out on the mountain, savoring the crisp blue day, the shivering gold of the aspen leaves, his own competence in the stalking, the quickening pulse as a form finally took shape through the bushes, the hammering heart as you drew down on the target. But Mitzy—Mitzy was a trout in a barrel, ready to leap into his arms.

Two weeks ago he'd been lonesome enough that he'd

thought he wanted that, if only for a few hot nights, but now… "Thank you," he said automatically as the dance ended. She tipped up her face and strained closer, and he realized she wanted a kiss. "Thanks for the dance," he repeated gently as he eased her out of his arms.

He walked her back to their booth with a hand on her back, her shooting him wounded and puzzled glances, then said, "If you'd excuse me a minute?" He fled to the men's room. *How long till I can decently take her home?* He'd been a fool to think this might work. A jerk to raise her hopes all over again.

But the men's room made a lousy refuge. Rafe knew from rueful experience that two women could swish off to the ladies' and stay gone for fifteen minutes or more, presumably while they dissected their dates or traded lipsticks. He'd always imagined a pink, frilly couch in there, crammed at any one time with three pairs of whispering, giggling women, while more waited their turn. Contrast that with the men's, where users went strictly one by one, and any man lurking there for more than the requisite two minutes was viewed with universal alarm.

So he used up his two minutes, then decided to kill a couple more on the phone. He could call Zoe and ask how her appointment had gone. And how she and Dana had hit it off on their own. Propping one shoulder against the wall, he had to smile as he pictured his tall redheaded daughter walking beside small, dark Dana. But his smile faded when no one picked up the phone back at Suntop. Zoe had estimated this morning, that Dana would have her back at the ranch by six-thirty at the latest. And now it was nine.

Took her telescope outside to look at the moon, he told himself. She'd been on an astronomy kick all last summer. Or perhaps she'd been shook by something Dr. Hancock had handed her this afternoon, and she was out walking and thinking. Give her twenty minutes, he decided, then try again. If she wasn't in by then, he'd call Dana. He hadn't spoken to her since Wednesday, when he'd yelled at her. After she'd sabotaged his plans that way, he'd been too angry to trust himself to be civil. *If you'd just see sense, Dana, I wouldn't be here courting a woman I don't even like.*

He was nearly to the booth when he realized they had company. A couple had joined Mitzy—the man's back blocked most of his view. Rafe smiled with relief. Four wasn't a crowd tonight; it was a welcome distraction. He reached the table, and smiled down at—Sean Kershaw and his missing daughter!

"Look who joined us!" Mitzy cried gaily. "You'd told me Zoe was a beauty, but I had no idea! And Sean, I'm so happy to meet you. What fun—a double date!"

"And what a surprise," Rafe said between his teeth, as Mitzy slid over to make room for him. He fixed his daughter with a stare that promised hellfire and brimstone when he got her alone. She'd broken every last edict he'd given her—Sean, off the ranch without permission, no doubt used the phone to set this up. Zoe tipped up her chin, giving him look for look, while she laid her hand over Sean's on the table. Rafe felt a reluctant flash of admiration beyond his outrage. She was no longer a child to be sent to her room, she was telling him. *Not my little girl anymore.*

"Where's Dana?" he asked, and felt another ripple of rage. Dana must have taken Sean along to the appointment, throwing the kids together even though she knew how Rafe felt about that.

"I told her you were meeting me here in town for supper, and that you'd drive me home."

"Dana's another of your little friends?" Mitzy cooed, not to be left out.

Zoe nodded, her gaze still locked on her father's. "And

I hope you'll drive Sean home, as well, since he rode down here on his bike.''

Rafe opened his mouth to say the kid could ride home thirty miles in the dark or sleep in a ditch, for all he cared—but there was Dana, who hadn't flouted his wishes, after all. Who probably this minute was worrying and wondering about her stepson's whereabouts. "I reckon I'll have to." Tied to his front fender like a trophy buck.

"So what brings you two to town?" Mitzy chirped. "A movie? Or a dance or…?"

"Actually, we came to meet *you*," Zoe said, and Sean nodded solemn agreement.

The devil they had! Rafe aimed a judicious kick under the table, but he bumped Mitzy's outstretched leg, instead. She twined it instantly around his calf and shot him a look that would have sizzled a snowman.

"I was wondering how you feel about children?" Zoe continued, studiously avoiding Rafe's evil eye. "Do you want a family?"

"Well, I—" Mitzy brought a hand to her low-cut neckline and giggled. "What is this, a job interview?"

"Zo-e." Rafe growled a warning. "Pay no attention, Mitzy. She's kidding." He glanced up to find their waitress standing at his elbow.

"Can I get you guys anything else?" She nodded at the newcomers.

"No!" snapped Rafe. "They're just leaving."

"Yes." Sean spoke up for the first time. "My date will have the spinach salad and I'll have a cheeseburger with fries. Ice tea for both of us." He looked Rafe straight in the eye. "And I'll pay for it."

You've got guts, kid, I'll give you that! The bruise on Sean's chin had faded to yellow-green. He'd put on a tie for this invasion. Rafe turned back to the murmuring women—to find Mitzy confiding, "Honey, I think family's the most important thing in the whole wide world!'' She nudged Rafe's leg with hers for emphasis.

''But do you want children of your own?'' Zoe persisted.

Mitzy shot Rafe a warily flirtatious look. ''Eventually. Sure. Doesn't everybody?'' She rubbed an open hand down the top of his thigh.

He captured it and brought it up onto the table. ''Could we change the subject, Zoe?''

''How about adoption?'' Sean chimed in. ''Have you ever thought about that?''

''Do you mean Zoe?'' Mitzy reached across the table to capture Zoe's hands. ''That's what all this is about? Honey, I would be so…so honored and *thrilled* to have you as my adopted daughter, if it ever came to that! Why, I— I can't tell you how—''

''Mitzy, let's dance!'' Rafe almost dragged her from the booth, then hustled her out to the floor.

''Oh, Rafe—'' Regardless of the surrounding dancers, she threw her arms around his neck and kissed him. ''I had no idea!''

''Neither did I, Mitzy, believe me.''

He managed to calm her down during the dance, though since he had no intention of explaining his daughter's antics, Mitzy ended up more bewildered than enlightened. He kept an arm anchored around her as they returned to the booth, to find that the kids had been served.

''I'm taking Mitzy home,'' he announced, ''and I'll be back here in twenty minutes. Don't budge from this booth. Not an inch.''

''I don't understand,'' Mitzy murmured, looking back over her shoulder and twiddling her fingers in farewell, as he marched her away. ''Did I do something wrong?''

''Mitzy, you're the only one here who did everything right.''

THE THREE OF THEM maintained an edgy silence most of the way to the Ribbon River. Rafe had exiled Sean to the rear seat of the cab, resisting the temptation to let him ride out back with his bike.

"Mr. Montana," Sean blurted suddenly, "I don't want you blaming Zoe for tonight. This was my idea."

"Was it?" Rafe knew his own daughter better than that.

"No, it was me, Daddy, you know it was me! But you said the other night you were serious about Mitzy, so we wanted to meet her. See how she felt about babies. See if we liked her."

"Just because I'm seriously seeing a woman doesn't mean I'm thinking about adopting your baby!"

"Doesn't it?" Zoe demanded, turning to face him and hooking an elbow over the backseat.

The problem was, she could read him like a book. When they sat down with the hands for a round of penny poker, she was the one he never could bluff. Rafe tried anyway. "It doesn't. Besides which, I'll thank you not to meddle in my…" *Private affairs* sounded too stuffy. "In my—"

"Love life?" Zoe suggested with a smirk. "But you can meddle in mine?"

"Till you're eighteen, you're damn right I can—and I will." He turned off the highway onto the unpaved road that led to the dude ranch.

Sean leaned forward. "You can let me out here, Mr. Montana. Uh, please?"

"Not a chance. I'm handing you over to your stepmother. She's probably been worrying herself sick wondering where you are." It was past ten-thirty.

"I'm not hers to worry about." He gripped the back of the seat with both hands. "Please, sir? You'll only wake her up if you drive up to the house. I can bike from here."

But if you don't want to see her, I do, Rafe realized. He could picture Dana roused from her bed, her soft hair tou-

sled like a child's, her long lashes drooping over her big,
dark eyes. *Bedroom eyes,* they used to call eyes like that.
He stomped on the brake. "Fine. Out with you, then. And
Sean?" Halfway out the door, the boy halted and swung
back. "Zoe is grounded, and from now on I expect you to
respect that."

"Mr. Montana?" Sean looked down, then up—straight
into his eyes. "I'll see your daughter whenever I can.
Thanks for the ride." He closed the door and walked
around back to lift out his bike.

Swearing heartily under his breath, Rafe reversed all the
way out to the highway. Zoe sat forward in her seat, arms
crossed, a tiny, private smile on her face, her gaze fixed on
her friend, who stood by his bike in the headlights' glare,
one arm uplifted in farewell.

"So..." Rafe growled after he'd driven a mile. "You,
young lady, are in trouble." Though how he was going to
ground her when she was already...

"That's what the doctor tells me," she agreed calmly.

The truck swerved, and he brought it back in line. "You
really are?" Deep down, he'd cherished the notion that
maybe this was all a Chinese fire drill, one of those—what
did they call 'em?—hysterical pregnancies. Had told himself that if he entertained the notion of marrying Mitzy, it
would not be necessary. So much for sacrifices.

"'Fraid so." Zoe crossed her forearms on the dash,
leaned her head on them and sighed.

"So..." No mercy from the gods. Now he would have
to do something. Find a way. "You went to all that trouble
to meet Mitzy Barlow. What did you think of her?"

"Umm." Zoe sighed again. "You know that drugstore
in Cortez that still has the old soda fountain? We stopped
there once years ago, and you bought me a cherry Coke?
With all that cherry syrup?"

Unable to gag it down, she'd offended the ancient proprietor who had made it special for her. Rafe grimaced. *You think Mitzy is syrupy?* So did he.

"She's really very nice," Zoe added hastily. "And if you like her, that's all that matters...I guess." The last words faded forlornly away.

She was picturing Mitzy raising Zoe's daughter in her own syrupy image. *Not gonna happen, sweetheart. I'll figure out something else.* He'd have to. No way could he see himself enduring eighteen years of pot roast and peas with Mitzy Barlow.

But he had to work something out, and soon. What had Dana said the other day—that no matter what choice was made, there was bound to be some heartache?

More and more, it looked like the trade-off would be Zoe's freedom—or his.

CHAPTER ELEVEN

From: RedColumbine@Westbest.com
To: SanDiegan@Pipeline.net
Sean Diego! Sorry I haven't written, but Dad has been
a GRIZZLY all weekend and he kept me on the run.
We rode up to the line camp Saturday to take the guys
some supplies, then looked over the cows and the
grazing. Took our bedrolls and slept outside the cabin.
You should have seen the stars. And I heard a cougar
scream near dawn—Harvard wouldn't have anything
to compare with that, not really. Sunday we came
back, then hung around the house all day. He's up to
something—making lists, talking to himself, growling
at the dogs and me. Locking the lists in his desk, so
I can't peek. Then this morning he called our banker
for an appointment and went into town. I've got a
NASTY suspicion that he's working out some sort of
prenuptial agreement for him and Mitzy—gagme-
withahoneyjar—Barlow. (Does she have something
I'm missing, or is Dad just too sex-starved to notice
she's a dweeb?) Uh-oh, he's driving up now. Gotta
go!! ZZZZoe+(?)

TUESDAY AFTERNOON, Dana had just put Petra down for
her afternoon nap, when she heard a car mounting the last
slope to the house. Drop-in tourists who'd seen her sign
out on the highway, she hoped as she went to the bedroom
window. Her cabins were only half filled this week.

Parting the sheer curtains, she saw, instead, Rafe Montana's black pickup truck dragging a horse trailer behind it. As the truck passed the house headed for the parking in the rear, Rafe looked up at her window, and their eyes met. He touched a finger to his Stetson and smiled.

What now, Rafe? They'd had no contact since that phone call last week, when he'd told her to keep her opinions to herself, and she'd hung up on him. She should have enjoyed being left in peace, she supposed, but instead it had been a week of surprisingly painful suspense—wondering what he meant to do about Zoe. Wondering how his ultimate solution would affect Sean's life—and hers. Wondering about that woman he'd said he was seeing seriously. *Wondering how I could have been so vain, feeling he might be attracted to me, just because he touched me once or twice...the way he looked at me.*

Still, she paused at the dresser mirror to brush the bangs back from her forehead. Petra had spit up on her shoulder, she noticed, so she hurried to her bedroom for a fresh blouse.

By the time she reached her kitchen, Rafe was knocking on her screen door.

"Coming!" *On his manners today,* she thought, since he'd waited outside. "Hello, Rafe." She smiled up at him briskly, to hide her embarrassment. An odd little jolt of pleasure went through her, seeing him standing there. Pleasure and surprise—he was always a little bigger and more vivid than she remembered.

"Dana." He lifted the brim of his hat an inch and lowered it again.

His very best manners. So he'd forgiven her. "You've brought horses," she noted, seeing a black tail switching within the nearest stall of the trailer and a cream-colored rump in the far one. And seeing Sean, who was just now retrieving his fly rod from the bed of the truck. Rafe must have collared him down at his favorite fishing hole by the bridge.

"I didn't know if you had any spare mounts, so I brought my own," Rafe explained. "Could I tempt you out for a ride?"

"Oh." His timing was perfect—Petra's afternoon nap time. No accident, she realized. Still. "I'd love to, Rafe." It had been months since she'd ridden. "But I can't leave Petra alone."

"Which is why I found you a baby-sitter." Rafe nodded at her stepson, who was glowering as he trudged up the steps. "I figure if Sean plans to be a daddy he could use all the practice he can get."

It wasn't fair, Dana told herself, that Rafe could demand cooperation from Sean that she only dreamed of. But why quibble with a gift horse? "Give me five minutes to change."

"This is Concha," he said a short while later, stroking the nose of a dainty buckskin. "She's gentle, and Zoe named her for her paces—she's smooth as a shell."

"She's lovely!" Her creamy coat contrasted dramatically with her black mane and tail and stockings.

Rafe held the mare's head while Dana gathered the reins and mounted, then he moved to her side. "Your stirrups are short." He caught her ankle and lifted her foot from the iron. "Let your leg hang."

She did so, her skin shivering at the feel of his hand encircling her. *He has a woman,* she reminded herself, staring straight ahead through the mare's black-tipped ears. He'd do this for Sean or for Zoe. It was only her panicked imagination that made the gesture seem significant, oddly possessive, as if he meant to stand there clasping her ankle forever.

He let her go and rebuckled the strap. "Two notches. I knew your legs were long, but I didn't…" He moved to the other side, extended that one, then mounted his big blood bay, his leg swinging up and over in an effortless arc as the gelding snorted and pranced in place. Settling his hat down over his dark hair, he said, "Which way?"

"Up!" She laughed. "I haven't been up on the mountain in *forever*." Not in more than a year, since her fifth month when she'd stopped riding.

Rafe kept the conversation strictly on horses as they made their way through the lower pastures; then the big wildflower meadows stairstepping toward the sky, slashed by forests of pale aspen and dark pine, outcroppings of raw red granite; then higher, silk-green meadows starred with columbine and Indian paintbrushes, a tapestry of crimson and blue and yellow. Once he'd satisfied himself that she could control her mount, he picked up their pace. They loped easily side by side, his ramping bay and her floating mare, smooth as a ride on a merry-go-round.

Finally Rafe lifted his hand, signaling a halt. Dana reined in beside him, and, as one, they turned their horses back toward the view. Far down the valley, she could make out one corner of her roof, a glint of the Ribbon River. "Beautiful," she murmured, stroking Concha's hot, sleek neck.

He nodded. "Almost as pretty as my land."

My land, said with such fierce, possessive pride that she wanted to smile, but didn't. *I bet he grew up poor.* She glanced at him sideways. He had an essential toughness, a harder edge than the men she'd grown up with, back in green, gentle Vermont—an upper-middle-class world filled with men who worked in offices and classrooms. *Nothing came easy to you,* she guessed. *No one handed you anything or smoothed the way.* Hence the pride in what he'd done by himself.

Still, she had her own pride. "I'd like to see anything prettier than this." She nodded toward the valley.

"Then sometime I'll show you." He smiled, but the

smile didn't reach his blue eyes as they roved over her face.
"I'm glad you ride."

What's it to you? Suddenly she'd had all she could take
of his scrutiny. She swung Concha uphill. Rafe followed,
jogging knee to knee with her. "What did you want to say
to me?" He hadn't brought her up here just to entertain
her. He'd brought her to his home ground, atop a horse,
because here he was most at ease—he wanted an edge, an
advantage. *Wants my help again, but how this time?*

"I..." He gave her a sidelong, enigmatic glance. "I have
a proposal for you."

She flinched inwardly at the word, then smiled at herself.
He didn't mean *that.* "About Zoe's baby?" When he nodded, she said, "I meant what I said before, Rafe. I know I
would be convenient for you, but I just can't do it. I'm
sorry."

"That was just an idea off the top of my head, but now
I've thought it through and I want you to hear me out."

She shook her head. "It's no good, Rafe."

"It could be very good," he disagreed, "for you and
Sean as well as Zoe, and here's how it would work. First—
and you can blame yourself for this part, Dana—we'd
marry."

"What?" The mare stopped dead as her hand jerked on
the reins. "You're—"

"I'm not crazy. You've convinced Zoe that her baby
needs two parents, not one—so here I am. Not exactly what
I had planned for myself, either, by the way."

Married to you. She couldn't look him in the eye,
couldn't look away. Her gaze snagged on his mouth—that
carved, full bottom lip curving ruefully...the breadth of his
shoulders...those capable, knowing hands. There was too
much of him—more man than any woman could use. And
she needed none. Certainly not this one. "No." She sent
Concha surging ahead.

Might as well try to outrun a centaur. He was beside her again in a moment, their knees only inches apart. "We'd marry and adopt Zoe's baby at birth," he continued, as if she hadn't spoken. "I'll live on my side of the mountain most of the time, and you'll live on yours."

And the other times? Or was she reading her own urges into this, turning a business proposition into something more?

"Whoa." Reaching over, Rafe caught her left wrist and pulled backward; at the same time, he reined in Tobasco, bringing them both to a halt. "Listen to me. I'll guarantee that you won't be overwhelmed, Dana."

With his big hand on her wrist, he'd guarantee. He must outweigh her by seventy pounds, and most of that muscle.

"You'll have all the child care you need or want, for Petra as well as Zoe's baby. A nanny or whatever you like, as long as the kids stay at home."

She had to smile in spite of herself. No, he wasn't exactly Mr. Day Care—not that Trueheart offered much in that line, anyway.

"As I said before, I'll assume all financial responsibility for Zoe's—and Sean's—baby." Reminding her that this mess wasn't all of Zoe's making. "Medical, living expenses, college when it comes time."

No small chunk of change he was talking there; still, that wasn't the point.

"Besides that, I'll bail you out, too." He let her go at last, as if his words alone could hold her.

"What?" She twisted in the saddle to stare up at him.

"You're not doing so well wrangling dudes, Dana. I understand you're two months behind on your mortgage payments."

"Who told you that?" Not even Sean knew that, so there was no way Rafe could have learned it through Zoe, which meant— "You talked to my banker?"

Rafe shrugged. "Doesn't matter. I made it my business to find out. What matters is that I'll pay off your debts and keep you out of debt."

"You did talk to the bank! Of all the arrogant, over-bearing—" She spun Concha back the way they'd come. "From now on, you can mind your own business, Rafe Montana!"

"Like you've been minding yours, Ms. Two-Parents-Are-Better-Than-One?" He trotted after her.

"Well, it's true!"

"Maybe, maybe not, but now we're stuck with it. So I want your help and I'm willing to pay for it."

"Eighteen years of mothering might come pretty high." Not that she'd even consider his proposition. She pulled down her hat, shutting him out.

"Then make it five years, if you prefer." He bent to peer under her brim. "Five would be enough to launch the kid. That would give Zoe time to make it through Harvard. After that, I could work something else out."

"Buy some other financially distressed mother?" she suggested dryly.

"Whatever. So what about five years? We'd draw up a contract—I mean to do that, anyway. At the end, you'd be free. I'd have your ranch running smoothly by then. There're lots of improvements that would make it pay."

She just bet he was itching to put his hand to her ranch. She'd seen the way he'd scowled at her corral, with its rotting rails, when they rode past. *Mr. High-handed, stomping across my land.* "Five years," she repeated, shaking her head. Not five years, not five minutes. *And I thought life had me overwhelmed?* A tornado didn't need five minutes to turn your life topsy-turvy, nor did a tidal wave, let alone Rafe Montana.

"Or less, if you found somebody you wanted to marry during that time."

She halted again and looked up at him. *So I can stop flattering myself. It's not me you want—not in that way.* "You'd release me—divorce me—if I met somebody?"

"As long as I approved him as a father for Zoe's baby, why not? She specified two loving parents. He steps in— that leaves me free to go." What he'd wanted in the first place. She felt a flicker of hurt, then a rising tide of anger, an impulse to lean over and shove him right off his horse. "How *convenient!*"

He nodded complacently. "As I said, works for everybody. Almost everybody."

She laughed—it was that or burst into angry tears. He was impossible! *Oh, yes, that works all right—for you!* But ridiculous as his proposal was, she found herself fascinated. He'd thought of everything. "What about Zoe, Rafe? If I adopted her child, it would be mine. I don't rent my heart out, not at any price. So what will happen if Zoe wants her baby back after she's made it through college?" She reined in, imagining the pain. *I've had enough pain to last me a lifetime.* "I couldn't bear that."

"And I wouldn't let that happen." Reaching across, he set a fingertip to the bridge of her nose and drew it slowly down to the tip. She sucked in a startled breath and her lashes shivered. "I promise. If you take the baby, it's yours forever." His finger moved on, down to her lips where it lingered. "And that's the kind of mother I want for my grandchild," he added huskily. "Somebody who cares like that."

She tossed her head, freeing herself of that touch, but it echoed along her nerve endings, sending tremors out to her fingertips. Her thighs tensed, setting Concha downhill at a flowing walk.

"So you're considering it," he said with satisfaction.

"No, I'm not." *You want somebody—not me, but somebody. Any mother would do. What about that woman you're seeing seriously—or did you try her and she's already turned you down?*

"Another thing I'd want. You have the best grazing on this side of the range, summer or winter, and it's all going to waste. Part of the deal would be that I can run cattle here. We'd work out some split, a way to share the profits on that. Sean could start earning his keep—he rides, doesn't he?—and learn a useful trade."

So now she understood why he hadn't gone to the woman he was seeing seriously and pitched his proposal to her. *She might make a mother for Zoe's child, but I bet she doesn't have land. While with me, he gets a two-fer—a double whammy.* His face almost glowed as he laid out his plans for her ranch. "You've thought of everything," she murmured ironically.

"I have. I'd want a long-term agreement on the grazing rights, by the way. They'd continue for eighteen years, with an option to renew, even if you go for the five-year plan, or if you remarry."

"Really," she said evenly.

"You see what that would do for your own operation, don't you? You'd have a lot more to offer, a much better draw. Dudes want to see cattle worked nowadays. They want to tag along on cattle drives, help out at the brandings, not just poke around the mountains on trail rides. So I'd put my steadiest, most easygoing cowhands over here, men who can put up with that nonsense and still do their jobs. You could start charging what the fancy guest ranches do. I figure we could double your take."

Which he probably knew to the penny! She urged Concha into a trot.

"So what do you think?" he asked, after they'd covered half a meadow and reached another stretch of forest.

"I think I'm a bit late—should be starting supper about now. I only have five dudes tonight—nothing compared with the *fancy* guest ranches—but they still like to eat. She touched her heels to the mare, and she and Rafe flew through the trees in single file, then down the next meadow to the gate of the home pasture.

Rafe opened the gate without dismounting, let her through, then reclosed it. "We walk from here. I don't want to load them up hot."

No way Dana could argue with that. She nodded tensely.

"Well, what do you think?" he repeated, a hint of exasperation creeping into his voice.

"I think…" Financial salvation. That was what he was offering her—bribing her with. And the sense of relief, as she imagined it, was startling. As if Rafe had lifted a half-ton pack off her shoulders that she hadn't realized she was carrying—till she was freed. But still. She shook her head.

"Whoa," he said, as they passed under the tallest tree in the pasture, a massive, spreading oak that the horses always favored for its pool of deep shade. "Let's have this out before we get back to the house."

And Sean's big ears. "All right." She reined in, and her eyes fell on the wooden treads hammered into the gnarly old trunk. Her eyes climbed them rung by rung to the weathered plank platform some twenty feet above, and the hutch perched on top of that. The tree house Peter and Sean had built, two summers ago. She'd almost forgotten it; she came this way so seldom. *Oh, Peter…how could I consider anything less than love for even a heartbeat?* "You said that you'd spend most of the time on your side of the mountain, and I'd stay on mine. What about the rest of the time?"

Dropping his reins on the neck of his gelding, Rafe took off his hat, examined its band with a faint frown, then dropped it over the saddle horn. "You're talking about sex…"

about love. She held his blue gaze and
ing within like a boiling tide.

ing to do here, Dana, is set up the most
minimal marriage I can arrange. One that's fair to you, that
doesn't clip my wings, but that satisfies Zoe's requirements.
That saves her future.''

''A marriage in name only, you mean.'' That would be
more lonely—infinitely more lonely—than what she had
now. A travesty of what she'd had before. But even worse,
it would be an obliteration. Because when a house burns
down to its foundations, and you build again on the same
spot, somehow it erases the original structure. You no
longer can picture the way it once was. *No, thank you. At
least now I have memories to warm me.*

''Maybe a sham marriage for a while, if you wanted,''
Rafe agreed slowly. ''But do you think it would stay that
way? There's something between us, Dana. I feel it. You
feel it, too.''

''I *don't.*'' Her heart was hammering in her chest, her
adrenaline pumping her blood toward rage at his hint of a
smile. ''Don't flatter yourself.''

''Oh?'' Though he hadn't picked up the reins, his big
bay sidestepped toward her little mare, edging Concha in
against the tree trunk. ''That's what I'm doing?'' He lifted
her hat off her head and dropped it over his on the saddle
horn. His hand reached to cover hers on the reins, holding
her horse in check. ''Did you ever watch a cat, Dana, when
she spots a mouse?''

Leaning back in the saddle, she felt her hair graze the
tree trunk, and stopped. His face was a handsbreadth from
hers, no more. She couldn't breathe with him this close.
Half hypnotized, she shook her head.

''Her pupils expand—the eyes go from green to black in
a second. Like *this.*'' He brought the back of his knuckles
to her eyebrow, brushed them slowly down her cheek,

across her trembling mouth. "Like yours go all dark whenever I get this close to you. Excitement is what that is."

"Or fear." Crowding her like this. Their legs were pressed together from knee to ankle. The blood thrummed through her veins like the bass notes of the Ribbon River in springtime, when the snow melted.

Laughing under his breath, Rafe shook his head. "You're not afraid of me. If anybody should be shaking in his boots, it's me."

"I don't know what you mean." Still, the words gave her courage. She reached for her Stetson, dropped it back on her head.

"No?" Taking her hat by the brim, Rafe adjusted its tilt to his own satisfaction. Then, obedient to some invisible signal, Tobasco sidestepped away. Concha snorted and tossed her head, as if she, too, felt the sudden easing of tension. "Just as well, maybe."

At least, that was what Dana thought he'd said, the soft words echoing like an unsolved riddle rattling around her mind, all the way to the house. *Just as well, just as well.* But was it?

"Well?" Rafe asked again, as they dismounted by his trailer.

She didn't have to think. "No, Rafe. Find some other way, but leave me out of it." She was up on her back porch and nearly to the safety of her kitchen door before she turned back. "But thank you for the ride."

AFTER THE HORSES had clopped on down the hill, Sean lifted his dozing half sister off his chest and sat up. She yawned hugely, opened her big brown eyes and blinked at him. "Wow!" he told her reverently. "Did you *hear* that?" Staring over the edge of the tree house platform, he could just see the riders rounding the corner of the barn—Dana and Zoe's old man, all right. He hadn't been dreaming. Who would have believed? "Some witness you are, Pet."

From: SanDiegan@Pipeline.net
To: RedColumbine@Westbest.com
Scoop of the century, Red! You are NOT gonna believe this. Do you know where your old man went today with those oat-burners, or what he was up to? Starts out with me fishing on the bridge. I'd just hooked into this rainbow, two pounds at least, when I look up and see...

CHAPTER TWELVE

RAFE UNLOADED TOBASCO first and led him over to the watering trough, then into the barn. It was drawing on toward suppertime; Zoe was probably up at the house, defrosting another of Mrs. Higgins's casseroles. *Wonder what Dana's feeding her dudes tonight?* Something better than frozen macaroni and cheese, he bet. His stomach grumbled at the thought.

Damn the woman, anyway. Too stubborn to see her own good. He'd offered her a sweet deal. The feel of her lips, trembling against his fingers, moved across his skin. The memory of her big eyes going dark at his touch. He'd wanted to lift her off her saddle and onto his, taste her sweetness right then and there under the oak, seal their bargain with a kiss. *A sweet deal for all of us, it could have been.* The best solution he could imagine to a nasty problem. And now what?

The sun gilded Suntop to the west, but the rest of the valley lay in shadow. He pulled the string hanging down from the barn rafters, switching on an overhead light, then looped Tobasco's reins over the rail and turned back for Concha.

"Daddy?" Zoe called from down the aisle.

"What are you doing out here in the dark?" He went to prop his forearms on the half door to Miel's stall. The palomino had gashed herself somehow out in the pasture. Always a greedy feeder, she'd probably leaned on the barbed wire fence in quest of a greener mouthful on its far side.

Zoe had discovered the wound on her upper leg yesterday, and Willy had stitched and salved it. She'd stay penned inside for a few days to limit her use of it.

"Just hanging out with my baby." Zoe lifted the curry comb she held. "With Miel."

Not a statement that would have needed qualifying a month ago, when Miel had been her only baby. A beloved horse was all the baby his daughter needed, or should have, at sixteen. Woofle rose from the straw in the back of the stall and came to rear against the door, stump tail wagging, with Trey right behind.

Rafe scratched behind Woofle's grizzled ears as he asked, "How's it look?"

"Beautiful. No swelling. Willy says it'll barely scar."

"He's the best." Rafe eyed the brush. When she was troubled, she often groomed Miel while she thought things out. "What about you? You all right?"

"Mmmph." She drifted out after him, stood watching him unsaddle Tobasco, then wandered out into the dark. He frowned, then relaxed when he heard the sound of hooves on metal as she backed Concha down the trailer ramp. She led the mare into the barn, tied her far enough from Tobasco that they both could work, then unstrapped the horse's cinch. "How was your ride with Mrs. Kershaw?"

Arms full of saddle and blanket, Rafe paused in the door to the tack room, looking back. "How'd you know that?"

A flash of mischief broke through her pensive mood. "Elementary, my dear Watson. Concha is a lady's ride. By my count, you know exactly two ladies right now. Mitzy Barlow has fingernails out to *here,* and reins would spoil them. And what do you bet she's scared of horses?"

A bet he wouldn't take. Still, Rafe smelled a bluff somewhere. "Have you been using the phone, by any chance?" If she'd talked to Sean in the past two hours... He'd stopped in Trueheart for some tractor parts on his way home, then a coffee, when he encountered a neighbor.

Zoe's red-gold brows shot skyward. "You said no phone. Or have you changed your mind?"

"In your dreams—and would you please answer the question?" He hadn't been a father for sixteen-plus years for nothing.

"I have not." She stomped off with Concha's saddle, then came back and snatched up her curry comb. They groomed the horses in silence for a while, Rafe wondering how she could possibly be indignant after the stunt she'd pulled last Friday, but go figure. A teenage girl's reasoning was a mystery to him. *And then they grow up to be women.*

Zoe ducked under Concha's neck and started on her other side. "I don't want you to do this."

Crouched at Tobasco's feet, Rafe looked up. "Do what?"

"I don't want you wrecking your life to fix mine. I won't let you do that, Daddy. It's not fair." Her hands flew over the creamy coat, her voice squeaked, perilously close to sobs.

"What are you talking about?" He finished the front legs and stood, staring at her hunched shoulders. How the hell had she guessed?

"I won't let you marry Mrs. Kershaw just to make a home for my baby!"

"You think that's what I was—" He forced a laugh that sounded fake even to him. "Don't be ridiculous."

"You were thinking about Mitzy Barlow, but when you saw how I felt about her, you changed your mind. So now you're hitting on Mrs. Kershaw, and I think it's rotten. Stupid!"

"You don't like Mrs. Kershaw?" How could she not?

"I don't like you cleaning up my mess for me. It's bad

enough I screwed up my own life. I'm not going to screw up yours.''

"Zoe, don't worry about it. I'm taking care of things.''

"By marrying somebody you don't even know? There's only one reason to marry, and that's for love.''

Ah, teenagers. Life was so black and white, so simple. *And that's how I want to keep yours for a few more years.* Give her a baby at seventeen, and she'd learn about life's compromises and limitations all too soon, as Pilar had. *So leave it to me, Zoe.* He wasn't looking to mess up his life— far from it. But if he did, it would only be fair—the debt he owed her mother. *Your happiness is how I clear the slate.*

"So just forget it,'' Zoe continued, when he didn't speak. "You don't have to marry anybody. I'm keeping my baby.''

No. You aren't. Rafe clenched his jaw while he brushed down Tobasco's hind legs, then his tail. "What makes you so sure I'm not attracted to Mrs. Kershaw—to Dana?'' he asked finally. *If I have to marry for love, here goes...*

"You just met her,'' Zoe pointed out.

"You never heard about love at first sight?'' A good case of old-fashioned lust, anyway.

"That's what you said about Mitzy Barlow last week.''

Had he? Well, something like that. "But this time I mean it. Dana's really something.''

Zoe turned around, leaned back against Concha's shoulder and cocked her head. "Really?''

Rafe crossed himself. "Cross my heart and hope to choke. She's very—'' *Sexy.* Each time he saw her, he got this irresistible urge to put his hands around her waist. His fingertips wouldn't quite touch, but they'd come close. He needed to find out how close. "Very pretty,'' he translated, for a female-teenage audience.

Zoe's mouth curled in her *gotcha* grin, the same smirk

she wore when she stomped him at chess. "So you'd marry her, anyway, even if I wasn't having a baby?"

Well...no. He wasn't in the market and didn't plan to be. But he'd still be thinking about taking her to bed. "Sure," he lied.

Zoe snorted. "Yeah, right!"

"I would." She was backing him into a corner, the way she did sometimes on the chessboard, harrying his king with an army of niggling pawns and a wayward knight.

She crossed her arms and grinned. "All right. So prove it. If you really mean that, Daddy, then go right ahead. Court Dana and marry her for love—not for me. Then, if you're still happily married when I deliver my baby..." Her smile wavered; her voice wobbled. "Then I'd be honored and very...very grateful for you to adopt it. But that's the bargain. You have to marry for love."

HOW DO YOU COURT a woman who doesn't want a man? Rafe had never even considered the problem before. Either the lady was willing, in which case the man tap-danced and showered her with little gallantries till she allowed him to win her—or she wasn't, in which case he tipped his hat and moved on. Since Pilar, he'd left his heart safely at home when he went calling, so the mating process had generally been pleasant, the risks not great, the rewards not enormous. Just pleasant. Sufficient unto his needs.

But now Zoe had changed everything. Rafe couldn't simply shrug off a loss this time and move on. He had six months in which to marry for love—at least, convince Zoe he'd married for love. And if he had to stick his head in the noose, he couldn't imagine that in six months of searching he'd find any local woman who'd do half as well as Dana Kershaw. A sexy, single woman with the best grazing in forty miles? A woman who rang his chimes every time he laid eyes on her? All his instincts cried that he should stop here, roll up his sleeves and make it happen.

But how?

All he could figure to do was skip over the courtship, since Dana wasn't having any, and start acting like a husband. Sooner or later, she'd get used to the idea—or he'd have to think of a better one. Rafe decided to start with her corral.

WHOK!

Dana opened her eyes to morning sunlight and blinked up at the ceiling.

Whok-whok. Crash!

Not a dream—but then what in heavens? She rolled out of bed and went to her window. Up by the barn, a familiar black pickup was parked, its bed filled with lumber. Beyond the rails of the corral, a tall figure moved, swung an arm back—whok! One end of a top rail flew out from its post. Rafe moved to the next post, applied sledgehammer again, and rail hit ground with a crash. *I don't believe it!* Rafe Montana, taking her corral apart.

Whok—crash!

He was demolishing her corral at—she glanced toward the clock on her bedside table—at seven a.m...? *I'll kill him!* She leaned out the window to scream at him, then thought better. Petra, still sleeping. Her dudes, probably wide awake by now. But at least she didn't have to add to the din.

Five minutes later she was storming up the hill, dressed and with teeth brushed, though she hadn't stopped to comb her hair. "Stop that!" she called. "Stop it now!" But Rafe was working on the far side of the pen—lumber crashing, hammer resounding—and he didn't turn.

He knocked out another rail, and she jabbed him between the shoulder blades. "What do you think you're doing?"

He swung around—just a little bigger and more vivid than she'd remembered—and smiled. "There you are." A rivulet of sweat darkened the front of his shirt. He swiped a bare forearm up his brow and grinned at her, like a small boy delighting in destruction.

"Here I am," she agreed, "asking what the *hell* do you think you're doing, wrecking my corral?" She crossed her arms and glared.

"I'm fixing it. We had some extra planks left from re-building our weaning pen. And I noticed last week this needed doing, so…" He turned away and walloped the fence.

"Will you *stop* it! You're waking my guests!" She swept an arm toward the far side of the meadow, where the cabins followed the course of the river.

"Oh." He looked, then shrugged. "Well, they should be up now. Missing the best part of the day."

"They're on *vacation,* Rafe. They can sleep as late as they like. So stop that."

"I can't stop here." He hooked a thumb at the fallen planks. "Corral's useless like this."

It was indeed. This was where her wrangler gave her dudes their riding lessons, when he deigned to do so. Where the horses were gathered for saddling each morning before the trail rides. "You'll have to fix it."

"What I intended to do." Frowning, he brushed a knuckle under her lashes. "Hey, it's nothing to cry about."

"I just…I just…" *I don't need this, Rafe! Don't need you here, larger than life, joggling my emotions.* She walked such a tightrope of calm nowadays. It was so easy to push her off.

"So I'll stop till you say it's okay to make noise. All right?" He caught her shoulder and walked her downhill toward her house. "But if I have to wait, could I fix myself a cup of coffee?"

WHEN SHE CAME downstairs again a half-hour later, with Petra yawning on her shoulder, the kitchen smelled of coffee. And baking bread. Rafe stood tall at the table, chopping onions on a block, while Sean worked at the counter, cracking eggs into a bowl.

"Coffee?" Rafe crossed to the stove and poured a cup. "Sean tells me that you make breakfast every morning for your wrangler," he said, handing it over. "So we figured we'd get a jump on the job."

We—right. Sean shot her a smoldering look, and kept on cracking. Dana didn't know whether to join her stepson in resenting this invasion, or rejoice in his discomfiture. "I see." She retreated to the table and sat. Miracles didn't happen every morning; might as well relax and observe this one. She sugared her coffee one handed, then sipped and wrinkled her nose—cowboy coffee, strong enough to peel paint. Hastily she added some cream from the carton he'd set out on the table. "What's in the oven?"

"Biscuits." His big hands wielded the knife deftly, whacking the onion into cubes. "Breakfast is my specialty. Mrs. Higgins and Zoe handle suppers."

He turned up the heat under a cast-iron skillet, added olive oil, then the onions, checked the biscuits, and said to Sean, "Five more minutes. Where's the damn wrangler?"

"He wanders in any time between now and nine," Dana volunteered. Depending on the state of his hangover. This was a Saturday, after all.

"That won't do. How the heck do you schedule his chores or your own if you don't know when he'll show?" He swung back to Sean. "Go get him. Tell him if he's not here *pronto,* we'll feed his share to the dogs."

"Don't have a dog," Sean growled, nevertheless heading for the deck.

"You ought to. How do you know when somebody's coming?"

"They knock on the door," Dana said dryly. *Or barge into the kitchen, like some people we won't mention.*

Rafe shook his head, disapproving, but willing to forgive. "City slicker. And I guess when you find the wrong person standing on your doorstep you call the police. But out here…"

He was right; the vast distances meant that a quick response was impossible.

"You ought to have a big, capable dog around the house if you don't have a man. I gave Zoe an Airedale when she was ten to keep an eye on her when I wasn't there."

She smiled, imagining little Zoe with an indomitable father on one side and a capable Airedale on the other. Safe as houses… It was a different world out here. *His world more than mine.* She shouldn't scorn his advice.

He stirred the sizzling onions, then brought the coffeepot over to pour her a refill. "What are you doing here, Rafe?" *I told you the other day, your idea won't work.*

His blue eyes moved over her face. "Being neighborly. That's another thing we do out here. We take care of ourselves, and we take care of our neighbors when they need help, because sooner or later we'll be the ones in need. Your corral needed mending, and I had the time and the lumber. That's all."

She doubted it, but how to challenge him without calling him a liar? "How's Zoe?" This all came back to her in the end. There'd be no tall, dark cowboy in her kitchen without Zoe.

"Still queasy most mornings, but the doctor said that's natural." He looked over from the stove for her confirmation. "I remember Pilar threw up every morning for the first three months."

"That must have been hard."

He grimaced. "You could say that." The back door opened, and Sean and Tim pushed through. "Just in time for breakfast,'' Rafe noted, holding out his hand. "You must be Tim.''

They ate well, but in silence. Sean was sullen, Tim morose and wary, Dana veering between wry amusement at the way Rafe dominated the table and dismay at the odd little riffles of delight that shot through her at unexpected intervals. It was so good simply to be allowed to sit back and relax. She didn't have to seize the day, because Rafe had seized it for her—by the throat—and was energetically shaking the dickens out of it on her behalf.

The moment Tim put down his fork, Rafe said, "You take the dudes for a trail ride at noon?'' Information he must have extracted from Sean.

"Was thinking about it,'' Tim allowed, erring on the side of caution.

Rafe's eyes narrowed as he put down his mug. "Yes...or no?''

"Uh, yeah. I reckon. If any of 'em want to go.'' Which was nonsense. The deal was that the guests were given a ride every morning, and that a picnic with a longer outing was supplied on Saturdays. Tim shoved back his chair and stood. "So I reckon I'll, uh...go look to the tack.''

Rafe conveyed incredulity with one lifted eyebrow. "It's not cleaned and mended and ready to go?''

"Um, most of it. Few things might need lookin' after.''

"So does your corral. When you're done with the tack, meet me there. You can put in a few hours digging postholes before you ride.'' Rafe gazed after the retreating wrangler for a thoughtful moment, then asked, "You're paying him full-time wages?''

"Just barely. Plus room and board. He's got one side of the shotgun cabin.''

"Full-time wages for half a day's work, if you're lucky,'' Rafe observed. "Life's too short to try to ride herd on a layabout. You'd be better off without him.''

Neighborliness didn't extend to hiring and firing her staff for her. "Not quite." Not unless she wanted to lead the trail rides herself.

He shrugged and dropped the matter—and turned to her stepson, who'd sat silent through this exchange. "Who washes the dishes around here?"

Sean's look of dawning alarm reminded Dana of a rabbit pinned in the headlights of an oncoming truck. "Uh, she does." He stood hastily and collected his plate.

"While you do what, instead?" Rafe inquired pleasantly.

"Um…" The red crept up Sean's throat, and he shuffled from foot to foot.

"What I figured. Well, today you can do them. Then come up to the corral and give me a hand." And now it was her turn. "A last cup of coffee out on the porch?" Rafe suggested.

He'd just knocked an hour's worth of chores out of her day. She opened her mouth to say that she could get used to this, then thought better and said, "Sounds lovely!"

CHAPTER THIRTEEN

SATURDAY RAFE FIXED her corral. The following Thursday he reappeared at her kitchen door, an hour after breakfast. Dana had just turned out a batch of bread on her pastry slab and her hands were sticky with dough, when he knocked on the screen door.

"Come in—oh, Rafe!" A little shiver of pleasure moved up her bare arms and across her shoulders. "What are you doing here?"

"Come begging a cup of coffee to start with." He nodded at the pot on her stove. "Mind if I do?"

After the effort he'd put into her corral last week—four new posts and a dozen planks or more? She was indebted much deeper than a cup of coffee. "Of course not. I'd take one, too, if you'd fix it for me."

That done, he settled across the table from her to watch, sipping slowly. How did he do it? One moment her kitchen was a prison, a place of lonely, endless drudgery. Now it felt as if the sun had swung around to this side of the house. As if life had a purpose once more, rather than simply a trudging sense of surviving each day, only to be faced with the next, then the next. A man around the house beat an Airedale any day.

Outside, a whinny sounded nearer than the pasture. "Yours?" she asked, cocking her head.

"Tobasco. And I brought Concha along."

Her heart lifted at the prospect of a ride, but she made a teasing face. "You just happened to have a couple of extra

horses, so you thought you'd bring them over? Right neighborly, pardner.''

''It is, isn't it?'' His blue eyes locked on hers—then
moved deeper, as if their foreheads, the tips of their noses,
touched, mind speaking directly to mind. *You know what
I'm doing and why,* his eyes said.

And you know my answer. She tore her gaze away and
dropped it to her hands, kneading mechanically. He knew
it, and yet still he sat here sipping her coffee. Well, he
couldn't say she hadn't warned him.

''I thought we'd ride your fence in the home pasture,''
he said finally. ''I noticed several posts rotted off at the
base the other day. One good push, and it would all come
down.''

''Maybe I like it that way,'' she muttered defiantly. She
couldn't let him do this; he had his own ranch to tend.

''Yeah, you'll like it when one of your horses tries to
step across the wire and tangles his feet and falls. It isn't
pretty when he starts struggling. And it's dangerous cutting
him out. Do you even own a pair of wire cutters?''

''There might be some up at the barn.''

He blew out a breath, not quite a snort, but merely said,
''I'll check.'' He swallowed some more coffee. ''Sean
should carry a pair everywhere he rides. I'll see he has
some.'' He went back to her coffeepot to refill his cup, then
put it back on the stove. ''Where is Sean, anyway? If he
doesn't know how to mend fence, it's high time he
learned.''

Her mouth tightened. ''He's out and about someplace.''
Hands on the spiraling dough, she could feel his eyes on
her face.

''He gave you trouble this morning?''

She aimed a breath upward, blowing bangs back from
her eyebrows. ''No more than the usual. We have this continuing battle about the computer.'' She tipped her head

toward a table pushed against the far wall, next to the ancient pie safe, where Sean's computer lived. "Peter gave it
to him, but he was very clear on the way he wanted it to
be used. He'd seen too many of his students turn into vir-
tual recluses, holed up in their rooms, cruising the Internet
for hours on end, visiting Web sites they shouldn't, playing
too many games, chatting with questionable strangers. He
said the best way to prevent that was to put the computer
in the family room, so you knew what your kid was doing.
It should be a tool for research, not a substitute for a social
life.''

"Makes sense to me."

"And to me, but not to Sean. And I do feel guilty lim-
iting his time, when he's stuck out here in the middle of
nowhere. When I first pitched our moving to Colorado to
Peter, I imagined it…differently.'' *I imagined Peter alive,
for one thing, with time to give to Sean.* Imagined Sean
adjusting well to his new school, making friends in the
neighborhood. "The distances out here—I don't guess
there's another boy his age within ten miles. And I don't
know that he's tried very hard to fit in. The only friend I
know for certain that he's made is Zoe.''

She watched Rafe's face cool and harden, then he looked
away. His eyes lit on Petra, who sat in the corner on a raft
of towels. Absorbed in the plastic containers Dana had
given her, she was pouring water from a quart container
into a butter tub. "Now, *she* knows how to amuse herself,''
he noted with approval. "Not such a hellraiser as Zoe
was.''

"Peter and I are—'' She swallowed. *Were.* "Quiet, patient types. She comes by it honestly.''

The water overflowed the smaller container. Petra
shrieked with startled laughter, put the quart down and
waved her hand at her achievement, glancing up to be sure
Dana had seen. "Wa!''

"More water than you planned on," Dana agreed, grateful for the interruption. "Why don't you show Rafe how you can pour it back."

Rafe stood, went over and hunkered down on his boot heels. "Show me, sweetheart. What have you got there?"

Even crouching, he must seem enormous to her daughter. Petra studied him earnestly, arrived at some decision and smiled. "Nuh-wa!" She picked up the butter tub and offered it to him.

"Mighty nice. Suppose we poured some of it in here...and some here?" Rafe poured half the water back into the quart container, the other half into a third tub. Petra stared, thunderstruck at this new concept. Rafe laughed, rubbed his palm lightly across her head and returned to Dana. "You're not drinking your coffee."

"Hands too sticky. I'll do it in a minute."

"Here." He picked up her mug and held it to her mouth.

"There's no need," she protested, drawing in a breath, as his hand fell on her shoulder.

"But who likes cold coffee?" Nudging her lower lip with the rim of the cup, he tilted it slowly. Eyes meeting his through the rising steam, she gave up and drank. Her heart must have been pounding all along, but suddenly she could hear it, a big, purposeful striding in her ears—taking her where? "Thank you," she whispered, as the cup drew back.

"My pleasure." Brushing a knuckle under her lip, he caught a drop.

It shouldn't be this way. She shouldn't be feeling what she was feeling.

"Ma-ma-ma-*ma!*" Petra called, demanding her attention. Peter's child. Dana slapped the dough into a ball and went to see.

ONCE SHE'D SET THE DOUGH on the warming shelf above the stove for its first rising, then taken Petra upstairs for a diaper change, she had a little time to spare. "Come with me," Rafe urged. "We're wasting daylight."

"I can't leave her, Rafe, and she won't be ready for a nap for hours."

"So bring her along."

"On horseback?" Dana shook her head. "If I fell with her…"

"Then let me carry her." His hands closed around the baby's fat waist. "Go change."

Not a good idea, she told herself as she returned upstairs, but the chance to be out in the mountain air, out in sunlight and flowers… *He knows how to tempt me.*

She found Rafe and Petra out back inspecting the horses. Rafe held the baby facing forward in the crook of his left arm while he showed her how to stroke Concha's velvety nose. Petra patted the mare and squealed. "A born horse-woman," Rafe declared, giving her back to Dana. He swung up on Tobasco. "Now, let me have her."

Dana bit her lip. "Rafe, I really don't think—"

His hands didn't fall. "I started Zoe at six months, Dana. I won't drop her."

This is his world and he knows it, she reminded herself, looking up at him. He wouldn't drop Petra, wouldn't let his horse run away, she knew that, but still… *I want her safe with me. He wants to show her his world and he's saying he can protect her.* She let out a slow, shaking breath and relinquished her daughter.

Petra's mouth formed into a pink *O* of astonishment, as Rafe settled her onto his lap, one hand curled around her stomach. She patted the saddle horn, reached beyond it to grab a swath of Tobasco's black mane. Giggling delighted-ly, she looked down at her mother to make sure she shared this moment.

A moment Rafe had given her, overriding her mother's

fear on Petra's behalf. *Thank you, Rafe.* The look on Petra's face was a gift surpassing six miles of new fence. Dana swung up on Concha and brought her side by side with the bay, as Rafe moved him out at an easy walk.

"Okay now?" Rafe asked huskily.

Eyes on her daughter's rapturous face, Dana nodded. "Very okay."

They rode most of the fence line, Rafe holding Petra while he instructed Dana to wiggle each fence post without dismounting. When she found a rotten or loose one, he gave her orange surveyor's tape, and she tied a bit of it to the wire. As they rode they talked of little things: Petra's first adventure with solid food—pureed carrots, which ended up on the ceiling; Sean's love of fly-fishing and photography; the spectacular crimson columbine Zoe had hybridized, which had bloomed for the first time last week. They talked a bit about their pasts; Dana's years teaching high school English in Vermont, then her two years with the Peace Corps in Pakistan; Rafe's early years as a cowboy after Pilar died, back when he lived in ranch bunkhouses, while Zoe stayed with Pilar's parents and he could visit her only on weekends.

How could you bear it? To be separated like that. To find each week that she'd grown, that you'd missed out on some crucial little triumph—her first bicycle ride, her first lost tooth? Dana wanted to touch his shoulder, as if touch could soothe the long-ago pain that echoed behind his matter-of-fact words. Unable to do that, she leaned, instead, to stroke her daughter's silky head. She glanced up at Rafe, and found their faces only inches apart—saw his pupils expand, his eyes changing from blue skies to storm clouds. *Excitement whenever we come close...* Who knew what her own eyes were revealing? She straightened abruptly.

"She's getting sleepy," Rafe said after a pause, rubbing her daughter's stomach. "In fact..." He shifted her so that she lay cradled in the crook of his right arm. "Gone, I'd say. Riding's as good as a car."

"You're not tired of holding her?"

"Not at all." He nodded ahead. "Now, there's a beauty."

While she leaned to tie ribbon to the sagging post, he said, "I've been meaning to say something...about Suntop."

She turned, surprised at how serious he sounded, then her eyes focused beyond him. "Will you look at that!" Sean, climbing down from the tree house in the oak tree at the center of the pasture. "So that's where he goes! I thought he'd outgrown it."

"Aha!" Rafe's eyes gleamed with satisfaction. "Think I will hand you Miss Sleepyhead for a minute."

"Then let me get down." Dana dismounted, accepted her daughter and watched Rafe lope purposefully in pursuit of Sean, who'd set off downhill, giving no sign that he'd seen them. Horse and rider came to a sliding halt in front of the boy, as if they were heading a stray calf. Observing the ensuing exchange, even at this distance Dana could see Sean stiffen, every angle of his body expressing outrage, while every line of Rafe's conveyed calm implacability. Her stepson threw up his hands abruptly and changed direction, trudging off toward the barn, shoulders slumped, kicking weeds as he went.

Dana bit her lip and looked down at her sleeping daughter. *Peter, am I doing wrong letting Rafe boss him around? But he's been so lost without you. Maybe a man in his life is what he needs.*

She waited, but no answer came, only the song of a mockingbird, far-off, trill upon triumphant trill. What had Sean himself said the other day when she was talking about the needs of a boy-child to have a man to follow?

I had that once, he'd said so wistfully that it had almost broken her heart.

Should I try to find that for him again, Peter? Or am I betraying you? Betraying his love for you?

No answer but the bird, spangling the day with notes of radiant joy.

The shadow of a horse and rider fell over her. "Looks like I've found my help, Dana. I've sent him for the posthole diggers."

She glanced at her watch. "And I should get back to my bread. But thank you for my ride. For Petra's first ride."

Rafe touched a finger to his hat and his slow smile crinkled his eyes. "Anytime."

From: SanDiegan@Pipeline.net
To: RedColumbine@Westbest.com
Zoe, your old man is driving me CRAZY!!!!!!!!!!! What's he trying to prove, anyway? The Ribbon R was doing fine without him. I've got blisters on top of my blisters. I guess he's trying to punish me for getting you pregnant, and this is the only way he can find to do it—death by posthole digger. From now on, how about warning me when he's headed this way? Anyway, I REALLY miss you. Saw a pretty columbine yesterday and I felt like breaking something. This SUCKS deluxe. What are we gonna do? Love you, Sean

From: RedColumbine@Westbest.com
To: SanDiegan@Pipeline.net
Hey, Seanster, don't take it personally. I think it's just his demented way of hitting on your stepmom. By the way, is she interested? I think he's a studmuffin myself, but maybe I'm prejudiced. Sorry about those blisters, but mending fence is a handy skill. I can do

it myself. Gotta run now. I've got five foals to exercise today. (He's working my butt off, too.) BIIIIG
HUG, Zoe+(?)

IT TOOK FOUR DAYS, spread over two weeks, to complete
the repairs to the home pasture fence line. Tim and Sean
did much of the work, but Rafe was the driving force behind everyone's labor. Each day Dana found herself falling
deeper and deeper into his debt, found herself both grateful
and dismayed by her growing obligation. Needing to balance the equation, she cooked hearty lunches for him and
his crew, but that hardly moved the scales, compared with
hours of backbreaking labor, setting posts and stringing
wire. Besides, she was fairly certain that Rafe didn't own
an endless supply of spare fence posts. She suspected he
was buying them somewhere, but when she demanded that
he let her pay for the materials, he laughingly brushed her
aside.

The least she could do was invite him to supper, but most
days he turned her down, citing a need to go home to Zoe.
The day they completed the job, however, he worked till
almost dark. Then, after he'd packed his truck, he appeared
at her kitchen door.

"It's done," he said briefly, looming tall against a red-
lavender glow—the sun had set. A cool wind blew, carrying
the smell of clean sweat and leaf mold and bruised grass
from him to her. He flexed his shoulders beneath his damp
shirt, easing sore muscles.

"Rafe, I don't know how to thank you."

"Step out here and see the moonrise. That would be
thanks enough."

"Hardly." Still, she slipped out for a moment to see an
amber moon creeping above the eastern peaks, chasing one
silver planet up the purpling sky. "*Beautiful*'s not a big

enough word,'' she murmured, after they'd stood shoulder to shoulder in mute fascination till it cleared the mountaintop.

He nodded. ''In Spanish, the word for heaven and for sky is the same. *Cielo.*''

See-EH-loh, she repeated silently. The word was liquid, sensual on the tongue. Pilar taught him that, she realized with the oddest twinge of—not quite pain, not quite resentment. She put it briskly aside. ''It's gorgeous, but we're just minutes from sitting down.'' Her guests were gathering in the living room, enjoying their hors d'oeuvres around the fire she'd kindled against the evening chill. ''I've tried before, but I'll say it again. You're welcome to stay for supper. You must be starving.''

''This time I reckon I'll take you up on it, if you really mean it. That lunch you made us seems about a hundred years gone.''

''Of course I mean it.'' Though she half regretted the invitation as soon as it left her mouth. He needed a change of clothes and a shower. Water was no problem, but she had no clothes to lend him. Peter's were up in the attic, packed away in boxes scented with sprigs of lavender and rose petals from her garden, against the day when she found the courage to give them away. She'd sooner Rafe come to her table in his birthday suit than in Peter's clothes. Not that they'd fit him anyway, she realized, looking up at him. He was taller, broader, longer of leg.

''I don't suppose Sean would have a T-shirt that would fit you.''

He laughed under his breath. ''No need. I always carry a change of clothes in my truck. Is there a hose out here I could use?''

''You know where the bathroom is upstairs,'' she reminded him. How long ago that seemed, and how he'd scared her that night! *If you'd just said, ''Hey, it's me, Rafe, stomping into your life,''* Somehow she felt she would have known that here was a friend, not trouble. ''Supper's in ten minutes, so you'd better hurry.''

She introduced him to her dudes that night as a neighbor—then gritted her teeth at the arch looks passing among some of the women. It didn't help that Rafe—by accident or inclination, she didn't know which—had chosen the seat at the opposite end of the table from her own. Not that he tried to pose as the host, but he had a natural authority to which people instantly responded. Before the soup course was done, the women were plying him with questions about Indians and rodeos; the men, about ranching and hunting. He didn't try to dominate the talk—far from it. His answers were delivered with a cowboy's dry humor and modesty, brief and straight to the point. Still, the conversation flowed around him. *I could hire him for the nightly entertainment,* she thought, watching him over the candles.

The only one who wasn't charmed by Rafe was Sean. Her stepson sat glowering, grimly shoveling food into his mouth till he'd cleaned his plate. Then, rather than waiting for his usual second helping of everything, he mumbled his excuses and retreated upstairs.

After supper, Rafe assisted in clearing away, then offered to help with the dishes. ''Going for sainthood?'' she teased him, and shook her head.

''*Cielo,* maybe, but not sainthood,'' he murmured, lounging against the counter next to the sink.

Dana kept her eyes fixed on her rubber-gloved hands. *What are you trying to do to me, Rafe?* He hadn't mentioned Zoe's problem in weeks, except to report that the morning sickness seemed to be easing at last. *So then, why are you here?*

You feel it, too, he'd told her weeks ago up on the mountain. And there was no denying it. Blindfolded, she'd still have felt his presence, as if the air had changed to warm velvet brushing against her skin, her nerves crisping with his nearness, the blood sliding through her veins like molten honey.

But even though I feel it, Rafe, it's no good. Even if you were offering me love, not sex, I'm still a coward. A chance of love didn't come without risk—and to risk losing again? She'd already had enough pain in her life. No. Whatever he was offering, she didn't need it. She kept her ambitions small and realistic these days. She'd settle for peace.

Rafe cocked his head. "Nice tune." He went to the swinging door and propped it open a few inches with the doorstop. In the living room, someone had found the CD player. The velvety tones of a Tony Bennett song drifted through the night. Dana glanced automatically at the playpen, but Petra slept on, bottom high under her blanket, sweet face a dreaming blank.

"I should be going," Rafe said regretfully, "but first I wanted to ask you something. Got a minute to come out front?"

"Sure." She drew off her gloves and followed him through the dining room, then paused in the archway to the living room. A new song had just started, and three couples were shuffling around the room.

"There you are, Dana!" Leo Shultz cried gaily. He was the most sociable guest of her current set. "Come dance with me." He drew her, protesting, out on the floor—she'd danced with no man since Peter, and didn't want to now. She glanced back helplessly at Rafe, mouthing a "Sorry," and found that he was scowling. Somehow that eased her own reluctance.

And Leo was the perfect partner with whom to break her long fast. His own cheery wife, Martha, was paired with Ira Kravitz from Aspen cabin, and Leo chortled and bumped hips with her every time they danced past. If Peter had been sitting on the couch watching them, he'd have been smiling. ''Marvelous dance, marvelous dinner, most marvelous vacation I've had in years!'' Leo declared at the end of the song, as he escorted her back to Rafe—as if she were a wheelbarrow he'd borrowed from a next-door neighbor.

''Sorry,'' Dana apologized, when he'd departed. ''What did you want to show me?''

''A question about paint, but it can wait.'' A new song had begun—''Till There Was You.'' Rafe settled a hand on her waist and drew her close. ''One of my favorites,'' he noted, clasping her hand and lifting it to his chest, just a hand span above his heart.

Not with you, Rafe, I can't do it! But how could she refuse, after she'd humored Leo? And she was already past the point of refusal, following his strong but simple lead, her body instinctively answering his. ''Is it?'' she said on a scrap of breath. Her heart had mysteriously ballooned to fill up her chest—all thuds, no oxygen. She felt dizzy, stunned sightless by his body heat and his nearness; all she could do was give herself to his hands and the music. Tremors filled her as if she were the guitar string quivering, as if the horn blew its shivering notes across her skin.

Rafe dipped his mouth to her temple. ''All right?'' he murmured huskily. His fingers slid around her waist to her back, splayed against her spine. Fanned upward in an absent caress, then down again.

I should be. It was only a song. Only a dance. It shouldn't shatter her. Shouldn't.

It ended before she could find an answer. His lips brushed across her hair. His fingertips followed her spine upward, exploring the shape and size of her, then dropped away when she stepped back. ''Thank you,'' she whispered, her throat aching too much for louder words.

They'd ended at the foot of the staircase. She reached out, needing to go, unable to do so without...something.

Some gesture. She fingered a button on his shirt. "Thanks, Rafe. And…good night." Avoiding his eyes—she knew they'd be dark, the pupils wide with her nearness, as hers were with his—she turned and fled up the stairs.

CHAPTER FOURTEEN

From: SanDiegan@Pipeline.net
To: RedColumbine@Westbest.com
So now your old man's REALLY messed us up. Our
wrangler quit a few minutes ago. Dana's gonna have
a COW when she gets back from the grocery store.
What happened was your dad showed up this morning
and announced we were going to paint the house. (Is
he always this hyper?) Tim said he was a wrangler,
not a house painter. Your dad said "Tough," that
while he was taking Dana's money, he could work
for it or walk. So the three of us scraped paint all
day—front of the house is more bare wood than paint
now. And megalousy work in the heat—the paint
chips and dust stick to your sweat and your arms want
to fall off. Tim finally threw down his scraper and
walked away about an hour before sundown. I figured
your dad would tear a strip off him, but he just sort
of smiled to himself and kept scraping. Then tonight,
I'm sitting here in the kitchen, hanging out with the
Pet-beast while Dana goes shopping, and Tim stops
by to drop off the key to his cabin. Tells me to tell
Dana to find some other slave—he's outta here. I
know just how he feels, too. If I had someplace to
go, I'd be gone for sure. Except for you, you, you.
You're the only reason I'm still here, Zoe. I don't
know what I'd do if my mom finally decided to take
me, like I've been bugging her to. (Want to run away

with me to San Diego? It beats this dump four ways from Sunday, I'm telling you.) WHUH oh, the BEAST is crawling this way—wants to know what I'm up to. Wants to help me play with the keyboard. Wants to sit in my lap—not with THAT diaper you don't, babe! Better sign off quick. I LOOOOOOOOOOOOOVE YOU, RED.

Your Sean Diegan

P.S. Like I told you last week, day after tomorrow is my birthday, the big 1-5. Is there a chance in the world he'd let you come to my party? Dana always makes this stupid fuss. It's way beyond embarrassing, with the dudes and all, but at least there's cake and ice cream. Think you could ask him? I REALLY miss you and I want to pat your freckled tummy. (Now that would be a birthday present.)

"TIM QUIT," Dana said flatly as she opened the back door to admit Rafe. She'd returned home too late from town the night before to call him then, and perhaps it was just as well. Overnight, her fury had cooled to manageable proportions, or nearly. "I knew he wasn't going to stand still for that!"

"For some honest hard work? No, I reckon that was too much to expect."

And you didn't expect it, did you? she thought, seeing the satisfied curl of his mouth. *I wouldn't let you fire him, so you persuaded him to walk.* The man's arrogance was boundless. "What do I do now? Some new guests checked in yesterday, and they're hot for their first trail ride." She wanted to bite her tongue as soon as she'd said it. Asking for Rafe's advice, she was playing right into his hands.

"You loan me your phone." He brushed the back of his wrist against her bare arm, nudging her aside.

Crossing her arms, she retreated to the far side of the

kitchen. Stood, stewing, while he punched in a number. She shrugged and went back to making pancakes. *All right. You got me into this mess. Let's see how you get me out.*

"Zoe?" Rafe murmured behind her. "I need to talk to Willy. Could you run get him?" He swung around to lean against the counter, tapping one boot.

Across the room, Petra looked up from the beach ball she was trying to chew. She flopped over onto hands and knees and made a scuttling beeline for Rafe. He dropped down on his heels. "How's my girl?"

Dana stiffened. *Not yours, Rafe. None of us is. You can't just annex a family, or a ranch, because you feel like it.* Still, she stole a glance every so often, watching him draw a clean red bandanna from his back pocket and tie it around her daughter's neck. Petra chortled and proceeded to pull herself up the leg of his jeans till she stood swaying against his knee, holding up her new adornment for his admiration. "Would you look at this?" Rafe called on a note of laughter.

"She's been doing that off and on all week," Dana told him, softening in spite of herself. How could you resist a man who thought your daughter was adorable?

"Be toddling before you know it—oh, Willy?" A few brisk words and the conversation was done. Rafe put down the phone, scooped Petra up and sauntered over to where Dana was whipping batter. "You've got a wrangler for the rest of this week. If you suit each other, maybe he'll stay."

WILLY PROVED TO BE a seventy-something cowboy with a shrewd-comical face and a salt-and-pepper beard that could have served as an industrial dust mop. Battered black hat in his hand, he stopped by the kitchen to introduce himself and ask her desires for the day. With that understood, he chucked Petra under her chin, then drove his truck and horse trailer—he'd brought his own mount—up to the barn.

"Ha!" Petra declared, watching as he backed a big, rangy chestnut down the ramp.

"That is a horse," Dana agreed. "Or did you mean Willy was funny?" And to be relied on, she admitted, hearing her own deep sigh of relief. If Rafe had chosen him, then Willy would do. "Blast the man, anyway, trying to run our lives for us, Pet."

But by lunchtime she'd forgiven him. Hard not to, when the whole house echoed to the sound of scrapers dragging across brittle paint. A job Dana had always hated herself. *I shouldn't be letting him do this.*

But just how did you stop an irresistible force? And if you only half wanted him to stop? *That's the real problem.* She wasn't wholehearted in her resistance, and Rafe knew it. *He manipulates me as easily as he maneuvered Tim into quitting.* But to what end? His original purpose? Or did he, too, find his original feelings subtly changing as the days passed, like the Ribbon River wearing rough stones to pearly smoothness? *I don't know. Don't think I want to know.*

She'd just completed the potato salad that would go with the chicken sandwiches for her paint crew, when Sean scratched at the back door. "Getting hungry?" she asked, coming to meet him, glad that he'd remembered the rule she'd made yesterday; Petra was not to be exposed to paint dust, since there was no way to be sure it was lead-free.

"Yeah, but I wanted to ask you something."

"Sure, what is it?" Anything. He'd been so sullen these past few weeks, with Rafe pushing him. Sometimes Dana felt as if their relationship had taken a giant step backward.

"I know what I want for my birthday present." He raised his gaze from his toes to her face.

Peter's brown eyes. "What's that?" she asked, though she'd already knocked the bottom out of her monthly budget, buying him a lens for the Nikon that his father had given him.

"I want Zoe to come to my party tomorrow night. Do you think Mr. Montana would let her if *you* asked?"

"Oh, Sean." *Ask me for the moon, why don't you?* Rafe seemed determined to keep them apart.

"Please?" He flattened a hand to the screen between them. "Will you, Dana?"

"Of course I'll try. But promise me you won't get your hopes up?"

Leaving Sean to eat his lunch on the back porch, with one ear cocked for Petra, who was dozing in her kitchen playpen, Dana brought a tray around the house to the front. Rafe stood up on the porch roof, dragging a two-handed scraper along the flaking clapboards between the dormers. The muscles clenched in his sweat-soaked shirt, then lengthened, clenched again. Muscles in her stomach, and lower, pulled tight at the sight of him. She stiffened her shoulders and called, "Lunchtime!"

They ate it down by the river, talking lazily of possible paint schemes for the house, and then of Willy. He was Rafe's oldest cowboy, his steadiest, hands down his funniest—just wait till she heard his yarns about the old days. "But he's getting a bit creaky for range work, though he's too mule-stubborn to admit it. If I could find him a soft spot where he still felt useful…" Somehow Rafe implied she'd be doing him a favor if she took Willy on.

"We'll see how he likes dudes," Dana promised. And now, if she was helping him out, then… "Rafe, did Sean tell you that tomorrow's his birthday?" Swiftly she made her plea. She couldn't take time off from the Ribbon R to give Sean any sort of celebration in town, not to mention the problem of money. So the affair would be simple—just an extraspecial supper, then cake and ice cream. "But he hasn't any friends that I know of to invite to the party. Except...Zoe.''

Rafe's brows shot together. "And whose fault is that? You said he doesn't make much effort to fit in."

"I don't think he knows how. He's a fish out of water out here. Half the kids in his class are ranch kids, so he's at a disadvantage being a city slicker. And the others are jocks, and he's not that, either."

"That's one of the hard lessons a man needs to learn in life—how to find his feet wherever he goes. How to make friends."

"I think, behind all his cockiness, he's fairly shy, Rafe."

"I reckon you're right, but still, he needs to learn."

It's not your place to teach my son, Rafe! Though she didn't doubt he meant it kindly. "But about Zoe?"

"I'm sorry, Dana. I want her heart-free and ready to go as soon as her baby's born. Zoe needs to get on with her life, not always be looking back over her shoulder."

"But Sean—" She stopped as he shook his head. The man was a rock.

"Your first concern is Sean, Dana. But mine has to be Zoe. The answer's no."

There was no use in fighting; she'd never win this one. And if he wouldn't oblige her in this, still, he had in every other way. *I tried, Sean.* One more time she'd failed him was the way he'd see it. She sighed and said, "How is Zoe, anyway? Is she showing yet?"

"She's taken to wearing baggy sweatshirts, so it's hard to be sure, but yes, I'd say so."

She watched the muscles quiver in his jaw, but pressed on. "What about adoption agencies? Have you looked into those yet?" *This is a test,* she realized suddenly. If he'd given up on her as the solution to his problem, then he must be addressing that. And she wanted to believe he'd given up. Wanted to believe that whatever Rafe was doing here, whatever kept bringing him back to the Ribbon R, it had nothing to do with Zoe.

His expression went a bit darker. "I spoke to a couple of agencies, but they say with Zoe's restrictions... Doesn't look promising."

"Maybe a private placement?"

"Maybe," he said shortly. "I've talked to my lawyer."

He had nothing further to volunteer on the subject, so Dana gave up prying. She stacked their plates on the tray and started to rise, but he put a hand on her knee. She subsided and cocked her head.

"I've been meaning to say something, and now I've got to," Rafe said. As if he'd forgotten it, his hand stayed in place. "It's about Suntop. I don't own all of the ranch— or even much of it."

"Oh?" *Why are you telling me this, Rafe?*

"I'm the ranch manager. Old man Tankersly owns Suntop. It has been in his family for a hundred-something years. But he had only daughters, three of 'em, and they all ran off to the city. He needed somebody to run the place for him—he moved down to San Antonio ten years ago, and he only stays up here for half of each summer, which is why I'm telling you this."

"Rafe, you don't have to tell me anything." Though apparently he felt he had to. His face was set, the muscles ticking faintly beneath his suntanned skin.

"I didn't want any...misunderstandings...false pretenses, is why. I own fifteen percent of Suntop, Dana, which is enough to bring me a very good living and always will be. Ben Tankersly thought the best way to keep me, and keep me working for his best interests, was to make them the same as my own. So once he'd decided I'd do, he paid me partly in land and partly in money, till I'd reached fifteen percent."

"I see." She nodded, not understanding the pain in his face.

"But that's all of Suntop I'll ever own, Dana. He'll never sell out to me at any price. He wants the ranch to stay in his family, and he wants it intact. His daughters don't care about the place, but they have two young sons among them so far. Tankersly's hoping that when his grandsons grow up…" He shrugged. "It's years before I'll have to deal with that, but I thought you should know."

"I see." Rafe was warning her that if she'd thought he was a rich man, she was mistaken. If anything, she liked him more for that, not less. Still, she felt a shadow creeping across her heart, a high, thin layer of ice-filled gray swallowing the sun. "Thanks for telling me. There was no need."

He grimaced. "Not the way I saw it. Besides, old man Tankersly took a notion to visit early this year. He phoned last night. He'll be flying in Thursday, which means I won't be able to finish painting the front of your house this week. Fact is, I won't be able to be around much at all, for the next month while he's visiting."

"Rafe, please, don't worry about it. But shouldn't you be over at your place getting ready for his visit?"

He stiffened as if she'd slapped him. "A well-run ranch is ready for an inspection at any time."

"Of course." She put a placating hand over his. "I imagine Suntop runs like a clock."

"As much as a ranch ever does." He'd stopped bristling. His eyes flicked down to their stacked hands, then rose to hers with a question stirring in their depths.

Hastily she gathered up the tray and stood. "I've stuck poor Sean with Petra."

AFTER SHE'D DISMISSED Sean, Dana took Petra upstairs to nurse and to nap. Lying in bed with the dozing baby cradled against her, eyes closed, she realized that her somber mood still lingered. Something Rafe had said? Picturing his face, hearing his scraper attacking the paint on the far side of the house, she felt a shiver start low in her stomach and rise to her breasts, her nipples hardening as if Petra still suckled. There was no denying her attraction. Was that the root of this sadness?

Something to do with what he told me… His chagrin at not owning all of Suntop Ranch…

That was it—land. He'd made it plain from the start that he'd like to lay his hands on the Ribbon R, but now she was beginning to grasp the extent of his desire. Fifteen percent of the county's largest ranch wasn't enough land for Rafe. He wanted more.

She had it.

When you're thinking—hoping?—that maybe his feelings are changing as yours are, just keep that in mind.

ONCE RAFE HAD LEFT for the day, she told Sean of her failure to move him regarding Zoe. He took it as she'd expected—slamming out of the kitchen and disappearing for the rest of the night. Not even supper lured him down from his room. At least she had plenty of privacy to bake a German chocolate cake—his favorite—and ice it.

THE NEXT MORNING her stepson's mood held steady—in the basement. When she wished him a happy birthday at the breakfast table, he grunted and shrugged. "Big wonderful deal."

As he was finishing his meal, Rafe's truck pulled into the yard. "Oh, *crap!* He thinks I'm gonna work on my birthday?"

He did indeed. "Best present a man could give himself" was Rafe's response. "Putting his own house in order. You own a quarter share in this ranch, Dana tells me."

Sean shrugged. "So what? I'd sell it in a heartbeat."

Standing in front of the stove, Rafe swung deliberately around, coffeepot suspended, one eyebrow raised. "Really? I'd like to buy it."

Dana sucked in a breath, as Sean rocked back on his heels. But before she could open her mouth, he'd recovered. "Sure, we could talk about that—if you'll let me see Zoe."

The hungry light in Rafe's face flickered and died. "Forget it." He smacked down his mug without refilling it. "Let's get to work. I want a coat of primer on the front by the end of the day."

"Whatever." Sean stalked out the door.

"And you can forget about cutting a deal with a minor," Dana said dryly, after he'd gone. "The terms of Peter's will say he can't sell without consent of his guardian, and that's me." *And I don't see you as my partner, Rafe.* Not if all he cared about was business.

CHAPTER FIFTEEN

WHEN SHE CALLED THEM to lunch out on the deck—paint chips still being forbidden in her kitchen—Dana found that the mood hadn't lightened. Sean was still mutely sullen. Rafe briskly ignored the boy's sulking, which was probably the best way to deal with it.

While they ate, Dana filled the edgy silence with a report on Willy's first day as a wrangler. Last night at supper, the guests had praised him to the skies. His stories were fascinating, his humor droll. He was a fount of natural history and cowboy lore. And apparently he liked to teach. He was currently up in the home pasture, showing some of the dudes how to rope a horse.

"If he wants to stay on after this week, we'd love to have him," she said.

"Up to him," Rafe reminded her. "Suntop has been his home for thirty years or more, so…"

"He said he'd rather continue living in your bunkhouse than move into the wrangler's cabin here," Dana said. "But maybe that will keep him from feeling homesick."

Sean stood abruptly. "Can I use the truck?"

"Didn't your mother ground you after your brush with the state police?" Rafe asked quietly. He knew she had.

"Yeah, but I want to go get the mail—all right? I could do it on my bike—I'd be glad to—but it'd take me an hour. I thought you wanted help painting."

"It's you who needs help painting," Rafe reminded him with measured calm.

"So, yes, but you should get back quick as you can," Dana cut in. "The keys are on the dashboard."

After the truck had rumbled away down the hill, Rafe said, "Not sticking to your guns. That's no way to straighten him out."

"Normally I'd agree with you, but today's his birthday. And there's one person he hasn't heard from."

Rafe scowled. "You mean Zoe?"

"Make that two, then. But I meant his mother. Margot."

Rafe blew out a breath. "That's nice. Damned if people should have kids if they don't want them." He stood abruptly and held out his hand.

"Well, I want him." She let him lift her to her feet. "He was the sweetest kid when I first knew him, Rafe." Now only Zoe, and sometimes Petra, saw that side of him. But Sean needed an outlet for his best instincts—if they were to live on.

"If you don't mind my saying so..." Rafe's thumb fanned across the back of her hand. "Sometimes he really seems to..."

"To hate me?" She nodded unhappily. "He thinks it's all my fault, Rafe. I'm the one who persuaded Peter to give up teaching and move here. And I'm the one who wanted a romantic anniversary weekend and insisted Sean stay home, so that he wasn't there to help." She pulled her hand away and hugged herself. "Plus, I'm the witch who taught Peter how to cross-country ski—he'd never tried it before we moved to Colorado. And then, after the avalanche—" She shivered as if she still stood knee-deep in powdery snow. "I had to choose between staying and searching by myself, or going for help. I looked—I really did—I don't know for how long..." She'd been half hysterical, in shock. "But there was just *nothing*." Nothing but white, white, a pall of choking white, burying all hopes and dreams beneath it. "Sean thinks I made the wrong choice."

Rafe drew her in, wrapped his arms tight around her. She buried her face against his warmth, and stood shuddering. "In an avalanche, sweetheart—" his lips brushed across her hair "—there usually isn't a right choice."

She nodded blindly against him. "I keep telling myself that. Peter would say that. But Sean—"

"Sean thinks life should have been otherwise, and you're the only one he can find to blame."

"Something like that." She lifted her head at the sound of her pickup wheezing up the hill, then stepped out of Rafe's arms. This wasn't the day to add to her stepson's bad mood.

"Any mail?" she asked hopefully, as Sean slammed the truck's door.

"Nothing." Sean headed around the side of the house, back to work.

Usually there was something, if only bills. "You sure it's come yet?" she called after him.

"The mailbox flag was down. We got zip. *Nada.* Crap-all!"

Rafe grimaced. "Happy birthday." He started to turn away—swung back and drew his fingertips down her cheek. "Hey, thanks for lunch."

THE MEMORY of Rafe's arms around her was like a wall between Dana and the blues for the rest of the afternoon. Things would work out, she told herself. They were bound to. If this wasn't Sean's happiest birthday, well, there would be other and better ones.

She came downstairs from putting Petra down and stepped out onto the front porch. The first-floor clapboards were primed a smooth, flat white. "Hey, this looks wonderful!" She went down the steps to check the porch roof. Sean was busily painting, with only a third of the second floor left to cover. "You guys are heroes!" She glanced around. "Rafe left?"

"Yeah," Sean said, his eyes on his brush. "Said he had to do something in town, but he might stop by later."

"Later," meaning the party? Had he taken pity on Sean, possibly changed his mind about Zoe? Dana didn't dare ask. "Terrific." She bustled into the house. Whatever Rafe's plans, she had supper and a party to put together.

From: RedColumbine@Westbest.com
To: SanDiegan@Pipeline.net
Happy birthday to you, Happy birthday to you! HAPPY BIRTHDAY DEAREST SE-AN, haaaaaaappy birthday to you!!!!!!!!!! I wish I could be there at your party, Sean. (I tried, I really did try.) But I and the whatzit will be THINKING about you all day, sending the most excellent vibes. And whatever you wish tonight, WISH BIG! I've gotta feeling it's gonna come true. So eat some cake for us, too. HUGS AND KISSES, Zoe+(?)

From: SanDiegan@Pipeline.net
To: RedColumbine@Westbest.com
Zoe, I don't know if your dad is stopping by Suntop before he comes back here tonight. But if he does, MAKE HIM BRING YOU. Or hide in the back of his truck? I'm so lonesome I could die. Your Sad Diegan. P.S. Thanks for my birthday card, but I want to TALK to you.

DANA HAD MEANT to give Sean his gift before the party, but she hadn't found the moment. Though he'd prowled in and out of the kitchen all afternoon once he finished painting, he'd been so glumly absorbed in his computer that she'd decided to wait. Perhaps a slice of cake would bump him into a receptive mood, if not a festive one.

At least the guests were in a mood to celebrate. Those who had stayed on the ranch for the day were boasting about their new roping and riding skills, thanks to Willy. The ones who'd gone into Durango had come back with glowing accounts of the steam train excursion up to the old mining town of Silverton. "Panoramas to die for!" proclaimed Suzie Shurman, one of their New York City dudes. "I bought the most beautiful postcards—oh!" She clapped a hand to her mouth. "Your mail!"

Everyone looked up politely.

"The postman was just putting it in the box when we reached the highway this morning. So we picked it up to save you a trip. It's still in the car." She turned to her husband. "Eric, would you run get it?"

Dana glanced at Sean's face and looked away. *Margot, if you haven't sent him at least a card, I will never forgive you.*

By the time she had cleared the salad plates, Eric was back. He presented a pile, mostly of bills, with a flourish and a panted "Sorry about that."

"Not a problem at all," she murmured absently, thumbing through them. *Come on, Margot. Come on—ah! Bless you!* "One for you," she noted casually, handing a large square envelope to Sean. The oversize, ornately self-conscious script on the return address was definitely his mother's.

He sat, turning it over and over in his hands.

"Love letter?" Suzie suggested slyly.

Sean growled something wordless and ripped it open.

"Oooh, a birthday card!" Suzie crowed, seeing the blazing birthday cake on its cover. "Is it your birthday, Sean?"

"It is," Dana said, covering for him. She'd meant to announce that anyway, to prepare them for dessert. Sean was sitting utterly motionless, except for his eyes. He'd opened them to their utmost width, as if trying to read in a dark room. Then he blinked, too deliberately, widened them again and closed the card. Folded it once, twice and jammed it into a pants pocket. *He's trying not to cry,* she realized. *Oh, Sean, I wish you'd waited to read that.* She stood. "Well, I trust everyone likes lasagna?" One of Sean's favorite foods.

During the meal she fielded most of the friendly questions aimed at Sean, until the guests gave up and the conversation turned to other topics. Her stepson ate mechanically, his eyes lifting from his plate only to focus on the window that overlooked the driveway, then dropping back to his food.

"More garlic bread?" Dana waved the basket under his nose.

"Um—uh, no. Thanks." Sean put down his fork. "Do you think he's coming back?"

"Who?" Then she realized. *He's waiting for Rafe.* Hoping for Zoe. She reached out for his cheek, then stopped herself. Too often he'd made it plain that he didn't like her to touch him. "I don't know, Sean. He didn't promise, did he?" Because if Rafe had, then sooner or later he'd be here. She'd learned that much about the man.

He brought a sigh up from his toes. "Guess not."

But as Dana rose to clear the main course, Sean jerked upright. "It's him!" A faint rumble of a big pickup truck climbing the hill sounded beyond the walls. He started to rise, but Dana shook her head. "If it is Rafe, he's probably just dropping off more house paint." *Don't get your hopes up, Sean.* He was building too much on so little.

Hands filled with her tray, she pushed through the swinging door—to find Rafe coming in the back one. The sleeves of his work shirt were rolled to his elbows; his hands and forearms, smudged with grease. "Sorry to be dropping by so late.'' He strode over to her sink and reached for the soap. ''I was down in Durango. Would have been here an hour ago, but I made the mistake of stopping to help an old gal with her car—flat tire. Then it turned out her spare was flat, so I had to—'' He shrugged. ''Anyway, here I am.''

With no Zoe in sight. Clearly, he hadn't even stopped by Suntop if he'd been down in Durango. She buried her disappointment. ''Well, you're just in time for cake and ice cream and coffee.''

''Was hoping I'd be.''

Carrying in the coffeepot, with Rafe following with the ice cream and bowls, Dana tried to prepare Sean with a rueful grimace and a little shake of her head. He didn't get the message. His eager eyes shot past her to take in Rafe, then swung beyond him—to a door that stayed closed. ''I'm afraid not,'' she murmured, drawing up an extra chair beside her own.

''Oh.'' Sean slumped back in his seat, his lips clamped and quivering.

He desperately needed a hug. If she'd offered one, he would have exploded. Dana stood, irresolute. *Will he feel worse if I bring in the cake, or neglected if I don't?* And meantime her guests expected a dessert and assumed it would come with candles. *Play it through to the bitter end,* she decided, and went back with a heavy heart to fetch it.

At first she thought they'd all carry it off. At the sight of the blazing birthday cake, the guests and Rafe broke into a hearty, off-key rendition of ''Happy Birthday,'' and somehow Sean mustered a shaky smile, then enough wind to blow out the candles. But while the slices were served out, he stared blankly down at his own portion, not eating.

Would his gift cheer him up or only sink him further in gloom? But Dana desperately wanted him to know she cared. Even though, in spite of all her efforts, everything had gone wrong, she cared. She drew the gift-wrapped parcel from its hiding place in the sideboard and set it before him. "Happy birthday, Sean!" she whispered under cover of the guests' cheerful chatter.

His mouth twisted, then stilled. "Thanks." He touched the bright paper, but made no move to open it.

Okay. At least she'd made the gesture. Perhaps opening it later was a better idea.

But her presentation had cued Rafe. His arm stretched past her, bearing a small, oblong package, also gift wrapped. "Happy birthday, Sean."

This one cut through Sean's daze. Mouth ajar, he stared at Rafe for a moment, then ripped into the gift.

Thinks it's from Zoe, Dana realized, her heart sinking, just as he drew the small object from its wrapping. A tool of some sort, like a big, multipurpose pocketknife, only larger. The gift one man would choose for another.

"It's got about everything you'll need," Rafe said beside her. "Wire cutters, a screwdriver. I carry one myself."

"Just what I'd want—if I wanted to be a dumb-ass cowboy!" Sean shoved back his chair and stood. "Thanks, but no, thanks!" He spun away, knocking his chair over, and slammed out through the kitchen door.

"Oops!" murmured one of the guests, breaking the pin-drop silence.

"Yeah, puberty," agreed another with a nervous chuckle. "If you could just lock 'em in a safety deposit box for five years or so, take 'em out when they reach twenty-one..."

The conversation turned determinedly general, everyone filling in the awkwardness in a rush, careful not to look at Dana or Rafe.

Dana put a hand over his fingers and squeezed. His face was red, but utterly expressionless. "I'm sorry, Rafe. Come out to the kitchen with me?" Sean would be long gone by now. Out to the tree house he and Peter had built, she supposed.

"I'm so sorry," she said as soon as the door had swung shut behind them. "You didn't deserve that." After a hard day's physical labor—labor that was a gift to Sean as well as her—Rafe had driven seventy miles round trip to buy a birthday present, one he'd chosen with obvious care. "He's had a rotten day."

"What the hell got into him?" Rafe moved past her to toss his gift on the kitchen table. He set her own, the unopened lens, carefully beside it.

While she washed the dishes, she tried to explain—the arrival of his mother's card, with its unknown, apparently disappointing message...his hope that he'd see Zoe...

"I gave him no reason to think that," Rafe objected.

"I know you didn't. Hoping against hope, I guess you'd call it. He's very lonely, Rafe, and somehow your daughter cut through that."

"Yeah, and look what it cost her."

"I know. I'm sorry." She was too heartsick to argue who'd done what to whom, who would pay for it most dearly.

Rafe reached past her to turn off the taps. "Speaking of which, I better be getting on home to her. Walk me to my truck?"

"Of course." She followed him out and across the deck. Crisp black upon gray, their shadows danced at their feet across the boards. She turned to look up at a silver-dollar moon riding high in a velvety sky. "Oh, wow!"

She felt his warmth at her back, then his arms came around her, snugging around her waist. "Beautiful," he agreed, his voice husky in her ear.

His jaw was bristly with a day's growth of beard; it rasped against her temple, and she shivered. Letting out a long, slow sigh, she allowed herself to relax and lean back against him—safe at last. And happy. Happiness blossoming like a moonflower in the dark. *Oh, Rafe...* Could anything that felt this natural and right be wrong? Reaching up, she cupped his rough cheek with her palm and whispered, "Rafe, I'm so sorry about tonight." He'd intended nothing but kindness.

"I'm not." His arms flexed, molding her tighter against him as he lipped her ear. "Not now I'm not." His heart was thundering against her shoulder blade. Shuddering, she arched her neck, and he kissed the corner of her mouth. Molten heat cascaded down her body, raising her nipples, roiling her stomach. Her hips rocked instinctively—he groaned and dipped his head to kiss the side of her throat. She drew in her breath in a stuttering gasp, sipping moonlight, then Rafe was turning her in his arms, clasping her waist, lifting her up on tiptoe.

"Yeah, *right!*" a bitter voice sneered from the near distance.

Gently, Rafe lowered her feet to the deck. "Sean," he said wryly, turning his head toward the yard.

Not good, not good, tonight of all nights! Dana tried to step back from Rafe's embrace, but his arms hardened around her, holding her there. He rested his chin on top of her head, as she turned to look at Sean. *Mine,* the gesture said simply.

"You are so *dumb,* Dana!" growled Sean, advancing up the steps from the yard. His hands were jammed deep in his pockets. "You think he really likes you?"

"That's enough, Sean!" Rafe snapped.

"He's doing this for *Zoe!* They made a deal—a bargain! She said she'd let him adopt our baby, but only if he fell in love and married you! So that's what he's pretending to do. But all he wants is what he wanted all along. A mommy for Zoe's baby!"

"Shut up, Sean!" Rafe brought his hands to Dana's

arms, pushed her away, but she grabbed his shirt with both hands.

"*No,* Rafe. Don't you dare touch him!"

"Sucker!" Sean jeered, ducking past them to the kitchen door. "Why would he want *you?*" The door banged, and he was gone.

Dana's fingers had gone numb. All of her was numbing, as if she'd wandered into a deep freeze and lost her way. Her hands slipped away from his shirt, and she shook her head.

"Dana..." Rafe said uncertainly.

"Is it true, Rafe? Was that the bargain?"

His hesitation was as good as a confession.

"I see." She spun out of his loosened grasp. "You'd better go."

"Dana, look, let me explain."

"I've heard enough, thanks!" For Zoe—he'd done it all for Zoe. "Please get out of here and *please* don't come back." She walked into the house—and locked the door behind her.

CHAPTER SIXTEEN

From: RedColumbine@Westbest.com
To: SanDiegan@Pipeline.net
Sean, whatever you said last night—how could you?
Dad landed on me like a ton of bricks. He thinks
we've been talking on the phone, which means he
thinks I'm a liar, which means now I AM a liar, since
I let him keep on thinking that. Thanks so much!
What happened over there, anyway? He came home
mad, woke up madder and drove off maddest to pick
up Mr. Tankersly at the airport. Did he fight with
Dana, too, or just you? Tell me quick. I've gotta
know. Zoe+((??))

From: SanDiegan@Pipeline.net
To: RedColumbine@Westbest.com
Zoe, I blew it. I saw them kissing and something
snapped and I shot my big mouth off. What happened
was this…

From: RedColumbine@Westbest.com
To: SanDiegan@Pipeline.net
Wow, gee, I don't know what to say. I'm sitting here
crying, with stupid Woofle trying to lick off my tears.
I guess you wrecked about everything, didn't you?
And I thought I had it all worked out. He was going
to fall for your stepmom, they were going to adopt
our baby and give it a wonderful home, you and my

dad were going to be best friends and I'd go off to Harvard only a year late and I could visit my baby whenever I wanted. Stupid me. I guess that's what I get for messing around with a dorky sophomore. I'd like to shake you within an inch of your dorkish life! So what now, smart guy? Got any better ideas? Z+((!!))

WAITING AT THE local airfield for old man Tankersly's chartered plane to arrive, Rafe stood in a phone booth near the window, punching numbers. "Dana," he said quickly when she answered. "It's me. We have to talk."

"No, Rafe, that's not necessary." Petra was crying in the background, water running. Her voice wasn't so much cold as flat. Tired. Drained of all warmth and emotion.

I did this to you. "Dana, please, if you'd just give me five—"

"*No!* There's nothing that needs explaining. Look, I can't talk now, so—"

"Then could I speak to Sean, please?" Any connection was better than none.

"Um." She made a humming sound of uncertainty, then called, "Sean?"

Intertwined with the baby's sobs, he heard the rise and fall of question and answer. So the kid was there in the kitchen. Rafe marshaled his words and his anger. *If not for you, Sean.* None of this would have happened. He'd never have hurt Dana.

Nor met her. He squinted as, beyond the end of the runway, a dark, insect-like shape banked into the final approach. Tankersly.

"Uh?" Sean grunted warily in his ear.

"What are you going to do about the house?"

"Huh?"

Rafe ground his teeth. "We've got the front of your

house prepped and primed, and now I can't help you. So what are you going to do, Sean?''

''Um...''

If he could have reached through the phone and grabbed the kid by the throat... ''What would your father do? Didn't he teach you to finish what you start?''

''Yeah,'' the kid said, so low Rafe barely could hear it, then added in a rush, ''Mr. Montana, I'm really sorry.'' *Click!*

Rafe held the disconnected phone out from his ear and glared at it. Then cradled it viciously. ''Not half as sorry as I am, kid.'' Yanking his hat down over his nose, he stalked out to greet the old man.

NO MORE SADNESS in her life. It was a promise she'd made to herself, made to Peter, months ago, and Dana meant to stick to it. She had to be cheerful for Petra, for Sean. It was the most important gift you could give a child, the habit of happiness. The expectation of goodness to come.

So now, just when she'd made it to a resting place on the climb back to contentment, to be thrown back to the base of the cliff! And to have humiliation heaped on top of sorrow. *How could I have been such a conceited fool, thinking Rafe was starting to...well, to like me a little? Me as a person. Me as a woman.* When all the time it was Zoe.

Worse than the stinging humiliation was the loneliness. He'd not been gone for a day, and already Dana missed him. Missed the happy, fizzing expectation that any minute he'd be knocking at her door, walking into her kitchen, bringing strength and laughter and vitality. That was over now. It had never really existed outside of her mind. He wasn't there for her; all along he was there for Zoe.

So now...how to get back to happy?

At this point, she should be qualified as an expert. *Take*

it one day at a time, she reminded herself wearily. Pretend she was recovering from a nasty case of the flu, not a wound of the spirit. Simply pace herself, focus outward on the most essential chores, not inward. Don't think, don't feel, just do. Start with the laundry, she decided, once the dishes were done.

UP IN SEAN'S BEDROOM, turning out the pockets of his jeans, stacking interesting pebbles, a bit of elk horn, a case of fish lures, a stub of pencil onto his desk, she came at last to a piece of card stock, folded to a tight, tiny square. Unfolding it, she saw the blazing birthday cake and drew in her breath. Margot's card. *Not yours to read,* she chided herself, unfolding it a final time. And if it hadn't hurt Sean, she would have left it alone.

Dearest darling Sean,
I know it's been months and months and months since I've written, but I've been having such a marvelous, mystical time at the spa, I'm sure you'll forgive me. I've been studying aromatherapy, and I've come to realize that—at last!—this is my Path in Life. (Much more on this later.) And I've found a lovely, lovable, clever man to share my life, who adores me and whom I'm sure you'll adore when you meet him. Which brings me to your question: I would *love* you to come and live with me. We belong together. But my house is so tiny, only two bedrooms, and I need one of those for my office and my extra clothes. So could you be patient just a little while longer, sweetheart? As soon as Ivan finds a job, and I start my aromatherapy boutique, we'll be moving to a larger house. Something charming on the beach, I think. Then I'll definitely send for you, my dearest darling, I promise. Meantime, have a happy, HAPPY, spiritual Birthday.
                                                        Your loving Margot

"You silly, stupid, heartless woman." Dana sank onto the bed. So this was why Sean had lashed out at her and Rafe last night. *The person who should love you most in the world clearly can't be bothered with you. Rafe deprived you of Zoe's affection. And then you stumbled on us, looking as if we'd found our way to love.*

For one foolish minute, that was just how she'd felt—loved. Safe. Her heart on its nest at last. *Dream on.* As Sean said, how dumb could you be? Squaring her shoulders, she sighed and refolded the note, then tucked it back into the pocket where she'd found it. Returned all his other treasures to the rest of his jeans. Dumped everything back on the closet floor where she'd found it. She'd do her laundry today, then ask Sean to bring his own dirty clothes down to the washer tomorrow.

BEN TANKERSLY WAS—how would Zoe put it?—a high-maintenance owner. One who required all Rafe's time and most of his attention.

Hadn't always been that way. In the years when Rafe first rode for Tankersly's brand, the old man had been tough—tough as an old cedar stump—but easygoing. You knew your job and you did it without him looking over your shoulder, or you were gone yesterday. And that was the basis on which he'd eventually made Rafe his manager—*Handle it, man, then tell me later what you did and why.*

But since Tankersly had moved down to San Antonio to live with his eldest daughter ten years ago, he'd changed. Misses Suntop, Rafe told himself, and had only six weeks each year to renew the love affair. Only six weeks to ride every inch of his land, see every cow, boss every hand, check every barn and outbuilding and hen coop. That was how the days went, and he wanted Rafe at his side, like a general wanted his aide-de-camp at his elbow while inspecting the troops.

That was how they spent their days. Evenings, after supper, were for sitting around in Rafe's den, drinking the finest whiskey money could buy—Tankersly flew in a case every year—and munching fried pork rinds (a treat the old man's daughter forbade him at home), while they went over bloodlines and breeding charts, last year's feed costs, next year's forecasts for the price of beef, maintenance schedules and water rights. And once they'd exhausted all that, he wanted to talk about the good old days.

Or sometimes the new.

LATE IN THE THIRD WEEK of his visit, the boss had invited himself to supper. Though he had his own professional "chef" up at the big house, who looked like an aging showgirl—Rena appeared mysteriously each summer, then vanished till the next—Tankersly often preferred Montana cooking. After Zoe had fed them a meal of macaroni and cheese, then retreated upstairs with astrophysicist Stephen Hawkins's *A Brief History of Time* under one arm, they'd settled with drinks before the fire, dogs snoring and twitching at their feet.

Tankersly took a considering sip of his whiskey, held the glass up to the firelight and gruffly observed, "Somebody knocked up your princess." *Princess* was a synonym for *daughter,* in the old man's vocabulary. He'd first come to fatherhood in his fifties and sired three of his own.

Rafe grunted and took a swallow. *Let's not talk about this.*

"One of your hands?" At eighty-two, Tankersly felt, if not entitled to pry, then entirely safe in doing so.

Rafe snorted. "I don't hire crazies or suicides."

"Damn sure hope not. Played doctor with a school chum, then? She always said she'd grow up to be a doctor."

"Hmm." Rafe rose, went over to the fire and added a log.

"If you want a name for the brat, I guess I could propose, but I don't reckon she'd have me."

Rafe turned and met the old man's eyes, as dark and inscrutable as a turtle's. He had wondered for the first years of his employment if he was perhaps Tankersly's bastard, the way he'd been singled out and brought along. Not that he hadn't worked his butt off to earn the bossman's respect. But selling Rafe a portion of his land, making him a partner in Suntop—that had been a gesture of either princely generosity...or implicit acknowledgment. Rafe had never dared ask him which, and it was too late to ask his own mother.

With the passing years, though, his first conviction had gradually faded. The old man dropped hints and allusions Rafe took to mean that they were not, after all, father and son. Now here was another. Tankersly would never offer to marry his own granddaughter, even in jest.

He smiled, resigning himself to the conversation. "Zoe would probably have you, but I expect Rena would snatch her bald."

The old man chuckled. "Or if not her, Luisa." Apparently confirming a rumor Rafe had heard years ago from Tankersly's middle daughter. That the old man had spent every Christmas for the past dozen years in Guadalajara. That there might be an entire shadow family down in Mexico.

"So what are you going to do with her?" Tankersly insisted, breaking Rafe's reverie.

What he'd been wondering every spare minute for the past three weeks, when he wasn't worrying about Dana. He should be making other arrangements for Zoe's baby if his original plan was a bust. As it seemed to be. He'd tried calling Dana every morning for the first week, till finally she'd stopped answering. Either Sean picked up the phone or—more embarrassing—Willy, who'd quickly discovered that breakfast at the Ribbon R beat bunkhouse chow any day.

I need to go see her.

But she'd told him to stay away, and she'd meant it. *She trusted me, and now she doesn't.* He felt that loss as if he'd been plundered, as if he'd reached into his pockets and found the bottoms sliced out, the floor fallen away below his feet. Something to stand on—to build on—that now was lost.

Trust was such a fragile emotion. And if by some unforgivable clumsiness or cruelty you forfeited trust, how did you ever regain it? Was it even possible?

If the answer was no, then that was Rafe's loss—his and Zoe's. But what kept him staring up at his ceiling night after night were Dana's losses.

Once upon a time, Dana had trusted love—then seen it snatched away in a torrent of snow. Then he had come, offering the shape of love, if not its substance—until Sean had declared it a fake, a pretense. And in all honesty, Rafe hadn't been able to deny the boy's accusation.

What had that second loss done to her sense of trust? Because something told him that unlike a man, a woman *needed* to trust love—was sorely crippled if she couldn't. *God, Dana, if I hurt you...*

And maybe what he'd done had cut even deeper than that. *Thanks to Sean—and thanks to me—maybe now she doesn't even trust her own desirability. She thinks I was courting her for Zoe's sake, not because she's a lovable, sexy woman.*

And worse, if she thought that, she thought right. Well, half right. When he'd started the courtship, it *had* all been for Zoe.

The memory of the pain dawning in Dana's big eyes as Sean's words hit home was enough to make Rafe leap up from his chair and walk out of the house. He couldn't sit still, when he remembered.

And he couldn't forget.

But neither could he figure how to make amends.

"If you're worried about folks talking," Tankersly said, "you could send her to me and Risa till she drops. She'd like San Antone."

"Thank you, Ben. I'll keep that in mind." People talking had never worried him much. But then, this was Zoe they'd be talking about. *Got to do something and soon.*

The only solution he wanted was Dana Kershaw.

WILLY LOOKED UP from the bowl of batter he was stirring, as Dana walked into the kitchen. "Mornin', Missus. Mornin', chipmunk." His name for Petra.

"Good morning, Willy." She'd given up asking him to call her Dana the first week of their acquaintanceship. Willy was of the old school, which meant she was Missus or Ma'am, or Missus Kershaw when he was feeling formal or disapproving. "Pancakes today?" If she was late coming down, he started without her. She set Petra in her high chair and poured herself half a cup of coffee.

"Yup. Banana-blueberry." He scowled down at the batter, stirring, stirring, then finally said, "You got a phone call, while back."

"I thought I heard it ring. Dudes?"

"Maybe." He stirred some more. "Sorta hard to say. The…um, woman was…tipsy, I reckon."

She'd known Willy nearly six weeks now, and this was the first time Dana had heard him refer to a member of her sex as anything but "girl" or "lady," "ma'am" or "missus."

"Really. A wrong number maybe?"

"She asked for Sean."

Oh. *Margot.* Dana walked over to the refrigerator, opened it and stood staring blindly into its depths. Margot, drinking at eight in the morning. So much for her latest spa cure. She sighed and reached for the bacon. "Did she get him?" *Tell me no.*

"Nope. He whipped through here on his way down to the river 'bout a minute before she called. Snagged a sandwich and said he'd be back 'bout noon."

Thank God for that, anyway. "Did she say what she wanted?" Margot had called a few times, raging and weeping and drunk after Peter's death, but not once in the past year.

"Well, she wanted Sean in the worst kinda way, and once I convinced her she wasn't gonna get him, no matter how ugly she cussed, she started askin' for you."

Margot never called except when she wanted something, even if it was only to vent. "Did you tell her I'd be down soon?" She reached for her cup and gulped; she'd need caffeine to face Margot.

"Told her I thought you mighta gone to town. Couldn't say when you'd be back." He grimaced. "Got a right earful for that."

"I'm sorry. That's Sean's real mother, and she isn't always…reasonable." Dana blew out a breath. "Would you do me a favor, Willy?"

"Yup."

"Don't tell him she called." *Whimsical* was Margot's middle name. By the time she'd sobered up, quite likely she'd have forgotten what she wanted, or whom she'd phoned.

No such luck. The phone rang again that night after supper, and when Dana picked up, the caller said briskly, "Dana? This is Margot Kershaw. I want my son."

THE LAWYER Dr. Hancock recommended to Dana, Durango's expert on custody cases, gave her a free fifteen-minute consultation the following afternoon—then suggested she post a thousand-dollar retainer so he could contact Margot's lawyer immediately. "Nothing like a preemptive strike in cases like this," he assured her.

"I...I'll have to think about this, then get back to you in a day or two," she said slowly, rising to go. *If I had a thousand dollars to spare, I wouldn't be two months behind on my mortgage.* "But thank you. You've been very kind."

She'd meant to shop for groceries after the appointment, combining errands as she always did, but when next Dana noticed her surroundings, she was speeding down the highway for home. Just as well, she told herself, and turned inward again. A thousand dollars...and that was just to get him started. *Willy could help me sell the horses.* They were easily worth twice that. But what was a dude ranch that couldn't offer trail rides?

Bankrupt. Not that they weren't headed that way anyhow. But sell the horses and they'd slip even faster down the long, slippery slope to insolvency.

There was no way the bank would give her a second mortgage when she couldn't quite keep up with the first. Neither could she borrow from her parents—schoolteachers who'd retired last year and were now touring Europe on bicycles. They'd earned their financial freedom through thrift and hard work, and they'd saved a modest margin for their pleasures. That was precisely what she'd be usurping if she asked for a loan—face it, a gift, since she didn't see how she'd ever repay it—the extras that made their retirement years worth living. And Sean might be Dana's son, but he wasn't their grandson.

So what do I do, Peter?

No answer, but a bird flew across the road, drawing her eyes. Toward a wide valley opening out to the north, a road winding up it. She was coming to the fork in the road, the right hand of which led past the Suntop Ranch. Sean had pointed it out to her more than a month ago. She had never passed this fork since without a pang. *Rafe.* He hadn't tried to contact her in weeks. Doubtless he'd made some other arrangement for Zoe by now.

But if he hadn't?

She pulled over to the shoulder of the highway and sat, hands clasping the top of the steering wheel, forehead resting on wrists, for a very long time. Then she straightened, started the pickup and chose the north fork.

CHAPTER SEVENTEEN

"COMPANY COMING," observed Anse Kirby from his higher vantage point, where he straddled the ridgepole of the barn. He and Rafe had commenced reroofing a week ago, partly because the building needed it, mostly because it was one of the few places old man Tankersly would leave them in peace. Now that they'd stripped the shingles off, they were committed to the job, even though the boss had flown off to Texas yesterday.

Halfway up the long ladder, with a load of shingles balanced on his shoulder, Rafe didn't look around. "Miguel?" The farrier should have arrived this morning, though his promises weren't worth a sack of cold cow chips. He did the best shoeing in a hundred miles, and knew it. He'd come when he pleased.

"In a cute little skirt and legs a man could die for? I sure hope not. Must be one of Zoe's friends."

Zoe was still grounded, forbidden company. Rafe heaved his bundle over the ends of the ladder and onto the footing board, then looked around. Dana Kershaw stood beside her old pickup, peering up, one hand shading her eyes against the sun. His heart lurched in his chest as if he'd missed a rung on the ladder.

"Dana," he croaked, and started down. He caught a glimpse of Anse's wide, white conspirator's grin, then the overhang of the eaves cut off his view. Dana. He'd been wondering what to do for six weeks now, telling himself he'd have to do something as soon as the old man headed south.

She made any and all alternatives he'd considered seem shabby. He'd never seen her in town-going clothes before—a white tailored shirt, a short, slim navy skirt and—his pulse ticked up a few beats—high heels. "Welcome to Suntop," he said huskily, halting before her. He'd forgotten how small she was. He had an impulse to walk right into her—simply duck his head till their mouths connected, while he shaped his hands to her trim bottom and pulled her up close and personal. *Reckon I missed you.*

"Rafe," she said simply. But there was no light to match his in her eyes.

Down boy. He eyed his palms ruefully—too tarry to even shake her hand—and said, "Let me clean up, okay?" He strode over to the horse trough, wishing she'd called ahead so he could have showered and changed.

Whatever had brought her to him, Rafe wanted to hear it in private, not out here in the barnyard with Anse leering down from the roof, or up at the house, where he'd have to share her with Zoe. "I was about to go check the year-lings. Come with me?"

Her skirt was a little tight for scrambling into a high truck. He opened her door, then, when she hesitated, sizing up the climb, he simply caught her by the waist and lifted her up. His heart was knocking as he walked around the truck to his side. *I want her.* One touch had reminded him how much.

They talked of this and that as he drove. She seemed a bit daunted to learn that the whole width of the valley and on up into the mountains to the west and north was Suntop. He felt a certain satisfaction that she was seeing his land at last. He might own only fifteen percent, but that was a small slice of a very large pie. *I didn't come to you as a beggar.*

The truck rumbled across a cowcatcher at an open gate and into the horse pasture. He honked the horn, three short beeps, then stopped the truck—as the yearlings burst over the hilltop, ears pricked, tails streaming, coats gleaming. Bucking and romping and full of themselves. Eager for oats.

"Oh!" Dana sat upright. "Oh, they're beautiful!"

"Sit here, while I feed them." He walked around back, scooped up a bucket of oats from the bin and strolled into the roistering herd. "Easy, there." A dip of a silken muzzle into the bucket. A pair of ears pinned back as another shook his head and shoved for position. "You, behave." He smacked a third on the shoulder. "Wait your turn, bub." They teased and jostled one another like kids in a cafeteria chow line, but they knew better than to shove the teacher. Five minutes, and everyone had had his treat.

Holding the bucket for a filly with a muzzle dainty enough to drink from a teacup, he looked up and saw that Dana was leaning halfway out her window, eyes aglow. *We feel the same about so many things.* He couldn't see why it wouldn't work. Hooking a hand under the filly's throat, he walked her back to the truck; she was as docile as if he held her halter. Zoe had trained her well last year. "Zoe named this one Arriba. Half Arabian, and it shows, doesn't it?"

Dana nodded, rubbing the little mare's dished face, the mobile tip of her velvety muzzle. "She's beautiful." Tears gathered in her gray-green eyes, and she blinked them away.

Something wrong here. Or maybe just too many emotions jostling for position at once, like the colts? He let the filly go back to her mates and waited for it.

"How *is* Zoe?" she asked, her eyes following the herd.

"Okay. Moody as all get-out," he added truthfully, "but

I reckon that's natural.'' Worried, as he was. Something had to be decided, and soon. "Not happy to be getting fat.''

Dana nodded. "That is hard. Especially if you don't...'' She shut her mouth abruptly.

"Don't...?'' he prompted, clenching his hands at his sides to keep them to himself. All his responses to her seemed to begin and end with touching.

"Don't have anyone telling you how beautiful you look pregnant, even when it isn't the truth.'' Her voice quivered with swallowed tears.

It was odd to feel liking for a dead man, especially when you were also glad he was out of the way. *Because I want your woman, Peter Kershaw, even if you were a good man.* A man who wouldn't begrudge him now, Rafe suspected. He'd want her cherished.

"I try,'' he assured her. "We all try. Too hard, maybe. She says the next cowboy who pats her stomach is going to have his hat jammed down around his jug ears. Getting a bit crabby, as I said.''

"Have you found someone to...adopt her baby yet?'' Her eyes flicked up to his and shot away, off toward the mountains.

His pulse quickened. She had a reason for asking, a reason for all this welling emotion. *Tell me, Dana.* "No,'' he said indifferently. "Tankersly left yesterday, and we've been pretty busy around here, what with haying and all, so... No. Not yet. But soon.''

"I see...'' Her hands crept toward each other along the windowsill; they connected, comforted each other. "Do you—'' She heaved a long sigh. "You remember that...proposition you made, that day we went riding up on the mountain?''

Goose bumps rose across his arms and shoulders; his blood surged. He kept his mouth even, his face relaxed, holding his excitement inside the way you did in poker when you drew a third ace. "The proposal I made?" he corrected her casually.

"That...yes." She let out another wavering sigh. "I was...thinking about it."

Were you, by God! Have you been lying in bed nights, thinking what I've been thinking? If so, she was hiding it well today, but women were hard to read. And it would be hard for her—he was glad it would be hard—to go from one man to another. She was that kind of woman. Nothing would come easily or be taken lightly. "What's changed?" he asked bluntly. *Tell me you missed me.*

"I...got a phone call. From Sean's mother, Margot."

Not what he'd hoped, but still. Rafe crossed his forearms on the edge of the window—her fingers retreated to safety—and said simply, "Tell me."

Half an hour later, he figured he had it all. Sean's mother had fallen off the wagon for the umpteenth time and lost her new boyfriend in the tumble. Apparently she'd looked to this Ivan to finance some new venture having to do with smells and how they made you feel—aromatherapy? Some sort of shop to sell these scents. So now Margot wanted Sean to comfort her, and since apparently Dana had had the foresight to tie up his college money in an untouchable trust, Margot wanted Dana to buy out Sean's quarter share of the ranch. Sean could be her partner in an aromatherapy boutique in San Diego, instead of a landowner in Colorado.

So he supposed Dana hadn't exaggerated—this wasn't just a tiff between a first and second wife. This Margot was clearly a nutcase, if she thought exchanging prime grazing land for a smelly little shop in the city was any kind of a reasonable trade.

On the other hand, bad as that would be for Sean, it wouldn't be bad for Rafe. He could buy a chunk of the Ribbon R free and clear, whether Dana wanted him as partner or not.

And if all he wanted was land...Rafe drummed his fingers on the steering wheel—he'd long since climbed into the truck to hear her out. *But I don't.* He wanted it all—Dana Kershaw in his bed, a mother for Zoe's baby, a prime chunk of land. *So throw for it all.*

But what he didn't much want was Sean, like a burr under the saddle blanket. Mooning over Zoe, making Dana unhappy no matter how she tried to win him over. "You know," he said, when he was sure she'd finished, "she is the kid's mother. And the lawyer has told you square that he can't guarantee you'll keep custody, no matter how hard you fight. Would it maybe be simplest to...hand him over?" Rafe didn't like himself as he said it. The kid was a sulky little son of a gun, but he had guts. He'd done his best to stand by Zoe.

Dana shook her head emphatically. "No. And if you'd heard her, Rafe... She doesn't want Sean, doesn't even ask about him—it's all *me, me, me.* What *she* needs, how lonely *she* is now that her boyfriend's gone, how Sean will be a help and a comfort to *her.* You see what I mean? She doesn't want her son so that she can love and protect him. Doesn't want him so that she can make sure he'll grow up true to himself and strong, then she'll launch him out into the world like some beautiful bird she's set free..."

He smiled to himself at the image. *We do think alike.*

"She wants a caretaker, a parent, a—a teddy bear to squash in her arms when it's dark outside, because she's lonely and afraid. And she wants his money, because she's too much of a child to try to earn her own. She wants to *use* Sean, not mother him! Peter would never forgive me, if I let her have him. It's just—no! Whatever it takes, I'm keeping him."

It could take more than she had. *On the other hand, you throw me into the mix.* There'd be money enough for the best lawyer. And the custody battle would be here, where

Rafe had…influence. You didn't run the biggest ranch in the county without making powerful friends. Tankersly had taught him that. Judge Baxter had hunting rights in perpetuity at Suntop. He'd brought down a bull with a twelve-point rack on Rafe's land last fall; its head hung in his courthouse chambers to remind him who his friends were. And they'd be going into court a married couple, able to prove that they could provide Sean with a stable home, against a single mom who couldn't, wouldn't, stay sober, who'd discarded all her custody rights once before when it suited her.

We could give it a damn good try. Even if Margot won in the end, delaying her for a year or two would give Sean a better chance to grow into himself. He'd be formed by seventeen if Rafe had anything to do with him—tough enough and old enough and strong enough by then to survive a bad year. But let a weepy, neurotic drunk get a stranglehold on the kid at fifteen, before he'd found his own way… "Okay," he agreed. "What else do you want?" *Let's get the terms on the table.*

"I…" She didn't like it that blunt. Dana hugged her elbows and stared through the windshield, a delicate pink creeping up her throat. "You…talked about giving me a divorce in five years if I wanted it. I think that would be best for both of us."

Why do you think that? And why should that gall him like a stone in his boot, when it was what he'd wanted, too?

"You wouldn't be giving up too much of your freedom that way, and who knows, by then maybe I'd want to re-marry."

You'd be married. To me. Though he'd offered this, hadn't he?

"I'd keep the child, of course. That's got to be understood. But you and Zoe would be welcome to visit whenever you liked.''

I wanted a good mother—I've found one, he thought wryly. ''Zoe wanted two parents for her baby, not one,'' he reminded her.

''I know, and the baby *would* have two parents for the first five years—the formative years. I...suppose if you insisted, we could split custody after that. If you had to do it that way...'' Her voice trailed away unhappily. ''I know that's not precisely what Zoe specified, but I have to consider myself—and you, too.''

Thanks, but I can take care of myself. ''There are also the grazing rights I wanted,'' he added, since they were bargaining. ''A lifetime lock, as long as you own the Ribbon R. A split of profits on the cattle I'll run there. I'll have to work that out, show you some figures.''

''Whatever. I think you're right. If the Ribbon R were a working ranch, I could attract twice the dude business that I'm doing now.''

He nodded. *So do we have a deal?* He felt both excited and oddly...flat, as if there should have been something more to this. *It's a good deal,* he told himself. *Works for everybody.*

''Just one more thing,'' Dana said in a tiny voice. ''Since...'' She clasped her hands in her lap till the knuckles showed white. ''Since we're agreed that we're doing this for Zoe, not for any other reason...there's no reason for this to be anything but a...marriage in name only.''

No *way.* He was giving up his freedom to chase other women—without getting Dana? What kind of a fool's bargain was that? Right up there with trading prime land for an aroma-thingummy shop! ''That doesn't sound very—'' *Fun.* ''Practical,'' he finished, voice carefully neutral. *Not a chance I could keep my hands off you.*

She bristled, reminding him of Zoe's little half-Siamese

cat puffed up to dog-chasing size. "Perfectly practical. You
wanted a business arrangement, Rafe, and that's what I'm
offering. You help me save Sean—I help you save Zoe."

*What about the fact that every time we come within kiss-
ing range, sparks fly? How long do you think we'll keep a
lid on that?* He was half tempted to reach for her and prove
his point, then and there. But she was stretched so tight at
the moment, if he stroked her once, she might fly to pieces,
blowing their bargain to kingdom come.

Still, he couldn't let it go. "Zoe's main requirement—
thanks to you, by the way—is a two-parent, loving family.
She's very clear on that. I don't see how I could sell her
on a make-believe marriage."

"You seemed to think you could before," Dana observed in a bitter, brittle little voice, looking off again toward the mountains.

Putting a finger to her chin, he brought her head around.
Her soft lips parted at his touch. "I meant to wed you and
bed you and make the best of the deal while we were together," he said fiercely. "I don't call that a sham."

Eyes flashing, she jerked her chin out of his grip. "Whatever you care to call it, I don't want it! I'm offering a
merger of interests—a business alliance, not a marriage
of...hearts."

Marriage. To Dana. Rings and lace and driving off with
tin cans clattering behind, hands clasped. *With my body, I
thee worship.* He didn't know about his heart, but his body
was ready and willing to worship hers. Too ready. He
shifted uncomfortably in his seat.

"Well?" she demanded. "Take it or leave it."

She was in no position to demand anything. But with a
five-month pregnant daughter, was he? *Begin in the way
you mean to continue,* his mother used to tell him. He
should never agree to something he couldn't hold to, didn't
mean to hold to.

Bottom line is, if I can't change her mind, can I live with the bargain?

If he had to, he could, but damned if he liked it.

So the key here was to change her mind. Or persuade her to *know* her own mind. He leaned close—and her eyes widened and darkened, her lips parted slightly. His heart leaped in glad response. He wasn't alone in this feeling, whatever she said. *So bargain for what you want.* "Marriage in name only, as long as it looks like the real thing to Zoe. That means same bedroom."

"Separate beds," she countered instantly.

It was a start. *Patience,* he reminded himself. You didn't saddle a filly the first time you showed her the halter. "You've got yourself a deal," he said huskily. "When?"

THERE WAS NO REASON to delay and plenty of reasons to clinch the deal *pronto*. Rafe hadn't much interest in the ceremony itself; he found himself looking beyond it— frankly, to the wedding night. And Dana seemed inclined to something cold and quick and businesslike—a justice of the peace, she suggested, afternoon appointment, so she could get back in time to cook for her dudes.

Zoe had grander plans. "You *have* to be married in church!" she cried, when Rafe told her about the J.P. The tears sprang to her eyes the way they did so often nowadays. "What will my baby think if you're not?"

How could someone who'd yet to even show his face run the show this way? Rafe remembered reading somewhere that you could see a hurricane was coming for days before it arrived by the ripples it sent ahead. "I doubt if he'll care one way or another." Somehow he'd convinced himself that his grandchild was a "he," though no one had a clue. Zoe had refused to be notified when she went for her ultrasound.

"She'll care immensely! She'll think you didn't love each other if you don't do it right."

What Rafe didn't want was *Zoe* thinking that. So far he'd avoided a quiz on just when and how he and Dana had fallen in love, how far they'd fallen and so on. Rafe hoped to keep on finessing the details. "Fine, if you think that's important, find us a church." Zoe attended sometimes with Mrs. Higgins or a town friend; Rafe, practically never. He had no need for a church while he had God's mountains to ride, or for a minister to tell him what any man could know if he opened his ears outdoors and used his eyes. But some people liked it formal on Sunday—and to each his own.

Zoe already had a church in mind, down in Trueheart. A girlfriend's father was minister, and a few phone calls determined he'd be delighted to perform the ceremony— Saturday after next happened to be free.

When Rafe presented Zoe's plan over the phone, Dana sounded taken aback, but after a long silence, she sighed and agreed. "If that's what Zoe wants, why not. It's all the same to me."

Rafe winced. She was going to take some thawing, but that would have to wait. "Good, I'll tell her." He gave his daughter a thumbs-up through the office door, then, as Zoe pantomimed her desire, said, "Um, I think she wants to talk with you."

"Mrs. Kershaw?" Zoe stroked her stomach nervously and looked up at her father. "I don't have a thing to wear, and I haven't a clue what I—" Her face shifted from worry to delight. "Really? I'd like that! Let me ask Daddy." She put a hand over the phone. "May I go shopping with Mrs. Kershaw in Durango?"

COMPARED WITH her last wedding, simple but heartfelt, this one might be a travesty, but Dana didn't have the heart to say so to Zoe. *I'm her proxy in this,* she realized, just

as Rafe stood for Sean. She could fight that all the way—
or she could give in and accept it with grace and good
humor. Somebody ought to enjoy the event anyway. So
Dana went with the flow.

Once she'd resolved not to spoil the day for Zoe, she
decided to make the most of it. Poor kid hadn't been off
the ranch all summer, aside from a few trips to the doctor.
Dana made an appointment for them both at the best salon
in town, prescribing a cut and a new style for Zoe—the
stylist took off six inches and layered the back, creating
bounce and fullness instead of straggling curls. Zoe walked
in a little girl—and walked out a sleek sophisticate.

For herself, she settled on a trim, along with some suggestions for the wedding day—how to make the most of
her own short and simple style with a circlet of silk flowers,
and subtle eye shadow to emphasize her eyes' natural color.

Once beautified, they went on to lunch at the fanciest
restaurant in town, per Rafe's recommendation, where
Dana ordered a Shirley Temple for Zoe and a glass of
champagne for herself. Somehow on the fumes of that single glass, they both managed to get giggly and girlish and
confidential. Rafe had reared himself a charming daughter—fierce and funny and passionately committed to a
dozen causes, from Save the Black Rhinos to Doctors Without Borders. She was brimful of plans and interests—everything from hybridizing wildflowers to Indian archae-
ology to piloting airplanes. *I can see why Rafe wanted her
free to fly.* Dana could also see why Sean had hitched his
wagon to Zoe's shooting star; the girl's enthusiasm was
catching.

But if lunch was a rousing success, choosing a dress for
the bride was not so easy. Zoe had set her sights on floor-
length white—lace, veils, all the trimmings. The fairy-tale
gown every young bride imagines.

"But I've been married before," Dana tried to point out. "It isn't appropriate the second time to—"

"This is the first time you've married my father," Zoe countered with a stubborn tilt of the chin. "And who cares about appropriate? You'd look gorgeous in white. Dad will be wearing black."

"How about this?" Dana suggested, holding up a simple amber silk, knee-length, dressy enough for cocktails.

Zoe wrinkled her freckled nose. "Too short, too...*uh-uh.*"

It was almost three-thirty, and Dana couldn't see how she could spare another day from her dudes for shopping. "Then what about this one?" A flowered print in pinks and burgundies—which earned itself another disdainful grimace. "Or this?" A pale-blue gown, too slinky for a wedding. She put it back on the rack before Zoe could veto it.

"What about a change of shop?" Zoe suggested.

This was the biggest department store in town, with far and away the best selection. But perhaps Zoe knew some boutique. It was really her wedding, after all. "Lead me to it."

Zoe led her to a hole-in-the-wall place on a street filled with used bookstores and consignment antique shops. A vintage-clothing boutique, where last year, Zoe confided, she'd found a fabulous black leather motorcycle jacket. Five minutes of rummaging the racks, and Zoe cried, *"Yes!"* She held her find up, and its pale satin reflected a rosy glow from her fire-engine curls.

Perhaps the dress had been white once and simply gone creamy-gold with age. It was simple, elegant, floor-length, a custom gown from the thirties, superbly cut on the bias so it hugged Dana's curves when she stood still and swirled when she walked. Zoe loved it, and, in truth, so did Dana. "We'll take it," they told the clerk.

"And so now that we've got that settled, what will my

bridesmaid wear?'' Dana demanded as she dove back into the racks. ''And *don't* tell me a motorcycle jacket.'' Somewhere along the way, the day had tipped from a rueful chore into delight.

CHAPTER EIGHTEEN

THE CHAPEL THAT ZOE had chosen for the wedding might have been drawn by an artistic eight-year-old. Perched at the top of a smooth green hill above the town of Trueheart, it was a tiny white clapboard box, with a graceful steeple pointing to the blue-blue late-August sky. There was a simple stained-glass window of Easter lilies to either side of the arched and varnished outer doors, presently thrown open to welcome all comers, and stone steps leading up to those doors.

Dana hardly could have accounted for how she had come to these steps, the shadowy threshold she must cross. The last two weeks had passed in such a blur. All that frantic activity, the endless, niggling decisions required for even the most modest of ceremonies—leading to this moment of doubt and stillness, with not a soul in sight but her and Sean.

No one to see if she decided to turn and go.

"Dana, we're *late*," Sean muttered, tugging at her elbow. "Come on!"

She gulped, nodded, counted the steps going up—*five, six, seven, eight*—then four paces across the darkened foyer to the inner doors and—

Here comes the bride, here comes the bride, insisted a wheezy little organ at the front of the chapel. A grinning cowboy usher held each door wide. And all eyes on both sides of the aisle turned toward the rear to see if it was truly so.

Couldn't be, Dana told herself, staring back at all those smiling, expectant faces. This *had* to be an incredibly vivid dream, complete with everyone she knew in Colorado. Willy, with his beard fanned out over a multihued patch-work vest. Most of her present dudes, in their vacation fin-est. Dr. Cassandra Hancock holding Petra, who was dressed in a blue frilly pinafore. Also Michele Minot, another friend from Trueheart. And a host of strangers—all Rafe's cow-boys and most of his neighbors—tanned faces and white grins under a hovering flock of cowboy hats. His house-keeper, Mrs. Higgins, and Zoe's best friends, Lisa Harding and Vickie Carter. Each and every one of them expecting her to walk down this aisle to where a tall man in a dark suit stood waiting at an altar ablaze with wildflowers.

"Dana, you gotta move," Sean begged at her side, tug-ging on her elbow. "Let's go!"

Sean, who'd dragged her into this dream, who now anx-iously stared at her with his father's brown eyes. *Peter, what am I doing here?*

Taking care of his son the only way she knew how. No dream, this; she'd made a bargain.

Come on! Zoe mouthed silently from the front of the church. Looking like a blushing bride herself in a pale-pink empire gown, vintage 1960s, she stood next to Rafe's best man and top hand, Anse Kirby.

Zoe looked frantic; Rafe looked...dangerous. He was wondering if she was going to chicken out on him now, at the last, most humiliating moment possible.

Petra had been staring at her, thunderstruck, rosebud mouth ajar, from the vantage of Cass Hancock's arms, and suddenly it must have hit her—who this vision in creamy satin must be. She pointed a chubby arm and yelled, *"Mama!"*

Dana burst into startled laughter, Rafe broke into a wide, rueful grin, the whole church joined in with relief, and, seizing the moment, the organist pumped the organ into the bridal march again. Suddenly movement was possible. Dana drifted down the aisle, homing in on her daughter, whose eyes widened to black-fringed astonished flowers as she neared. Coming even with her, Dana touched her petal-soft cheek and floated past. And now it was Rafe she steered by, his blue eyes like a beacon drawing her to port.

Blue eyes that swept her from head to toe and back again as she neared—this was the first he'd seen of her gown. And then she was standing by his side, amazed as always to find him a little taller, more vivid than her memory served. Or perhaps that was only the heels on his western dress boots.

He offered his forearm, and she curled her fingers around it—hard and warm and solid—the first time she'd ever taken his arm. *We've never even really kissed!* With second, third and fourth thoughts about the bargain they'd struck, she'd done her best to avoid him these two weeks, burying herself in the details of the wedding, thanks to Zoe's constant suggestions and proddings. But here he was at last, this stranger who was about to become her husband.

And do you, Dana Kershaw, take this man to have and to hold... The familiar words twined in and out of her mind, a golden thread sewing other ceremonies, other faces in her past, to the present dreamy moment. There came an expectant pause, and Rafe nudged her and muttered, "You do."

"I..." He placed his other hand on top of her fingers and stroked them once, and she sucked in a long shivery breath, and said, "I do." His fingers settled down over hers, warm, comforting...possessive.

"I do," Rafe said clearly, when his time came.

"Then you may now kiss the bride," prompted the beaming minister.

She stood frozen, staring up at the man. This was it, the

moment when past intersected the present and ricocheted off into an unknowable future. *This* was the defining moment, not the rings, or the words, but the kiss—a gesture of pure emotion to seal a strictly business arrangement. *Can't do it. Not for the first time. Not with everyone watching!* Rafe's hands slid across the buttery satin at her waist, clasping her firmly. He drew her in, but for a moment she couldn't move her feet—she bent like a willow at the waist, though her face lifted imploringly to his. She bit her bottom lip, and from only inches above her, he smiled, his eyes crinkling.

"It'll be all right," he whispered, and rubbed his nose along hers.

"Oh, will it?" she whispered back, aching to believe him.

For answer, his mouth settled softly over hers. "Yes." He spoke into her. "Oh, yes." His tongue touched hers for an instant—she shuddered and instinctively moved closer— and he lifted his head and smiled down at her. "It sure will be."

Dimly, beyond his words, she heard the congregation cheering, saw from the corner of her eye Zoe, all freckles and tears, and Sean, caught between a smile and a frown.

Then, to the triumphal strains of "The Wedding March," they paraded back down the aisle, man and wife, Rafe's arm around her waist. They came even with Petra, and she held out both arms and demanded, "Mama!" in a tone that brooked no denial.

"That's my name," Dana laughed as she lifted her out of Cass's hold. And that was how they walked out of the chapel—a threesome, with Zoe and Sean arm in arm at their heels. A *family,* Dana told herself, as confetti and glitter showered down upon them.

THE REST OF THE AFTERNOON whirled past in a happy blur—photographs on the steps of the chapel, cake and champagne at Michele's restaurant down in the town. Dana was introduced to a flood of congratulatory strangers and kissed by too many cowboys to count. She met Zoe's great-aunt Emilia, who'd come all the way from Phoenix; the local veterinarian; Sheriff Noonan; an Indian archaeologist who was excavating a site on Suntop land; one of the Tankersly daughters. Finally, late that afternoon Rafe put a hand to her back and said, "They won't leave till we do, so what do you think? Shall we go?"

I can't. Her heart rose into her throat.

Because if Zoe had shaped their wedding, Rafe had crafted its finale. He'd put his boot down when Dana had proposed going back to the Ribbon R for the first night. "You've been running around like maniacs, you and Zoe, all week. This is *your* night to relax. The dudes can do without you for once," he'd pointed out, insisting she find someone—Cassandra, as it turned out—to stay over and keep Petra.

Since her baby had been born, Dana had never slept farther from her than the next room. Though Petra was essentially weaned now, apparently her mother was not. The thought of a night apart made Dana feel so helplessly homesick, she wanted to cry. And layer that emotion on top of all her fears and her shyness… *I've married a man I don't know, not really.* They'd made a bargain, but what about tonight? Trapped with him in a strange hotel, far from all she knew and held dear?

At the expression on her face, he smiled and brushed a slow knuckle across the underside of her mouth. "Trust me?"

His touch went through her from lips to toes, and she trembled. For all that she didn't know about him, everything she *did* know was straight and true. And it was much

too late to turn back now. Wide-eyed and solemn, she nodded.

His eyes crinkled. "Then, Mrs. Montana, that's a good
start."

RAFE HAD RACKED his brains about how to do this—their
honeymoon night. Had it been his choice, if this had been
a normal marriage, he'd have proposed they ride up into
the mountains to one of the line cabins, his favorite one by
an alpine lake. They'd spend half a week up there, loving
and lying in bed till noon, then rising to cook simple meals
on a wood-burning stove, fly-fish or ride or walk a little,
then back to a bearskin by the fire. Flowery meadows to
roll in by day, stars by the millions to wish on at night,
and no one for miles and miles around. That was his idea
of a honeymoon.

Maybe next year, he consoled himself.

This year, he'd figured Dana needed something
less…threatening. All that time to fill, with nothing but
each other? Rough way to start a marriage in name only—
he almost snorted at the phrase. And she was doubly fraz-
zled, putting a wedding together in two short weeks and
leaving her baby overnight for the first time. *Patience,* he
reminded himself.

"You're sure you reserved a room with two beds?"
Dana dithered as they walked down the hotel corridor. This
was the third time she'd asked since they'd left their reception.

"It has two beds." Only one of which would need making in the morning, he sincerely hoped.

"Oh! Where's our luggage?" She'd hurried off to the
telephone to call the Ribbon R, while he checked them into
this hotel, the oldest and grandest in Durango.

"I sent it on ahead." With a hefty tip for the bellboy,
and the request that he be sure the champagne Rafe had

ordered was on ice, then make himself scarce. Because of one of the groom's prerogatives, Rafe had determined he wouldn't be cheated. And he didn't want an audience.

"This is it," he said, stopping before a numbered door on the top floor—a suite, but not *the* bridal suite, with all that heart-shaped foofaraw to spook her. Luxurious but understated, he'd specified. He fished the room key out of his coat pocket and handed it over, and she looked up at him, startled.

"Need both hands for—this." He scooped her up, smiling as she squeaked and threw an arm around his neck for fear of falling.

No fear of that; she didn't go a hundred and ten; he could have carried her to Paradise and back without breaking a sweat—at least, not that kind of a sweat. Her legs kicked over his arm; her lips were parted in startlement and dawning outrage. *"Rafe!"*

"Mrs. Montana, this might be a marriage in name only—" reminding her that he hadn't forgotten "—but all the same, it's a marriage." He hoisted her a little higher in his arms. Every muscle in his body was flexed, standing to attention, ready and eager to pounce. His heart was stretched out in a dead run, headed for the barn. "And since every last man in Trueheart got to kiss you today—what the heck—what's one more, and that one your husband?"

"Rafe..." she said on a note of warning, shaken with laughter.

"Open the door, Dana." He almost sang it.

She shook her head, her hair brushing his arm. "I...don't think so. Maybe we need to review our terms here."

"You promised to love and obey, Mrs. Montana."

"*Not* obey," she pointed out, trying not to smile. "They took that out years ago. And as far as—"

He didn't want to hear she didn't love him. He pretended to drop her, and she yelped in alarm. "The *door,* Dana,

before my arms break.'' An out-and-out lie, that, but it got
her attention. She clucked her concern and jammed the key
in the lock, then opened it.

He maneuvered her over the threshold, careful of those
slender legs, so long for her height, then nudged the door
shut behind them. Leaned back against it. ''Well...'' He
looked around approvingly. If it had to be a city hotel, this
one would do. And there was a fireplace, with a fire laid
ready for lighting.

''So now you can put me down,'' Dana prompted, tossing the key onto one of the two king-size beds.

''There's the matter of that kiss,'' he reminded her huskily, dipping his head.

Her eyes were huge; her lips, half curved into a smile.
She was scared nonetheless. ''Rafe, we had a bargain.''

''Sure did, surely do. But I don't recall one clause that
said no kissing.'' He touched her lips with his own, the
lightest of teasing contacts, then backed off a hairsbreadth,
hovering. She shivered in his arms and sucked in a shaky
breath. Made no further protest. *Good.* He closed that tiny
gap and brushed his mouth across hers, as light as a butterfly landing on a flower that trembled in the wind. Then
just as slowly back again, soft as silk, his heart thundering.
Oh, Dana, let me in.

She made a murmurous sound deep in her throat, and
the tip of her tongue crept into view—flicked nervously
along the tremulous gap, then vanished.

Taking that for the shyest of invitations, he closed his
lips over her bottom lip, plump and dark as a berry—he'd
been aching to do this for months. She moaned something
wordless, seemed to lengthen and soften in his hold, while
her arm tightened around his neck, drawing her up and him
down.

He slid his tongue into her—wet, warm...delicious.
Gently, gently, he reminded himself, even as he hardened

below. He was shaking with the effort not to plunge into
her, all his instincts crying that he should plunder and sack
and make her his own, and do it *now*.

Dana was shaking, too. She pulled away and stared up
at him. "Put me *down*, Rafe."

He set her on her feet immediately, but couldn't make
himself let her go. His hands smoothed up her arms, restlessly down again. Her eyes were pools of darkness to
drown a man. "Dana?"

She shook her head and backed away. "Remember why
we're doing this?"

Because I'll die if I don't have you this minute?

"For Zoe," she reminded him, when he didn't speak.
"And for Sean."

Still punishing him for the way he'd deceived her. He
got it. "You're a hard, hard woman, Dana Montana."

Slowly she relaxed into a smile. At least his forbearance
had earned him a little more trust. "You're just finding that
out?" She turned her back on him—at the sight of her trim
hips, he almost groaned aloud—and said, "Have I got time
for a bath before supper?"

"You've got all night, if you want it." And one hell of
a honeymoon night it was looking to be. "Save some cold
water for me."

HE PROWLED THE ROOM blindly for a while, ears tuned to
the thunder of water in the bathroom. With the taste of her
on his lips, it was impossible to control his imagination.
He saw himself stripping off his clothes and joining her in
the tub, picking up that bar of soap... *Down, boy.*

He halted before the fireplace, stared at it till it took
meaningful form, replacing the inner visions, then knelt and
lit the fire—saw them loving before it, Dana kneeling
astride him, all wet, sliding silk...rising and sinking in ex-
quisite slow motion. *Stop,* he told himself desperately. Yes,

he'd had his hopes for tonight, but he'd sworn to be a gentleman, come what may. Hadn't realized he'd catch fire this way. That it would be so damn hard. He glanced down at himself and grimaced.

Once he had the flames leaping, he realized it had been a while since the water stopped. She was soaking, he supposed, and his mind conjured up a mound of foamy bubbles with treasure below. Whatever she needed, *he* needed a drink.

A moment later he gripped the stems of two crystal flutes in one hand and knocked on the bathroom door. "May I come in?"

He heard a squeak of alarm and a startled splash. "No!"

She must have meant "Go." He opened the door. "Champagne, Mrs. Montana?" He got one heart-stopping glimpse of her sitting upright, yanking frantically at the shower curtain—then the show was over.

"Sorry," he said, unrepenting. "Champagne?" He pushed his hand and one glass through the curtain's gap, waggled it invitingly.

She sighed and took it. "Thanks."

"What shall we toast?"

"Privacy," she growled.

"Back rubs," he suggested. If she'd just let him get his hands on her, he could make her sing.

"Not a chance. Um…five years of fruitful friendship?"

Five years like this would kill him. He finished his champagne in a gulp. "So…are we ordering in or going out?"

Her sigh sounded as if it came up from the bottom of the ocean. "I'm so tired, Rafe."

"Fine. Come to bed."

"Just what I'm planning to do. Which one did you choose, the one near the windows or near the fire?"

Yours. He'd hoped—somehow convinced himself these past few days—that, womanlike, she meant to punish him

for hurting her pride, then graciously relent after he'd
wooed her humbly and long. Now he was beginning to
wonder.

When she came out of the bathroom, he had his answer.
Dana wore a terry-cloth bathrobe, supplied by the hotel,
over her own pajamas. He closed his dropped mouth with
a *snap*. A pair of flannel pajamas with a pattern of blue
teddy bears! She looked maybe twelve—adorably jailbait
twelve—but her message was crystal clear. No real bride
would have been caught dead in such an outfit. If she'd
meant to let him win her in the end, she would have come
gift-wrapped in silk and lace for their wedding night. This
package said, in mile-high letters, Keep Off!

She'd meant what she said—marriage in name only.

He sat down on his own bed with a frustrated *thump*.
"You want to order pizza or burgers?"

SLOWLY HE ROLLED OVER on top of her—a living roof of
hard, warm muscle, encircling arms—sheltering her from
the cold, empty world. He filled her, and she arched her
back and murmured with the shattering sweetness, rocked
her hips, begged for more of him, *more, please more...*

A faint *rattle* sounded nearby. Warm, red light probed
her closed eyelids. They were loving in the morning then,
though it had been night only a moment ago.

Her breathing steadied and slowed as the sensation of his
solid weight faded...spun away to nothingness, like dust
motes spinning in sunlight... Her loins throbbed, empty and
unfulfilled. *A dream,* she realized at last, eyes closed.

A dream—and the man hadn't been Peter; it had
been...Rafe. Rafe Montana. She shuddered—a long throbbing release of pent-up tension. Rafe...she'd married him
yesterday; *that* had been no dream. Dana lay motionless,
pictures of yesterday taking on color and form behind her
eyelids—the church, the ceremony, Zoe and Sean waving

and smiling as she and Rafe drove away. *No dream; it really happened!*

But loving him? She drew a forearm over her eyes, shutting out the light. *Did we?* She could remember he'd wanted to—he'd made that very clear—but after champagne and pizza, she'd gone to bed alone.

But sometime in the night? Had he joined her? Her hand drifted in slow exploration down her chest, down her stomach, skimming over her pubis—her flesh leaped alive at her touch, meltingly eager for more…

No loving in the night, she realized with a long sigh. Only incredibly vivid dreams of loving. But she had none of that satisfied heaviness; those delicious aches; no lingering, irrepressible smile. Her body walked a brittle razor edge of desire this morning. Tears of frustration hovered behind her lashes. *Oh, what have I done?*

And where was Rafe? She opened her eyes—to sunlight. Someone—Rafe—must have pulled back the curtains to welcome the day. Water was running in the bathroom. Her husband…readying himself for the morning. She grabbed a pillow and pulled it over her face.

So…*what do we do today?* Somehow she'd never envisioned the day-to-day reality of marriage to Rafe when she made her bargain. How would they fill the time today, on this honeymoon that wasn't a honeymoon? *Do we act like tourists, go see all the sights?* Sit down and have a marathon heart-to-heart? There was so much she didn't know about him.

She wanted neither tourism nor talk—wanted to go back to the Ribbon R, go back to Petra, go back and pretend this wedding had never happened.

Because there had been no unknowns or uneasiness in that life before Rafe, if no real happiness. Better that than this feeling of being utterly lost and alone…trapped between her old life and an unworkable new.

The phone rang at her bedside—she winced and hugged the pillow closer. Who? Then realized—Cass had the name of their hotel! *Petra!* She threw off her pillow as the phone rang again—and Rafe sat down on the edge of her bed, lifted the receiver.

"Yes?" he said curtly.

She half sat up. He was dressed in a pair of new jeans and nothing else, his chest hair curly and damp, his face half shaved, half covered with foam. He glanced down at her and his scowl faded. "That's all right, Cass. What's the problem?"

Dana grabbed for the receiver, but he shook his head and leaned away, so she scrambled up and knelt beside him, her temple almost touching his. "Uh-huh," he said, absently hooking an arm around her waist to steady her there.

At his touch, her body reacted instantly—throbbing within, ready and eager to resume what she'd only dreamed. She felt her nipples rise to brush painfully against the flannel of her pajama top. She could hear Cass's voice, but not the words. "Is Petra all right?" she whispered frantically.

"When?" he snapped. "Does it look like he slept in his bed?" He put a hand over the mouthpiece. "Sean took off sometime in the night—took your truck."

CHAPTER NINETEEN

"THAT KID is nothing but trouble!" Rafe swore, not for the first time, as they drove under the rising sun name board of the Suntop Ranch. He'd tried to phone ahead, but at eight-thirty in the morning he'd reached no one at his own house; and not one of his hired hands, who should all be outdoors.

"I don't know what got into him," Dana fretted. "He seemed all right yesterday—not exactly happy, but..." Not entirely sullen, either, she'd thought, when he'd solemnly kissed her and wished her happiness outside the church. "If he's run off to Margot..." The lawyer had told her that possession was nine-tenths of the law and that a sympathetic judge was the rest of it. If they had to battle for Sean's custody in San Diego...

"This is where he'll be," Rafe said grimly, "and when I get my hands on him—"

"You'll leave him to me."

"Don't count on it. This isn't a mistake. It's willful disobedience."

"If you'd arranged for someone to spend the night with Zoe..." In the flurry of all the preparations, she hadn't thought to ask, had never *dreamed* he would leave his daughter alone after the wedding.

"She's almost seventeen, Dana. Has gone camping out in the hills by herself, with her dog, since she was twelve. There were eight Suntop men within calling range if she needed help—any one of 'em would stand between her and a bear—and it wasn't my choice, anyway. Her great-aunt Emilia decided to visit friends while she was here in town, and Mrs. Higgins flew out to her daughter's in Oklahoma after the party.''

But even if Zoe had been safe by herself, still, last night of all nights she must have been lonely. Rafe and Dana had celebrated the wedding that should have been hers, and, as far as Zoe knew, had been joyfully consummating that union last night. Had she and Sean decided to celebrate their own reunion?

"I don't see my pickup," she said worriedly, as they roared up to the backyard of the ranch house.

"Anse would check on any strange trucks around the place, and Zoe knows it. If Sean's here, he'll have parked out of sight. In the barn, probably."

He stomped into the house with Dana scurrying at his heels, through a mudroom, on into a large kitchen—where Zoe stood scrambling eggs at the stove, a radiant smile on her face.

"Hi, you guys! You're just in time for breakfast."

Sean sat across the room, straddling a chair backward, his Nikon, propped on its backrest, aimed at Zoe. The camera shutter clicked, then he looked around at them with an odd mixture of a child's wary defiance and a young man's serenity. "'Morning, Dana. Rafe."

Dana pulled out a chair beside him and sat down with a sigh. He was growing up before her eyes, and there wasn't a darn thing she could do about it. She and Rafe had climbed aboard the roller coaster ride and there was no stepping off. But at least Sean was still *here* to be mothered, however badly she did it.

"Breakfast sounds wonderful." She didn't dare ruffle his hair as she wanted to, but when she touched his shoulder, he didn't withdraw.

AT LEAST THE PROBLEM of how to fill her first married day had been solved. After a breakfast during which Rafe sat glowering while Zoe prattled on and on about the wedding and Sean prudently kept his eyes on his plate, Dana had driven her stepson back to the Ribbon R. Rafe would see her sometime later, he'd said, not specifying when, or even which day. Had some issues to discuss with his daughter, he'd growled; he meant to settle this once and for all.

Short of leg irons, she couldn't imagine how. "That wasn't a very good idea," she murmured to Sean, as they drove away. "You know he wants you two to…" How to tactfully put it—break up? Drift apart? Go back to being children? But his willful Pandora had opened the box and now… "Whose idea was this, anyway?" Zoe's, she'd bet.

"Mine. I wanted photos, Dana." He touched the camera on the seat between them. "I want to remember it. How she looked, carrying *my* baby. She's so *beautiful*."

"Yes, but you broke the law driving over there without a license."

"I don't give a *damn* about the law!" His voice cracked, and he glared at her as if this were her fault along with everything else. "I *love* her. You gotta clue what that means?"

"Yes," she murmured, eyes on the road, "I do, Sean. Hurts like a bear sometimes, doesn't it." *No punishment,* she decided, because how did you punish love? But perhaps there was some way to disable the truck so he couldn't do this again. She'd have to ask Rafe.

Whenever I see him. The road blurred for a moment before her, as a feeling like homesickness swept through her. And it wasn't the Ribbon R or Petra she was missing.

BUT ONCE HOME, the Ribbon R swept her up in her usual round of chores and demands—a baby who had sorely missed her and now, in compensation, whined to be carried around all day as if she were six months old instead of ten. Dudes to be waited upon—one bunch checking out and their cabin to clean, then a new bunch checking in. A flurry of phone calls from hunters for the fall season. She turned them all down—no hunting on *her* land—and found herself grateful that now, with Rafe's financial backing, she could afford to follow her conscience on that. She baked for the week, cooked and served supper and ate it with her guests, her ears tuned all the while for sounds of a truck mounting the hill.

They hadn't discussed yet how they were going to blend households, though he'd insisted on their sharing a bedroom. But maybe he'd meant only when he felt like it—a few nights a week?

Or maybe less—maybe he'd changed his mind entirely— now that she'd made it clear that she meant to stick to the terms of their bargain.

By bedtime, she was exhausted and trembling, on the edge of tears. If Rafe hadn't come by now, he wasn't coming. She bathed, changed to her oldest, most comforting nightgown, soft as chamois, sheer as silk from years of washing, and climbed into bed. Lay there with the lights out, staring up at the ceiling, as lonely as she'd ever been in her life. Missing him—could it be? Not Peter this time, but Rafe...

Oh, Peter, what have I done?

No answer...as if somehow her bed was a boat and she'd gone adrift from the shore, floating out into dark, uncharted waters. Tears trickled; she brushed them angrily aside. Who'd made this bargain, anyway?

And what did you really want from it? So far he'd given her everything she'd asked for. Taken nothing she wasn't willing to give in return. So why these blues? Exhaustion, she told herself—and sleep answered.

THUMP.

Through her lashes she saw a golden light, a tall, stumbling shadow. Rafe, across the room. He'd switched on the lamp by the daybed and now stood awkwardly at its foot, hanging on to the brass bedstead. *Thump.* His second boot hit the floor.

"Rafe," she murmured, turning on her side to watch, smiling drowsily. *You came.*

"Sorry to wake you. First thing I'll need around here is a bootjack."

He meant to stay—to move in. His hat rested upside down on her bureau. Her eyes blurred and her smile widened. "We'll get you one tomorrow. What time is it, anyway?"

He padded over and sat on the edge of her bed. "Past twelve. I've been down in Durango at the airport, seeing Zoe and Emilia off to Phoenix."

"You sent her away!"

"For a few months. Seemed like the best I could do. She's bored, she's lonely, she ought to have a woman around. But I can't bring her to you, with Sean living here. And she won't promise me that she'll never see him again—we banged heads half the morning on that one. Don't know if they had sex last night or not—she says it's none of my business—but either way, that's not how to break off their attachment. So…" He shrugged. "Bye-bye, Zoe."

She covered his hand on the bedspread with her own. "I'm sorry, Rafe."

"Me, too. I'd rather airmail Sean to Patagonia. No return address."

No use arguing that one. She smoothed her hand up his wrist, marveling at the rugged size of it compared with her own, and its warmth, the crisp, curling hairs. "Did you eat?" At least she could feed him.

"I did. Down in Durango. Figured I'd get in too late to bother you."

"Would have been no bother at all." She found herself wanting to take care of his needs. Most of his needs. Those that didn't conflict with her own.

His other hand moved to cover hers. "I'm ready for bed is what I want. So where do I sleep?"

"Here." She sat up and took back her hand.

He leaned closer and cupped her cheek. "You mean—"

She shook her head. "I mean the daybed's too short for you. If I'd known you were coming…"

"This is crazy, Dana, you know it?"

I know it. She didn't speak. But how else could she protect herself?

Warm and gentle, his hand smoothed down her face. His palm shaped to the curve of her neck and drifted lower, raising goose bumps. "I like this better than your teddy bear pajamas." His eyes roamed over her body with shameless approval. "Seems a little more—" Reaching her collarbone, he drew the flat of his fingers slowly, deliberately across the soft, clinging fabric—the tops of her breasts beneath it—and smiled as her body responded, her nipples rising for his touch. "More welcoming?" His eyes rose to hers with the question.

"It isn't." She slid out the far side of the bed, and his hand fell away. "Shall I change the sheets for you?"

"Don't you dare." His fingers moved to the placket on his western shirt, and he watched her steadily as, snap by snap, he bared his chest.

She retreated to the daybed and sat, weak-kneed. He was too beautiful.

He hung his shirt over a bedpost, then reached for his belt buckle, his eyes locked on hers.

"No...um, pajamas?" She'd fallen asleep last night when her head hit the pillow. Hadn't seen.

"Not since I left my mama's house at seventeen, no, ma'am." The zipper of his Wranglers was coming down, its sound a sexy snarl in the late-night stillness.

"Oh." She flipped back the covers on the daybed and slid in, primly turned her back—and watched the enchanting shadows moving across her wall, then his silhouette growing taller...wider...heroic or monstrous or both, climbing up to the ceiling as he advanced. She sucked in a breath and held it. If he kissed her...

The light on the table behind her flicked off. "'Night, Mrs. Montana."

She blinked and let out her breath. "Sweet dreams, Rafe."

He snorted; the bed creaked; she smiled, closed her eyes...and slept.

From: RedColumbine@Westbest.com
To: SanDiegan@Pipeline.net
Hey, Sean-*de-mi-corazón,* here I am at last, writing you on a Phoenix Public Library computer. Aunt Emilia doesn't have one, and had a hissy-fit when I asked if I could set up a local server through her phone line for my laptop. *Invención del diablo,* computers, and that's that. So I won't be able to write you every night, as you've probably noticed, but hey, you know how I chop through the books. Should get here a couple of times a week, anyway.

I cried for two days straight after Dad put me on the plane, but that's no good for Ms. Ariel Bliss (I'm SOOOOO glad you like that)/Mr. Peter Rafael (tho that ain't gonna happen—she kicks like a girl). (Oh, yeah, she kicked for the first time on the plane, with glee, it felt like. Gonna be a pilot like her momma someday, you bet.) So I decided to stop whining and, as Dad always says, make the most of it.

Emilia and I've spent the past few days down in Tucson with my grandparents, the Cavazos. I told you they retired out here, didn't I? Lots of love and LOTS of clucking disapproval at my tummy—*¡qué lástima! ¡qué vergüenza, niña!*—my grandfather wanted me to go to Harvard even more than Daddy did, since that's where my mother meant to go.

They lightened up a bit when I explained that I still mean to go, that the dean sent me the book list for all the classes I would have been taking and that I'm doing the reading on my own. (Plan to ace 'em next year.) And Abuelo Paco suggested that since I have all this time on my hands, I should look into auditing some classes at the junior college near Emilia's house. Brilliant idea. I mean to do it.

Meantime, how'z it feel to be a mighty junior? Did you get Hendricks for English? What about your other courses? And how about Yearbook—you are going to sign up again, aren't you?

OOOPS, look at the time! Emilia will be picking me up any minute, and I haven't checked out a single book. So write me and tell me EVERYTHING— school; if you're happy or sad; how are Daddy and Dana? (Does my dad seem happy with her? That's REALLY important—a deal breaker, far as I'm concerned, if he isn't. He calls me a couple of times a week, but it's like trying to quiz a clam, and I can't tell what he's thinking if I can't see his face.) Meantime, *muchos abrazos* (we speak only Spanish at Emilia's and I'm trying to think in it), Zoe+((Ariel Bliss)).

From: SanDiegan@Pipeline.net
To: RedColumbine@Westbest.com

Red, don't you EVER do that to me again! I was giving you one more day to write, then I was going to hitch out there and find you, though I didn't remember your aunt's last name, and your dad gave me the Evil Eye the one time I tried to ask him. (What is her last name and what's your address, just in case?)

School's a bummer, just like I figured. Didn't get Hendricks, got Franz, and she's snooze-city. Or would be, except she alphabetized me into a seat in the middle of a nest of goat-ropers (sorry, cowboys), who have a thing about city slickers like you-know-who, so I'm too busy ducking spitballs and Copenhagen juice to doze off.

Did sign up for Yearbook and the newspaper. Shooting pix is the only worthwhile thing I do around here.

About your dad and Dana, dunno, it's sorta weird. He's sleeping here every night, though he leaves way early and comes back late, except the days he works over here. At first they laughed a lot, but lately it seems sort of tense. You know how you can feel the lightning coming on top of a mountain? Like that—prickly air whenever one of 'em walks into the room. And he can't take his eyes off her, the same way I watch you. But I don't hear anything late at night, which is a relief, but sort of strange. Maybe grown-ups do it quieter, or only in the day when I'm gone? YUK! Turns my stomach to think of it. Meanwhile, here comes Dana to start supper, so I guess I'll split before she asks me what I'm doing. (Why do women DO that?) I wish to God I'd been there with you, Zoe, when our baby first kicked. I miss you so much I can't even talk about it. Everybody here has somebody but me—Willy's got his horse, the Pet's got Dana, Dana and Rafe have each other—and here I sit, without you.

Please, please, PLEASE try to take some photos of yourself, even if it's just one of those throwaway cameras. I'm missing everything—MISSING YOU. Your, Sean

RAFE LEFT THE HOUSE most mornings at seven to make the forty-five minute drive to Suntop. What he'd do when the cold weather closed in Dana couldn't imagine, didn't want to think about. But meantime, she'd taken to rising with him, sending him off with a hot, hearty breakfast, though he insisted he could cook his own.

So he could; still, she liked doing for him. Liked sitting across from him at the table, sleepily sipping her first cup of coffee while he ate, asking him what his plans for the day might be. She didn't get to talk with him as much as she might have wanted to these days, four weeks into their marriage. The lazy pace of summer was picking up as September drew to a close. Each morning Rafe stood out on the deck with his face turned to the sky, studying clouds, sniffing the cool breeze. Soon it would be time for fall roundup—a crucial matter of timing, he'd explained. Bring the herds down from the mountains too early and they'd cut into the winter's grazing in the home pastures. Bring them down too late, and Rafe risked doing it in the snow, losing cattle or even men.

A hard life, ranching, she mused, as she washed their breakfast dishes, but Rafe seemed to love every part of it— working outdoors, making his own decisions, something new to do every day. He never slacked off and he never complained. When he wasn't working at Suntop, he was slowly whipping the Ribbon R into shape—meant to have it ready for cattle by the spring.

She jumped, as he loomed up behind her smelling freshly of toothpaste, his hat settled in place for the day. "I'm gone now.'' His hands landed on the edge of the sink, either side of her waist.

He was standing too close for her to turn around, so instead she turned her head. ''Back for supper tonight?'' Usually she fed him later.

''I'll try to make it, but don't hold it for me.'' Bending, he kissed her nape.

Heat starred out from the warmth of his mouth—searing down her spine to tighten her hips in a reflexive curl, rushing out her arms in a flurry of goose bumps. His lips brushed back and forth in a hot, leisurely caress, then roamed up to her earlobe—lava pooled in her stomach.

''Hey,'' she protested weakly. He didn't do this often.

For just a second, the zipper of his jeans nudged her hips—an electrifying touch—then he edged away. ''Hey yourself, lady.'' He caught one end of her apron bow and pulled it free, stood fingering the string as she turned and leaned against the sink, at bay, looking up at him.

Oh, Rafe, don't do this to me.

''When?'' he demanded huskily.

On the day I believe you're here for me—not because you need a substitute mommy for Zoe. And not because you need a woman, and I'm the closest available. Her pride wouldn't let her say that. Love had been no part of their bargain; it was too late to demand it now. She shrugged. ''When the cows come home?''

Amusement and frustration warred in his tanned face. He tugged her apron string once more, and when she didn't budge, he draped it over her shoulder. Laid one fingertip to the corner of her mouth. ''Might be sooner than you think, Mrs. Montana. Wind's blowing from the northwest.'' He traced the line of her lips to the far corner and turned away.

Whatever that means, she thought, retracing his caress

with one fingertip as he banged out the door without a goodbye. She turned back to the sink and the dishes.

It was getting harder to resist him every day. But to simply give in? She thought she knew where that would lead.

Straight to bed—and straight to heartache. Let Rafe love her, and she'd end up loving *him*. She had no doubt of that anymore. Something in him spoke to her, touched her. Had from the very start. Let him all the way in, and he'd own her, body and soul.

While he remained unowned, untouched. With the freedom he'd always said he wanted intact, unsurrendered.

Dana couldn't imagine a lonelier fate than to go down love's road alone. She brought the back of her hand to lips that still tingled. *Touches me, wants me, oh, yes. But doesn't love me.* She'd come to realize, these past few weeks, that when she'd made that bargain with him, she'd inadvertently set him a test.

And Rafe had failed it.

Because if he loved me, he'd never have agreed to divorce me in five years. Never have agreed to let me go. Love didn't come on a five-year plan.

Neither would he have agreed to the condition she'd set; that this be a marriage in name only. Dana grimaced. Not that he wasn't doing his best to wiggle out of *that* clause!

But without giving what she needed in return. He was kind to her always, passionate often.

He'd spoken not one word of love.

SOMETIMES RAFE THOUGHT he'd made a mistake opting for patience. If he'd kissed her past resistance that first night, seducing her in a hot rush as he damn sure could have done, then he'd have gotten them over this hump, to put it bluntly. By now they'd be easy with each other, smugly confident, lost in all the wonderful ways that man could please woman, or woman enslave man.

Instead, he'd held back on their wedding night—and a simple difference of opinion had grown as high as the San Juan Mountains, with no pass in sight.

Maybe I could have, maybe I should have, he told himself, scowling at the highway unreeling before him, leading him east to Suntop, *but I didn't.*

Because he'd been afraid. Worried that if he rushed Dana off her feet and into loving, but couldn't carry her past regret—where would they be then? What if she woke up the next morning feeling that she'd betrayed her love for her late husband?

Not a good start, he'd figured. Much better to take it slow and patient. He wanted Dana to come to him in her own sweet time, and to mean it when she came.

Sound arguments, he'd thought at the moment, but now Rafe wondered if he'd simply been a coward. And giving in to fear was always such a damn mistake. Not just that it belittled a man, but that tactically it never worked. Bold paid off, where timid went wanting.

And he was wanting bad nowadays. With no end in sight.

CHAPTER TWENTY

From: RedColumbine@Westbest.com
To: SanDiegan@Pipeline.net

Sean Diego, that last letter was a real whiner. I know you think you've got it bad, but THINK about it. Who got to stay home with his family in Colorado, and WHO GOT EXILED? Here I am without my dad or my dog or my horse, and anyway I'm getting too fat and ugly to ride. Oh, yeah, I got my first STRETCH MARK this week, and my face and hands and feet look all puffy—and you think YOU'VE got problems? I'm sorry, I'm sorry, I'm a raving grump tonight, a mopey wreck. For once it's raining, and Aunt Emilia won't let me drive across town to the bio class I'm auditing Tuesdays and Thursdays. The old girl's going deaf, so she turns up her game shows full blast, and I can't even THINK, much less study. I finally snuck out the back door and squelched off to the library (for which she'll give me grief later) and got your latest. I'm sorry to hear the creeps at school are bugging you. Somehow you've gotta learn to laugh it off and joke back, Seanster, or you've got to warp into some parallel dimension where the trogs can't touch you, like I used to do. Your prob is that they think you think you're better than they are. (And you are, but don't EVER let 'em know you think so.) And also, they're scared that the girls are going to realize what a hottie you are (which they will, if you ever talk to 'em), so they're trying to whittle you down to size before you steal all the women. So don't despair. I know it seems like FOREVER, but the year will be over before you know it—here it's October already!!!!—and then you'll be a senior. (And a father, sort of.) You know, nobody has discussed that—at least not with me, WHO SHOULD BE IN ON ALL THIS, BUT WHO SOMEHOW GOT DUMPED OUT IN LEFT FIELD—but what are Dana and Dad and you and me going to tell Ariel Bliss? You think it will confuse her if we tell her the truth? Would she be happier and more secure thinking she's my half sister and your stepsister? Whoops, my time on the computer is up; they only give you half an hour here. Gotta go. Anyway, cheer up, Seanster, and look at it this way—you could always be SEVEN MONTHS PREGNANT!

Biiiiiig Hug, Zoe+((A.B.))

P.S. Yeah, I'm taking pix, though trust me on this, pink-freckled watermelons are not particularly scenic.

FOR ONCE HE'D BE on time—early, even—for supper, Rafe thought, turning in at the sign for the Ribbon R. He'd spent the afternoon, he and half his hands, helping his neighbor Tripp McGraw round up a herd that had gone astray after a border fence came down. They'd scattered up and down the state highway, a danger to traffic and themselves. Rafe and his men had taken the south end of the problem, while McGraw and his brother took the north. Except for a nasty fall Rafe and Tobasco had suffered as they scrambled to head a panicked calf off the road while an eighteen-wheeler bore down on it, blasting its airhorn like an idiot, the drive had gone smooth as butter. After the last straggler had been eased back through the gap and onto McGraw land, Rafe had called it a day. His left side, where he'd landed on it, was stiffening up. Home early and a hot shower, he'd promised himself, and here he was.

Home... His eyes swept past the low concrete bridge over the river to the white ranch house tucked into a bench in the rising hills. Not his home, this place—he still didn't feel that—much preferred Suntop. But the woman *inside* that house... That was where this feeling centered, this feeling of homing. Where he was taking his battered body and the memory of that evil wind that had sucked at him and Tobasco as they crashed down on the edge of the pavement and the truck had thundered past not three feet beyond Rafe's outstretched arm. *A close one.* Too close to tell her about it in any detail, but all the same he needed her smile to wipe out that moment of blank acceptance when he'd thought he was a goner. When you were shook and bruised and a little bit rattled, you went home for comfort—wherever, whoever, home was.

Gunning his truck for the last rise, he saw Sean working up on the scaffolding he'd helped him set up last week. Second side of the house coming along nicely to match the front, which Sean had finished all by himself before the wedding. Had to hand it to the kid; he had grit and persistence when he put his mind to a goal. Rafe grimaced. *Which is why it's just as well I sent Zoe away, much as I miss her.* "Looking good," he called as he drove past. The kid's shoulders jerked, but he didn't turn—just kept on scraping paint.

Rafe frowned as he parked the truck and trailer. The boy was generally polite these days, though he had his moods. Walking around back to unload Tobasco, he changed his mind and strolled on till he stood looking up at Sean. "When do you figure to paint this side?" *Talk to me, boy.* He kept too much inside.

"Sunday," Sean muttered without turning.

"Want some help when you get to it?" Last thing Rafe

felt like doing, but he'd bullied Sean into this chore. "What?" he demanded when the kid growled something over his shoulder.

Sean turned around. "I said I can do it my*self!*"

Rafe let out a grunt of surprise. The kid had a shiner— a beaut. His left eye was half closed and purpling fast. "*Nice one.* Where'd you get it?"

The boy shrugged. "School, where else."

Rafe stifled a sigh. So much for his long, hot shower, then a cup of coffee at the kitchen table while he watched Dana cook. "Get down here, son."

WHEN SEAN DIDN'T COME to set the supper table, Dana went looking for him. He wasn't out on the scaffolding— wasn't anywhere in sight. But Rafe's pickup, with trailer attached, was parked out back, hours before his usual arrival. She had twenty minutes to spare till the roast chicken came out of the oven. So...up in the barn or down by the river? Since he'd brought a horse along, Dana guessed uphill. A few feet from the open door of the barn, she heard Rafe's voice.

"Good, good, carry it through. Punch *through* it, Sean, like you're nailing something a foot behind your target. *Yeah,* like that."

Bared to the waist, her two males shuffled around each other, fists upraised, heads weaving. Dana crossed her arms and stared. On the far side of the barn, Willy slouched on a bale of hay, a chaw of tobacco bulging one bushy cheek. "That a way, *yeah,* clean his clock for him, boy!"

Sean advanced on his opponent. Rafe retreated, flicking lazy jabs at his head. Blocking a punch with his forearms, he taunted, "That the best you can do?"

"*Uhh!*" Sean lunged for him.

Rafe slipped inside Sean's fist to tap the boy's chin. "Knockout," he announced, then grabbed his shoulders.

"Let me tell you *again*. If you open yourself up like that—"

Sean had swung around in his hold—the last of the daylight touched his face. One eye was swollen shut, turning eggplant purple.

"*Rafe!*" she exploded. "How could you?" He glanced around, surprised, then pleased, to see her. Not for long he wouldn't be. She dug an elbow into his ribs, shoving him back from her stepson. "How *dare* you?" She cupped Sean's jaw in her fingers, sucked in a breath.

Sean laughed delightedly. "He didn't do it, Dana. Honest!"

"Then who?" She swung around, her eyes lighting on her husband's magnificent torso, then rising till she met his amused blue eyes.

"Not me," Rafe assured her, hands held palm up in surrender. "We've just been sparring."

Her eyes focused on his left shoulder, and the thundercloud bruise that stretched from elbow to biceps. "You call this sparring? You lunatics!" She put fingers to it, and he winced.

"And Sean didn't do that. Fell today is all that is."

"It's cut, too—abraded," she said accusingly, cradling his arm with both hands as she studied it.

"Nothing to speak of. Just a concrete burn."

"Utterly certifiable, the both of you." She hooked her fingers over the front of his belt and tugged him toward the door. "Let's get this cleaned up—*now*. And you, Sean, are due for an ice pack. Sorry, Willy, the show's over, but stay for supper?"

LATE THAT NIGHT, after Rafe had soaked in the tub, then padded into their bedroom in his old flannel bathrobe, Dana checked his arm again. "You've definitely had a tetanus booster in the past five years?" He was seated on the bed, near the lamp, and she'd peeled his robe off his shoulder. He smelled deliciously of soap and warm man.

"Mmm," he agreed in a sleepy growl.

She moved the light closer, making sure she was seeing only scabs, not embedded gravel. "What happened?"

"Fell."

She smiled in spite of herself. An easterner would have given her a ten-minute report, a Californian a half-hour saga, including every emotion he'd felt throughout the experience, climaxing with a life-altering epiphany—but a Colorado cowboy? "Fell *how?*" She ran a fingertip up an unabraded patch of skin, taut over swelling muscle, and he shifted restlessly.

Word by word, she dragged the story out of him, till she knew enough to guarantee herself a good nightmare—the truck thundering past within inches of the flailing horse and trapped rider. Also, "If Tobasco fell on his left side, then—" she reached for the hem of his bathrobe "—what about this leg?" Lifting it above his knee, she cried, "Oh, Rafe!"

"Just bruised," he protested, putting a restraining hand over hers. "I was wearing chaps."

"Let me look at it." She pulled the hem out of his hold and rucked it up nearly to his lap—then realized that the contours beneath had changed radically—substantially. She bit her lip to stop a laugh, but it shook her voice, anyway. "Show me."

"Be glad to." His voice had gone all husky. "But it might be more than you can handle."

Do not giggle, she warned herself. "Oh-h-h, I doubt it. When I was in the Peace Corps, I took several courses in first aid."

"That's just what this needs—first aid…last aid…all the aid in between you can possibly give it."

If only I dared. She cocked her head, then said with quick relief, "Petra's crying. I'll have to go see." She ran a hand lightly up his thigh, glanced up questioningly as he groaned, then realized and smiled. "It does look okay." The leather chaps had protected him from the concrete, though not a thousand pounds or more of struggling horse. "As long as you're sure it's not broken…"

"Got the full use of it, as I could show you."

I bet you could. Still, the thought of the oncoming truck, how close she'd come to never seeing him again—a wave of raw emotion swept through her. *This arrangement may be an emotional disaster, but I like you sitting on my bed, Rafe Montana. Thank God you came back to me!* She pressed her lips to his thigh, then rose hastily and stepped back. His hand that had been reaching for her hair was left hovering midair.

She returned from soothing Petra—with a glass of water, two aspirin and a renewed resolve. Giving in to Rafe would be a joy now—and certain heartbreak later on. And she'd promised herself no more heartache in her life. Her growing attraction didn't change that one essential fact of her existence.

So she gave him his painkillers and backed off from the bed. She'd stayed away long enough that he'd lost his man-on-the-prowl look, gotten sleepy. Also naked, she noted, seeing the bathrobe hung on his bedpost. "I think you should stay in bed for a day or two," she said, while he swallowed his pills.

"Keep me company?" Smiling, she shook her head, but he didn't smile back as he set his glass aside. "Then, no. I've got a ranch to run. Roundup starts this Saturday if the weather holds."

She moved across to the daybed and sat. "Wish I could go with you." To ride high into the mountains with Rafe… The late-autumn flowers, the crystalline air, the elk bugling their mating calls… Maybe she could ride above all her worries and fears up there, simply be a woman with her man.

He let out a long breath. "Maybe next year."

Will we have a next year? By then, surely, he would have lost interest if she still wouldn't share his bed. He'd have found some other, less cowardly, woman by then, someone willing to risk her heart and damn the consequences. While she... *I'll be here, keeping my half of the bargain.* "By next year I'll have my hands full with Zoe's baby."

He grunted—though whether it was agreement or dissent she couldn't tell—and eased himself down under the covers. She switched on her own lamp, then rose to switch off his. If he was too stubborn to take a day to recover, then he needed his sleep.

He turned carefully onto his side to watch her. "While we're talking about it, I've been thinking...I mean to take Sean along."

"On roundup? But he wouldn't be back on Monday for school, would he?"

"Nope. But school's where he got that shiner."

She ran a hand up through her hair, tousling it distractedly. "I know, I know. I don't know how to help him, Rafe. He's not making friends."

"Doesn't know how. Kids are devils always—and at this age? I imagine they're riding him pretty rough. But he takes it too much to heart. He's got to learn to take his knocks and come up laughing, then hassle 'em back."

"That's what you were teaching him out there in the barn? Advanced social skills?"

"That's part of it, yeah. A week out on the mountain with my hands, and he'll learn more. More than he would in a year of schooling. He's got to learn to get along with men, Dana. Somehow he's missed out on that."

He'd had Peter, until nineteen months ago. But Peter had

been a schoolteacher, a man who moved easily through a kinder, gentler world than this. "Maybe for your world, he does. But it's just as likely that he'll go back to the coast when he's grown. Work in computers, or some such. He needs to learn to get along with *people*."

Rafe yawned and stretched mightily under the covers, trapping her eyes, drawing them down the long, rugged length of him, then shook his head against his pillow. "If he's lucky, he'll live among men and come home to women. A woman."

"That's how you see the world, men and women apart?" Married to Rafe, sometimes she felt like a captive dropped into a savage Indian tribe.

"No, ma'am," he murmured. "By no means. But men— real men—can't live in a woman's world and be happy. Though we sure like to visit." Their eyes held, speaking when there were no words left to say, till she broke first and turned away. After a moment, he switched off the light.

RAFE WAS PREOCCUPIED and busy over the next few days, preparing for roundup. Dana hardly saw him, but his words lingered on in her mind. *We sure like to visit.* So there he was, condemned by his own words. That was what he wanted to be in her world—a visitor.

Fine for him. But this time she wanted someone who'd stay. Who wouldn't allow himself to be called away, not on any account. Not by death. Nor by that mindless male urge for unencumbered freedom that had broken so many hearts—most of them female. Dana didn't need it—didn't need Rafe, if that's what he was. But, oh, she could miss him.

RAFE HAD ALWAYS rated himself pretty high in the patience department—he bowed to no man when it came to breaking

horses and breaking them kindly—but now he was beginning to worry. Maybe Dana would outlast him.

Usually the easiest of men, he was starting to notice his
own temper. It was fraying around the edges, tightening his
muscles when he moved, putting an edge to his voice when
he spoke. Hard to say if that was really temper—he had no
one to blame but himself for this fix, so how could he
justify anger?—or sheer, untapped testosterone looking for
release.

Whichever, he didn't feel like a gentle man, much less
a gentleman, nowadays. So till he'd mastered this mood,
he did his best to avoid Dana. No more smiles or sexy
teasing in the bedroom. No more kisses stolen in the
kitchen on his way out the door to work. Because he
couldn't guarantee anymore that once started, he could stop
if she asked him to. Couldn't guarantee that if he *could*
stop, he could without words he'd later regret.

A few days apart would do them both a world of good,
he told himself. He always did his best thinking up in the
mountains.

From: SanDiegan@Pipeline.net
To: RedColumbine@Westbest.com
Hey, Red, guess what? Your old man is taking me on
roundup! We leave in the morning from Suntop. I'm
sleeping over here tonight, since I had to go to school
today, but he's spending the night over at your
place—last-minute prep, I guess. Then Dana's driving
me over at dawn. So Yippie-yi-etc and it's me and
the little dogies. I'm REALLY stoked. Beats school
any ol' day. And how, by the way, is your dogie?
Taken any pix this week? I've got the one of your
bellybutton that you asked Lisa to pass on to me in
my wallet. I kiss it nightly—in case you feel any tick-
ling, that's me, not A.B./P.R. So gotta run. Still

haven't packed my saddlebags yet, and Dana's fussing about if I have enough clean Jockey shorts (wimmin). But please, please remember this. I LLLLLLLLLLLLL-OOOOOOOOOO VVVVVVVVV EEEEEEE You, Zoe Montana! Your Colorado Cowman, Sean.

THEY WERE RUNNING LATE on this day of all days—very late.

Racing to get ready, his arms piled with clean clothes from the dryer, Sean had stumbled over Petra—she'd taken a nasty tumble, bumping her head and bruising her feelings. She was fine now, but the fall plus the change in their usual routine had left her tearful and grumpy, demanding to be held, throwing tantrums, then furiously determined not to be bundled into her coat and shoes when they were ready to go.

Then, on top of Petra's toddler tactics, Dana's old pickup chose this frosty morning not to start—perhaps the battery needed replacing? Sean had coasted it down the hill, trying to pop the clutch, and had succeeded for a minute—then it wheezed and died again. Luckily the mountain bikers in Cottonwood Cabin had already been up and about. They'd jumped her battery from their sports ute, and that had done the trick.

So here they were at last, an hour late, wheeling under the Suntop name board. "What if he left?" Sean dithered, his nose nearly touching the windshield.

"He wouldn't do that." Dana wasn't as certain as she sounded. Rafe had been awfully brief these past few days—worrying about something, the drive perhaps. And he didn't suffer fools when it came to his ranch work. He'd told Sean to be here at dawn, and they'd blown it. *Please, please Rafe.* She hadn't seen Sean so happy or excited in months.

The truck roared around the last curve, over a creek lined with aspens, then the manager's house and the barns rose up before them. The yard was filled with neighbors' trucks hitched to trailers, saddled horses, men mounting up. And the still center to all this swirl of activity, Rafe, sitting his blood bay, Tobasco.

His eyes nailed them as she parked the truck and slid out. No smile of greeting, though she hadn't seen him for more than a day. Leaving Sean to gather his gear, Dana hurried across the yard, as he swung down and tied his horse.

"You're late," he noted, as she halted awkwardly before him, fighting her urge to not stop until she hit his chest.

"My fault," she said immediately, "I'm so sorry." *But please don't blame Sean.* Don't let him start out on this adventure scolded. In the privacy of her kitchen, she would have touched his arm and explained the events of the morning. But not out here with half a dozen hands standing around, watching the boss with his new wife.

His face colder than she'd ever seen it, Rafe shrugged and looked away, to where Anse Kirby was helping Sean tie on his saddlebags and his blanket roll. Some silent message was passing among the gathered men. Spurred boots stepped up into stirrups—they were cowboying up, as Willy would put it. Dana spotted her wrangler, as she thought of him, seated on the top rail of the corral, chewing furiously to hide his wistfulness at being left behind.

Anse had mounted. Sean swung up on Concha—good, Rafe had assigned him a gentle but lively mare. Rafe turned and tightened Tobasco's cinch, then untethered the gelding's reins and swung back to face her. "Well…"

She was missing him already, more than she could say, especially here, among strangers. "Take care of Sean for me," she begged in a low voice, laying a hand on Rafe's arm. She felt his muscles flex at her touch.

He nodded curtly, a muscle fluttering in his cheek below his eye.

"And of yourself." She was beginning to realize that it would look strange if she just waved goodbye. Would feel awkward and hypocritical if she offered to kiss him, something she'd never done before. It was Rafe who'd initiated all kissing till now.

"Don't worry about me."

But she would; so many things could happen up there. "Of course not. Well…"

His face hardened and he jerked away, gathered the reins. *Don't go like this, mad at me.* Dana slid a hand to the top of his shoulder. "See you in a few days, then?" She stood on tiptoe to kiss his cheek.

His free arm snagged around her, hauling her close. She gasped in surprise at the suddenness of his response, its latent violence. His mouth came down on hers with none of the gentleness he'd always shown her before—demanding this time, arrogantly taking what she'd offered, then more. His tongue swept roughly into her; his heart was slamming against her breast; he'd bent her so far backward that she had to grab for his shoulders. Dimly, she heard someone whistle, then he brought her upright, dropped her flatfooted and swung away.

Shock gave way to hurt, then furious humiliation. *Why was he so mad at her?* Just for being late or— But this was no time to demand an explanation. His boot was already swinging over Tobasco's rump. He found his stirrup, straightened his hat and called loudly, "Let's move on out!"

She stood glaring up at him—ignoring the grinning cowboys that filed past—daring him to meet her eyes.

"'Bye, Dana!" Sean called, and trotted after Anse Kirby, who touched his hat in farewell.

Rafe's eyes swung down to hers, and they were nearly

black with emotion. Tobasco pranced in place, and she stepped back.

"What was that about?" she demanded in a quivering undertone.

He laughed aloud, one harsh incredulous bark, then brought Tobasco sidestepping alongside her. "See you in a few days." Reaching down, he touched her trembling mouth, and for just a moment he softened. Then he was past her, loping away after his men.

He didn't look back, even once.

CHAPTER TWENTY-ONE

IT WOULD HAVE BEEN bad enough if they'd parted in perfect amiability. She still would have missed him. But to have Rafe leave her like that, in anger—an anger she couldn't explain—was far worse. Dana drifted around her empty house all weekend, restless and blue and confused.

Forget it, she tried to tell herself. She'd simply crossed him at the worst possible instant—when he had a roundup to organize, a dozen urgent issues competing for his attention—and he'd lashed out. The first time he'd ever really lost his temper with her; that's why it cut so deep.

When he returned, all would be forgotten, forgiven. They'd be just the same as before, warily tender and always aware of each other, but most of all—most precious of all—*liking* each other.

She'd come to depend on that more than she'd realized; the contentment of having a friend around the house. Someone to listen to how her day had gone and to tell her of his. Someone to share a laughing glance when Petra did something marvelously silly, like the time she played dress-up with his Stetson and her brother's sunglasses. Someone to share her concerns about Sean.

If I lost that... Emptiness all over again, even deeper and darker than before.

But don't be silly, she'd tell herself, shying away from the abyss. She was exaggerating one moment's petty irritation into something permanent and awful. In a few days Rafe would return, and life would be as before.

Somehow it didn't feel that way. That bruising kiss felt like some sort of...divide. *He's angry at me, and not because I was late.* But for what, then? Because she refused to share his bed?

When she wondered about that, Dana grew angry herself. They'd made their bargain, and sex had been no part of it. If now Rafe was blaming her for that, he was being unfair.

She didn't think of Margot till her letter came on the Tuesday.

ADDRESSED TO SEAN, of course. Sitting in her pickup, which she'd pulled over just beyond the highway mailbox, Dana held it up to the light, but the envelope was opaque. She studied its childish, disturbingly erratic script for a moment, then grimaced and tossed it back on the pile of mail. Trouble, whatever it was, she told herself, and fought the temptation to not deliver it. But much as her instinct told her to shield Sean, there were some things one couldn't do. He had a right to mail from his own mother.

Margot...Dana had been waiting for her next move. Expecting it for weeks now. The custody expert she and Rafe had hired—Rafe had paid the thousand-dollar retainer with barely a grimace—had contacted Margot's San Diego attorney the week before the wedding. There had been some preliminary legal posturing and declarations, both sides claiming swift and certain victory in any eventual encounter; then each had withdrawn to his respective corner. Papers would doubtless be filed and soon, Dana's lawyer had assured her, then the real fireworks would start.

Instead, there had been a resounding silence until now, this letter.

It wasn't until Dana placed it on Sean's desk that the thought occurred to her. It was Margot who had pushed her into this marriage, who'd sent her running to Rafe to save Sean.

But for seven weeks now, Sean hadn't needed saving. *I must look like the little boy who cried wolf!* Rafe had rescued her from…precisely nothing. At least, nothing so far.

Could he possibly think—no, surely not—that she'd invented the whole Margot threat out of thin air? Dana sank down on Sean's bed, starting to feel like a fool. Could this be the source of Rafe's bad temper? He was beginning to wonder if she'd tricked him into this marriage, using Margot as her excuse?

Don't be ridiculous, she chided herself. It was Rafe who'd first proposed their arrangement, for Zoe's sake.

But two months later, it was she who'd finally set the deal in motion, citing Margot's threat as her reason.

I wonder what arrangement he'd have made for Zoe if I hadn't come begging his help? Had she perhaps barged in unknowingly on other plans he'd been making? Plans of some sort that Rafe now regretted he hadn't completed?

Maybe, happy as she had been with this arrangement, she was starting to seem a bad bargain to Rafe. That could account for his temper.

HE'D BEHAVED BADLY, very badly, taking out his temper in a kiss.

He *wanted* to behave badly with Dana Montana—his own wife, damn it!—for a good nonstop week or more. Maybe that would shut off his mind, let him sleep again at night. A sound sleep—not like the ones he was having these days, where he woke from torrid dreams, unsatisfied, on the sweaty point of explosion. *I signed on for five years of this?* He must have been out of his mind!

Still, Rafe was missing her, his thoughts moving faster than the damn cattle down the mountainside. Going to have to work something out when he got home.

Home… There the thought was again, and that was the problem. How did you give an ultimatum—insist on a revision of terms—when she held all the aces? What was the use in threatening to walk out, when he wanted her and she didn't want him? Where was his leverage?

Or his pride if he stayed?

From: RedColumbine@Westbest.com
To: SanDiegan@Pipeline.net
Seanster, You probably won't get this before you go, but I'm SO GLAD Dad took you on roundup. I'm sitting here with tears dripping down my silly nose, thinking of how beautiful it is up there, and how I'm missing it, Miel and Woofle and the guys, the campfires at night, the frosty mornings, the aspens all shivery golden. Not that I'm not having a good time here, too. Finally meeting a few kids over at the college. I borrowed some study notes from a guy, that night I missed. He's pre-med, too, hoping to transfer to Stanford next year, so we had a lot to talk about. Kinda neat to meet someone who shares your dreams. Ouch!—now THAT was a kick, Ariel Bliss, you beast. Guess she's telling me it's time to check out a book and go, soooo… Hey, one last half-a-thought, Seanster. About the L word? I don't think we should use that anymore. It was never really part of the plan, you know. This was just s'posed to be some friendly scientific inquiry, till the big OOOPS! You know how I feel about you—you'll always be my very, very, very BEST FRIEND. But I think we should remember, that's just what we are—amigos. (Besides, now that Dana and Dad have married, it's practically incest, isn't it?) So anyway, that's all. I love you, too, but with a little l. Talk to you soon, Cowboy. Your pear-shaped pal, Zoe+((((((AB))))))

HE DIDN'T KNOW what he wanted anymore from this bargain. Take the long view had always been his approach, but with Dana filling up his whole horizon, that wasn't working. Hard enough to look past tomorrow when all his thoughts circled around tonight, Rafe admitted as his truck closed the final few miles to the Ribbon R.

"Do I *have* to go to school tomorrow?" Sean shifted restlessly on the seat beside him. "I'm awful tired."

Rafe smiled to himself. First whine he'd heard from the kid all week. Sean had done well for a tenderfoot. Had taken to heart Rafe's advice to keep his mouth shut and his eyes wide open. He'd tried hard to pull his weight without getting in the way, and mostly he'd succeeded. The men had accepted him, not because he was the boss's stepson, but because he'd made it plain that he wanted to learn and that he knew nothing. That they had something valuable to give him. The older men in particular couldn't resist that attitude, and the young ones followed their elders' leads.

"Sure you do. Have to pay for your pleasures."

How could he pay for his own? What coin would Dana accept? Six days up on the mountain had calmed his temper, but the separation had only whetted his desire. And for once, the high country had granted him no clarity. He knew how he'd gotten himself into this mess—all for Zoe—but where was he now? Where did he want to go with it, beyond Dana herself? An image of himself lying between her slender thighs, her long legs wrapped around him, made him clench the wheel. His eyes whipped guiltily toward the boy, then back to the road. *Yes, oh, yes—but beyond that?*

He didn't know what he wanted anymore, only what he'd wanted before—his freedom. Only knew now that somehow this had changed.

But wherever it is we're going, sex has to be one of the stops along the way. One of the necessary steps toward…whatever. Dana had to trust him, had to accept him, if they had any prayer for any kind of a future.

Maybe, if she'd missed him as much as he'd missed her, she was seeing that now.

DANA WAS HALFWAY THROUGH the supper dishes, when the back door burst open letting in an icy draft—and her two cowboys, tall and rumpled, Sean carrying his saddlebags slung over his arm as Rafe did, his hat tipped to precisely the same angle.

"You should have called," she cried, whipping off her rubber gloves. "I'd have held supper."

They were sunburned and looked as if they'd slept in their clothes for a week. Sean wore a jaunty grin on his face that she hadn't seen in a year or more. *It was a success,* she rejoiced.

"Rafe didn't want us to barge in in the middle." Sean dumped his bags by the washing machine. "So we stopped at Moe's."

"I could have fed you a real meal if you'd come home. You probably haven't had a vegetable all week, not counting ketchup."

Sean shot Rafe a triumphant smirk. "What'd I tell you she'd say?"

"He had a double order of onion rings, along with his three cheeseburgers, so reckon that's vegetables enough for tonight," Rafe assured her.

"Reckon it is," Sean declared with satisfaction, heading for the front of the house.

"Son, take your bags with you," Rafe called. "You unpack your own dirty laundry."

"Right." Sean scooped them up and went.

Without a sour look or an argument! "Thank you, Rafe," she said softly. He'd given her stepson something precious, a gift beyond her own giving. "But how did he get so dirty?"

"Green hands always ride drag in a cattle drive. He's been eating dust for three days."

"And loving it, it looks like."

"He got along fine." Rafe wandered over to the coffee-pot. "Any left here?"

She joined him at the stove. "Let me make you a fresh pot."

"Nope. Just want a swallow to wash Moe's cooking out of my mouth."

"You should have come home," she told him. *Let me take care of you.* They were standing very close, and his eyes were more dark than blue.

"Well, here I am," he said gruffly.

"Yes." *Here you are, and I missed you so.* But nothing had changed, really. Her head still said one thing—stick to the bargain and stay safe—and her heart quite another. She touched a snap on his shirt and turned away for a clean cup. "How was it up there? Did you have snow?"

He sat down at the table and told her, while she finished the dishes. Upstairs, she could hear the water in the pipes—Sean showering. Down here, Rafe was painting her pictures—lowing cattle, a night of shooting stars, a bear that might have been a grizzly he'd spotted across a valley, though they'd not been seen in these hills for a generation. "And what about here?" he asked after a while.

So she told him, knowing that her bits of news and gossip didn't really matter; it was the unspoken message under her words and his that counted. *We still care about each other.* Whatever his reason had been for anger, it seemed to be gone now, and he was saying he was sorry. Saying also that he still wanted her, the way his eyes followed her around the kitchen.

And still, I don't know what I want. Or didn't know how to take it and be safe. The tension was building in the room, his eyes speaking one question—the big one she couldn't answer. She snatched up a folded stack of towels from the top of the dryer. "I'll take these up for you. He's finished now."

Passing the open door to Sean's bedroom, she saw him seated on his bed, dressed already in his pajamas, his face bent low over an unfolded sheet of paper. Margot's letter. Damn, she'd forgotten it! Biting her lip, Dana stacked the towels in the bathroom linen closet, set out a fresh, fluffy one for Rafe on the towel rack, then returned, stealing a glance as she passed. Sean sat as before—and this time she saw his face. All traces of his earlier happiness had vanished.

Oh, damn you, Margot. And on tonight of all nights! She slipped into Petra's room to check on her, and stood watching her sleep. *I will never, ever hurt you,* she swore fiercely to her daughter, reaching down to brush a soft, dark curl off her cheek. Not a promise she'd keep, she knew, thinking of her own mother, their rows and blowups over the years. Love and hurt seemed to be two sides of the same golden coin—open yourself to one and you made yourself vulnerable to the other. *But if I ever hurt you, sweetheart, they'll be little hurts. Hurts meant kindly, with your best good in mind and with the best of my intentions.* Not hurts delivered blithely, obliviously, by a mother who could see only her own needs and wants, no matter how they might damage her child.

She raised her head as booted feet passed the door—Rafe, heading for the bathroom. *And how do we hurt each other, you and I, while we're guarding our hearts?* Rafe, who had taken her stepson under his wing, who'd offered her his protection. *And for all that generosity, what have I given him in return?* The comforts of a home, yes, but not what he really wanted.

My body. She stood in the dark, very aware of it—a feeling like hot honey flowing through her veins, sweet and heavy and golden, amplifying the endless stride of her pulse.

He wanted her body and she'd have given it gladly, except that it came attached to her heart. *Oh, Rafe, if you'd say one word about loving me...*

WHEN HE ENTERED their bedroom at last, she sat on her daybed, dressed in a nightgown that telegraphed her ambivalence. Simple, almost virginal white, but so soft it clung to her every curve. She ran a hairbrush through her short hair, the stroke of the bristles a comfort and a torment. She needed to be touched, maybe as much as he did.

"Margot wrote him a letter," she said, when he paused at the foot of his bed to study her.

"Oh?" He sat down and frowned. "What did it say?"

"I have no idea. He's just read it. Looked miserable when I peeked in his door."

"Blast the woman," Rafe said quietly. "Damn and blast her."

"Maybe I should go talk to him?" Already she was accepting him as her authority on Sean.

"I wouldn't. Don't want to crowd him. I'll see if I can get him to talk in a day or two." Rafe blew out a long breath. "There was a message for me back at Suntop on the answering machine. Kelton called. Said to drop in to his office any day this week."

Their lawyer, down in Durango. "So he's had news?"

"S'pose. I'll go down there tomorrow. Need some ointments, anyway. Want to come along?"

She shook her head regretfully. "I have two cabins checking in, a hiking club from Denver."

"Then I'll take care of it."

A wave of warmth moved through her. To have someone else to rely on, taking care of the things she couldn't get to or handle. More and more he felt like her partner, her…husband. Her hand dragged the brush again. "I've been thinking, Rafe."

"Mmm?"

"It's time you brought Zoe home. She's coming into her eighth month—and she's living with an elderly old maid. That's not right. She should be here where I can keep an eye on her. Where she can see Cass Hancock if any problems arise." She watched Rafe's smile fade and his face harden.

"I agree, but what about Sean? He's stopped mooning around, or at least he's hiding it better—but to throw them together again?"

"I know, but—"

"And there's the problem of space. I'm sure Sean would be delighted to share his bedroom, but—"

"But she *has* to come home, Rafe. She could be starting Braxton-Hicks contractions any day now. They're terrifying if you don't know what they are, and—"

"So what about this—?" Restlessly he stood, walked over to the bureau, reached for his hat. Stood fingering it and frowning. "Sean lives here for the next few months with Willy. And I'm sure Mrs. Higgins would be happy to come in a few days a week to beat back the bachelor dust, cook for 'em. You and Petra and Zoe and I move back to Suntop. I've been meaning to speak to you about that, anyway. Once the heavy snows start, I have to be on the ranch to feed the stock. Can't depend on getting through from here if there's a blizzard."

She couldn't see leaving Sean. She'd promised to love him, guide him. Might as well send him back to Margot if she couldn't do the job. She ran the brush through her hair thoughtfully. "Or I suppose Petra and Sean and I could stay here." *Like before.* The old desolation crept through her at the thought. The house would feel empty, no one coming home to her in the evenings. "And you and Zoe could go back to Suntop.'' She looked up and met his eyes. *This is a test, Rafe Montana. If you love me, you'll never consent to our parting.*

He scowled and shook his head. ''What's the use in having Zoe home if she doesn't have a woman to look out for her these final months? I'll need you at Suntop.''

For *Zoe.* Not because he loved her, needed her by his side, couldn't bear to let her go—but for the safety and comfort of his precious daughter. *Nothing's changed but my stupid, gullible heart!* Imagining that what she needed and wanted was so.

But it wasn't.

She smacked her brush down on the bedside table, snapped out the light. ''Guess we'll have to think about it.'' Though no way would she abandon Sean. That was where her loyalty belonged.

''What's the matter?'' Rafe padded closer in the dark— became a tall, looming blackness over her bed, smudged by her trickling tears.

She wiped her eyes angrily. Didn't trust herself to speak.

He sat down on the edge of her bed. ''Dana?''

If only you wanted me. Me—not a mother for your grandchild, a woman when you needed one. ''Nothing,'' she muttered. ''G'night, Rafe.''

A big hand dropped down out of the dark, fumbled for the top of her head, stroked her hair. His fingertips rotated in tiny circles against her aching skull. ''Nothing...'' he repeated with husky disbelief. ''Your time of month?''

She let out a *hiss* of outrage and jerked her head away from his caress. ''That's none of your business!''

''It's the business of any man who lives with a woman to know when to get his head down and lie low,'' he disagreed, laughing under his breath. ''Is it?''

''No! Go to bed.''

Hot and callused, his fingers slid around to her nape,

massaged her gently. She could feel the faintest tremor below his strength. "I'd like to."

Like, not love. That was all he was offering. That—and a night she'd never forget. Might never recover from. To open her heart would be to let in a pain that might kill her this time. His invisible fingertips played across her cheek, found her lips, sought the dampness within. She shook her head—*no, Rafe*—even as her hips rocked upward, the rustle of covers belying her thoughts.

His fingers found her chin, traced a lingering line down the arch of her neck. She'd have to refuse him in words, but they snagged in her throat. Then his hand lifted away, and she sucked in a breath of relief.

His fingers alighted again—on the swell of her breast. Her skin came alive, roughened, electrified—it was now or never. "*No,* Rafe." She sat up abruptly, just as he cupped his palm to her—she filled his hand to overflowing. He groaned aloud and buried his face in her neck.

"I said *no!*" She twisted away, pushed herself over against the wall, since he blocked the route to the floor. "I mean it!"

"I heard you." The bed bounced as he stood. "You don't have to yell, believe me."

She was panting with emotion, her hands cupping her own aching breasts, her tears scalding. *Rafe*... It wasn't that she didn't want to give to him, but if he wouldn't take— didn't want—what she was really offering... "I'm sorry," she said miserably, wiping her eyes.

"Me, too," he said from somewhere above her. "You know, one of these days I'll stop asking."

Stop asking and simply take? She'd almost—*almost*—be relieved if he robbed her of the choice she couldn't make. Should not make. Though she'd never forgive him.

Across the room, his bed creaked, covers rustled. Her

tears wouldn't stop streaming, her heart galloping. Slowly she sank back to stare up miserably into the darkness.

Someday I'll stop asking.

She blinked as it hit her, what he meant. He meant something far worse than that someday he'd insist. He meant that someday he'd stop wanting her. The thought cut like a dull knife, pressing down on her heart. She couldn't bear for Rafe to stop wanting her.

But, then, what does that make me? A tease?

SOMETIME AFTER MIDNIGHT, Dana accepted defeat. There was no way she'd sleep tonight, at least not in this room. A glass of warm milk, perhaps, then she'd try the living room couch. The first few months after she'd lost Peter, that was where she'd bedded down. Something about its mushy softness, or the fact it held no associations, often did the trick when all else failed.

Rafe didn't stir as she crept from the room. She tiptoed past Sean's room, then Petra's, then on down the stairs. But as she passed through the dining room, she paused. A crack of light showed under the swinging door. Surely she'd switched off the lights.

Some sense of caution made her open the door an inch, then peek through its gap. Across the kitchen, Sean sat at his computer, typing furiously. The desk lamp beside him traced a glistening line of moisture down his cheek.

Oh, Sean. And what would Rafe tell her to do?

She could hear him as clearly as if he stood beside her, one comforting hand on her shoulder. *Mind your own business.* Letting the door fall back into place, she padded back to the couch—and finally slept.

From: SanDiegan@Pipeline.net
To: RedColumbine@Westbest.com
What the HELL do you mean, don't use the L word?

I LOVE you, LOVE you, LOVE YOU with the biggest L in all the world! You know it, I know it. I've never tried to hide how I felt. You never stopped me till now. What's changed, Zoe? Dana and your dad marrying means nothing to us. It doesn't count and you know it. Are you just being blue and crabby tonight, or do you really mean it? If you do, I don't see how I can live without you, or why I'd want to. We aren't just best friends—you're my ONLY friend. The only woman I'll ever want or love. I think I should come out there and we should talk about this. If you don't write me soon, I guess that's just what I'll do. Mom is asking me anyway to hitch home to San Diego. Saves her the money it would cost her to use a lawyer, to fight for my custody. (At least somebody, somewhere out there, wants me.) And Phoenix is right on my way. So write me—or plan to find me knocking at your door sometime soon! Your LOVER—never your brother—Sean.

CHAPTER TWENTY-TWO

WHEN DANA WOKE on the couch in the morning, Rafe was gone. He'd somehow walked past without rousing her, then out of the house. His words hung like a pall over her heart. *Someday I'll stop asking.* Was this that day already? He hadn't even asked her for his breakfast.

Sean, too, was gone, she found, though there was evidence on the counter that at least he'd made himself a peanut butter sandwich. Must have ridden his mountain bike down to the bus stop on the highway per his usual routine.

They'll both be back tonight, Dana told herself. *Please, God.*

The weight on her heart said they would not. That happiness had fled forever.

But premonitions didn't clean cabins or make beds or change dirty diapers. She tucked her heartache away and went to work.

She'd just checked in her hiking club and sent them to Willy to sign up for trail rides, when the phone rang. *Rafe!* Her heart gave a joyous leap.

No. Mr. Haggerty, principal of Trueheart High School. "Mrs. Montana? I'm afraid we've had a problem down here with Sean. Could you come in and see me?"

"AFTER HE'D KICKED IN his own gym locker and half a dozen more, he went down to Mrs. Lindstrom's class and called Mike Andersen and Joe Petit out into the hall," said Mr. Haggerty.

"The two boys who Super-Glued his locker closed with all his clothes inside while he was in the shower," Dana summarized, determined to keep the facts straight, in the principal's mind more than in her own. The man seemed determined to blame Sean entirely for the brawl. "Mrs. Lindstrom didn't stop them?"

Mr. Haggerty drummed his meaty fingers on his desktop and fixed her with the glare he must use on rebellious students. "Mrs. Lindstrom is a student teacher," he growled finally. "And Andersen and Petit are 'backs on our football team."

"Not inclined to obey a woman's orders, plus they're both bigger than Sean, then," Dana guessed. "Also older?"

"They're seniors, but that's entirely beside the point. Sean bloodied Andersen's nose and he loosened a few of Petit's teeth. What the dental bill will be is anybody's guess."

"And Sean?"

"Sean has a black eye and a ripped shirt."

"Did they black the same eye they did last week, or were they kind enough to alternate?" she asked icily.

"We don't know that last week's fight was with the same students as this week's. Your boy seems to have quite a chip on his shoulder."

"I presume, if someone locked *your* clothes away, Mr. Haggerty, you wouldn't take it kindly, either? Or would you?"

He reddened and shoved his chair back from his desk. "Maybe I should discuss this with his father. Where's Rafe? Is he reachable?"

"He's down in Durango this afternoon." She'd tried to call him at Suntop herself, before she left the Ribbon R, but Anse Kirby had answered the phone. "I'm not sure when he'll return. May I see my son now?"

Haggerty assumed an expression of smug righteousness. "That wouldn't be advisable for discipline, Mrs. Montana. He has been suspended—in house, of course. I don't hold with rewarding misbehavior with a vacation. And he's upset, you know. A good cooling down period—"

"I'm very upset, too, that you're unable to protect my son from bullies." *Shut up, Dana, shut up,* she advised herself. She'd taught in public schools long enough to recognize this breed of petty disciplinarian. Once his mind was set, it was set in concrete. She'd do her stepson no favors by demanding special treatment on his behalf. *Calm down.* Maybe sending Rafe to bat for Sean was the smart thing to do. Quite likely the two men had known each other since grade school. And to be brutally honest, Rafe could walk into this office and command a level of attention and respect that a five-foot-three indignant mother would never be accorded.

"All right," she said levelly. "When *may* I see him?"

SEAN WAS TO BE DELIVERED into her custody in the principal's office at three-fifteen, it was decided, a few minutes after school let out for the day. Which would give Haggerty a chance to dress Sean down in her presence, Dana suspected, then gloat over his sentence—five weeks in-house suspension.

That gave her three hours to drive in to Durango and back again. With any luck, she would find Rafe at their lawyer's office and bring him back to help her deal with Haggerty. Gritting her teeth at the thought of her stepson sitting forlornly alone in some windowless room with torn shirt and blackened eye, she marched off to her truck.

RAFE PICKED UP the pinkeye ointment, an antibiotic salve that Willy swore by, and some parts for the tractor. He encountered his banker at lunchtime, and took him along to a better restaurant than he'd have chosen alone. But while his boots carried him about the town on his errands, his thoughts were elsewhere, back at the Ribbon R, back with Dana.

Coming home to her last night had been so sweet. There'd been those few moments she'd endured his loving—his hand still tingled as if he held her, his groin muscles jerked tight at the memory—and then it had turned so bitter. *This has got to stop.* His own needs shamed him. *You don't keep on offering what the other doesn't want.* He was acting like a schoolboy, like Sean mooning after Zoe—not like a man who knew the ways of the world. There were some things that wanting could never change.

After a lunch he hardly tasted, he dropped by the lawyer's. Because whatever he decided for himself, it didn't alter his obligations. He'd told Dana he'd help her fight for Sean's custody, and so he would. Besides, the kid had shown himself sensible enough to grasp the value of what Rafe and his men had offered him up in the mountains. The life of a free man. Sean deserved a helping hand.

At least the news at the lawyer's was good. "You've got yourself a kook, there," Kelton announced, his three-thousand-dollar lizard skin boots propped on his half-acre desktop, his hands clasped behind his head. "A pure, prime, California kook. We ever get her in court, we'll eat her alive."

But it looked as if Kelton wouldn't have the pleasure. He'd finally pinned down Margot's lawyer by phone and gotten the story off the cuff. The woman had pulled a tantrum in her lawyer's office two weeks ago, demanding that he work for her on spec, his eventual legal bills to be paid out of Sean's inheritance—once Margot had been granted custody and Sean's portion of the Ribbon R had been sold

When her attorney had suggested that no reasonable man would work on such a basis, that some cash up-front would

be an excellent spur to his progress, she'd flipped out, as
Kelton put it. Had accused her own man of a gross lack of
compassion, creativity, comprehension of the finer points
of the law, to say nothing of justice. Had called him a
sexist, a fascist, a money-grubbing shyster and a left-
brainer, to boot. Then informed him that his office had
lousy *feng shui,* whatever that was. In short, Margot's lawyer had suggested she take her business elsewhere, and
she'd flounced out of his office in tears.

"And my guess is that's the last you'll hear of her in an
official capacity." Kelton swung his boots down to his silk
oriental carpet.

"Unofficially, that type has more lives than a slasher in
the last reel," Kelton continued. "She'll pop up and scare
you every six months or so, but she's strictly short attention
span. Wait three weeks and she'll wander away again." He
lifted a file off his desk. "Did put a P.I. on her as you
asked me to do, and there's plenty of ammunition if we
ever do need it—which we won't. As of Saturday night,
she's shacked up with a new boyfriend, bar pickup, and
he's a beaut. Want the particulars?"

Rafe grimaced and shook his head. "File it in case of
need and take your man off her tail." He himself was in
need of fresh air.

Coming down the stairs from Kelton's office, he was
already considering how much he'd tell Dana. Enough to
ease her mind, but not enough to pain her. He knew her
well enough by now to be sure she didn't wish Margot
Kershaw any harm. Wouldn't be happy to hear that the
woman was self-destructing. He hadn't told Dana he'd
played hardball, setting a private investigator on Sean's
mother, and there was no reason to tell her now. He shoved
through the downstairs back doors—and stopped short.

"Why, Rafe Montana!" Mitzy Barlow stood beaming at
him, one long-nailed hand pressed to her heart. "How *are*

you? It's been months since—'' She tossed her hair and smiled. "Well, it's been too long!"

He let out his sigh slowly between his teeth, hoping it looked like a normal breath, and offered his hand. Sending a message. "Mitzy, it's good to see you." Any other day he wouldn't have minded. She was always easy on the eyes, and how could you dislike a woman who tried so hard? Here she was doing it again, turning his handshake into something that would have caused one man to punch another.

Still, he stood patiently, courteously, hoping his eyes weren't glazing over as she rattled on. A chatterer compared with Dana's quietness. A magpie compared with a mourning dove. How he ever could have seen himself bedding her... But back then he hadn't known there was someone like Dana Kershaw in the world, waiting around the next corner.

But not waiting for me—missing her husband. That was his whole problem, Rafe was starting to think. He'd rushed in when he should have waited. Had only himself to blame for his sorrows.

"...So when she told me you were married, I almost swallowed my ice cube!" Mitzy declared, regaining his wandering attention. "And I know it's late to be wishing you all the happiness in the world, but Rafe—" She fluttered her eyelashes as she stood up on tiptoe. "Do I still get to kiss the groom?"

THE PARKING LOT behind Kelton's office was almost full. Pulling into a slot in the last row, Dana looked around. No sign of Rafe's truck. Either she'd missed him or he'd yet to arrive. She could ask Kelton's secretary, she decided, and reached for the door handle—then paused. A tall, familiar shape stood in the shadows outside the back entrance—Rafe. Facing a smaller, curvier figure—a woman dressed in a mauve business suit that hugged her like a second skin. High heels that propped her bottom up at a preposterous angle. *Woman on the prowl,* shrieked that outfit, and right now her body language was announcing the prey.

Dana's husband.

But Dana hadn't claimed him, made him her own. And now, watching this huntress fling her arms around Rafe's neck and do her best to dive down his throat, Dana sat frozen, the first shards of ice piercing her heart. *Too late,* said a bleak little voice inside her. *You waited too long to know what you really want, and now it's too late.*

Rafe had stopped asking. Asking *her,* anyway.

Long after he'd straightened, patted Ms. Mauve on the shoulder and strode off toward the street with a silly grin plastered all over his face, Dana sat motionless, blinking back her tears. She had nobody in the world to blame but herself.

AND BAD AS IT HAD STARTED, this miserable day wasn't quite done with her yet. When Dana walked back into Mr. Haggerty's office at precisely 3:10 p.m., he fixed her with an accusing eye. "Where's your son, Mrs. Montana?"

SEAN HAD WALKED OUT of in-house detention at precisely 3 p.m., with orders to wait for his mother in the principal's office. That was the last anyone had seen of him.

Dana drove home, assuming he'd caught the bus, would be sulking somewhere around the Ribbon R. But a search of his room showed his fly rod propped in its usual corner, his camera on the desk. He wasn't in the barn, his tree house or down along the river.

By dusk she was starting to worry. By nine, she was frantic. She'd searched all of Trueheart, plus the little airport between the ranch and town, and she'd done it alone. Because Rafe was missing, too.

Please, God, let them be together. They'd bumped into each other someplace near the school, she told herself, and Rafe was listening to Sean's troubles—had taken him out for a male-bonding supper of junk food somewhere down in Durango.

When Rafe's truck finally rumbled up the hill at eleven that night, she flew out of Petra's bedroom, down the stairs, to meet him at the back door. "You have Sean, don't you?"

His face, which had just started to lighten to a wary smile, went back to somber. "He isn't here?"

IT WAS PAST 1:00 A.M. by the time they'd searched Trueheart again, then all the ranch buildings at Suntop, then spoken with Sheriff Noonan. Past two by the time Mrs. Higgins arrived to care for Petra and cook for the dudes, until their return. A starless night of lowering clouds, as they drove southwest bound for Phoenix.

"Maybe we should call Zoe," Dana suggested, not for the first time, but again Rafe disagreed.

"He's got eleven hours' head start, but the road's rough and it isn't direct. And drivers don't pick up hitchers late at night. She won't have him yet, even if Phoenix is where he's headed."

"It is—has to be." The more she thought of it, the more certain she grew. Whatever was paining him, the fight or something else, Sean had taken his woes to the one person he really loved. His wise woman and lucky charm, Zoe Montana.

And this time, Dana wished he'd borrowed her truck. God, let him be all right! He was only fifteen, and not half as tough as he thought. To hitchhike some four hundred miles, through harsh high desert, mountain passes, across the Navajo reservation, with the threat of an oncoming blizzard for most of the way?

"All Zoe could do is sit there and worry. That wouldn't do her any good. With any luck we'll find him shivering beside the road between here and Flagstaff."

They didn't—though they drove with agonizing care, gritty eyes sweeping each side of the road, stopping in each dusty little town they passed to speak with the local law, asking them to keep a watch, then halting at every truck stop to question the sleepy waitresses. Each time Rafe passed a patrol car, he pulled over and walked back to talk. "Snow's coming," he said grimly, the third time he returned to the truck.

Sean had worn only a light jacket to school that morning. No proof against a blizzard. *Please, please,* she prayed, but said only, "Shall I drive for a while?"

West of the state line at Four Corners, the blizzard socked in. The snowplows had yet to turn out, and Rafe slowed the truck to a crawl, windshield wipers frantically sweeping. Rafe reached out and took hold of Dana's hand for a while, but the road was too dangerous for that. Instead, he drew her over beside him, and they drove like that, pressed together for comfort.

THE FIRST RIDE he'd caught had been the best. A battered old pickup with a tarp-covered bed. He'd untied the cover and crawled beneath it while the truck was parked outside Moe's Truckstop. That ride carried him through most of the freezing night, all the way through the reservation and out the far side. Too far. In spite of his shivering, Sean had fallen asleep after Flagstaff, and when he woke near dawn, the pickup was pulling into a gas station halfway to Kingman, fifty miles out of his way.

He'd scrambled out and taken half the morning to retrace his route east to Flagstaff, then south. By the time he reached Phoenix and figured out the bus routes, it was ten in the morning. He was grubby and exhausted and hungry enough to eat a horse, but any time now he'd see Zoe, and everything would be fine.

"SHE'S NOT HERE," said the tiny old woman with the black, snapping eyes, who opened the door to his knock. "Who are you? You're that boy she keeps talking about?"

He had to smile. "Yes, ma'am, I guess I am."

She sniffed. "You look too young to be studying to be a doctor, but what do I know? Everybody's too young, and their manners—*huh!*"

It wasn't him she meant—and suddenly Sean wanted to sit down and cry. "Could you tell me where I could find Zoe, Miss Cavazos—please, ma'am?"

Aunt Emilia directed him to a junior college halfway across town. Zoe should be sitting in on some science class there, or maybe in the student union. Who knew, with that girl? Like her mother, Pilar, who wouldn't settle down, head always off in some book.

An hour later, Sean stood in the doorway to the student union, scanning the crowded tables. She'd be here. Had to be here, when he needed her so. *Zoe, I love you with a big L. If you love me...*

His eyes focused like his zoom lens—on a head of blazing red hair across the room. He let out a cry of relief, then stopped short as he realized. That was his Zoe, all right, but she sat huddled over a table, her temple pressed to the cheek of the boy sitting beside her. Except he was too big, too old, to be called a boy—years older than Sean. Zoe sat with a young *man,* whose arm was draped comfortably around her shoulders while they read a book that lay open on the table.

As Sean stood paralyzed, Zoe turned to say something.

The man listened, nodded gravely, then kissed the tip of her freckled nose.

"Hey, why don't you just stand in the doorway?" Somebody bumped into Sean from behind.

Ready and eager for a fight, he whirled to shove back, but the kid had already passed by. *Love* had passed him by—just like that. The only woman he'd ever love in his whole life loved somebody else now. Sitting there, radiantly beautiful and ripe as a pear, with his unborn baby in her lap, she was loving somebody else.

Sean didn't look back. Blind, numb, his heart just starting to break, he walked.

IN FLAGSTAFF, the Navajo police directed them to the hospital. A young, unidentified man had been struck by a hit-and-run driver sometime the previous night and taken there. They lost nearly two hours gaining permission to see him, and when they did—*thank you, oh, thank you!*—it wasn't Sean lying there with a hangover and two broken legs. Dana's heart went out to the boy's mother, wherever she was, waiting and worrying.

Grateful and subdued they drove on, to reach Phoenix at last at eight that night.

ONCE ZOE HAD STOPPED laughing and crying and hugging them, the news was not good. She hadn't seen Sean, she reported with a startled, stricken face.

Her great aunt Emilia might have done so. A young man with manners better than most young men nowadays had come asking for Zoe sometime that morning—or was it perhaps the morning before? No, no, no, this one, because she'd been watching *General Hospital* when he'd come to the door. She couldn't say quite what he looked like, and as for age, well, they were all young these days, weren't they? But she'd sent him on to the college where Zoe wasted her time most days.

"I didn't see him," Zoe repeated, wringing her hands. "But if he missed me there, he'd try back here, wouldn't he?"

Aunt Emilia made them sit down while they waited and eat a meal of meat loaf with green salsa and instant mashed potatoes. By ten that night, they all had to admit, if that really had been Sean at the door earlier, he should have returned by now.

"Unless he hitched on to his mother in San Diego," Zoe said worriedly. "She'd been begging him to run away to her, he said."

"Said?" Rafe repeated ominously.

"E-MAIL!" HE GROWLED an hour later, as they drove east across the desert. "They've been talking all this time by e-mail?"

Dana kept her smile to herself. Rafe was so superbly competent in his own hands-on world, he tended to dismiss technology—till it reared up and bit him.

"Did you know that?" he demanded.

"No. Oh, no." Though she'd had her suspicions once or twice, and when she'd seen Sean typing so furiously at the keyboard the night before last…*I should have guessed trouble was coming.*

Rafe snorted, then let it go. Drove for a few miles in silence, then said, "I still think you should have stayed back there at Emilia's, in case he shows up in the morning. Gotten a good night's sleep. Let me go on to Margot's by myself."

"No." *You've stood by me all this way. I'll stand by you.* It was another four hundred miles to San Diego. "If he shows up, Zoe will sit on him." They'd told her they'd check back by phone every few hours in the morning.

Meanwhile, it was crucial that they head off Sean before he reached Margot, persuade him to come home. Possession was nine-tenths of the law, Kelton had warned them. Let him reach San Diego, and they might never get him back.

"At least we don't have to worry about him out in the snow now." Rafe was following his own thoughts. "And clearly he's road smart. He made good time to Phoenix, given the conditions."

"Yes." Her earlier frantic anguish had settled to a grinding worry, but Rafe was right. Sean had passed through the most dangerous terrain in his first leg of the journey. Not that there weren't a hundred other dangers still to fear, but she put them all doggedly from her mind. Sean was clever and determined, and he had her and Zoe's and Emilia's prayers—and Rafe's tireless energy—working on his behalf. *We'll find him. I promise you, Peter, we'll find him.*

Rafe rubbed her shoulder with his free hand. "Why don't you try to sleep. If we take it in turns and stay fresh, we'll have a better chance of spotting him."

So she lay on her back, with knees bent and, gladly giving in to Rafe's suggestion, pillowed her head on his thigh. Lay that way for a long while, infinitely comforted by his warmth and the vibrations of the road rising up through the seat. After a while, his right hand came down from the wheel to cradle her forehead, and her eyes swam with tears. He'd backed her so completely in this ordeal, without question or complaint. *Oh, Rafe, what would I do without you?* Reaching up and back, she found his wrist, brought his hand down to her lips and kissed it. "Thank you!" she whispered.

"My pleasure." Heavy and warm, his hand lay in her hold, not demanding anything, but not retreating.

She kissed it again, then brought it down and tucked it beneath her chin, smiled once—and fell fast asleep.

SUCH A BITTERSWEET sensation, having her rest her head in his lap. Rafe's muscles were jammed tight with her nearness, his hand almost trembling with the need to smooth on down over her breasts, exploring and claiming and worshiping every inch of her he could reach. His heart was heavy and full, just that she trusted him this far. *Oh, Dana.* His woman, even if she didn't know it.

Not long after they'd crossed the Colorado River, the border between Arizona and California, he glanced down to find her eyes wide open, pools of gleaming darkness in the truck's dimness. He moved his hand slightly, and she let it go. He was brave enough to bring it up to her mouth. To draw a fingertip across her softness, which curved at his touch to a smile, then replace it below her chin in a paradise of neutrality. "Can't sleep?" he murmured.

"Off and on. Was lying here thinking..." Her fingers twined about his, and she sighed. "You've never told me about Pilar, Rafe. What was she like?"

CHAPTER TWENTY-THREE

MILES PASSED under the truck's wheels, till she was sure he wouldn't speak—then suddenly he did. "They don't look a bit alike. Zoe's hair comes from my mama, and her height from me, I reckon, while Pilar was tiny like Emilia, and dark. But their...intensity, that's the same. The quickness. And the curiosity—Pilar was interested in a thousand different things. She'd plow through the books, researching this or that. She was so smart she was scary, and she was smart in the right way. Not just knowing facts and figures—she put facts and figures *together* to come up with ideas about the way things or people worked. Wasn't one of those types who memorize the world tree by tree—she saw the forests. Would have *planted* forests someday if she'd had the chance."

You admired her. That came through in every word he spoke. *But what about love?* Perhaps he'd loved Pilar so much that he could never love again, not all the way, not the way she needed. "So that's Pilar," she said softly, rubbing his hand with her thumb. "What about you and Pilar?"

"Us together?" Rafe shifted beneath her, then stilled. More miles passed. "There's not much to tell," he said abruptly. "I wrecked her life."

The offhand pain in his voice brought her rushing to his defense. "Who said so? Pilar said that?"

"Often." One bleak little word, barely audible above the hum of the tires.

"But what did she mean by that?" How could having a man like Rafe Móntana in her life ever be anything but a blessing?

He laughed under his breath without humor. "She meant I was the cheap young cowboy who bought the economy-price condom that burst at the wrong moment and changed her whole life. Wrecked it."

"How could she blame *you* for that?" No one had forced Pilar to risk teenage sex.

Rafe laughed that bitterly unhappy laugh again. "Easily. Whenever it hit her that there she was, living in a shabby little trailer with a baby crawling around her feet and a no-account husband who could hardly put food on the table, no matter how hard he worked. When, instead, she could have been off at Harvard, studying to become Dr. Cavazos, the way her father had hoped and planned for her. She didn't just feel a failure, Dana—she felt she'd failed her whole family. And family was big to Pilar."

Reaching back, she rubbed her knuckles along the top of his thigh, desperately needing to comfort. To heal a wound she couldn't touch. "But you didn't do it to her. I mean, not by yourself."

He shrugged. "Pilar didn't see it that way. Guess I did want sex more than she did. She never let me forget that I'd promised—sworn to her—that nothing would go wrong if we loved each other."

"But even so, Rafe, even if you did—and what eighteen-year-old boy doesn't, in the heat of the moment?—afterward, she had a choice. She could have gotten an abortion."

"Pilar didn't see it that way," he repeated so softly it sounded as if he spoke to himself. And so they'd married, and now it was hitting Rafe that his first marriage had been very much like his second.

He'd always been able to satisfy Pilar, make her sing

like a little mockingbird and then beg him for more. And Dana—somehow he knew, if she'd only let him, that she'd answer him like music. Like rock to river or moon to sun. They'd be good in bed together—so much better than good.

But no matter how he'd tried with Pilar, he'd never been able to make her losses up to her. She'd never forgiven him, and in never forgiving, had never given him her love. Not love as he thought of love—a mating of bodies and souls.

And now, a dozen years later, here was Dana—the same way—holding back the one part of her that really mattered. That she wouldn't let him into her bed signified something much deeper—that she wouldn't—couldn't?—make room for him in her heart.

Maybe it's something in me. Because Dana, at least, had loved before. Time and time again, she'd made that clear.

Up ahead, the lights of a truck stop pierced his inner blackness. Rafe sighed with relief and slowed the truck. "Maybe he'll be here."

BUT ONCE AGAIN they came up empty, and when they drove on, Dana insisted on spelling him at the wheel. Rafe folded his coat to a pillow, leaned back in the angle of seat and door and stretched out his cramped legs. "Wake me the minute you get sleepy," he warned her.

"I will, but tell me one more thing before you nap." Dana tipped up her chin as she did when she was facing something hard. "Tell me what happened. How she died."

You're not asking much. But it was Dana who asked. Rafe stared at the lines in the highway sweeping under them and away. "One night...in our sixth year together, I came home dog-tired and Pilar showed me a letter from the dean of admissions at Harvard. Without telling me anything, she'd reapplied to go there. She had grades and test scores off the charts. And she was a minority, which they like to recruit. They'd said sure, we still want you, and here's full financing to boot.''

''What about you?'' Dana asked quietly.

''She said I could do what I liked. I could go with her or I could stay, but we both knew what that really meant. There was no job that I'd take in Boston. I couldn't live riding subways instead of horses, working inside a concrete box, breathing canned air. Fluorescent lights instead of the open sky? It wasn't possible. I asked her why she couldn't study in Denver or Boulder, someplace closer where maybe we could have held it together.''

''But she wanted her old dream back.''

''That's right. Like our years together had never happened. Just erase the nightmare and get back to reality—like that. So I told her fine, if that's what you want, go on. But I'm not waiting back here with my hat in my hand, hoping, for five years or eight years or however long she stayed away. I said I'd want a divorce.''

Dana nodded to herself. ''And how did she take that?''

Why the hell are we talking about this? He shifted angrily. ''She burst into tears. Not that the discussion had been exactly calm till then—our fights never were. We were both shouting and swearing, and poor Zoe was hiding in the bedroom. She hated it when we fought. Well, Pilar saw my ante and raised. She said fine, she'd take that divorce, but she wanted her daughter.''

''Oh,'' Dana said on a note of quiet pity.

''And I said I'd see her in hell first. I said there was no way she was getting Zoe, no way she could care for her properly if she did—not and be a full-time med student. And Pilar kept insisting that she *had* to have her daughter, that she'd work things out, she could put Zoe in day care. And I'm yelling that no child of mine is going to be raised by strangers, cooped up in some lousy city, when she could live in Colorado with her own pony and dog, free to ride a hundred miles in any direction. No way! I'd fight her for custody every inch of the way, and by God, I'd win. She could go if she wanted, but Zoe was staying.''

He was speaking in almost a shout, he realized, the old passions echoing down through the years, with the power still to stampede his heart and his breathing. He rolled down the window and leaned his head out into the icy slipstream till his lungs ached, then he rolled it up. *Let's drop this, can we?*

''And so?'' Dana prodded. She'd removed a splinter from his palm a few weeks back with this same grave-faced determination.

''So she smashed a dish against the wall and screamed she hated me and out the door she flew. And I...never saw her again. Her car hit a bridge abutment out on the highway, not five miles from our trailer.''

''Oh, Rafe!'' Dana reached for his hand.

But to his mind, he deserved no comfort, wouldn't take it now. He pulled away. ''I figure maybe she was crying so hard she didn't see it.'' He let out a long, slow breath between his teeth. ''Or maybe...maybe she did.'' Pulling his hat down over his eyes, he slouched lower in the seat. ''I need some sleep.''

She had to be careful her own tears didn't blind her. Dana wiped her lashes and drove on. *And now I know why you're so determined for Zoe to fly free and high. To live to her full potential. You're paying Zoe the debt you think you owe her mother.* Oh, yes, love was a two-faced coin.

''HE'LL BE HERE,'' Dana said the following day with passionate conviction, as they drove down a street in a San Diego suburb. ''Oh, let him be here!''

If he wasn't, Dana was going to fall apart, Rafe realized, as he scanned the address of each bungalow they drove slowly past. She hadn't had a real sleep in—what?—two days now? This must be Sunday, he calculated, his mind sluggish with exhaustion.

"There it is!" Dana pointed at a bungalow no different from the rest, except that nobody had picked up the wind-blown trash. Bits of bright plastic and wadded paper were snagged in the rock garden that was its front yard. Crushed beer cans were tossed helter-skelter on the gravel.

He parked the car, then caught Dana's wrist as she tried to leap out. "I'll do this, Dana." From everything Kelton had told him, he figured Margot was a flake.

An absent flake, ten minutes of hard knocking proved. Rafe knocked so hard that finally the next-door neighbor popped his head over his bleached cedar fence. An older, white-haired man, with wire-rimmed glasses and a pinched mouth. "She's gone, as anybody could see," he snapped, and bobbed down again.

Rafe walked to the fence and looked over. Old Crabby was rearranging his own rock garden—potted cacti, a spade and a bag of soil set out beside him as he knelt in the gravel. "Know when she'll be back?"

The old man sat up on his heels. "You better believe I do! Same time she always comes home—two hours after every sane person on this block has gone to sleep. And now she's taken up with that biker trash? Last week the thug chained his Harley to my car's back bumper. When I complained to Margot, she laughed and said he was afraid somebody would rip him off. What about me, I said, who can't use his own car? If that isn't ripping—"

"Actually, we're looking for Margot Kershaw's son," Rafe broke in. He glanced aside, as Dana took his arm and leaned over the fence.

"He's only fifteen," she said, voice quivering. "Have you seen him?"

Mr. Crabby pushed his glasses up his nose and sniffed. "Young Sean? Well, of course, I have. He sat there like a stray pup on her front steps last night, till finally I came out and told him she wouldn't be home till long after midnight.''

"Where did he go then?" Dana cried.

Mr. Crabby gave her a look of exasperated contempt. "Why, here, of course. He ate an entire pound of my hot dogs and all my potato chips, thanked me kindly, then went back to sitting on her steps. I guess she let him in when she came home at two. I always look at my clock when she wakes me."

BUT AS TO WHERE Sean was now, Mr. Albert Hinkley wouldn't hazard a guess. Margot and her sleazy boyfriend had rumbled off a couple of hours ago in the company of several other bikers—all of them three sheets to the wind in her neighbor's humble opinion, though who asked him? But the old man insisted, with increasing indignation in the face of Dana's pleading to be sure, that they hadn't taken the boy along.

So perhaps the kid, still exhausted after 800 miles of hitching, was sacked out inside his mother's cottage. While Dana sat, near tears, in the truck, Rafe walked around the bungalow, peering through the curtainless windows. The place was a pigsty, but he saw no sign of Sean.

"Wait here?" Dana said faintly, when he returned.

"Let's think this through," Rafe suggested. "If he was expecting any kind of warm welcome from his mother, doesn't sound like he got it. And there's not a lot of space for a guest in there." And how would the kid feel, sharing his mother with a drunken biker? Or the biker feel, sharing Margot with her son?

"And she didn't make time for him today," Dana murmured thoughtfully. "Went off with her friends, instead. Oh, Rafe—after he went to such trouble to get here. What he must be feeling!"

"Yes," Rafe agreed, taking her hand. "So he's blue and tired and nobody loves him, is how he sees it. Is there anybody else Sean might turn to, feeling that way? An old school buddy or—"

Dana let out a laugh that was halfway to a sob. "There's Margot's father!"

A retired plastic surgeon, living north of the city in San Clemente. Dana had never met him. Knew almost nothing about him, except that he'd divorced Margot's actress mother when Margot was five. Every year he sent Sean a birthday card with a handsome check, and another check for Christmas. Not once since she'd married into the family had he asked to visit his grandson. But it was her best guess.

Rafe consulted a map, and they drove.

THE SUN WAS SINKING into a blue, blue Pacific when finally they stood on the doorstep of a pink stucco, Spanish-style house that was two-thirds of the way to mansion, in a neighborhood where every second dwelling seemed to have a pool out back or a Mercedes coupe in the garage. A neighborhood where nobody tended his own lush garden, Rafe was sure.

"*Be* here," Dana murmured as she jabbed the doorbell.

A tall, lean, bald man in his late sixties opened the door and regarded them without enthusiasm. "If this is a solicitation, then please don't—"

"Dr. Swenson?" Dana cut in eagerly. "My name is Dana Kershaw...Montana. I'm—"

"Sean's stepmother!" Swenson warmed rapidly. "I've been trying to reach you all afternoon."

"He's here?" Dana cried, as he swung the door wide.

"Out back with my dachshund. Please come in."

THE TWO MEN STOOD at a picture window looking out over a flowery, terraced backyard. Sean sat on the grass at the far end, slump-shouldered, head drooping, rolling a tennis ball for a fat red dachshund, which waddled after it.

Dana came into view walking toward the boy, who didn't see her yet. "She wants him?" murmured the surgeon, eyes fixed on the scene.

"We both want him."

Sean's grandfather let out a long sigh and nodded. "Then that's a load off my mind. I've been sitting here telling myself that it's never too late to be a father. Since I botched it so badly with Margot—was too engrossed with my career to be there for her when she needed me—I told myself this would be my last chance to get it right. But frankly, Rafe, it's a young man's job."

"A job I want," Rafe said softly. "He's a good kid."

Dana had come to a halt some twenty feet behind the boy. The dachshund, trotting back with the ball, spotted her first, dropped his prize and barked. Sean turned, and Rafe watched his head jerk up in surprise.

Rafe didn't think Dana spoke as she closed the gap between them. When the two stood eye to eye, she hesitated for an endless, agonizing moment, then she reached out— and folded the boy into a fierce hug. Sean stood frozen, his face working, then slowly at first, then faster, his arms rose till he hugged Dana back.

They were still standing that way, arms locked around each other, foreheads touching, when Rafe and the doctor finally turned away. Dr. Swenson let out another long sigh, then gave Rafe a broad smile.

"Well...that seems to be settled. So come have a beer and tell me where he got those black eyes and why he ran."

"DO YOU KNOW what he said to me?" Dana murmured, waving as they drove away. Sean stood on the front porch under the arm of his grandfather, waving back with a tired, shy grin. "He said, 'You guys came all this way just for me?'"

Rafe caught her hand and squeezed. "And you said?"

"Oh, something about 'of course! Where do you think you belong, you silly goose, but with us? Will you please, please come home?'" She sighed contentedly and sagged against him, her head coming to rest on his shoulder. "So…thank you, Rafe, for finding him for me."

"For us." *If there is an us.* Tonight, with her head on his shoulder, they felt a couple, really married.

"You think we did right letting him stay?"

"Absolutely." Dr. Swenson had asked to keep Sean for a visit now that the boy was there. Had promised to fly Sean home in his private plane the following weekend. The way Sean's face had lit up at that, Rafe figured that was worth a month of makeup homework. "Sends the right message—that he's welcome home, not that we're dragging him home by his collar."

"And you don't think we have to worry about Margot?"

"Sean's no fool. I think he's learned his lesson there, for good and all." And Margot's father had privately promised Rafe that if Margot ever changed her mind again and decided she wanted her son back after all, he'd cut off her monthly allowance till she reconsidered.

"If all the therapy I'm paying for ever takes effect and she suddenly grows up, now that would be a different story," Swenson had added sternly. "But I'm afraid it's a little late for that."

In return, he'd asked that they allow Sean to visit him once or twice a year, and he would serve as the safe bridge to Margot, so that some sort of emotional connection between mother and son was maintained.

Swenson, seeing their exhaustion, had also offered to put Rafe and Dana up for as long as they liked, but Rafe had thanked him and asked for a recommendation to a nearby hotel, instead. A single room with his own wife beat a palace with company any day, to his mind. *Whether we share a bed or not.*

THE HOTEL WAS A LOW, Spanish-looking affair, built on craggy cliffs above the ocean. Would have made a nice spot for a honeymoon, Rafe found himself wistfully thinking. They took a room with a balcony overlooking the water. Rafe ordered sandwiches sent up, while Dana showered. Then he opened the sliding glass door and let the sound of the waves fill the room.

Then it was his turn for the bathroom, and when he came out, clean and shaved for the first time in days, he found Dana fast asleep under the covers of the bed nearest the balcony. He stood longing to join her. Imagining himself pulling her close and curving to fit her warm backside, kissing her nape, then sinking into delicious sleep, the sweetest of dreams, with his face buried in her fragrant hair.

But not without an invitation. Somehow the inviting was more important than the party. He sighed, pulled back the covers of the other bed, crawled in, fell asleep before his head hit the pillow.

SHE WOKE—somehow knowing it was near dawn—to the sound of waves combing up a beach. Dana stretched luxuriously and turned her head. Rafe was a long, dark, motionless shape on the other bed.

Shouldn't be over there when I'm here. They'd been so close these past few days. *Why are we apart?* At 4:00 a.m., she could find no logic to it. Trying to live her life avoiding pain—what kind of a life was that?

A rotten one if it kept her apart from Rafe Montana.

And if she'd thought to protect herself from pain, she could see now her resolution had been foolish, utterly useless. He hadn't needed her body to claim her heart. Rafe

had it now, and there was no going back. She loved him—
would love him always, whether she let him into her bed,
or slept cold and lonely forever.

And in loving him, yes, she'd suffer heartache. When
her man hurt, she'd hurt, too. If he ever left her, by choice
or as Peter had gone, well, she might not survive it this
time.

But still…*he's here now and so am I and I love him.*
However much time she was granted, it wouldn't be
enough, so why was she wasting it? The night was full of
a rushing peace, the certainty of waves, time out of mind,
caressing the shore. Dana slid her legs out of bed before
she could second-guess herself, stood paralyzed with fear
for a hundred heartbeats or more—then an especially large
wave hit the sands with a shuddering roar.

She slipped back the covers and slid softly in beside her
husband.

RAFE CAME HALF-AWAKE to the feel of kisses on his chin,
his cheek, his shoulder. He'd dreamed this too many times.
Grumbling, he turned away onto his side and relaxed again.

Soft and warm and deliciously damp, the invisible lips
returned to kiss his nape…between his shoulder blades—
he was suddenly wide-awake and hard as a rock. He sucked
in a startled breath.

"Just me," she murmured at his back, and brushed her
nose across his skin.

"Dana?" Couldn't be, he was dreaming.

"Who else?" she laughed in a husky whisper. "No—
please don't answer that."

His body was revving like a tractor engine, testosterone
raising his goose bumps and all else, his head not getting
enough blood to comprehend just what had inspired this
miracle. He didn't dare move. "Couldn't…um…sleep?"

She kissed his nape again—driving a ragged shudder

down his spine to curl his toes. "I just...wanted to thank you. For everything, Rafe. Not just these past few days with Sean, but...everything you've done for us...for me."

If he turned, she could reach other parts of him.

But he might scare her off. An agonizing dilemma, but bold paid off where timid went wanting. He turned, bending one knee up discreetly to tent the covers. His heart was racing. She kissed his shoulder, and he sucked in his breath, held it while her lips brushed delicately down the line of his jaw. "That's...all you wanted?" he asked casually—except his voice was shaking.

"No-o-o," she admitted in a sassy purr he'd never heard before.

It brought an incredulous smile to his lips. No dream. This was happening. *At last...*

She rose up on one elbow to lean down over him in the dusk, and found his nose. Kissed the tip of it. "I want *you.*"

The miracle was not his to question. Not right now, anyway. Rafe shifted around to face her and cupped the side of her warm face, thumbed her moist, smiling mouth and laughed shakily as he kissed it. "Mrs. Montana, you've had me since the first time I walked into your kitchen."

AFTER THEY'D LOVED, she fell asleep to his kisses—tiny skimming kisses covering every inch of her sweat-slick, quivering skin. She stretched and purred, and exhaustion sucked her down into a smiling dream. She woke only when Rafe entered her for the second, or was it the third, time? They didn't keep count here in Paradise.

He covered her like a hunk of sheltering sky, kissing her eyelids, her smile. Filling her to trembling ecstasy, he remained ruthlessly, rigidly, motionless, pinning her hips to the bed as wave after wave rumbled up the shore, till she was shuddering with need, begging for release, fighting his control.

Then he moved one inch deeper and the universe shattered, and she could hold it inside no longer. "I love you!" she panted—cried it again as his mouth came down over hers—*I love you*—in a moan that he swallowed with a victorious growl. He moved faster, harder, deeper, and she wrapped herself around him and wept it. *"I love you!"*

WHEN HE HAD TAKEN IT ALL—everything she had to give— every emotion, every last arch and thrust and heart-slamming convulsion, Rafe lay atop her, his weight on his elbows, his big hands framing her face, heart speaking softly to heart. He kissed her eyelashes, the tip of her nose. She smiled blindly.

"Did you mean that?" he whispered above her. "Really mean it, or was that just—"

She reached up and put a hand over his mouth. Looked deep into his eyes. "Truly." Forever and ever.

Within and without her, she felt his satisfied sigh, and he nodded.

Do I get to hear it back? Though somehow she knew it already. What he'd shown her tonight, what he'd been showing her all along if her fear hadn't blinded her, was all about loving. He was a man of deeds more than words.

"Then I reckon that means I can renegotiate a few terms of this bargain," he said with rich satisfaction.

She arched her back and stretched—then smiled, as he gasped and his hands tightened on her. "Marriage in name only? I'm afraid we've already broken contract on that one," she said.

"I was talking about that five-year clause. *No* divorce, Mrs. Montana. Not in five years. Not in fifty."

She brushed a hand up through his thick hair, then cupped his cheek and said with solemn mockery, though the tears trembled on her lashes, "Oh-h-h, I think I can live with that."

PEGGY NICHOLSON

THEY STAYED THERE for two days, leaving their room
to walk hand in hand on the beach, speaking only to ⌐
and Mrs. Higgins by phone and to the smirking bellboys
who dropped the breakfast, lunch and supper trays off at
their door. Finally, on the third morning, while Dana was
scrubbing Rafe's back in the shower, she said, ''It's time
to go home. And why don't we pick up Zoe on our way?''

CHAPTER TWENTY-FOUR

ZOE GAVE BIRTH on the twelfth of December, three days
after she turned seventeen. For a first delivery via natural
childbirth, it went better than most. Dr. Cass Hancock ex-
pressed the opinion that horsewomen were tougher and
more flexible than their city sisters.

At the height of the pain, the mother did express some
rather heated opinions about the young father, who'd gotten
all the fun and none of the work...her know-it-all stepmother, whom she'd chosen to assist her in this birth-
ing...and her own shamefully neglectful father, who really
should have warned her about boys—or at least locked her
away till she turned twenty-one. Also lambasted was the
physicist Stephen Hawkings, who, now that Zoe thought
about it, didn't know piffle about the nature of time. *"Try
childbirth, Stevo, then come back and tell me!"*

But all was tearfully, laughingly, totally forgiven and forgotten when eight-pound Peter Raphael Montana finally
made his debut nine hours after the first real contraction.
Zoe shut up and stared with rapturous wonder at the squall-
ing baby they'd placed on her freckled stomach. She ran a
timid fingertip over his downy, dark skull, smiled
broadly—then burst into tears. Looked up at Dana and cried
piteously, "But what am I going to *do?*"

"Sleep on it, sweetie," Dana advised, and kissed her
cheek. "Sleep and then think."

IN SPITE OF ALL RAFE'S protests and tirades, Zoe demanded
that she be allowed to nurse her son on the first night of

his birth, and Dr. Hancock backed her up. She was nursing him again the next morning, when Sean tapped on her door and came in alone.

"Hi." He kissed her cheek, inhaling the scent that to him would always be Zoe. Then he stroked his son's head, sat staring at him spellbound for several minutes. Drawing a deep breath, he said, "Mind if I take a family portrait?" He'd left his Nikon and tripod out in the hall.

Her blue eyes glistened, though she smiled. "Family, Sean?"

"Whatever you decide, yeah. We were—are—a family." He hadn't meant to sound so fierce. He patted her hand, and when finally she nodded, he went for his gear, began setting up his tripod at the foot of the bed.

"Remember how we started all this?" she said softly behind him. "You were doing me a favor…just a bit of friendly, scientific inquiry into human sexuality. Helping me smooth out the rough spots before I went off to college. You can't take this so hard, Sean. It was just an accident."

"Penicillin was an accidental discovery, wasn't it?" he said gruffly, and wiped his nose.

"Yeah, it was. And maybe we've made something even better. But Sean Diego?—you've got to promise me one thing."

"I don't have to promise you anything, Red." He fixed the camera to the tripod, hooked up the shutter cord, wiped his eyes and turned.

"But would you?" she coaxed. "If you love me, would you promise?"

"You know I do." His eyes wouldn't stop. He dropped down on his knees beside her and buried his face against her arm. "You know how I feel!"

She ruffled a hand through his hair, back and forth, back and forth. "Then *promise* me you'll get over me. Get on with your life. I'd just die, Sean—really die—if I thought my stupid experiment messed you up. Don't you *dare* do that to me. You're my best friend in all the world.''

''I don't *want* to get over—'' She smacked the back of his head, and he shut up, groped for her hand and kissed it.

Zoe pulled gently away and ruffled his hair again. ''You know what Lisa Harding told me last week?'' she murmured after a while. ''She said she saw you and Karen Peabody sitting together in the library, laughing like a couple of hounds.''

''Lisa's a lying, nosy, run-off-at-the-mouth little—'' He winced as she smacked him again, then he lifted his head and snarled at her. ''Hey! Cut that out!''

Zoe's grin was wide and triumphant. ''So it's true!''

He shrugged sullenly. ''She likes me, I couldn't care less about her.''

''So try harder, best friend.'' Her eyes filled again. ''You *better* be happy, Sean Kershaw, or I'll never, ever forgive you.'' She jerked her chin at the camera. ''So are we going to do this or what?''

THEY'D COLLECTED their mail on their way into town, and now Dana sat reading it while Rafe paced up and down the waiting room. ''By God, Dana, if this falls apart now!''

She glanced up from her letter and smiled. Touched his hand, as he stomped past her. ''Then we'll love her anyway, and we'll work it out.''

He swore and paced on, and after a few minutes she folded her letter and tucked it back into its envelope with the colorful foreign stamps. ''Cat got word from the institute, and it's exactly as she predicted, given Zoe's grades. As long as we pay her way, they'd be delighted to take her through the summer.''

Catherine Danner, a fellow schoolteacher who'd worked

with Dana in the Peace Corps, was now a biology instructor on the tall ship *Peregrine,* an education and research vessel for the Winslow Institute of Oceanographic Studies. The ship carried a crew of some thirty college students and instructors on voyages around the world. For the next few months they'd be stationed in the Caribbean, while they did a census of humpback whales. Then they'd head on through the Panama Canal for the South Pacific.

Rafe had insisted that if Zoe was to relinquish her baby, she couldn't be near little Peter for the first year. And quite probably he was right. Send her to Cat, had been his wife's suggestion. Distract her with a lifetime adventure under the nurturing wing of a warm, wise woman before Zoe went on to Harvard in the fall.

"Great. Good. That's in place, anyway." Rafe stopped, thumbs hooked over his belt, frowning back at her. "Now all we have to do is sell her on the idea. You shouldn't have let her nurse."

"Not my choice to make, love." Setting her papers aside, Dana stood and went to her husband; she slid her hands around his lean waist to lock them behind his back.

Rafe resisted her embrace, then, glancing toward the doorway, which remained empty, gradually relaxed. He dropped his head, to rest his chin on top of her hair. Let out a long, deep sigh. "I know," he muttered. "But still…"

"Just remember, whatever happens, I love you. We love her. We'll work it out."

RAFE KNOCKED ON THE DOORJAMB, then pushed through the half-open door to find Zoe, sitting up in bed, cradling her son. She glanced up at him, and her smile faded. The baby let out a startled grunt as her arms tightened around it.

"How's he doing?" Rafe asked, hating that hunted expression in her eyes. He sat down beside her on the edge of the bed.

"He's doing everything perfectly. He's…he's perfection, Daddy. Look at his fingernails! And his eyes."

The baby blinked in Rafe's direction, then yawned hugely with an admirable tongue. Rafe laughed and held out his hands. Zoe bit her lip, then handed him over— giggled tearfully when her father cradled the baby on one forearm and offered a fingertip, which was immediately clutched in a tiny red fist. "Hi there, stranger." He didn't resemble Zoe at that age, though Sean insisted he did. Rafe thought possibly he looked like Sean; Dana had been reminded of the baby's namesake, Peter Kershaw. *You're your own self entire, hotshot, but you'll learn to love horses if I get any say in the matter.*

Peter Raphael yawned mightily again, looking like nothing so much as a wrinkled pink bullfrog, and fell fast asleep. They admired him in silence awhile, both of them scared to speak, till finally Rafe said, "So what do you figure?" He looked up in time to see the first teardrop fall, then too many more. *Damn it. Do I ever get to stop hurting the people I love?* "What do you want, sweetheart?" He reached with his free hand to wipe a tear off her freckly nose.

"I don't *know,* Daddy, I don't, I don't, I just—" She shrugged helplessly and the tears dripped faster. "He's *so* beautiful, but…"

That one little word gave him the courage to go on. "You used to trust me once upon a time," he reminded her. "I realize a lot has changed…but I'm still the man you used to listen to. Want to hear what I think?"

She sniffed, reached for some tissues on the bedside table, held them to her nose, then nodded over them. "Uh-huh."

He met her woeful eyes, then gazed down at her son,

nestled in his arm. "I think you did the right thing at the wrong time, baby. I know I did, and I've never regretted you—not for one single, solitary moment. But it was *hard,* sweetheart, so hard." Harder than he could ever make her understand, he feared. "I'd like life to be easier for you. Easier for this little guy, too."

"But it *hurts!*" She grabbed the whole box of tissues and hauled it into her lap.

"I know, I know, sweetheart, I know it does. But think, when was the last time it hurt this bad?"

She considered, balling a tissue in her fist. "You mean...yesterday?"

Nodding, he smoothed a palm over the baby's velvety, fragile skull. "Pain's about gone now, though, isn't it? And see what you've got to show for it."

"It's not the same!"

"No? Then what about when we wean the foals? You'd swear their hearts would break, theirs and their mamas, when we move them apart." His tenderhearted daughter practically lived in the weanlings' pen, consoling the frantic babies for the first few days. "But within a week or two, you know how it always is. The colts are off in their own herd, romping and kicking up their heels together, having the time of their lives. The mares are off grazing, not a worry in the world."

"You think it'd be that easy?" she whispered bitterly.

No lies between us. He shook his head. "I think it'd be the toughest thing you've done yet in your life. But I think it's the right thing."

"I don't *know!*" she wailed, then held out her arms. "Give him to me!" Hugging the baby to her breast, she covered his fuzzy head with kisses.

Rafe wished desperately that he could call Dana for help, but she'd steadfastly insisted she had to stay out of this.

Cheek pressed to her baby's head, Zoe stared off into

time and space. "If I…gave Peter to you and Dana—I'm *not* saying I will—but…if I did…what would you tell him about me?"

Rafe felt the first faint stirring of hope. "How 'bout the truth? That you're his mama, and you loved him more than life itself, but you were too young to do right by him. So you chose the very best parents for him you could find."

"And when I come home to visit?"

"He'll know you're his mama and that we're his grandparents, Rafe and Dana, who love you both."

She sniffed and knuckled her nose. "You really… think…it would work?"

"I know it would. Peter would have more folks who love him than most kids, that's all."

Letting out a long, shivering sigh, she looked down at her son. "I just don't *know*."

Rafe stroked her baby's hot cheek, her damp one, then rose. "Don't reckon deciding will get any easier the longer you wait." Zoe closed her eyes and bobbed her head in agreement.

"And there's one thing more you need to think about while you're deciding," he said finally, dreading it. "One thing you have to promise me if we do this, and that's that you won't go back on your decision, Zoe, later on. Once you've given him to us, Peter stays with us. I won't have you breaking Dana's heart someday or taking your son from the only home he's ever known. This is a once-and-for-all decision. Understand?"

"Yeah," she murmured bleakly. "Sure, I do. I understand."

There wasn't much more to say. *Time to pray.* "Want to think some more?"

Zoe shook her head emphatically. "No. I've decided."

THEIR PLANE WAS LATE touching down on the Caribbean island of Martinique. *Peregrine* was scheduled to sail at three o'clock, and Rafe feared they'd miss it.

"Maybe it's fate," said Zoe, half hopeful, half dismayed, while she sat tensely beside him in the back of the cab that raced past cane fields, then shantytowns, then stone city streets, toward the harbor at Fort de France. But for the first time in six grim weeks, her eyes were alive with interest—taking in the vivid tropical flowers, the lush jungly greens, the laughing people in every shade from ebony to coffee-with-cream. The cab came to a screeching halt at the base of the stone quay, and she let out an audible gasp. "That's *her?*"

At the end of the pier, two masts raked the sky above a long, low white hull. Rafe realized the ship's scale when he noticed the tiny figures up in the rigging. "I reckon so." Definitely the school ship—a steel brigantine of 135 feet. He'd been studying boats this winter for his own peace of mind.

"Hurry!" Zoe shoved her door open, grabbed her backpack and camera and slipped out—to stand jittering beside the cab.

Rafe smiled as he paid the driver. For six long weeks he'd worried that he might be doing the wrong thing. Wondered if he was breaking her heart for all the wrong reasons. Six weeks while he'd lived alone with his daughter at Suntop, making sure she'd recovered in body, if not entirely in spirit. While Dana had cared for young Peter at the Ribbon R with the full-time help of Mrs. Higgins. A cold and bitterly lonely and doubt-filled winter for them all. But now…maybe…

"Daddy, look!" Zoe pointed overhead. Far up in the impossibly blue tropic sky soared an enormous bird like none Rafe had ever seen. Pure white, trailing a long, graceful scissor tail. "And—*oh*—there! Could it be Mont Pelée?"

Far off beyond the old colonial town, their bases shrouded by clouds, reared razor-toothed mountains—one of them a volcano, he'd been told.

Hoisting her duffel bag to his shoulder, he walked beside her. She moved like the old Zoe he feared he'd lost forever—long, jaunty strides, at almost a run. She seemed as taken as he was by the fantastic colors, the strange smells of bananas and seaweed and flowers and fish and diesel fuel. *Peregrine*'s engine was already idling, he realized, hearing its muffled vibrations as they neared. People—kids of both sexes, and adults—bustled around its decks or bounded up the shrouds into the rigging.

"She's so big!" Zoe muttered. "I never thought..."

He dropped his free hand on her shoulder and bent his mouth to her ear. "Remember, sweetheart, I want you to give it a try for a month. Then, if for any reason you can't stomach it, call us from wherever you are, and we'll send you a ticket home. Or if you want, I'll come get you."

"Okay, Daddy," she agreed absently, her head tipped back as her gaze followed a young man moving along the foremast yard, some sixty feet above deck.

Glancing down at them, the sailor must have caught her eye, because he grinned and waved. Zoe smiled shyly and lifted a hand. Rafe narrowed his eyes at the kid in warning—and was blithely ignored. *That's one lesson she's already learned,* he told himself, crossing his fingers.

"Zoe?" called a woman hurrying down the gangplank. A honey-blonde matching Dana's description of her friend Catherine Danner. "Zoe Montana? You are? Thank heavens—we're about to sail! Come on board. And you must be Rafe—Dana's husband." Her handshake was firm as a man's; her green eyes, kind and ruefully laughing. "I meant to invite you aboard for a tour of the ship and to see Zoe's cabin, but as you can see, we're sailing, so..."

Two tanned and T-shirted young men bounded down to

the quay to untie the ends of the gangway, then stood wait-ing—and eyeing his daughter. *She's grown, she's grown,* Rafe reminded himself. "Well..." He shrugged. Maybe it was better this way. He hated goodbyes. "Then good to meet you, Cat, and take care of her for me. For us."

"You bet I will!" She lifted the strap of Zoe's duffel bag off his shoulder and onto her own. Gave him a warm, wide smile. "She'll be fine, Rafe, I promise you." Cat turned and walked up the gangway, then hopped down to the deck.

"Well, Zoe?"

And then she was in his arms, tears streaming, mouth tremulous and widely smiling. Hugging him so hard he thought she'd crack a rib.

"Bye, Daddy! Tell Dana thank you for—for everything. And...and kiss my baby for me?"

"Every night!" he promised huskily, his throat aching. "And remember—"

"Hey, Montana, come aboard!" bellowed a bearded man of Rafe's own age, hooking a thumb toward the deck.

"G'bye!" One last kiss on his cheek, and she was run-ning lightly up the gangplank. Hands were casting off the dock lines, then jumping aboard. Rafe watched the gap be-tween ship and shore gradually widen from one he could have leaped...to one he couldn't. Watching Zoe's pale, freckled face...her wide, tearful, shining blue eyes... growing smaller, ever smaller, below her frantic wave—till she was a tiny, gawky, frantically waving figure topped with a patch of fire-engine red.

In the outer harbor, a quarter-mile out, the boat seemed to pause. To raise sails, Rafe realized. Great wings of white, rising and opening one after another from the stern toward the bow. Then the two yards on the foremast rising—clouds of billowing white spreading slowly to the warm trade-winds. Wings to carry her off to sea, right over the edge of the curving world. He stared, almost grudging to blink, as the ship gathered way and moved off. Soaring on and on and on…

"Fly away, Zoe," he whispered. "Fly…" He blinked once more—and she was gone.

He stood for a moment more, squinting against the hard, hard tropic blue—then let out a long, deep breath and turned for shore.

Back toward the plane that would take him home. To a woman who waited. A family that needed him. *Some fly free, some fly home to the nest.* And that was another kind of freedom.

A smile crossed Rafe's face. His steps lengthened, then lengthened again—till he was as close to running as a grown man could justify.

Little Girl Lost

MARISA CARROLL

CHAPTER ONE

THE CALENDAR SAID it was November, but the scudding gray clouds and lowering sky made it seem as though winter had arrived in southern Ohio. The maples and slippery elms had long ago lost their leaves. The mottled trunks of the sycamores blended into the white and gray of the storm clouds. Only the oaks held stubbornly to their tattered brown leaves, the way she had been holding stubbornly to her grief.

No, not stubbornly, Faith Carson told herself as she trudged along the path that skirted a small lake and ended at a tiny, hidden roadside park bordering her farm. "Surely six months isn't too long to mourn a dead husband?"

She wasn't talking to herself, not really. She'd addressed the question to her two-year-old Shetland sheepdog, Addy, trotting at her heels. She'd found Addy at the local animal shelter a few weeks after she'd moved into the echoing old farmhouse that Mark had inherited from his grandparents, and which, until three weeks after his death, Faith had never set foot in. Addy was the only friend Faith had at the moment. The little dog pricked her ears at the question and gave a yip of sympathetic agreement.

Six months. Not nearly long enough when that sorrow was coupled with the aching loss of a child barely conceived. Surely six months was only a beginning. Faith blinked hard to hold back tears as icy raindrops touched her cheeks. She had nothing left in her but a sense of bereavement so deep and unrelenting she sometimes felt as though she had died, too, on that mountain road in Mexico.

They had been vacationing, their first real vacation since their marriage, looking for the remote area where thousands of monarch butterflies came to spend the winter. Mark was a computer programmer whose passion was butterflies. It was a trip he had wanted to take for as long as she had known him. But a washed-out section of road and a blown tire had caused their rented Jeep to roll over.

Somehow, for some reason, her heart had gone on beating when Mark's had stopped as she held him in her arms and their baby's life drained away between her legs. A loss like that scarred the heart so much the healing might take six years, or sixty—or never come.

She walked out of the trees just behind the rustic two-sided building that, along with a pair of old-fashioned outhouses and a rusty jungle gym, were the park's only amenities. An expensive, sporty blue car was parked in the graveled lot at the edge of the small body of water the county had named Sylvan Lake, but that was still known to the locals of Bartonsville, Ohio, as Carson's Pond. A young couple, the boy's arms wrapped around the girl, her head resting on his shoulder, sat on one of the picnic tables near the blackened fieldstone fireplace that took up the entire north wall of the building. Faith halted, half-hidden by a huge pine whose low branches brushed the ground, and acted as a windbreak on one side of the small picnic shelter.

She hadn't expected anyone to be in the park on a day like this, certainly not a pair of amorous teenagers. She took a quick step back, deeper into the shadow of the pine. They hadn't seen her. She could melt back into the woods, retrace her steps through the frosty grass and be home before the raindrops that were now falling steadily changed to sleet. Addy growled low in her throat.

"Shh." Faith knelt down to fasten the leash she carried in her pocket to the dog's collar before Addy could begin barking in earnest. She scooped the small dog into her arms and prepared to depart. The teenagers were absorbed in each other and didn't look in her direction, but some trick of sound brought their words to her ears.

"Beth, we can't stay here. There must be a town close by. Maybe it's big enough for a hospital."

"If we go to a hospital they'll call your parents." The girl cried out, a moan of pain and fear. These weren't just two moonstruck teenagers making out. Something far more serious than that was going on. Addy whined nervously and squirmed in Faith's arms. The boy turned his head and stared directly into her eyes.

"Help us," he said, his face as gray-white as the

clouds and the sycamore trees. He was blond, broad-shouldered, square-jawed, seventeen or eighteen at most. A good-looking kid, or would be if he weren't half-scared to death. "My girlfriend's having a baby. And I don't know what to do."

Faith couldn't believe her ears, didn't want to. He couldn't have said what she thought she had heard.

"Please," he said, raising his voice so there could be no doubt as he repeated the words. "She's having a baby. I don't know what to do."

Instinctively Faith shook her head. "I don't, either," she murmured, but he couldn't hear her above the moaning of the wind in the trees. And she did know what to do. That was one of the things that made her own loss so hard to bear. She was a nurse. She had the skill and knowledge to help save lives. Once, she had even delivered a baby herself. But that had been five years ago in the hospital emergency room where she'd worked while Mark finished up his graduate studies. She had been young and fearless, then. Now she was not. She hadn't even set foot in a hospital since three days after her miscarriage.

The girl shifted her position, and Faith took a better look at her, her heart sinking. Her arms were wrapped around her swollen middle, which strained against the fabric of her pale-green sweater. She wasn't wearing a coat and shivered in the cold air. She was very, very pregnant. Her face was white, her eyes dark with fear. "I—I hurt so badly. I can't walk."

Feminine instinct and medical training took over,

marching Faith forward on stiff legs. She tied Addy to a sapling at the corner of the shelter and hushed her with a stern warning. The little dog dropped to her belly on the cold ground whimpering with anxiety, sensing the tension in the humans around her, but obedient to Faith's command.

Faith looked from one terrified young face to the other. "She needs to be taken to the hospital." She took off her all-weather coat and draped it around the shivering girl's shoulders. She was wearing the sweatshirt Mark had given her for Christmas the year before, a heavy black one covered front and back with butterflies so she would be warm enough without her coat.

"No!" The girl panted, then bit her lip and groaned, a low, guttural sound. The sound of a woman who was almost ready to give birth. Faith's heart hammered. This couldn't be happening. Not today of all days. The day her own child should have been born.

"Your baby is coming, and it shouldn't be born out here in the cold. I'll give you directions to the hospital in Bartonsville. When you get there the nurses can notify your families—"

Silvery strands of gossamer-fine hair danced in the cold air as the girl shook her head. "I don't have a family," she said defiantly. "Only my brother in Texas."

"What about you?"

"I—I don't have any family, either," he said miserably.

He was lying, but before Faith could call him on it another contraction rippled across the girl's belly. Less than two minutes had passed since the last one. She had to move quickly or the situation would get out of hand. "I'm Faith Carson. I live just down the road at the bottom of the next hill. What's your name, honey?"

"Beth."

"And you are?"

"Jamie." No surnames. Faith let the omission pass. For the moment there were more pressing matters.

"You're the baby's father?"

He nodded, his Adam's apple working up and down in his throat. "Is Beth going to be okay?"

"She needs expert care. You know that, don't you?"

"We were looking for a hospital. We got lost. I'm—I'm not used to driving in the country. The road's go every which way."

"It's okay. You're only a few miles from a good hospital. I'll give you directions, but you must leave now. Your baby's going to be born very soon if I don't miss my guess."

"How do you know it's going to be soon?" Beth was gasping for breath, clutching at Jamie's arm with both hands. He stood beside the table, ramrod straight, breathing almost as hard and fast as the mother-to-be.

Faith sighed. "I'm a nurse," she said. "I know."

"First babies take a long time, I've heard. This—this only started about an hour ago."

"Has your water broken?"

For a moment Beth looked puzzled, then nodded. "Yes," she said. "I didn't know what it was at first, then I remembered from health class. It was this morning. Then the cramps started." She began to sob. "I hurt so bad. I just want to get this thing out of me." The sobs turned to a groan, and she dropped her hands to the tabletop, lifting herself into a crouch, straining against the contraction.

"Don't push," Faith ordered automatically. "Try to breathe through the contraction. Like this." She made an O with her mouth and panted.

Beth tried, but she was too upset and in too much pain for the exercise to do any good. She cried out and her knees buckled.

Jamie had gone from looking scared to terrified. "Help us. I don't know what to do. The doctor at the clinic in…back home…told us the baby probably wasn't due for another three weeks."

"Have you had regular prenatal care?" Faith asked.

"I—I just went twice. I had a test where they rub a wand over your stomach—"

"A sonogram," Faith supplied.

"Yes. My baby's a girl. But they wanted—" Beth broke off what she was about to say. Faith guessed it was that the clinic doctor wanted to notify her family. She was a little thing, and if she wore baggy clothes, like the sweater she had on now, she probably had been able to hide her pregnancy. "If we go to the hospital they'll take my baby away." Beth's eyes sought Faith's. They were blue Faith noted, as blue as a country sky on a cloudless June day.

"No they won't. Not unless you want to give the baby up."

"I want my baby." Beth bit down hard on her lower lip as another contraction began.

"Beth," Jamie said, his tone edged with desperation. "We've gone over this and over this. We don't have any money or jobs or a place to live. How can we take care of a baby?"

"Other girls have. I can, too. You don't have to marry me. You know that, Jamie. Your parents don't want you to, anyway."

"I—I just don't know how we'll manage—" He broke off as she cried out again. "Do something," he pleaded to Faith.

"Do you have a cell phone?" she asked.

Jamie wouldn't quite meet her eyes. "We lost it."

So much for the easy way out.

Faith took one more look at the car. It was a two-seater. Warmer than the open shelter, certainly, and out of the wind, but with little room to maneuver. If there was a problem with the birth she would be at an even greater disadvantage shoehorned inside it than she was now. Beth moaned again, leaning against her young lover, straining.

"Don't push," Faith said sharply. Beth's labor was progressing rapidly. Even if she left Addy behind and they all squeezed into the car, the baby's arrival would probably occur before they reached the hospital. "We're going to have to deliver the baby here," she said with false calm.

Beth started to cry harder. "I think so, too."

Faith reached out and touched her fingertips to Beth's cold cheek. She couldn't think about her own grief, couldn't remember that she should be laboring in the same way as this girl, bringing the baby she had longed for so desperately into the world.

"It's going to be okay." She swallowed against the familiar lump of sorrow in her throat, made her voice as soothing as she could manage. "I'm going to deliver your baby and Jamie's going to help."

"Me?" He swallowed audibly. "I... What can I do?"

"Do you have any blankets in the car? Towels?"

"We have sleeping bags. And I have a couple of clean sweatshirts. Will they do?"

"Yes. We can wrap the baby in them. How about a pair of scissors?"

The last of the color drained out of Jamie's face as he made the connection. He shook his head. "No scissors."

"Not even cuticle scissors? A penknife, then." Faith held on to her composure with both hands. It wouldn't do to let these two terrified kids see that she was almost as afraid as they were.

"I have a penknife." Jamie pulled a small one out of his pocket. "It's sharp."

"Good. That will do."

She'd been burning trash earlier that morning so

she had matches in her pocket. She could sterilize the blade to cut the umbilical cord. But she would need something to clear the baby's nose and mouth, and something to tie off the cord. "Do you have any cotton swabs? Dental floss?"

"In my makeup case," Beth groaned. "I have floss and Q-Tips. Will the baby be all right being born outside like this? It's so cold." She was shivering, but not entirely from the cold. Her legs were shaking hard, another sure sign she was far along in her labor.

"Everything will be fine," Faith assured her, but she had no such assurance for herself. "Give me the knife." She held out her hand. "I'll deal with Beth's clothes while you get the things we talked about."

Jamie took off for the car at a run. Faith looked at the shivering girl on the wooden picnic table. It looked hard and uncomfortable but the only alternative was the stone floor. Thankfully Beth was wearing thin leggings and not jeans. If the penknife was sharp enough Faith thought she could split the crotch and panties and at least protect the girl's legs and feet from more exposure to the cold.

She told Beth her plan and the girl nodded, lifting her hips off the table. Faith said a little prayer of thanks that Jamie's knife was indeed sharp. The baby had not yet crowned but Faith was certain that one more contraction would bring the top of its head into view. She couldn't risk examining Beth anymore closely for fear of infection later; she had no way to sterilize her hands. Washing them in the icy water of the old-fashioned pump outside the shelter house would have to do. But she couldn't leave the laboring girl exposed on the table. She would have to wait on Jamie's return to do even that much.

"Try to relax," she said.

"Are you really a nurse?" Beth was half sitting, half reclining against Faith's arm. But her weight was slight.

"Yes."

"And you've delivered babies before?"

"Yes," Faith assured her. That it was long ago and far away needn't be said.

"You're wearing a wedding ring. Do you have children?"

"No. I'm a widow." The words came out tight and hard. There was no way she could stop them.

"I'm sorry for your loss," Beth said politely.

"So am I."

"I have to push again." The sounds Beth made deep in her throat were no longer quite human.

"Jamie, hurry!" Faith called over the rising wind and the sharp tattoo of sleet on the metal roof. Tiny icicles were already forming along the eaves, and the pine tree's needles had begun to chime slightly whenever the wind set the branches swaying. Addy turned her back to the wind and dropped her head on her paws.

Jamie started the car and left it idling. He ran up the slope to the shelter, slipping a little on the icy crust forming on the brown grass. His arms were full of two down sleeping bags, a couple of red sweatshirts and a small plastic case, pink and sparkling—the kind of case teenage girls used to keep their treasures safe, emphasizing again how young they both were.

"Good thinking to start the car," Faith praised him. "We'll move Beth and the baby inside as soon as we can." The baby was crowning and there was only time to lift Beth enough to slide one of the sleeping bags beneath her and to wrap the other around her as best they could. Faith murmured encouragement, forcing her breathing into a normal pattern, steeling herself not to show any of her own fear and uncertainty.

Another contraction, another long unearthly moan, and the head emerged. No one saw but Faith. Beth was staring fixedly at the butterflies on Faith's sweatshirt, and Jamie was watching Faith, too, not wanting to look between his girlfriend's legs.

Faith's cracked and bruised heart began bleeding anew as she cradled the baby's head in her hands. *Oh, God, why did you have to ask this of me today of all days?*

Aloud she said only, "Okay, honey. You're doing fine. Just rest now, wait for the next contraction."

Beth groaned. "When will it be over? It hurts too much. I can't stand it any longer."

"Yes, you can," Faith said soothingly. "This will do it. Her shoulders will come out and the rest of her body will just slide along. I promise. Just push slowly and steadily so you don't tear. You can do it, come on."

"Please make it—" The word ended in a long drawn out moan as the baby's shoulders came free and the rest of her small body slipped into Faith's hands.

"You have a daughter," Faith said. *Mark had wanted their first child to be a girl.*

"The baby's not breathing," Jamie whispered.

At the words, Beth—who'd dropped her head against his shoulder—jerked upright. "She's not breathing. She's all blue. What's wrong?"

"Nothing's wrong. She's cold, that's all." Faith said another silent prayer that she was speaking the truth. She wiped the baby's face and head with one of the clean sweatshirts, then bundled her into a second, careful not to entangle the umbilical cord. She took a cotton swab and cleaned out her mouth and nostrils as gently, but as thoroughly as she could. It wasn't ideal, she really needed a suction bulb, but it would have to do. She tapped her middle fingernail against the soles of the infant's feet, then a second time a little harder. The baby's eyes popped open and she looked directly at Faith. She blinked once, then opened her mouth, took a deep breath and began to wail. The cry was weak and thready but the most beautiful sound Faith had ever heard.

"Look. She's turning pink," Beth murmured. "May I hold her?"

"Of course you can."

Faith placed the baby in her mother's arms, pulling the edges of the sleeping bag more closely around them both.

"She's awfully tiny." Jamie's voice cracked as he spoke.

"She's perfect," Beth murmured. "Just perfect."

Faith handed the matches to Jamie, who couldn't seem to take his eyes off his daughter. "Here, sterilize the knife blade with these. The afterbirth will be coming soon and we'll need to get the cord cut and tied. Do you want to do it?"

He shook his head. "You do it." His expression was suddenly grim.

Faith didn't press the matter. Beth was already beginning to breathe heavily with the beginning of another contraction. "This won't be as bad," Faith promised. "It's the afterbirth, the placenta."

Beth shook her head, smiling down at the tiny infant in her arms. "It's okay. I can handle it. Now that she's here, it's worth it. Oh, Jamie," she whispered, looking up at the boy with love shining from her sky blue eyes. "She's beautiful, isn't she?"

Jamie didn't smile back. He looked as if the entire weight of the world had shifted onto his shoulders. "She's so tiny. How will we take care of her?"

"We'll manage," Beth declared.

Jamie didn't speak again.

Faith delivered the placenta a few minutes later. It appeared to be intact and there was little bleeding. She recited a silent prayer of thanks. With any luck she would have her charges safely in the hands of the competent staff at Bartonsville Medical Center in a very short while.

She bundled the afterbirth into the oldest looking

of the sweatshirts Jamie had brought from the car. ''We should take this along to the hospital for the doctor to check. You do realize that Beth and the baby need to be seen by a doctor? Your daughter is very tiny,'' she said quietly, so that only Jamie could hear. ''She seems to be healthy but she might have some difficulty with her breathing, or regulating her temperature. Newborns sometimes do. She should be where she can be monitored.''

''Problems breathing?'' His nostrils flared and he swallowed hard. ''Like needing oxygen and everything?''

Beth had overheard. ''No. She's fine. We don't need to go to the hospital.''

''Even if she is okay, we don't have any bottles or milk or diapers—''

''We can get them. And I'll nurse her,'' Beth said defiantly.

''You don't even know if you can. What if she gets too hungry? Or something like Mrs. Carson just said happens? We wouldn't know what to do.''

''We'll learn.''

''I've never even held a baby. She's so tiny.'' There was real panic in his voice. ''We only have about sixty dollars left.''

''It will have to do,'' Beth said, her eyes glued to the baby.

''That's barely enough for gas. No way can we stretch it to buy food and formula and diapers. I don't even know what else we need. I can't use the credit card—'' He broke off realizing that he'd probably

said too much. He glanced at Faith and his eyes were
desperate, the reality of responsibility overwhelming
any joy he felt at his child's birth. "Maybe it would
be better if we—"

"No!" Beth's refusal cut off what he meant to
say.

Faith interrupted. "We can work everything out
when Beth and the baby are safe at the medical center." The ice storm had hit in earnest while Faith had
been preoccupied with the baby's birth. Already a
silvery sheet of ice covered everything in sight. It
was going to be tricky walking home for her car, but
there was no way she and Addy could fit into the
sports car for the ride to the hospital.

Beth looked up from the baby to the car in the
parking lot. "I don't know if I can carry her that
far," she said. "I feel all wobbly."

"Give the baby to Mrs. Carson. I'll carry you."

"Please be careful with her, Jamie. If you should
slip on the ice..." Faith let her voice trail off.

"I'll be careful," he promised. His face was chalk
white. Once more he refused to meet her eyes.

She ought to press him for some answers now that
the immediate danger to mother and child was past.
Where had they come from? Where were they going?
The infant cried out again, and it sounded weaker
than before. She had waited this long to ask those
questions, surely a few minutes more wouldn't make
any difference. When Beth and the baby were safely
in the small, but up-to-date maternity ward of the
hospital there would be time for answers.

Beth had eyes only for the baby held tightly against her breast. Faith brushed her hand softly against the infant's cheek. Her baby's skin would have been this soft and rosy if she'd lived. There was dried blood under her fingernails just as there had been that awful day six months before. She dropped her hand quickly.

"It's time to go."

Beth's blue eyes darkened to the color of a twilight sky. "Couldn't we stay with you? You must live nearby. Just for a few hours..."

Faith shook her head. She couldn't have a baby in her house. Not today. "We might get trapped there by the storm. There's a bad one coming." She gestured to the icy scene beyond them. "It's already here. I promise you I'll come to the hospital as soon as I can get back to my home and get my car. There's no room in yours."

"We'd better get going," Jamie said. "I'm going to carry you, and Faith will bring the baby."

Beth's mouth tightened but she didn't protest again. "Okay." She lifted the small bundle toward Faith as though offering her the most precious gift in the world.

Faith swallowed hard again, but this time against the tears she could not let fall. How wonderful the fragile little body felt cradled against her breast. A tiny hand worked its way out of the folds of the sweatshirt and clamped onto Faith's cold finger. The baby was a fighter, stronger than she looked. She could feel the baby nuzzling, searching for nourishment. Warmth pooled in her womb and her heart, melting a bit of the ice that sealed her emotions away.

Jamie scooped Beth into his arms, sleeping bags and all, and started down the slope at a quick pace. Faith looked down at the baby she held. ''I wish you were my baby,'' she whispered very, very softly. ''I would love you and care for you as best I could if you were.''

But she was not. Faith's baby was dead. Her husband was dead and she was alone.

That was the reality of her life.

Addy began bouncing up and down, straining at her leash, barking in short, frantic yips. Shelties were herd dogs, bred for centuries to protect their flocks. And when they didn't have sheep to watch over they transferred those instincts to their human companions. She did not want to be left behind by her mistress, and she wasn't shy about letting Faith know. ''Sh, Addy. It's okay. I'm not leaving you. I'm just taking the baby to the car. Then we'll take the shortcut home through the woods.''

Faith turned her back on the indignant dog and stepped out from under the shelter into the stinging sleet just in time to watch Jamie open the driver's door and look back at her over the roof of the car. ''We can't take her with us, Mrs. Carson. Not all the way to Texas. I know you'll take good care of her. Keep her for us. We'll be back. I—'' His voice broke. ''I promise.''

What happened next would stay in Faith's memory

until the day she died. The sleek blue car sprayed ice
and gravel from its back wheels as Jamie roared out
of the parking lot and fishtailed down the steep, narrow drive toward the county road that led to the state
highway. For a split second Faith saw Beth's face,
her hands pressed against the window as if she were
trying to escape, her mouth open in a soundless
scream of anguish and protest.

"Don't go! Don't leave the baby."

But they were already gone.

Faith was alone in the storm.

But not really alone.

For she held in her arms the one thing she
wanted most.

CHAPTER TWO

Two and a half years later.

HUGH DAMON RESTED his forearms on the steering wheel of his much traveled Blazer and looked out on the tapestry of farm fields that stretched toward the low hills on the horizon. In the shallow valley below him a century-old brick house sat squarely in the middle of a grove of massive oaks and maples.

Painted Lady Butterfly Farm and Guest Lodging, stated a tasteful white-and-gold-lettered sign on the grass verge of the sleepy county highway he'd been driving since he'd left Cincinnati an hour ago. He hadn't expected his search to bring him this far east, but it had.

The house itself was a monstrosity of Victorian overindulgence that made the engineer in him cringe. Elaborate gingerbread gables and bay windows abounded. There was even a widow's walk on the roof. But the native red brick had mellowed with the years, allowing the building to blend into its surroundings, and the ornate trim was painted a pale cream instead of white, softening the effect still more.

On the other hand the red, clapboard barn behind the house was a masterpiece of function and design. Set on a native stone base, it was large and imposing, with a high-pitched slate roof and the same cream paint on the doors and windows. A working barn from the looks of it. Through the open double doors Hugh could see a big green tractor and what looked like an even bigger combine, dwarfing a minivan. Farmers didn't build barns like that anymore. They couldn't afford to, and it was to the owner's credit that she spent the necessary money for its upkeep.

Beyond the barn were fields of soybeans and corn, the beans barely higher than the lush green carpet of lawn that abutted them, and the corn knee-high only to a small child at this stage of growth. There was also a pond complete with a small dock and an angled telephone pole with a long rope attached, just perfect for swinging out over the water on a hot summer's day.

A large fenced-in area several acres in size directly behind the big house wasn't planted in any cash crop, as far as Hugh could tell, but seemed to be left as meadow. Spindly, dried pods of milkweed provided sentinel posts for red-winged blackbirds. Red, pink and yellow flowers bloomed among the waving grasses. At the very edge of what he now recognized as a naturalized garden, there was a greenhouse-type building.

The butterfly house he'd read about on the Internet, he supposed. Along with the three small, fifties-era tourist cabins to his left, it gave Painted Lady Farm and Guest Lodging its claim to fame.

Butterflies.

Beautiful, ethereal, innocent. And in many cultures said to represent the souls of lost children.

The stuff of his sister's nightmares.

They were what had drawn him to this place.

Did it hold the answers he sought? Or was it just another dead end?

He'd find out soon enough. He turned his attention to the vintage cabins, one of which, the largest, he'd already reserved. They were painted the same cream color that highlighted the house and barn, but were accented in pine-green with window boxes filled with red geraniums, just coming into bloom. Round-backed, metal lawn chairs flanked the front doors inviting weary travelers to sit a spell and watch the sun set behind the hills.

The cabins, a reminder of times when travel cross-country was an adventure, not a blur of fast-food restaurants and strip malls glimpsed from a super-highway, were as carefully preserved and maintained as the barn and house. It was just good business to keep the place in top-notch shape, Hugh reminded himself. It was no indication whatsoever that the owner was a good and caring person who loved the land and its buildings. None at all.

A small sign, hanging beneath the larger one, proclaimed the farm and cottages the property of one Faith Carson and directed guests to the butterfly

house for check-in, or to the back door of the main
house if the butterflies weren't in season. But butterflies were very obviously in season this late May
afternoon. A big yellow school bus was parked in
the gravel lot beside the barn. Small children raced
around the yard, some brandishing what appeared to
be large, colorful foam butterflies attached to sticks,
the boys attempting to fight duels, the girls swirling
around like ballerinas. It seemed he had arrived in
the midst of an elementary school outing to see the
butterflies that Faith Carson raised.

Now was probably not the best time to announce
his arrival. He wanted to meet the object of his search
alone. If he had to wait until nightfall to gain that
advantage he would.

He put the Blazer in gear and drove up the gentle
rise to the top of the hill. An old but well-maintained
cemetery occupied the crest, weathered marble
stones warming in the sunshine. The lettering on
most of the markers was so faded he couldn't read
them from the road except for the newest one. The
name engraved on the granite stone was Mark Carson
and the date of death, just days short of three years
before. It was the grave of Faith Carson's husband.

Hugh pulled the Blazer onto the grass and opened
the door. The air was humid, filled with the scents
of newly turned earth and the sound of birds. A gi-
gantic red pine shaded the oldest of the stones. As
he walked, he realized many of the graves belonged
to Carsons, some predating the Civil War if he was
reading the faded numerals correctly. Probably all

related to the dead man whose headstone drew him closer almost against his will. Hugh had no idea what it was like to have roots this deep.

He'd left home at seventeen. And after their mother had died in a car accident five years ago he'd had no one but his half sister, Beth, in his life. To his eternal regret he hadn't returned to Texas to take care of her then. Instead he'd sent her off to the father she'd barely known in Boston. She'd been miserable and lonely, and like many miserable, lonely teenage girls she'd gotten pregnant. And run away. The flight had ended in a terrible accident that had killed her boyfriend and robbed Beth of her memory and almost her life.

And had sent him in search of a child she didn't remember.

A newborn baby that had disappeared without a trace.

Hugh hunkered down on the balls of his feet and peered more closely at the lettering on the stone.

Mark Carson
Beloved Husband of Faith
and
Father of Caitlin

The question that had driven him to this place wasn't whether the dead man was the father of Faith Carson's two-and-a-half-year-old daughter. But whether Faith Carson was actually her mother.

Or was the child she called hers, really his sister's baby?

That was what he'd come to Painted Lady Farm to find out.

Faith waved the Bartonsville Elementary School bus out of the yard. Having 35 eight-year-olds underfoot for an hour and a half was exhausting. She wondered how teachers could do it all day, every day. Still, she enjoyed having the school groups come to the butterfly house. It was the kind of thing Mark would have loved to see happen.

She turned back to the T-shaped glass-and-metal building that had been specially designed by an entomologist friend of her late husband. The top portion of the T was a greenhouse, open-sided now that the weather was warm. It contained a small gift shop where she sold butterfly and hummingbird feeders and figurines along with gardening books and paraphernalia. It also contained tables of colorful bedding plants and shrubs that especially appealed to butterflies and hummingbirds, along with vegetable plants and kitchen herbs.

The butterflies themselves were housed in the back half of the building in a gardenlike setting that Faith had spent the entire winter after Caitlin's birth creating on paper, and the summer after bringing to reality with hours and hours of backbreaking work.

It had taken a sizable portion of Mark's life insurance settlement to build the greenhouse and butterfly habitat. Perhaps too much, but it had been for the best that part of her comfortable nest egg had been spent, since that had forced her back into working two days a week at the Bartonsville Medical Center. And being back at work had forced her back into society, which was important for Caitlin if not for herself.

At first she had avoided anything to do with the small farming community where members of her husband's family had lived for four generations before his grandparents had moved to Cincinnati after the end of World War II. Now she was the only Carson who shopped along Main Street, belonged to the garden club and attended the church where one of the stained-glass windows had been dedicated in the family name, but she felt at home. She had put down roots. No more crisscrossing the country as Mark moved from one troubleshooting systems project to the next for the huge software conglomerate he'd worked for. Next year she'd enroll Caitlin in Sing, Giggle and Grin Preschool two mornings a week. Her daughter was bright and quick for her age. A slender, elfin-faced bundle of energy with silver-gilt hair and her own green-gold eyes.

The center of her universe appeared at the back door of the house. "Hi, Momma," Caitlin called in her piping, toddler's voice.

"Hi, Kitty Cat," Faith called back, lifting her hand to shade her eyes from the bright spring sun. On the western horizon storm clouds had begun to form, not an unusual occurrence for this time of year, but it wouldn't hurt to check the weather forecast when she got back into the house. It was tornado season after all. But for now the spring afternoon was perfect, warm and only a little humid.

"I awake," Caitlin announced unnecessarily.

"I can see you are."

"She did take a nice nap." Faith's older sister, Peg, appeared behind Caitlin and hooked her finger inside the collar of the child's pink Winnie the Pooh embroidered sweatshirt to keep her from tumbling headfirst down the porch steps. "And she went potty like a big girl, too."

"You did?" Faith clapped her hands, making her tone excited and incredulous.

Caitlin nodded vigorously. "Big girl."

"You are a big girl. Mommy's so proud of you." Faith opened the wrought-iron gate that separated the old herb garden she was slowly restoring and Caitlin's play area on the other side of the brick walkway, from the rest of the yard.

Faith gathered the little girl into her arms and hugged her tight. Caitlin was the most precious thing on earth to her. Her whole life revolved around her daughter. Having her to love was nothing short of a miracle.

Caitlin hugged her back then wriggled to be free. "Cookie," she said emphatically. "I want a cookie."

"I could go for a cookie myself. How about you, Aunt Peg?"

Peg glanced at her watch. "No cookies for me. I'm dieting as usual." Peg was two inches taller than

Faith and full-figured. She had their mother's dark-brown eyes and rich auburn hair. She was five years older than Faith's thirty-one, and had dropped out of college to raise her younger sister when their mother had died of kidney failure when Faith was fifteen. Their quiet, hardworking father had died just a few years later—of a broken heart, Faith often thought.

A year and a half earlier Peg and her two boys had moved to Ohio from upstate New York to be closer to Faith and Caitlin. At Christmas she'd married Steve Baden, who farmed Faith's acreage for her, and whose large and close-knit family had taken all three of them under their wing.

Peg was also the only other person who knew that Caitlin was not Faith's biological daughter.

They walked back into the kitchen, and Faith went to the cookie jar.

"Two cookies," Caitlin demanded.

"I think I'm raising a Cookie Monster here," Faith lamented, handing over the demanded treats.

"Are you kidding? She's an angel compared to Jack and Guy at that age." Peg rolled her eyes. Her boys were seven and nine and every bit as ornery as their mother proclaimed them to be.

Peg looked at her watch again. "I'd better be going. Steve's cutting alfalfa at his uncle's place, and I should be home when the boys get off the school bus, or they'll trash the kitchen making snacks."

"I really appreciate your watching Caitlin this afternoon."

"I love watching my adorable niece." Peg had

never once let slip by word or action that Caitlin wasn't Faith's daughter. Despite her profound misgivings over Faith's actions, she'd accepted Caitlin completely. "What's on your agenda for the rest of the afternoon?"

"Caitlin and I are going to gather up the feeding dishes in the butterfly house to wash them for tomorrow, and then we're going to walk up the lane to make sure the big cottage is ready for our new guest. He's supposed to be checking in this evening."

Peg's eyebrows went up a fraction. "Is he by himself?"

"I haven't the slightest idea. Why do you ask?" But Faith thought she already knew the answer to that question. Peg worried about her.

"Just curious. You're so isolated out here."

"I'm not isolated. You spend too much time watching those women-in-jeopardy movies on the Lifetime channel. I'm as safe here as you are a mile down the road."

"I have a husband. You're alone."

"But not lonely," Faith said, firmly, if not altogether truthfully. She had loved Mark, and with that love she had given him faith and trust and honesty. She couldn't envision a relationship that didn't contain all those elements, and she could never be honest with a man again, not completely. She had a secret to keep. Now that Peg was married again it added another layer to Faith's burden. Because of what she had done two and a half years ago, Peg could never be totally honest with her new husband—for her sister's sake.

"Okay, I know when to change the subject."

Faith shook off her heavy thoughts. "And if my guest puts one foot wrong I have a vicious watchdog to protect me don't I, Addy?" At the mention of her name, the sheltie pricked up her ears and wagged her tail. She'd been pouting a little all afternoon because Faith had made her stay in the house while the schoolchildren were visiting. Not all of them appreciated being herded around the yard by a wet nose.

"Watchdog, my fanny. She'd let the devil himself inside if he called her a pretty girl," Peg snorted. "Well, I'm off. I need to run into the IGA and pick up some bread and milk to feed the horde. Anything you need I can drop off on my way back out of town?"

"Not at the moment, but thanks for asking."

"Bye-bye." Caitlin, her mouth still full of cookie, hugged Peg's plump thigh.

"Bye, sweetie. See you Friday."

Caitlin ran to the breakfast nook's bay window and watched Peg get in her pickup and drive off. "Watch *Blue's Clues* now," she announced as the sound of the rough-running engine faded away.

"I have a better idea. Want to go see the butterflies?"

"Yes." Caitlin clapped her hands and nodded so hard one of the little butterfly-shaped clips in her hair came loose and the silken strands floated around her face. Faith sold the clips in the gift shop in a myriad of sparkling colors. They were very popular with the little girls who visited. "See 'flies."

Faith smoothed Caitlin's hair back from her face and secured it with the retrieved clip. "Come on, then. We'll go before any more customers drive up the lane. We'll have them all to ourselves." She carried Caitlin outside and into the greenhouse, then placed her in the lightweight folding stroller she kept just for this purpose. Caitlin loved the butterflies, but the insects were far too fragile for the toddler to be let loose among them.

They crossed through the greenhouse and Faith opened the first door to the butterfly sanctuary, automatically glancing to the left into her tiny cubby-hole of a breeding room. An array of gray-and-brown chrysalises hung from a foam board in an alcove, carefully suspended from a pin with a head color coded to the species waiting to emerge. To a casual observer they appeared wizened and dead, but inside they pulsed with life and in a few days a new batch of jewel-winged butterflies would be ready to release into the habitat.

This was her second shipment of tropical and ornamental butterflies this season. Their life spans were short, and she needed to restock the habitat every few weeks with specimens she ordered from a breeder in New Jersey. Someday she would like to raise the exotic forms of the species herself, but she would need a much larger operation and more disposable income to house and winter over the specific plants each species needed to breed.

Caitlin chuckled as the gentle puff of air from the specially designed door—which blew air back into the habitat so that the butterflies couldn't escape— lifted the fine strands of her hair. It was very warm in the glass house, more humid than the outside air, at least for the time being. Faith turned on the exhaust fan in the far gable of the building. The opening was covered with fine netting so none of the butterflies could be sucked outside.

"Pretty!" Caitlin squealed, reaching for a huge blue morpho as it glided swiftly by. The spectacularly colored tropical butterfly was one of the visitor's favorites.

"Daddy liked them, too," Faith said. To everyone else, Mark was Caitlin's father, just as Faith was her mother, and it wouldn't be natural not to talk to her about him. Above all else Faith wanted everything she did for Caitlin to seem natural.

She glanced through the chrysalis-room window that gave a view of the parking lot. It was empty. She'd probably have a spate of customers again in the early evening if it didn't rain, but now the two of them were alone.

She picked Caitlin up and sat down on one of the rustic wooden benches that were scattered throughout the habitat. She'd made the butterfly house as near to a tropical garden as she could manage. There were paving stone pathways, raised beds of verbena, impatiens, butterflyweed, rudbeckia. The plants all in shades of pink and blue, purple and yellow that butterflies loved. She'd added large specimen plants, ferns, small trees and host plants like dill and parsley, Queen Anne's lace and African milkweed, to encourage the laying of eggs and as food for emerging caterpillars.

Steve and Peg had helped her build two waterfalls of lightweight landscaping rock—it was how they'd first met—a small one directly across from the door, and a much larger one that climbed almost to the ceiling in the farthest corner of the house so that the sound of falling water was everywhere. She loved this place, and Mark would have loved it, too. If he'd lived.

But if Mark had lived she would not have Caitlin.

She seldom let herself think of the dark days after Mark had died anymore. She preferred to believe her life had started the day Caitlin was born. It was a task she was mostly able to accomplish.

The sun disappeared behind a cloud and the butterflies disappeared from the air almost as swiftly, settling on leaves and flowers and feeding dishes to await the sun's return. Faith stood up, deciding to come back for the dishes later, and set Caitlin back into the stroller, then checked her backside in the long mirror beside the door. Butterflies often landed on visitors unawares and had to be carefully removed before anyone left. Today no colorful hitchhikers had attached themselves to her.

A rumble of thunder came rolling across the fields, so faint and far away it was felt more than heard. The wind had shifted while she was inside the butterfly room and the big baskets of red and white impatiens and trailing blue lobelia were swinging wildly from their hangers.

"Darn, I should have asked Steve to take them down for the afternoon when he was here earlier," Faith muttered half to herself, half to Caitlin. The hanging baskets were some of her best sellers and she didn't want to see them ruined by a storm. Her brother-in-law was six foot five and he'd hung the baskets high enough so they weren't a hazard to the skulls of customers, but they were out of Faith's reach, even standing on her tiptoes.

"Stay put like a good girl and I'll take them down," Faith told Caitlin, wishing she'd remembered to bring a cookie along with her. Caitlin had been an inquisitive baby and now, in the midst of the terrible twos, she was always on the go, poking her little snub nose in every nook and cranny the moment Faith's back was turned.

Faith retrieved the big stepladder that she used to open the vents in the roof of the greenhouse and set it up under the hanging baskets. But she'd positioned the ladder just a little too far from her objective and had to lean precariously to reach the first basket. To make matters worse the chain refused to come free of the hook. "Drat," Faith muttered, wishing she could give voice to something a little more stress-relieving, but she'd learned the hard way that Caitlin was a perfect mimic when it came to swear words.

She wrestled the first basket free, making a mental note to get Steve to lengthen the chains, customer liability or no, and reached over to take down the second. A flicker of movement from the direction of Caitlin's stroller caught her eye at the same moment a dusty black Blazer turned off the road and started down the lane. A last-minute customer stopping in on the way home from work, or the man who had rented the cottage? It didn't really matter who it was, she'd rather not be seen struggling down off the ladder with the two heavy baskets swinging from each hand.

"Caitlin, honey," she said over her shoulder. "Are you being a good girl and sitting still for mommy?"

A tremor of movement and a piping voice directly below her sent Faith's heart into her throat. "I help you." A small hand tugged on the leg of her slacks. Caitlin had crawled out of her stroller and climbed up the ladder. Now she was perched a good four feet off the ground, and blocking Faith's way.

"'Fraid," Caitlin mumbled suddenly, clinging like a limpet. Faith would have to lower the heavy baskets by their chains as far as she could, let them drop the rest of the way to the floor, then twist around and pull Caitlin into her arms. But as she shifted her weight one of the ladder's legs began to sink into the soft earth. Faith let out a gasp as she pitched forward.

"Can I help you with those?" a male voice asked.

Faith looked toward the source of the voice. The occupant of the black Blazer was standing just inside the greenhouse entrance. He wasn't a tall man, but solidly built with broad shoulders that tapered to a narrow waist, and long blue-jean clad legs.

"No, don't bother." Faith swallowed to ease the lump of anxiety that had lodged itself in her throat. She could feel Caitlin wobbling on the step behind her as she attempted to look around at the stranger. "It's...it's what's behind me I'm worried about." She was going to have to drop the heavy baskets, there was no help for it. The ladder was sinking more deeply into the soft earth each time she shifted her weight. In another few seconds it would tumble over taking both of them with it.

The stranger in the doorway took two long steps forward to see what she was talking about. His eyes widened a moment at the sight of Caitlin clinging to Faith's pant leg.

"So that's what has you treed. Come here, little one," he said, his voice slightly rough around the edges, but with a Southern lilt underneath. "Time to get down."

"Hi," Caitlin said, brightly and to Faith's surprise she held out her arms to the stranger.

"Hi, yourself." He lifted her up into one arm and steadied the ladder with the other.

"I climb high," Caitlin informed him smugly.

"Too high." Faith started down the ladder. It was still tilted at an awkward angle, but she made it without making a fool of herself by falling, even when he reached out and laid a steadying hand on her elbow.

A strange shiver went up and down her spine. Not because his hand was cold or his touch too personal. It wasn't. His hand was warm, slightly rough against her skin and he let go of her the moment she was steady on her feet. But still his touch unsettled her.

"I go high. I big girl."

"You are a very brave girl," he said in a wondering tone. He had a strong face, stern looking, all masculine lines and angles. Not a handsome face, but an intriguing one. As she watched, it softened and relaxed as Caitlin's laughing giggle coaxed a smile to his lips.

"I Caitlin."

"Hello—" he hesitated for a brief moment, "—Caitlin."

Caitlin wrapped her arms around the stranger's neck. She was a loving child, but she was usually reserved around people she didn't know, especially men. Caitlin planted a kiss on his cheek. "I like you," she said.

Faith dropped the heavy baskets and held out her arms. A rush of protectiveness coursed through her. The instant connection between her child and this stranger unsettled her even more than his touch. "Thank you. I'll take her now."

He placed Caitlin in her waiting arms. "I don't think she's suffered any harm from her climb."

Faith's sudden anxiety attack faded away once she held her daughter. She tried to summon a smile and thought she mostly succeeded. "She climbs like a monkey."

"And you're all right, too?" he asked, fixing his dark gaze on her directly for the first time. His eyes were blue, like dark, still water, or the color of the sky at twilight. "You look a little pale." Once more Faith's breath caught in her throat. Whatever had made her think he wasn't a handsome man? When he smiled it took her breath away. She would have to be a dead woman not to respond to that smile. "No strains or sprains? Those baskets look heavy."

"I'm fine, really," Faith insisted, although her left shoulder was aching a little. She fell back on formality to hide her continuing confusion. "Thank you for your help. I'm Faith Carson." She shifted Caitlin's slight weight and held out her hand.

He gave her his. "Hugh Damon. I've reserved one of your cottages for the week."

"Yes, Mr. Damon. Please wait a moment. I'll get you the key." She attempted a smile of her own. "Let me thank you for your rescue of me and my daughter one more time. And, of course, welcome to Painted Lady Farm."

THE STORM ROLLED through quickly leaving the air fragrant with the scent of wet grass. Twilight lingered a long time, the sky shading from red to orange to dusky pink and purple-gray, before the stars twinkled to life in the east. Hugh stood beneath the shelter of the high-pitched overhang at the back of the cottage. Beneath his feet were fieldstones that formed a small patio edged by a low stone wall and flowering plants, fragrant with scents that were heady but unfamiliar. He stared down at the lighted windows of Faith Carson's house.

He'd almost given himself away earlier, when he'd

let his reaction to seeing Beth's child for the first time get the better of him. She was Beth's child; he was convinced of it, although he couldn't say how he knew.

Caitlin Carson looked a great deal like his sister had at that age, the same elfin shape to her face, the gossamer fine hair. But Caitlin's eyes were not blue, like Beth's, like his. They were green-gold and changeable, exactly the same color as the woman who called herself her mother. Otherwise there was little resemblance between them. Faith Carson's hair was brown, her face more rounded. Her figure, too, was rounded. In all the right places he had to admit, but her body type was not the same as Caitlin's, who would grow up as slender and petite as Beth. But if he commented on that fact Faith Carson would say her daughter took after her dead father, not her mother, and her suspicions would be aroused.

She was Caitlin's mother according to all the laws of the land. He'd seen a copy of the child's birth certificate. Everything about it seemed to be in order. But still he knew his hunch was right. Even though the accident that had killed Jamie Sheldon and taken Beth's memory, had occurred a hundred miles away in another state, he was convinced she had been in this place. Here she'd given birth. And for some reason she'd left her child behind. Despite all the damage to her body and her mind, that memory had not been completely erased. She remembered the baby crying in the snow. And she remembered butterflies.

It was the slightest of hunches that had brought

him here. A baby born to a woman alone, during a terrible ice storm. A woman who was a nurse. A woman who could have delivered a frightened teenager's baby. A woman who raised butterflies. A young widow who, perhaps, despaired of ever having a child of her own and who would take the desperate risk of keeping another woman's baby.

He didn't know the details, but nothing he had learned led him to believe that Faith Carson was a cold-blooded baby snatcher. He was determined to find the truth for Beth's sake but he had to proceed carefully. He didn't want to bring the law down on his sister for abandoning her baby, anymore than he wanted to see Faith Carson jailed for kidnapping— at least not yet. The whole situation was a minefield. One misstep on his part could spell disaster for all of them.

Faith Carson was wary of him, and he would have to be careful to earn her trust before he brought Beth here. He was convinced his sister's well-being, and certainly her happiness, depended on learning the truth of the events that were the basis of her nightmares.

But he wasn't the only one searching for Beth's baby. Jamie's parents were determined to learn the fate of their lost grandchild. And they would not stop with merely learning that truth. They wanted the baby. And they were rich and powerful enough to take her from Beth, from Faith Carson. From him. If they discovered where she was.

CHAPTER THREE

"CAITLIN SEEMS TAKEN with your renter," Peg said, peering out the window above the kitchen sink. Hugh Damon had been staying in the cottage for several days now, over the long Memorial Day weekend, and the third anniversary of Mark's death.

"She's taken with anyone who spends time swinging her." Faith was standing in front of the open refrigerator, enjoying the blast of cool air as much as searching for juice for Caitlin's afternoon snack. It was 85 degrees, and the still air was heavy with humidity and the threat of approaching storms.

Faith snared the plastic bottle of apple juice from behind the milk where it had been hidden and shut the refrigerator door, coming to stand beside her sister. She had made up her mind to ignore her first disquieting reaction to Hugh Damon, but it didn't mean she was comfortable talking about him.

Faith watched him push Caitlin in her tire swing, as Addy lolled in the shade beneath the picnic table. The muscles in his back and shoulders moved smoothly beneath the light fabric of his shirt. His thick, dark-gold hair lay heavy and straight against his forehead. He wore no jewelry except a service-able-looking wristwatch. That was another direction she didn't want her thoughts to take. He was a good-looking man, who didn't wear a wedding ring.

"She's usually a little shy around strangers," Peg observed, running cold water into a glass she'd taken from the cupboard. Peg had started a wallpapering and painting business when she'd moved to Bartons-ville and it was doing well. She was on her way home from a job and was wearing paint-splattered jeans and an old, long-sleeved white shirt of her hus-band's. Her hair was tucked up under a ball cap and the smell of solvent and paint scented the air around her.

"She likes him," Faith admitted. She rubbed the back of her neck with her hand. A storm coming always affected her that way, a tightness in her mus-cles, pressure behind her eyes.

"She's female. Even a two-year-old woman can spot a stud like that one."

Faith laughed. "Hey, you've only been married five months. You aren't supposed to be ogling other men already."

"I'm married, not blind. Steve's a dear but not fantasy material. Put a leather kilt on that guy, give him a sword and he'd give Russell Crowe a run for his money any day."

"Does this mean you're taking back your warning about renting the cabins to single men?"

Peg drained her glass and shook her head as she set it in the sink. "Nope." She tilted her head in Hugh's direction. "Men as good-looking as that one are trouble. I ought to know—I married one the first time around, remember.''

"Men like that one are engineers,'' Faith said, putting two Oreos on a paper plate for Caitlin.

"Engineer? I admit that sounds respectable enough.'' If Peg had been a grasshopper her antennae would be quivering. "What kind of engineer?''

"The kind who build shopping malls, I guess. He's working on that fancy new complex they did a feature on in the *Cincinnati Enquirer* a couple of months ago. You know, the one with all the high-end stores.'' He'd told her that much the afternoon he'd inquired about continuing to rent the cottage for the month of June, since his work on the project would last several weeks.

"Has he asked you out yet?''

"No. Of course not.''

Her sister didn't look convinced but she didn't say any more. Faith had perfected the talent of sounding very sincere when she lied. And this was just a little white lie, not a universe-size one, like taking another woman's child to raise as your own. Hugh Damon hadn't asked her out on a date. Not officially, so her conscience was clear.

But he had offered to take her and Caitlin out to eat. It was while he was helping to rehang the baskets the day after he'd arrived. They had talked as he worked and she tallied the day's receipts. She was alone in the greenhouse and it would have seemed churlish to refuse his offer of help. Or so she told herself.

He'd been wearing an old University of Texas T-shirt that stretched tight across his chest and shoulders, she remembered, and faded jeans that hugged his long legs. "Where do you find a good meal in Bartonsville?" he had asked. She brought out muffins and bagels, orange and grapefruit juice, and made coffee in the greenhouse every morning for herself and Steve and Peg, or whoever was around. Guests at the cabins were welcome to them, as well. Painted Lady Farm was as close to a bed-and-breakfast as you got in Bartonsville.

She had replied without hesitation. "The Golden Sheaf. It's run by a family of old order Mennonites who make everything from scratch. The mashed potatoes are my daughter's favorite. I'm surprised you haven't found it already. All you have to do is follow your nose down Main Street."

Caitlin had been sitting at the small table Faith kept for her behind the counter coloring in a *SpongeBob SquarePants* book. "Eat," she'd said at the mention of food.

"Maybe the two of you could join me for dinner there this evening?" Hugh had said as he tested the strength of the chain extension before rehanging the planters. The invitation was offhand, but it caught Faith by surprise and she immediately said no. The refusal hung harsh and unfriendly in the air between them and she hurried to soften its uncompromising sound. "I mean, thanks, but I already have dinner started."

"Some other time then. Do you recommend the meat loaf?"

"It's the specialty of the house."

He'd looked pleased. "Homemade meat loaf. Nothing better."

"Don't forget to try the pies. The coconut cream is to die for."

"I'm a banana cream man myself," he'd answered with a smile.

Faith had managed a smile in return. Her eyes had been drawn to the hard muscles of his thighs as he worked, and suddenly, from out of nowhere, she remembered the feel of legs and bodies tangled together in lovemaking, and she nearly dropped the stack of receipts she held in her hand. The flash of eroticism had come and gone in a heartbeat, but the aftereffect left her shaken. In her vision the arms holding her hadn't been Mark's. They'd belonged to this man.

She'd mumbled something about liking banana cream, too, and made some excuse to leave the greenhouse. Her legs were wobbly as she picked Caitlin up to carry her to the house, her breath coming in quick little gasps that couldn't be blamed on the heat or the slight weight of the child in her arms. It was lust. Something that for three years had been completely absent from her thoughts.

That incident wasn't the last erotic thought she'd had about Hugh Damon, but it was the last one she had let get the best of her. Perhaps because she also couldn't quite forget the disquieting certainty that he was here, not just to avoid spending several weeks at an interstate off-ramp motel, but for some secret reason of his own.

A rumble of thunder announced the arrival of the storms that had been predicted all day. Peg angled her head to check the sky visible between the branches of the big maple outside the kitchen window. "Nasty-looking clouds," she said, forgetting, at least for the moment, her fixation with Hugh Damon. "I have a feeling we're going to get a real bad storm out of this cold front."

"I think you're right," Faith agreed.

"You're sure you don't need me to watch Caitlin Wednesday and Thursday?"

Those were the days Faith was scheduled to work at the hospital. It was going to be her last week of duty until the fall. She would be busy with her own businesses from now on and had taken a leave of absence until September. "No, thanks. Martha's going to watch her." Martha Baden was Peg's mother-in-law.

"Well, then she'll probably end up at my house part of the day anyway."

"Probably." Faith laughed as they headed outside.

"Introduce me to your engineer," Peg said under her breath as she held the screen door open for Faith.

Faith continued on into the yard, setting the paper plate of cookies and the sippy cup on the picnic table. She introduced her sister to Hugh Damon and then followed her to her truck to say goodbye.

"My Lord, he's even better looking up close than

he was from the kitchen window,'' Peg said fanning her cheeks with her fingertips. ''If he asks you out while he's here, you go. You've been alone for three years, that's long enough.''

''I don't want another man—''

''That's what I said, too, until I met Steve.'' Peg switched on the engine and drove off. She loved having the last word.

Faith walked slowly back to the big maple. Caitlin dragged her little sneakered feet in the wood chips layered under the tire swing to slow its movement. She was wearing a pink top and darker pink shorts. Her fine silvery hair was in pigtails, and she looked like a spun sugar angel to Faith. An angel, but a mischievous one.

''Juice,'' she squealed as Hugh stopped the swing so that she could hop out and come dancing across the grass to Faith. ''I want juice. I'm hot.''

Faith bent down and gathered her daughter against her heart. ''That's because it's hot outside and you've been swinging and laughing and talking real hard.''

''Hugh's hot, too.'' *That went without saying.* Faith was glad she had her face buried in Caitlin's neck. She was having more and more trouble controlling such unsuitable thoughts. ''He needs a juicy,'' Caitlin declared.

''I'll settle for a drink of water.'' Hugh moved toward the old-fashioned hand pump that stood by the gate. Once there he took the antique ladle off the hook and began working the long handle up and

down. The well was as old as the house, but the
water was pure and spring fresh. Faith had it chan-
neled into the greenhouse to water the plants and
keep the waterfalls topped off.

As soon as a steady stream of water began to rush
out of the pump into the shallow stone trough that
had once held chicken feed a century before, Caitlin
wiggled out of Faith's arms and darted over to Hugh.
''Swim,'' she said loudly. ''Let's swim.'' She squatted down and started to untie her shoes to wade in
the trough.

''No way, Kitty Cat. The water's too cold and I'm
too big for the basin.''

Faith followed Caitlin to the pump. She wondered
when Hugh had started using her pet names for Caitlin. The endearment came so naturally to his lips she
felt churlish in mentioning anything about it. ''No
playing in the water now. It's going to storm and you
have to help Mommy bring in the plants and shut up
the greenhouse.'' Peg had offered to help before she
left but Faith knew she was anxious to get home
before the rain so had assured her she could manage
on her own. Besides, she didn't want to answer any
more questions about Hugh Damon. Since she'd remarried, her sister's mind was focused entirely too
much on sex, especially Faith's lack of it.

''Would you like a drink of water?'' He rinsed and
refilled the ladle and held it out to her.

She took it gratefully. It was hot and she was
thirsty for something that wasn't full of sugar or caffeine. Her hand brushed his knuckles and she felt a

tremor like a tiny earthquake rattle her bones, just as another long rumble of thunder boomed overhead.

"It's getting close," Hugh said, raising his eyes to the sky.

"I have a feeling the cold front is going to get here ahead of the weatherman's prediction." She handed the ladle back to him. "Please excuse me, Mr. Damon. I think I'd better batten down the hatches in the greenhouse."

"I'll help. And I think we've known each other long enough to drop the honorifics. My name's Hugh."

"Thank you, Hugh." She liked the way his name sounded on her tongue. "And please, call me Faith."

Addy grabbed her much chewed Frisbee in her teeth and trotted along at Hugh's heels as they walked toward the greenhouse, obviously hoping for a game of catch. So Faith could add her faithful sheltie to the list of females at Painted Lady Farm who had fallen for her guest.

"I can manage," she started to say, but he was already moving the remaining flats of bedding plants off the old farm wagon she used to display them. It had grown noticeably darker in the ten minutes they'd been standing in the yard. And the clouds were moving fast, roiling like water in a saucepan. The green cast to their undersides was more pronounced than ever, a sure sign of hail.

Faith deposited Caitlin at her table behind the counter and went to help Hugh. They were both soaked by the time all the bedding plants were inside.

She struggled to close the wide panels that were usually folded back against the side of the greenhouse. Hugh reached a hand over her shoulder and unhooked the panel, then tugged them into place. He had just closed the final one when the hail came pelting down.

The roof of the greenhouse was made of the same industrial weight plastic as the sides and the hailstones, small ones thankfully, bounced off harmlessly. But the roof of the butterfly habitat was made of glass. It was reinforced and supposedly shatterproof, but so far it hadn't been put to the test. Faith picked up Caitlin and hurried into the chrysalis room. The sound of hailstones on glass was deafening. She'd reached for the handle of the pressurized door when Hugh spoke from behind her.

"It might be better if we get back to the house in case there's a tornado."

"Oh, God, don't say that." Ohio wasn't technically a part of Tornado Alley, but they still had their share of the deadly storms.

"Back in Texas this is the kind of weather that has us heading for the nearest storm cellar. You do have a cellar, don't you?" His tone was ordinary, for Caitlin's sake, Faith realized. There was even a tinge of laughter beneath the faint drawl, but his eyes were grim.

"Yes, there's a cellar. Have you always lived in Texas?" Faith kept her tone as light as his. She was determined not to allow her own fear to be transmitted to Caitlin.

"From time to time," Hugh said. He turned to go back into the greenhouse. "My dad was in the military. We lived in a lot of places, but Texas was where I went to high school and college. My mom and my half sister stayed on there after I left home. When I got back to the States last time it seemed as good a place as any to hang my hat."

"Back to the States? You build malls overseas then?"

His laugh was short and held little amusement. "I've only been building malls the past couple of years. Before that I worked all over the world. Dams in China, bridges in South America. Never more than a year or two in one place, and most of them were pretty far off the beaten track."

Faith wanted to ask him more about what sounded like a fascinating life, but a blinding flash of lightning and the earsplitting crack of thunder that accompanied it brought her back to the situation at hand. This was no time for conversation, fascinating or otherwise. She gave one more troubled glance through the chrysalis room window into the habitat. The insects were on their own now. She couldn't risk injury to Caitlin staying where they were. But how was she going to get her daughter safely back into the house?

The hailstones weren't that large but they were coming down so thickly she had to shout to be heard. And the wind was picking up, too. There would be blowing leaves and twigs, perhaps even falling tree branches to contend with between here and the house. She didn't even dare to consider what damage the storm was doing to the crops in the fields. "I can't take Caitlin out into the storm." She indicated the sleeveless top and shorts her daughter was wearing. Caitlin had her face buried in Faith's shoulder. She didn't like thunder and lightning, but she wasn't unduly afraid of them. That might change if she had to go out in it unprotected.

"No umbrella or raincoat in the greenhouse?"

"Nothing like that." The radio on the counter began to vibrate with the sirenlike alert that signaled a weather update. A disembodied voice announced a funnel cloud had been spotted about ten miles west of Bartonsville. It was moving northeast at thirty miles an hour. Everyone in the area was to take immediate cover.

"If it stays on course it will probably miss us but we need to get into the cellar," Hugh said. She didn't for a moment question the accuracy of his pronouncement. It had taken Faith weeks to orient herself to the land around Bartonsville after she'd moved to the farm, but it appeared Hugh had had no such difficulty.

She racked her brain for something to use to cover Caitlin. "I suppose we could wrap her up in one of the those nylon garden flags. They're heavy enough to give her some protection."

"It's better than nothing." Hugh reached out to slide the nearest off its pole, a springlike design of pink and yellow tulips on a green background. Faith's eyes flicked past the display to the shelf of hummingbird and butterfly statues.

"Wait a minute. I have a better idea." Faith darted around the counter. She pulled out a roll of packing material. "Bubble wrap! I keep it around to pack the figurines. We can wrap her in it."

She was rewarded with one of his heart-stopping grins. "Great idea. Here, give her to me."

Faith didn't let herself hesitate. She couldn't hold on to Caitlin and wrap her head and shoulders at the same time. Hugh held out his arms and Caitlin tumbled into his embrace. "Bubbles," she giggled. "Poke the bubbles."

"You can poke all the bubbles you want in the house, Kitty Cat," Faith promised. "Just hold still now like a good girl." Thirty seconds later Caitlin grinned out at her from a cocoon of packing material.

"Hey, you're Cocoon Girl now," Hugh said admiringly.

Faith laughed despite the anxiety that made her hands shake and her throat close. "Not Cocoon Girl. She...she needs to be Chrysalis Girl. We don't want to take the chance that she'll hatch into a plain old moth. We want her to be a beautiful butterfly, don't we, sweetie?" She leaned forward and touched noses with her daughter. The spontaneous movement brought her close enough to feel the heat of Hugh's body and the evocative smell of his soap and aftershave. She straightened quickly, taking a step back.

Hugh didn't seem to notice her awkward movement. "Okay, Chrysalis Girl it is. Up, up and away!"

Faith tugged open the main door, the swirling wind working just as hard to keep it closed. Addy

started barking, backing away, stiff-legged, as hailstones clattered on the paving stones just inside the
door. ''C'mon, dog. Move,'' Faith ordered, but Addy
was too excited and too frightened of the storm to
be her usual tractable self. Faith made a dive for the
sheltie but Addy bounced out of range. ''Addy!
Come. Or you're going to get blown to Oz.'' This
time Addy obeyed the stern command and Faith
lifted the little dog into her arms.

Hugh motioned her through the open door first and
then pulled it shut with one hard jerk. The sting of
hailstones against her cheek and head made Faith
gasp. She took off across the gravel parking lot at a
run, the dog squirming and whimpering in her arms.
Hugh's Blazer was parked under the big maple that
shaded the back yard. Faith hoped a limb didn't come
down on it. Thank heaven, her own dependable Car-
avan was parked in the barn.

The ground was an inch deep with marble-sized
hailstones. The footing was treacherous, almost as
bad as it had been the day Caitlin was born. What a
terrifying trip home that had been, the tiny newborn
clutched tight to her chest, nothing to protect her
from the sleet and wind but the sweatshirt she was
wrapped in.

Faith didn't dare look back to see how her daughter was faring in Hugh's arms for fear of turning an
ankle and ending up on her bottom with an armload
of indignant sheltie. She shoved open the wrought-
iron gate to the yard and went directly to the house.
Inside the kitchen she motioned Hugh to follow her

down the steep, narrow cellar steps. The big white-washed room contained her washer and dryer, the hot water heater and a huge old boiler that she was hoping would provide heat for one more winter before it died. Otherwise, the low-ceilinged, stone-floored room was empty except for some of Caitlin's toys, an old castoff sofa and a small TV and VCR. She often brought Caitlin down here to run around and let off steam on rainy days. Faith hit the light switch inside the door. Thankfully the two overhead lights came on.

She kept a powerful flashlight and some candles and a lighter on a shelf by the stairs for an emergency such as this, but she hoped they didn't have to use them. She turned on the TV, and muted the sound so that Caitlin wouldn't become alarmed by storm bulletins. A map of the county filled the screen, and a dark red blotch, the indication of the strongest storm cell, was superimposed over Bartonsville, but it had begun to move off to the east. "I think the worst of the storm's passed, thank goodness." She glanced out one of the small windows, placed high in the thick, stone walls of the cellar. The hail had stopped; now it was only raindrops hitting the wavy glass.

She turned back to find that Hugh had set Caitlin on her feet and hunkered down beside her to unwind the bubble wrap cocoon.

As soon as she was free Caitlin bolted for the stairs. "Need Barbie."

"Oh, no, you don't." Hugh's long arm shot out

and his fingers curled around the child's wrist. Faith's heart leapt to her throat. Caitlin was such a tiny thing, her bones so delicate he could easily hurt her and not even realize it. She almost cried out, but she needn't have worried. His grip on Caitlin's wrist was so light it scarcely touched her skin.

"I think I see Barbie over there." He pointed to the seat of the old couch and let Caitlin go skipping off to retrieve the doll.

"She's smart and fearless, isn't she?" he said with a note of wonder—*and love?*—in his voice that sent shivers through Faith.

"She was born in the middle of a terrible ice storm." Faith hadn't meant to let that slip. She had perfected her story of Caitlin's birth, but she never volunteered details. His actions had thrown her off balance, and it was too late to take back the words.

"Tell me about it," he said, standing up, towering over her it seemed, although there was no more than three or four inches difference in their heights. The tone of his voice didn't change, nor the look in his eyes, but Faith felt compelled to answer as though bidden by some unspoken command.

Suddenly she was afraid, completely and unreasoningly afraid, and the fear had nothing to do with the storm, but was caused by the man before her. She felt for a moment that he could see right through her and that he knew what she would say next was a lie. Her throat closed and the litany of carefully constructed half truths and fabrications that was her fortress, as well as her prison, wouldn't come.

CHAPTER FOUR

FAITH OPENED HER MOUTH but no sound came out. She was suddenly thrust into the midst of her worst nightmare. In it, she was standing in a huge echoing chamber. Stern, shadowy figures sat in judgment of her, demanding to know why she had taken another woman's baby. No matter how eloquently she tried to explain her actions, her motivations, no matter how she many tears she shed, slowly, inexorably, one of the shadowy figures would pluck Caitlin from her arms and melt away, leaving her alone. She would wake in terror, tears running down her cheeks and only a trip to Caitlin's room and the warmth of her baby's skin could dispel the dread.

It was the middle of a late May day, and she was wide-awake. This was not her dream. This was reality, and she had told the story many times before. Today would be no different, unless she allowed it to be. "There was no one to help me when Caitlin was born," she said as lightly as she could manage. "My husband had died six months earlier. I...I was here alone."

Raindrops glistened in Hugh's dark-blond hair, the harsh light catching steaks of lighter gold that she hadn't noticed before. He didn't seem menacing any-more, although his dark gaze held hers. "You must have been very frightened."

"It was terrifying." The words were heartfelt. She had woven as much of the truth into her story as possible. She had become a very good liar, but she did it only when necessary.

"Did you try to contact the emergency squad? Bartonsville has one, I imagine."

"There wasn't time." She forced herself to keep eye contact. She was back in stride now, back on script. "Contrary to conventional wisdom about first babies, labor went very quickly. The ice storm hit and a broken tree limb brought down the phone line. Thank God, the electricity stayed on." That was true, too, but it had happened *after* she made her night-marish trek across the ice-slick fields to the house, with the tiny infant barely clinging to life in her arms.

Faith couldn't help herself, her eyes sought her daughter across the room. She was seated in front of the old TV, oblivious to their conversation and the dying storm, engrossed in an episode of *Rugrats.* "We were cut off from the outside world for the first three days of Caitlin's life."

She had made diapers from an old flannel blanket she'd found in a back bedroom. Then she'd taken a plastic sandwich bag and poked a hole in one corner with a pin. She'd dissolved a little sugar in warm water and put the glucose solution in the bag, twist-ing it into a cone, as though she were a chef preparing to frost a fairy cake. She had coaxed Caitlin's tiny mouth open with the tip of her little finger and pushed the makeshift nipple inside. Fortunately, Caitlin's sucking reflex was strong and Faith was patient. Eventually the baby swallowed an ounce of the liquid.

After she'd held the newborn close to her breast and wrapped them both in blankets until the worrisome blue cast to the baby's skin had been replaced by warm pink. They'd stayed snug and warm in their isolated cocoon as the storm raged, and when they'd emerged a transformation had taken place that was as complete and life-altering as that of a caterpillar changing into a butterfly.

Caitlin had become Faith's child as surely as if she had given birth to the infant. She had labored to bring her to safety through the storm. She had fed her and bathed her and held her close so that she slept against the beating of Faith's heart.

She'd loved her.

But she'd known she couldn't keep her.

The ice melted the fourth morning after the storm, and life began to return to normal, but Faith remained closeted in her big, old house.

She knew Beth and Jamie would lose custody of the infant the moment Faith stepped into the sheriff's office and told her story. The baby would go into the system, into foster care. If she was lucky it would be to a loving home. But it could be months, even years, until all the technicalities were sorted out. Sometimes bad things happened to children caught up in the system. Faith didn't want to think of that. So she stayed put, telling herself it was still too dangerous to drive. She would wait for the phone to be repaired and to give Jamie and Beth time to change their minds. For a little longer she could make believe she had what she wanted most—a child of her own.

And then the newspaper had come.

Faith closed her eyes and could see as clearly as if it were still in front of her—the headline about the ice storm. Below it was a sidebar of storm-related deaths in Ohio and surrounding states. In Indiana, the story read, a hundred miles from Bartonsville, there had been a pileup on the interstate during the height of the storm. Eleven cars had been involved, but as of press time there was only one death, a seventeen-year-old male from Massachusetts. His companion, a teenage girl, was not expected to live. The couple was identified as Jamie Sheldon of Boston, and Beth Harden of Houston.

Jamie and Beth.

Was it only a coincidence that the first names were the same? Or was the child in her arms an orphan?

There were no further details of the accident that she could find. No mention of Beth having recently given birth, or any indication that a search for the infant had been started. Faith waited all that day and the next for someone to come and claim the child. With each passing hour it became evident that it was not going to happen. The young parents had died without telling anyone about their baby.

It was as if she didn't exist.

It was as if she were really Faith's.

And in the end it had been remarkably easy to make Caitlin legally hers.

In Ohio, she learned from the Internet, either parent could register the home birth of a child simply by appearing, within ten days, at the records office of the county in which the birth had taken place. No other witnesses were required, no medical records were needed. Only her own declaration of parenthood. That was her first lie, but one she told gladly. Within fifteen minutes of arriving at the courthouse she'd left with a birth certificate that declared Caitlin Hope Carson was her daughter.

She became aware she had been silent a long time, too long. As it sometimes did the guilt at what she had done burst out of the locked corner of her mind. She didn't want to talk about Caitlin's birth anymore. She didn't want to lie to Hugh anymore. "The storm's passing. I think it's safe to go back upstairs."

He made no objection so she turned off the TV and took Caitlin in her arms. Once back in the familiar surroundings of her yellow-and-white kitchen she felt her confidence returning and the guilt retreating.

"Do you have other family in the area in addition to your sister?" Hugh asked, leaning back against the granite countertop, arms folded across his chest. His shirt was still damp from the soaking they'd gotten. It pulled tight across his chest with the movement and Faith's mouth went dry with need and wanting. She carried Caitlin to the bay window that faced the fields and watched as the dark menace of the retreating storm clouds broke into tatters of gray smoke.

"My husband has a few distant cousins in the area, but otherwise, no. Peg and her boys are my only living relatives."

Caitlin wriggled to be free, so Faith set the little girl on her feet. Caitlin then bounced over to Hugh where she began to tug on his pant leg. "Cookie, please."

"She wants an Oreo. They're behind you."

Hugh swiveled his head and shoulders and spotted the big plastic jar filled with cookies. "May I?" he asked.

Faith nodded. He didn't look out of place at all in her kitchen. He leaned down and lifted Caitlin into his arms, letting her open the cookie jar and extract two of them all by herself. "Bite for you," Caitlin said and pressed the cookie to Hugh's lips for him to take a bite. Hugh went very still for a moment, then opened his mouth to nibble on the cookie. Caitlin shoved the rest of the cookie into her mouth. "Good?"

"Very good." He lifted one hand and smoothed it gently over her hair. "Thank you, Caitlin." Faith went all shaky inside. It looked so right somehow, Hugh holding her daughter in his strong, tanned arms.

He put Caitlin down and she raced through the archway into the dining room, where they never ate, but where she kept many of her larger toys.

Silence stretched between them, and it made her nervous. She returned to the subject of family because she couldn't think of anything else to say. "You mentioned a half sister, I remember. Do you come from a large family?"

He grew very still. "My parents are dead."

"I'm sorry."

He nodded shortly. "Beth is my only sibling. She's twenty."

"Beth? Is it short for Elizabeth?"

"No, just Beth."

A little shiver skittered across her nerve endings. She could never hear that name without associating it with Caitlin's sad and pretty mother, especially when she had just been thinking of her such a short time ago. "It's...it's a pretty name. Are you close?"

"As close as she'll let me get." This time she didn't imagine the pain in his voice. It was raw and real. "She's got a lot of problems right now, both physical and emotional. She was in a bad accident some time ago. It's been a long road back. I wasn't there for her when I should have been and now..."

"And now she won't let you be there for her?" Another Beth. Another accident. Another stinging memory evoked.

"Not as much as I want to be."

"I'm sorry." Impulsively she laid her hand on his arm and immediately wished she hadn't. His skin was warm as sunlight. The feel of rough hair and the solidity of bone beneath her fingers reminded her that she was a woman who had been alone for three years. "I know it's none of my business but perhaps, it would be better if you spent the next few weeks with her instead of remaining here."

"She's in Texas. I need to be available to the architect in Cincy on two hours' notice, or I would go home."

"She has no one else?"

"Her father." His brows drew together in a scowl. "My stepfather is living, but he and Beth are estranged."

"I see." His expression warned her not to inquire further. "You could bring her here." She spoke the words without thinking.

He looked down at her hand, then lifted his gaze to hers. He watched her for a long moment, his eyes as shadowed as the stormy sky had been. "You mean that, don't you?"

"Of course I do. This place brought me comfort and peace after Mark died. It might do the same for your sister."

"Comfort and peace. She could use both of those."

"She would be most welcome."

He leaned closer and Faith felt herself drawn to him as though by an invisible magnet. He reached out and she held her breath certain that he meant to touch her cheek or even to take her in his arms. But she was mistaken. Hugh let his arm fall and took a step backward, leaving Faith feeling chilled. He was silent a long time, then his jaw tightened and he gave a short, sharp nod, as though coming to a decision that had been difficult to make. "You're right, Faith. I think it's time I brought Beth to Painted Lady Farm."

HUGH PROPPED HIS FEET on the knee-high, stone wall that bordered the tiny patio behind his cabin and leaned back in the red metal lawn chair, slouching down far enough in the seat to rest his head against the round back. It was getting to be a habit sitting out here at twilight. The only other guests, a middle-aged couple in a car with Michigan plates staying in the unit next to his, seemed settled in for the evening, and he had the place to himself. He looked up at the faint scattering of summer stars. Off in the west the last of a glorious orange-gold sunset had faded into purple and gray. The storms of the afternoon had passed off to the north and east, taking some of the humidity from the air.

He'd been sitting in the same spot for the past hour observing Faith go about the business of closing the greenhouse. He'd watched as a tall, dark-haired man and two small boys in a pickup had driven down the lane and walked to the edge of the cornfield with her. He could hear the boys whooping and hollering in the backyard, running up to the pond to throw something into the water, then scurrying back down the bank. Caitlin had followed close on their heels, her small legs pumping to keep up.

Faith had called out a warning to the boys and obediently they had each taken Caitlin's hand and led her back to her mother. Faith gathered the toddler into her arms. She'd waited, cuddling her daughter, as the boys ran off again, and the man waded into the rows of new corn to check for damage. Steve, the brother-in-law, Hugh had decided, and the boys would be his stepsons, Faith's sister's children.

When the man left, driving slowly back up the lane in a gray pickup that had seen better days, he stopped and got out. The boys, both towheads with dark eyes and noses too big for their faces, hung out the open window as the older man approached.

"I'm Steve Baden," he said. "Faith's brother-in-law."

"Hugh Damon." Hugh held out his hand.

Steve took it. His palm was callused, his grip strong. He gave Hugh the same once-over he'd gotten from Faith's sister. "Thought I'd introduce myself since Faith says you're going to be around the place for a few weeks."

"A few weeks," Hugh agreed. "I'm working on the Spring Meadow Mall project north of the city."

Steve nodded, frowning. "I've read about it. Supposed to bring a lot of business into the area. The outfit that's developing it bought out three family farms to put it up, I heard."

"I don't know the details," Hugh said carefully. Steve Baden was a farmer. It was obvious he didn't like the idea of all that farmland being paved over. To tell the truth Hugh didn't much, either, but he kept his opinion to himself. If developers didn't build malls Hugh would be out of a job.

"Well, I can see why you'd prefer staying here

than at one of those highway motels. Nice country around here. Quiet. Peaceful. I see to the cabins for Faith. If you need anything done she can give me a holler. My place's only a mile down the road.''

''Thanks, I'll remember that.''

The boys had begun to wrestle in the pickup. ''Jack. Guy. Settle down,'' Steve called, without even turning his head. The boys untangled themselves, but continued to bounce up and down on the seat.

''Jack tried to wipe a booger on me,'' the youngest shouted out the window.

''Did not.''

''Did too.''

Steve shook his head and grinned. He pointed his finger at his stepsons. ''I said settle down.'' Tranquility followed, but the youngest folded his arms across his chest and stuck out his lower lip in a pout. ''Time to get these two hellions home to their mother.'' He held out his hand again. ''Good meeting you, Hugh.''

''You, too.''

As the sound of the truck's engine died away Hugh returned to his chair. Faith's brother-in-law hadn't stopped to introduce himself just to be neighborly. It was obvious Steve Baden felt responsible for Faith and Caitlin. He was checking Hugh out, but he didn't mind. He'd have done the same thing in Steve's position.

He wished there had been someone to perform that service for his mother. Instead, after his Green Beret father had died in a training accident she'd married Beth's father. There was nothing really wrong with Trace Harden. He just wasn't Tyler Damon. The marriage had lasted only long enough to produce Beth, then Trace had taken off and mostly stayed out of the picture, until their mother's death in a car accident when Beth was fourteen.

Thinking it was for the best Hugh had sent her to Boston to live with her likable, but weak-willed father and his third wife. He'd thought Beth needed two parents to raise her, not one brother who was out of the country, and sometimes out of touch, for months at a time. It was a decision he'd regret until his dying day.

Hugh surged from the chair and stepped over the low wall into the wet grass. Mosquitoes rose up in swarms around him. He batted them away and walked out onto the gravel lane and headed up the hill.

The stars were bright and he stared upward, looking for the Big Dipper, but he was really seeing Faith. She had beautiful hair that brushed her shoulders, a rich mixture of gold and brown that defied description. The closest he could come was likening it to sunlight shining through a glass jar of honey. Her skin was honey-colored, too, and as soft as thistledown. He'd damn near made a fool of himself when she'd touched him. He'd wanted to pull her into his arms and learn for himself if her lips and skin tasted as sweet as they looked.

He couldn't think of any better way of making the

whole situation even more complicated—except to take her to bed.

By the time he reached the old cemetery, the moon had risen, dimming the stars. He wasn't afraid of the dead, but he didn't go inside the intricately patterned wrought-iron fence that marked its boundaries. The Carsons and the Bartons and the Badens buried there had earned their rest, and he had no intention of disturbing it. Instead, he leaned on the gate and looked past the burying ground to the lights winking in Faith's upstairs windows. He already knew which was her room, the second on the right. And Caitlin's was beside hers.

Caitlin. Once more he felt her slight weight in his arms. Her skin was even softer than Faith's, her bones more delicately wrought. Only her eyes were the same as Faith's.

He no longer believed that Faith Carson had kidnapped Beth's child, if he ever had. For reasons he might never know, he now believed his sister and her boyfriend had left the child behind. And whatever justifications Faith Carson had made to herself to keep the baby, it had been a good decision for the child. She was a loved and loving little girl. His niece? If she was, he could never claim her. Even making the attempt could cause more problems than he could ever solve.

What if he brought Beth to this place? Would it help her to remember what had happened those hours before the accident? Would she somehow recognize

Caitlin as her child? Or was he only indulging his own obsession?

Perhaps he should leave well enough alone. Caitlin was healthy, happy and loved. Beth was working on building a new life for herself. She was young. He had every hope she would find someone to love and have more children one day. He had no business playing God.

Hugh turned away from the moon-shadowed cemetery and walked back down the hill to his cabin. As he opened the old-fashioned screen door and stepped inside, his cell phone rang.

He picked it up off the table and put it to his ear. ''Damon,'' he said.

''Hugh?'' Beth's voice sounded lost and faraway, but not because of the connection. Hugh felt his gut tighten. She always seemed glad to hear his voice, but she almost never initiated a call.

''Hi, Beth. What's up?'' He tried to keep his tone from reflecting his uneasiness.

''I'm okay, I guess.''

''You don't sound okay. Bad news on your finals?'' Beth had been taking courses at Baylor. Her first semester. She still required physical therapy on her leg. She had had to learn to walk and talk all over again, but she was getting better.

That is until a few months earlier when the dreams had begun.

''No, I did great on my finals.''

''You don't sound great.''

There was silence on the other end of the line.

"Beth? Tell me what's wrong."

"You're doing the big brother thing again." She gave a tiny little laugh, that was half giggle, half sob. Hugh balled his left hand into a fist.

"I am your big brother. Tell me what's wrong."

Beth took a shaky breath. "Jamie's mother called me again today. She...she wants to pay for me to start seeing a hypnotherapist."

Damn the woman. Harold and Lorraine Sheldon had all the money in the world. They could buy and sell him a hundred and fifty times over. And they weren't averse to using that money to get what they wanted. What they wanted was their grandchild, no matter what the cost to Beth. They'd been playing on her guilt and uncertainties almost since the moment she'd regained consciousness three weeks after the accident.

"They say this woman is incredible. They say she can help me remember everything that happened those last weeks. They don't believe I'll never remember everything. What should I do, Hugh? I have a child somewhere. A little girl. And I wouldn't even know that fact if it wasn't for my diary. I—I don't even really remember being pregnant. I just don't know..." She was crying now, quietly, hopelessly, and heartache for his sad little sister warred with Hugh's desire to throttle Harold and Lorraine Sheldon.

"You're not going to do anything you don't want to do, Beth. Remember the doctors told you that making yourself ill trying to recall what happened before the accident will not help." Her brain had been damaged from trauma and loss of blood. Her amnesia was complete and irreversible.

"But maybe they're wrong." Her tone was a blend of wistfulness and fear. Although the doctors had said miracles did happen, that there were no absolutes when dealing with the human brain, they didn't hold out much hope Beth would regain the lost portions of her life. That knowledge haunted her day and night, and her sadness and guilt fueled Hugh's remorse and frustration. "If I do as she asks we might learn what happened. If we find the baby alive they would have something left of Jamie. And if we don't, at least they will have a body to bury alongside Jamie—" Her voice broke and Hugh gritted his teeth against a sudden urge to howl along with her.

"God damn that bitch." Hugh usually kept his low opinion of Lorraine Sheldon to himself but he felt goaded beyond endurance. The investigation after the accident had turned up no leads, no clues to the baby's fate. Beth had never been charged with a crime, but the case was still open. It was another burden she carried.

Beth's voice was weary. "Hugh, we both know the baby must be dead. Why else would I dream of crying babies and blood and butterflies in the snow, unless some part of me remembers…hurting my baby?"

"That's enough, Beth." She would spend the night huddled on the couch in his apartment torturing herself with doubts and fears if he didn't stop this. "Put it out of your mind," he commanded.

"I can't." He could hear her sniffle back her tears and he suddenly remembered her at four, doing the same when she'd scraped her knee and had come running to her big brother because he could fix everything. God, how he wished that was true.

"Yes, you can. Remember the relaxation techniques Dr. Webster taught you." Beth's therapist was a jewel of a woman, but she'd told Hugh the last time they'd talked that there was not much more she could do for Beth. From now on her healing must come from within.

"My favorite's the triple scoop of double-chocolate-chip-mocha ice cream exercise." Her voice quavered but grew stronger with each word.

Hugh swallowed his own emotion and said, "I might even start seeing a shrink if that's what she recommends."

"Oh, Hugh." She managed to laugh. "I miss you. I know I don't tell you that often, but I do. I wish you were here to back me up with Jamie's mother. As soon as she walks in the door I'll be so nervous I'll agree to anything she asks, I can't seem to help myself." There was real fear underlying the lightness of her words.

Hugh felt his hand ball into a fist again and deliberately made himself relax. "You mean Lorraine and Harold are coming to Houston?"

He could almost see Beth's earnest nod, her silvery hair swinging against her pale cheek. "They'll be here day after tomorrow."

Hugh made up his mind in a flash, shouldering aside his own doubts about the wisdom of what he was planning. "But you won't be."

"What do you mean?"

"Get your suitcase packed. I'll call from here and get you on the first available flight into Cincinnati."

"But Hugh, it's too late tonight." She sounded hopeful despite her objection.

He raked his hand through his hair. "Okay, first plane out in the morning. You're coming to Ohio to stay with me."

"But what about—"

"Harold and Lorraine Sheldon can go to hell."

He wondered what Faith would say when she learned that Beth would be coming to Painted Lady Farm. What reaction would she have to the sight of his sister? And if his gut instinct was right, and Caitlin was Beth's lost child, would the woman he was coming to care about more than he would admit, ever willingly speak to him again?

CHAPTER FIVE

BETH PROPPED her good leg on the dashboard of the Blazer and surveyed the view through the windshield. She was feeling less anxious now that they'd left the interstate behind and were traveling east along a county highway that Hugh informed her would take them within a mile of their destination. She knew it wasn't logical to feel this way but it had spooked her more than she wanted to admit to find some of the road signs giving the mileage to the town in Indiana where the accident had occurred.

Of course, she hadn't a single memory of the accident or the town, but that didn't seem to matter. Now she calculated they were at least a hundred miles east of that terrible place, and she tried not to think about it anymore. She was getting good at not thinking about things that troubled her. At least some of the time.

"You're sure it's all right with this woman if I share the cabin with you?" The question was out of her mouth before she could stop it.

"It's fine. I told her you were coming this morning before I left for the airport."

"I've asked you that already, haven't I?" Her

mind still played tricks on her like that. She would blank out on a word, or an object, stuttering and stammering as she tried to bring the errant image to mind, or she would forget whether or not she had asked a question, or received a reply, until she heard herself repeating it. Kind of like having Alzheimer's at twenty, she often thought with a shudder.

"Yes, but only once since we left the interstate."

"There's a sign for Painted Lady Butterfly Farm. Two miles straight ahead." She pointed out the window, pleased that with all the stress of the past forty-eight hours that her mind hadn't decided to play tricks on her eyes, too. She knew she was blessedly lucky that other than the amnesia, she had very little residual brain damage.

She shifted position on the hard seat. Her hip was throbbing and she could feel a cramp coming on in her calf. She was glad they'd be arriving soon. She needed a good stretch. "Pain is good," she mumbled, massaging the incipient cramp. She'd probably never be comfortable wearing shorts or a bathing suit in public with all the scars from the surgeries. But, at least she was wasn't walking on an artificial leg.

And she wasn't dead and buried like Jamie. *And their baby? Was she dead and buried, too?* As usual those kind of thoughts threatened to drown her in guilt and sadness. She fought to beat them back.

"Leg bothering you?"

She took a deep breath and sat up a little straighter. Hugh was with her; this time the darkness wouldn't win. "Just a little."

"We're almost in sight of the place. I'll help you walk it off. Then I'll take you into Bartonsville for the meat loaf special at the Golden Sheaf."

"I don't eat red meat."

"I know. I'll eat yours. You can have the salad and mashed potatoes. I don't suppose you've sworn off banana cream pie, too?" His grin was devilish. Hugh was a really good-looking man, even if she was prejudiced in his favor. He looked a lot like pictures of his father, who had been a Green Beret. He'd died when Hugh was eight, six years before she was even born. She used to pretend he was her father, too, instead of Trace. Trace wasn't father material at all.

"Don't even think about it. Especially if it has whipped cream on top instead of meringue."

"It does."

"I'll fight you to the death for it." The exchange brought them to the cabins. Beth opened the door of the truck and was engulfed by the steamy heat of an early June afternoon. "Whew, it's hot."

"Yeah, but not as hot or humid as Houston."

"Nowhere is as humid as Houston. So this is our new abode?" Beth looked at the cabin and liked what she saw—steep-pitched roof, green window boxes overflowing with spicy-scented geraniums, funky red lawn chairs and a real wooden screen door. She got stiffly down from the high seat of the Blazer. "This place is stuck in the fifties."

"Faith will be thrilled to hear you say that. I think she worked hard to get that ambiance. Wait until you see the refrigerator. It's vintage *Happy Days*. And it doesn't keep ice cream. You'll have to get your double-chocolate-chip-mocha fix at the Dairy Barn in town.'' Hugh pulled her bag from the back as she limped past the cabin to stare down at the farmhouse. There were big trees in the yard and an even bigger red barn, a pond with a swinging rope and green fields stretching for miles in all directions. A woman was out in the yard picking up branches, probably from the hailstorm Hugh had told her about.

She was being followed by a dog that looked like Lassie, only way smaller, and a little girl. A toddler, dragging a stick almost as long as she was. She appeared to be two or two and a half. The same age as her daughter would be. Comparing children of similar age to her lost baby was a habit she needed desperately to break. She turned hurriedly and saw Hugh coming back out of the cabin. The screen door slapped shut with a bang.

''That sounds like the one on *The Waltons,*'' she said too brightly. She watched a lot of classic TV shows when she couldn't sleep.

Hugh's eyes moved past her, and spotted the three figures in the yard. ''That's Faith Carson and her daughter,'' he said. ''Do you want to meet them?''

''Sure.'' Hugh had told her the owner of Painted Lady Farm was a young widow with a little girl. Faith was her name, and the little girl was Caitlin. She shouldn't have trouble remembering those names.

''You're sure the butterflies aren't going to be a problem?''

She wasn't going to let them be a problem. It was a weird coincidence that the place where Hugh was staying was a butterfly farm. And her nightmares had come to be filled with images of blood and butterflies, but she could handle it. She used to love the damn things. She had even wanted to be an entomologist once, a lifetime ago. That was the kind of useless thing she remembered with no problem at all.

Hugh was looking down at the woman and child, his expression guarded. "You've asked me that before," she said, giving him a little punch on the arm. His muscles were rock hard and she winced. "You've been working out, again."

"I've been working. Period."

"To tell you the truth I'm looking forward to being a lady of leisure." She was amazed to find she meant it. The time since the accident had been like running a nonstop marathon—on crutches, rehabilitating her body and mind, getting her strength back and staying one step ahead of her nightmares. Now she just wanted to do some reading, walk the trail along the creek Hugh had told her about, swim in the pond, even if the fish did nibble her toes. Maybe she'd even go in the butterfly house. If facing your demons was something you had to do, she could think of worse ways to go about it.

"Ready?" Hugh tucked her arm through his. "Just take it slow until you get the kinks worked out." She was surprised to see a flicker of nervousness in Hugh's dark eyes. Hugh never looked nervous. Almost against her will her gaze skated past him to focus on the woman and her little girl still picking up sticks in the yard. She shivered and didn't know why. A premonition?

The scene before her looked like something out of a Norman Rockwell painting. Nothing threatening except a glass house of butterflies, which she could stay out of if she wanted to. She was just tired, that's all. Time to suck it up and move on. "I'm ready," she said. "Introduce me to Faith Carson and her little girl."

IT WASN'T ONLY CHANCE that made Faith look up from her task of collecting downed twigs and branches to see Hugh and a slight, blond woman walking arm and arm toward her. She had spent entirely too much time watching for them…no, for him, over the course of the last hour, and entirely too much time thinking about what might have happened if he'd taken her in his arms the other evening. She'd dreamed about it, as well, and her dreams had gone much further than a kiss.

He had come to the greenhouse early that morning, while the mist was still on the meadow and the sun barely over the horizon. Caitlin was asleep in the house. Faith was relying on the intercom that connected her daughter's bedroom to the greenhouse to give her warning when Caitlin woke up.

Hugh had accepted a cup of coffee, black, no sugar, but declined a cranberry muffin. He'd explained his sister was coming in on a flight from Houston in the afternoon. There had been a sense of urgency about him, a grimness in the hard line of his jaw, or so Faith had fancied. She had attributed it to worry for his sister, and approved of his concern. Family was important to Faith. She was glad to know it was important to him, too.

Faith's heart almost stopped beating as the young woman stepped out of the glare of the sun and could be seen clearly. She was the last person on earth Faith expected to see.

She was Caitlin's mother.

The girl Faith had thought dead two and a half years before.

"Hi," the apparition said in a light, sweet voice that Faith recognized even without the overlay of pain and fear it had once had. "I'm Hugh's sister, Beth Harden. Are you okay? You look as if you've seen a ghost."

"I… No," she said, and forced a smile onto her face. "I…I straightened up too quickly, that's all. I'm fine. It's…it's nice to meet you, Beth. Welcome to Painted Lady Farm." Inside she was shaking so hard she thought her knees might buckle, but her voice sounded almost normal.

"It's nice to be here, Mrs. Carson."

"Faith. My name is Faith." She heard the echo of her words that stormy November day and wondered if Beth recalled them.

"Thanks, Faith. My brother said you had quite a storm go through here yesterday." Beth looked around the yard, noting the broken twigs and branches, the mud-splattered pansies in the bed at their feet. "Hugh also said Painted Lady Farm was a lovely place. He was right."

"Thank you. I've worked very hard on it the past three years." Faith could scarcely form sentences. Why the polite small talk? Why didn't Beth and her brother get it over with, state their claim to Caitlin and end Faith's life?

"I can tell."

The young woman's smile was pleasant, but distant, a stranger's smile. Sudden unreasoning hope hit with the force of a blow. Was it possible Beth didn't recognize Faith as the woman who had delivered her baby? How could that be?

Behind her, Faith could hear Caitlin crowing with laughter as she played tug-of-war with Addy. The moment she had dreaded for two and a half years had arrived and passed. The sun hadn't fallen from the sky, the world hadn't stopped turning. The slender ghost from her past hadn't pulled Caitlin into her arms claiming her as her own.

Still, the urge to grab Caitlin and run away, as far and as fast as she could go, was strong. But Faith knew if she made any move toward Caitlin at all, Hugh Damon would notice. Her first impression of him had been the right one. He *knew,* and nothing she said or did would convince him otherwise. Her world was in danger from this man. She should have heeded her intuition and sent him packing the moment he had first set foot in the greenhouse.

But she hadn't, and now she had no other choice. She would have to play the game. "Let me show you around.'' She forced the muscles of her mouth into a smile and lifted her hand toward the greenhouse. Everything around her had taken on an aura of unreality, except for the steady regard of Hugh's eyes and the gurgling laughter of Caitlin playing with her dog. ''There are no other visitors at the moment. Would you like a tour of the butterfly house?''

Now Beth looked as if *she* had seen a ghost. ''I...I'm a little tired from the flight,'' she said, glancing up at her brother. She was as slender and petite as Faith remembered, but her hair was no longer the color of moonlight. It had darkened to gold, the same color as the highlights in Hugh's dark hair.

''Perhaps tomorrow morning, then? The butterflies are early risers and it will be cool enough to sit for a while and enjoy them.''

''Thanks. I...I'll think about it.''

Addy had tired of playing tug-of-war with Caitlin and had come prancing over to sniff at Beth's pant leg. Caitlin followed close on the sheltie's heels. She wrapped her grimy little arms around Faith's leg and peeked up at Beth. ''Hi. I Caitlin.''

Faith didn't dare look down at her daughter. Her reluctance was mixed of equal parts wariness and fear. Wariness that Hugh was watching and cataloging her every reaction. And fear that Caitlin would feel some connection to Beth, and with the complete honesty of small children voice that emotion and bring down Faith's carefully constructed web of lies.

Beth leaned forward but didn't stoop to Caitlin's

level. "Hi. I'm Beth." Her smile was warm, genuine, but still one of a stranger.

Any lingering doubt Faith had as to Beth's utter obliviousness of her relationship to the two of them vanished. She could not be such a good actress that she could suppress all emotion at the first sight of the child she had lost.

Faith glanced at Hugh and saw doubt and shock flicker across his face before he mastered the emotions. Had he thought the same as Faith? That Beth couldn't possibly fail to recognize her own child? Now that she hadn't had he been thrown off balance?

"My dog," Caitlin said, pointing to Addy. "Watch out. She'll smell your bottom."

"Caitlin." Faith's admonition was automatic.

Beth's laughter was as unguarded as Caitlin's comment. "I'll remember that. She's a nice dog." Beth leaned a little farther forward, holding out her fingers for Addy to sniff. A spasm of pain crossed her face and she stumbled slightly. Hugh was beside her in a moment, steadying her with a hand under her elbow.

"Are you okay?"

She jerked upright, color rushing into her pale cheeks, a look of annoyance on her face. "I'm fine. My knee just gave out on me. It still does that sometimes. I should have worn my brace, but I didn't want to get stopped going through security at the airport."

"Would…would you like to sit down for a few minutes?" Faith gestured to the Adirondack chairs under a nearby oak. The last thing she wanted was to spend more time in their company but she had to play her part. She had to carry on as if nothing was out of the ordinary. Instead of ordering the two of them off her property and out of her life, she would have to be the gracious hostess without a care in the world beyond their comfort.

"No, thanks. I think I'd like to go back to the cabin."

"I'll go get the Blazer." Hugh's expression was unreadable. Once more she had the impression that this meeting had not gone as he had expected. How had he tracked her down? Something had brought him to her doorstep. Some scrap of knowledge, some tidbit of detail gleaned from Beth, perhaps? She would never know because she would never dare to ask.

And she would never dare to be alone with him. She wasn't fool enough to think that he intended to let matters stand as they were. He would confront her with his knowledge at the first opportunity. And, God help her, she was as loath to lie to him now as she had ever been.

"YOU'RE UP EARLY." Hugh came out of the cubicle-size bedroom of the cabin the next morning, pulling a shirt on over his jeans. It was barely daylight, the sun just peeking over the rolling farmland to the east. Beth was sitting at the small Formica-topped table with a bowl of cereal in front of her and orange juice in a vintage jelly glass in her hand.

"I'm always up early these days," she said not

quite evasively. There were faint shadows under her eyes, but she didn't look as if she'd spent a sleepless night tossing and turning, the way he had.

He didn't question her any further. He wasn't quite sure what to do next. He'd acted on impulse the past couple of days and that was sure as hell the last thing he should have done. He'd brought them both to the edge of disaster yesterday, and today the risk was just as great. *Engineers* and *impulse* were not words that belonged in the same sentence.

"I made coffee." Beth gestured over her shoulder with her spoon. "This place is seriously retro, but it's got a modern-day coffeemaker. Although I was kind of hoping I could take a crack at making it in one of those old aluminum pots with the little glass domes on top. You know, like the ones in the old Maxwell House commercials."

"I need a cup. I don't care how you made it." The floor was linoleum and cool to his bare feet, but the day promised heat and humidity.

"I bet you do." Beth let the spoon drop into her empty bowl and stood up. "You tossed and turned all night. Bad dreams?"

"No. Just a hard mattress," he lied. The wide-awake memories of introducing Beth to Faith and Caitlin the afternoon before were nightmare enough. Deep down inside he simply hadn't believed the doctors. Couldn't believe that Beth wouldn't have some remembrance of what had happened to her once she confronted the woman who was raising her child.

Whatever other doubts he had he still believed that Caitlin was Beth's child.

Beth moved over to the sink to rinse her bowl and glass. She was wearing long-legged flannel pajamas even though it was too warm for them in the barely air-conditioned cabin. She was still sensitive of the scars on her leg. Four surgeries, eleven pins. She was lucky to be walking at all. Not lucky, Hugh reminded himself proudly. She'd worked damn hard to come this far.

"What do you want to do today?" he asked.

She paused with the bowl suspended under a stream of water. "I...I don't think I'm quite ready for the butterfly tour yet."

"Did you have the dream again last night?" he asked too sharply. She turned her head and gave him a considering look. His guilty conscience was working overtime and she'd picked up on the vibes in his voice.

"No. I don't remember dreaming at all."

What did that mean? Hugh wondered, but he was relieved that Beth didn't seem to have suffered any psychological damage from his aborted attempt to jump-start her memory. Still, he didn't want her around Faith Carson until he could find the words to tell his sister why he'd brought her here. And how he was going to do that, he had no idea. Except he couldn't do it at Painted Lady Farm. "We could do some sightseeing today if you want. There are a couple of antique places nearby. And a farmer's market. The strawberries are coming out around here."

"You hate antiquing." On the other hand she loved poking through the nooks and crannies of antique shops.

"For you I'll brave the dust and mildew of every junk shop we can find in a fifty-mile radius."

"Great. I'll jump in the shower and be ready in fifteen minutes."

He'd brave more than a couple of musty antique shops to see her smile that way. They'd spend the day together. He'd find some way to ease into the subject of her lost baby. And then, later, he'd strap on body armor and track down Faith Carson to have it out with her.

He wasn't joking about the body armor. He had no illusions whatsoever that the woman was now his enemy. He had seen it in the fierce protectiveness in her eyes yesterday, in the way her hands had tightened into fists on the branch she'd held. She would fight him to the death to keep what she claimed was hers.

His pager went off. He grabbed it off the counter. "Damn. It's Higgins at the site. I'll have to call in."

He punched in the number on his cell phone and thirty seconds later he was listening to the half-hysterical voice of the site boss. The EPA inspectors were on their way and his secretary hadn't passed on the message the evening before. Hugh had to get his butt to Cincy before the Feds arrived or there would be hell to pay.

There was no getting out of it. Hugh was going to

have to spend the day on site. He'd have to take Beth with him.

But when she came out of the shower ten minutes later, dressed in a sunny-yellow top and thin white cotton slacks, she surprised him by shaking her head and turning down his offer of a day in the city. "I've had enough sitting around in airplanes and trucks. I think I'll rent a bicycle and take off on my own."

"Rent a bicycle?"

"Yeah, from Faith. How long have you been here? Haven't you read that note on the end of the cupboard?" She wrapped the towel she'd been using into a turban and marched over to tap a pink-tinted fingernail on the sheet of paper tacked to the cupboard. "Faith rents bicycles. It says here there's a bike trail that starts at a little roadside park—" she tilted her head and then pointed west "—just down the road. I'll check with her and see if any of those antique shops are close enough to go to on my own."

He opened his mouth to protest and she cut him off.

"Don't thank me, big brother. I know how much you hate poking around in dusty shops while I try on vintage hats and paw through stacks of old table linens."

"You just got here. I haven't seen you for weeks." He felt like a jerk for trying to manipulate her this way, but the last place on earth he wanted her to be today was in close proximity to Faith.

"You can take me out to dinner tonight to make up for it. They're featuring fresh strawberry pie at the Golden Sheaf. I saw it on the menu last night. Besides, I want to get to know Faith better.''

''What?'' He searched her face for any clue that she had recalled something, but he saw only a hint of laughter and mischief in her eyes that brightened them to the color of the sky on a midsummer afternoon.

''I want to check her out. See if she's good enough for you.''

''What the devil are you talking about?''

''I think you're just the teeniest bit interested in our landlady,'' she said.

''What gave you that idea?''

''Woman's intuition, I guess. Something about the way you look at her. The way you talk about her.''

''I was making conversation. Filling you in on what it's like around here, that's all.''

''If that's all you were doing then why are the veins standing out on your neck? And your face is turning red.''

He made a grab for her. She'd always been ticklish, and when she was little he'd used it to his advantage when she was teasing him.

''I'm too old for this,'' she giggled, wriggling like a fish, as he reached out and reeled her in for a bear hug.

''You're not even twenty-one.''

''I will be next month.''

''Practically an old woman,'' he growled, noting how light she felt in his arms.

She went quiet very suddenly. "Some days I feel like an old woman."

He set her gently on her feet. "Beth, honey—" Once more words failed him when he needed them most.

"No poor-Beth talk. I shouldn't have said that. I'll be fine, really." She clasped her small hands around his wrists and squeezed hard. "Go do your job."

He had to tread very carefully. He'd foolishly brought his sister to this place, and introduced her to the woman who might hold the key to her past without learning the truth from Faith first. But today he had nothing to fear. Unlocking that mystery was the last thing Faith Carson wanted. He was convinced of that. She had become his unwilling ally, whether she liked it or not.

CHAPTER SIX

THIS TIME she was ready for the appearance of Hugh's sister. Faith was watering the last of the flats of red, white and what passed for blue petunias that were always popular for bedding plants in and around Bartonsville, not only because people liked to wave the flag, but because the Bartonsville high school sports teams were known as the Patriots. Beth's limp was less noticeable this morning, a slight hesitation in her gait, the only indication of the accident that had almost taken her life.

"Good morning," Beth said, shoving her hands into the pockets of her white slacks. The high for the afternoon was predicted to be ninety. Even though she had paired the slacks with a sleeveless yellow T-shirt she was going to be uncomfortable in the outfit before long.

"Good morning. I hope you slept well. Have you had breakfast?" Faith was proud of the nothing-out-of-the-ordinary tone of her voice, but she hoped her smile didn't look as forced as it felt on her lips.

"Yes and yes." Beth's answering smile was genuine and free of guile.

Faith relaxed a fraction. She had lain awake most

of the night reliving the moments of their first encounter, searching her memory for any inkling of recognition she might have missed and had found none, but still she worried. And with good reason. Hugh Damon didn't suffer from amnesia as she'd begun to believe Beth did.

"And your brother?"

"I'm afraid he has to spend the day on site in Cincinnati. Something about the EPA and drainage variances." She lifted slender shoulders in a shrug. "He left almost an hour ago." Faith knew exactly when he'd left. She had watched the Blazer drive away as she'd gone to feed the barn cats.

"Then you've come to see the butterflies. It's a good time. I'm just getting the feeding trays ready."

Beth was standing before a table of garden herbs. She had picked up a small clay pot of rosemary to sniff, but now she set it down with a thump. "I...I don't think so. Thanks, anyway. Actually, I came to see about renting a bicycle for the day. The flier in the cabin mentioned a biking trail."

"Yes, it starts at the park about a mile from here and follows an old railroad right-of-way. About two miles farther on it crosses the river on a trestle bridge. It's a very pretty ride at this time of year."

"Sounds exactly right...if the grades aren't too steep."

"Nothing steeper than the lane from here to the road."

"I think I can mange that." She went back to examining the herb pots, as though she needed something to do with her hands. Beth appeared restless and on edge, although she tried not to show it. Faith wondered how much of that edginess might be caused by the first faint stirring of returning memory?

"I'm afraid I don't have much of a selection of bikes. Only a couple of old three-speeds, but you really don't need anything fancier around here." Faith turned off the wand sprinkler and motioned for Beth to follow her toward the barn, where the bicycles were kept.

"Mommy," Caitlin yelled, hopping down the back steps, pulling thirteen-year-old Dana, Steve's niece, and Peg along with her. Her daughter tugged free of Dana's grasp and flung out her arms as she ran, apparently as thrilled to see Faith as if they'd been parted for twenty days instead of twenty minutes. Peg and Dana followed more sedately and nodded pleasantly to Beth.

"I got Barbie shoes on. See." She held up one little foot shod in a pink Barbie sandal. "I'm be-oo-ti-ful."

"You are beautiful." Faith picked her up. "Are you all ready to go bye-bye with Dana and Auntie Peg?"

"I go potty like a big girl. I brushed my teeth." Caitlin gave Faith a Cheshire cat grin that showed two rows of shiny white teeth.

"Good girl."

Caitlin wrapped her arms around Faith's neck and gave Beth the once-over. "Hi," she said, growing suddenly shy. Again Faith felt a sharp lance of anxiety pierce her. Was it possible for Caitlin to feel some connection, however tenuous, with the woman who had given her life?

Beth's smiled wavered for a moment but the darkness passed quickly and the smile returned. "Hi, Caitlin. Do you remember me? I'm Beth."

Caitlin nodded, looking over Beth's shoulder, then up the lane to the cabins. "Where's Hugh? I like Hugh. Get him."

Beth's laughter was high and tinkling. "Uh-oh. Sounds like my brother's made another conquest."

Faith didn't want to talk about Hugh. "Beth Harden, this is my sister, Peg Baden and her husband's niece, Dana."

"Hello, Beth," Peg said. "Welcome to Ohio."

"Hello," Beth said politely. "It's nice to meet you."

Dana added a shy hello, which Beth returned.

"Baby school." Caitlin started to fidget. "I go baby school."

Beth's expression was puzzled. "Baby school?"

Caitlin nodded vigorously and then went limp, hanging over Faith's clasped arms, her silvery-blond hair floating around her face as she reached for the ground. With a little grunt Faith set her on her feet. "Go," the toddler demanded, tugging on the hem of Peg's denim skirt.

"Caitlin, that's not polite. Remember we must use our manners. The grown-ups are talking. Please be good and wait until we finish, or you'll have to stay home," Faith said as sternly as she could manage.

"Caitlin is going to be Dana's study subject for her baby-sitting certification course at the junior high school," Peg explained. "Evidently potty-trained, two-a-half-year-olds are very desirable specimens."

Dana nodded. "Brittany Weisman can't use her little sister because she's still wearing diapers. Her mom says she's not going to bother to potty train her until summer's over."

"You'll graduate with honors if you last two days with Caitlin," Faith added.

"It sounds like fun," Beth said.

"Go now, Dana. C'mon, Peg-peg." Caitlin was dancing up and down again. Beth was watching Caitlin's antics with interest, but nothing more, no hint of recognition or connection showed on her face.

"All right already." Dana scooped Caitlin up and swung her onto her back.

"Yay! Piggyback." Caitlin giggled.

"I put her new Barbie and her favorite sippy cup in her bag and the phone number's in the side pocket."

"I've got everything in the van already," Dana assured Faith.

Peg rolled her eyes. "I don't think it's Caitlin that's having separation anxiety here."

Faith felt her color rise. She tried hard not to be overprotective, but today she couldn't help it. She wanted to shut Caitlin safe in her bedroom and throw away the key.

"We'd better be on our way. Steve is watching

the boys, but he has work to do so I need to get back. Nice meeting you, Beth,'' Peg said.

Faith excused herself to Beth and followed Peg to the van. ''Are you okay?'' Peg asked as Faith buckled Caitlin into the safety seat.

Faith snapped the harness into its lock and didn't look up. ''I'm fine.'' But, of course, she wasn't, and Peg had noticed. Her sister, although only five years older, had been more of a mother to her than the frail, pretty woman who had borne them. Faith had made up her mind not to tell her sister who Beth was. She couldn't add that extra burden of secrecy to Peg's marriage. She was going to have to face this alone.

Peg climbed into the driver's seat and stared at Faith as she brushed Caitlin's hair behind her ears. She spoke quietly while Dana strapped herself in beside Caitlin. ''You're all jumpy. You've got big circles under your eyes. You look as if you haven't slept in days. Are you coming down with something?''

''No. I'm fine, really. But you're right. I haven't been sleeping too well.''

''Take a nap this afternoon. I'll keep Caitlin until after supper.''

''You don't have—''

''I know I don't have to.'' Peg gave her a saucy grin. ''I promise we won't keep her too late. And I won't let the boys feed her too much ice cream.'' A trip to the Dairy Barn at the edge of town would be the highlight of Caitlin's day. There was no way Faith could say no.

"Okay." She leaned over and gave Caitlin a peck on the cheek. "Bye-bye."

"Bye." Caitlin gave her a happy wave.

She watched her sister drive away, then turned to find Beth wheeling a bicycle out of the barn. "Do you want me to leave the deposit with you?" Beth asked. She pulled a couple of bills out of her pocket and held them toward Faith.

"No need. You're welcome to the bicycle."

"You can't make money that way."

"I don't need the money. Let's just call it a perk for long-term guests. But I do have to ask you to sign a waiver. My insurance company demands it."

"No problem." Beth leaned the bike against a post and followed Faith to the greenhouse.

"You're welcome to tour the butterfly house whenever you like," Faith said as she showed Beth where to sign the simple liability form. "In fact, if you're interested now would be a good time. It's sunny. The butterflies are always more active when it's sunny."

Beth spoke quickly, shaking her head. "Maybe tomorrow. I'd really like to ride this morning."

"All right."

The note of uneasiness had returned to Beth's voice. It was faint but evident. She didn't want to be around the butterflies. Faith wondered why. She was finding it too easy to talk to Beth, and she mustn't allow herself to drop her guard that way. The girl's next words confirmed the wisdom of that internal warning.

"Your little girl's adorable. I wish I had hair that color."

"You do have hair that color," Faith said, swallowing against the sudden constriction in her throat.

"I used to have hair that color. Now it comes out of a bottle. So do my eyelashes and eyebrows. Your little girl has lovely eyelashes and eyebrows, darker than her hair."

"She...she takes after her father." Jamie had been blond, with dark eyelashes and eyebrows, Faith recalled. But if Beth couldn't remember Caitlin's birth, or Faith, had she also lost her memories of her baby's father?

"She's lucky, believe me. After my accident my hair got dark, but my eyebrows and eyelashes didn't. I looked weird. Of course, for six months I didn't know how I looked. And I couldn't have complained about it if I had. Every word that came out of my mouth made no sense." Beth had been running her fingertip along the edge of a hummingbird figurine on the shelf just inside the door. She broke off suddenly. "I'm sorry. You probably don't want to hear all this, do you?"

"No. Please. I—I'm a nurse. I know a little about brain injuries. You don't have to go into detail if it makes you uncomfortable, but please feel free to do so if you want to."

"Thanks. I—I don't usually care about that anymore. It's—" Beth shrugged and set the little figurine back on the shelf very carefully. "This will sound silly but this is as close as I've been to where the accident happened. Seeing the road signs on the interstate gave me the willies." She rubbed her hands up and down her arms.

"Where did your accident happen?"

"A little town in Indiana. About a hundred miles or so from here. You've probably never heard of it."

"Probably," Faith agreed. "I only moved here three years ago after my husband died. Were...were you alone?"

"I was with my boyfriend. He was driving. There was a terrible ice storm."

Faith caught her breath and knew she must speak. "Caitlin was born during an ice storm. I was here by myself."

Beth's face was suddenly very white. "When?"

There was no way Faith could avoid answering. "She'll be three in November."

"I thought she m-m-must be about that old. T-t-two and a half." Beth seemed to force each word from her lips, her stutter was very pronounced.

"Yes, she is."

"That's when my accident happened."

"It was a very bad storm. It covered most of three states, all the way from Chicago to Cleveland. Caitlin and I were trapped here for days." Faith waited for Beth to ask Caitlin's exact birth date, her heart beating hard and fast in her chest, but the question didn't come. Instead, Beth reached out for another figurine. Her hand was shaking badly enough that Faith could see the tremors from several feet away. She busied herself straightening a stack of invoices before putting them in the drawer below the cash register. She needed to change the topic. But first she must learn all she could without Hugh's hard, seeking gaze pinned on her. She could never show such interest in Beth's past in front of him.

"Were you and your brother living in Indiana at the time?" She was taking a great risk. Anything she said could lead to the younger woman remembering everything.

"No. I was living with Father and my stepmother in Boston. Hugh was out of the country. My boyfriend was killed. A semi truck jackknifed and started a chain reaction. W-we were running away from our parents. His parents mostly." The words were defiant, but the slighter stutter betrayed Beth's agitation. She gave a harsh, quavering little laugh that betrayed her still more. "I still am. I came here to get away from them. They keep badgering me…about things I can't remember."

"I'm sorry." Faith bent down to the little refrigerator so that Beth couldn't see her face. She wasn't especially knowledgeable about brain injuries, but one thing she did know was that there were no absolutes. Faith's whole world was in danger from any of a thousand small associations that could bring about the return of Beth's memory.

She brought out a plate of watermelon and orange slices and set them on the counter with a thud. Her hands were shaking as hard as Beth's had been. She rubbed them together and reached for the paring knife and plastic container of wooden skewers she kept beside the refrigerator.

"What are you doing?" Beth asked. If she wanted to change the subject, Faith would go along with her. She had had enough of this dangerous game.

"I'm getting ready to feed the butterflies. They love fruit. Especially watermelon."

"Maybe because it's the closest to nectar?"

It was an astute observation. "I sometimes think that myself, although there's plenty of nectar flowers blooming in the habitat. And I set out nectar feeders, too." While Beth watched, Faith threaded pieces of fruit onto the skewers and placed them in a grid pattern to hold them up off the plate, giving the butterflies more surface to feed from.

"Butterflies taste with their feet and hear with their antennae."

"That's right. The school groups always get a laugh out of me telling them if they were butterflies, they'd have to stick their bare toes in their hot fudge sundaes to taste it.

"I remember all the oddest things," Beth said softly. "I wanted to be an entomologist...until the accident. Bits and pieces of things I used to know pop into my mind all the time. But I can't—" She stopped abruptly. Faith held her breath wondering what she would say next.

I can't remember what happened to my baby?

"But huge chunks of the most important months of my life are gone." Her voice trailed off. "I really am sorry I've dumped all this on you. It's strange. I don't usually talk about the accident. And I never ramble on this way. Especially—''

''With a stranger?'' Faith was slightly ashamed of herself for putting the words in the girl's mouth.

''I was going to say with someone I just met. *Stranger*'s such a hard word.''

''It is, isn't it?'' Faith said softly, speaking from her heart. Beth looked so lost and confused. Only a monster wouldn't feel compassion for her. And Faith wasn't a monster, just a mother terrified of losing her child to another woman. ''I don't think we're strangers anymore, either. Would you like to help me feed the butterflies?''

''No.'' Once more the denial was swift and immediate. ''No. I think I'd better get on with my ride. It's getting hotter by the minute. Where did you say that little park was?''

''It's at the bottom of the next hill. Go out to the road, turn right past the cabins. First you'll see the cemetery and at the bottom of the hill a road off to the right. The park's at the end of it.'' Faith gestured with a skewer. ''It's only a half mile or so across the fields. You can't see it from here because of the woods that run along the creek. But you can't miss it. There's a sign. The county renamed it Sylvan Lake, but everyone around here still calls it Carson's Pond.''

''Turn right. Cemetery. Bottom of the hill. Sylvan Lake.'' Beth's eyes were huge pools of blue misery.

Faith began to be alarmed. Perhaps she shouldn't let her go off by herself this way.

"Beth, what's wrong?" She couldn't stop herself from asking. It was hard for her to see this girl in such distress, even though self-preservation prevented her from offering too much comfort.

"I—I'm afraid of butterflies. Isn't that a hoot? I dream about them. I'm cold and scared and hurting. There are thousands of butterflies. And they drop into the snow and turn to drops of blood—" Once more she stopped, as though torn between wanting to tell Faith what was on her mind, and in fear of doing so. "I told you it was weird." She squared her narrow shoulders and started backing toward the door. "I recommend never getting your brain scrambled in a car accident."

"Beth."

"Don't worry about me. I stammer a lot and get words all mixed up. But I'm not crazy, even if I do rattle on. And look, if I said anything earlier to make you believe my brother's some kind of lady-killer, he's not."

"What?" Faith was taken off guard by her words. "Your brother?"

"When Caitlin asked for him. I—I made some comment about him being a lady-killer. It's the truth. But it's not because he encourages them. I don't think he's even had a date since I got hurt. I don't want you to get the wrong idea about him."

"Your brother...has been the perfect gentlemen since he arrived."

"He's a great guy."

"I'm sure he is." It was Faith's turn to be evasive. She shooed away an inquisitive fly from the fruit plate with a wave of her hand.

"I'll go now so you can feed the butterflies."

"Beth."

She had already reached the doorway of the greenhouse by the time Faith spoke. She turned back, her defiance melting away, as though she expected to be told to take a pill and forget all the things that tormented her.

"Have a good ride."

Beth held her gaze for a long moment. So long Faith was tempted to look away, lest Beth read the secret she kept so carefully. "Thanks," she said, a tiny curve of a smile touching the corners of her mouth. "I'll do that."

IT WASN'T EVEN ten o'clock and it was already as hot as a Houston summer morning would be. But the humidity wasn't as bad, at least not yet. Beth leaned the bike against the wrought-iron fence of the small cemetery and looked back at Painted Lady Farm.

"God, what a fool you made of yourself this morning." She talked to herself when she was alone. It wasn't something that she'd started doing since the accident, though. She'd been talking to herself since she was a little kid. Hugh always used to tease her about it, peering behind the curtains and lifting up the cushions on the couch to find whoever it was she was talking to.

"Oh, Hugh. I still think I'm losing my mind, no matter how hard you try to convince me I'm not."

She looked down. Her hands were shaking and dark spots danced before her eyes. Her therapist would be mad at her for getting this upset. If she didn't settle down before Hugh got home he'd insist she take a sedative, and if she did that the dreams would be back in earnest.

She couldn't go on like this. She needed exercise. Exertion would lead to oblivion. She had to find the bike trail and go as fast and as far as her unreliable leg would take her. She coasted down the slope of the cemetery hill and found the gravel lane leading to the park just where Faith said it would be.

The lane angled up another gentle hill, winding through a grove of big oaks and maples and finally opening into a small parking lot. The trail head was clearly marked, a wide asphalt-paved path that would make for easy riding. It was shaded by a row of small trees and big sumac bushes at this time of day, and inviting. There was only one car in the lot, a beat-up looking Buick that had to be at least as old as she was.

A set of steps led up a steep bank to where the ground leveled out again. Beth decided to take a look at the park, maybe find a fountain or a spigot and get a drink of water. She'd taken off in such a state that she hadn't stopped at the cabin to get her pack. It would be a hot ride without water, but she wasn't about to use that as an excuse to turn back and spend the rest of the day pacing in the cabin's cramped main room.

She topped the rise, puffing just a little from pushing the bike up the banked slope, and looked down on a meadowlike setting. The lake was very small, more like a large pond really, narrow at one end and rounded at the other. A little hump-backed bridge crossed a marshy stream at the narrow end and a path led to a stone and wood picnic shelter. There was a play area for children on the shore of the lake, a big wooden jungle gym, swings and a slide. Primitive outhouses stood against the tree line.

There was an old-fashioned pump with a long handle in front of the shelter like the one she'd seen in Faith's backyard. She would get a drink before she began her ride. She started down the slope, pushing her bike, when a sudden wave of vertigo washed over her, leaving her shaken and sweating. Bright spots danced before her eyes, the sun whirled in the sky, and somewhere far away she heard a baby crying. Not now. Not the dream. This had never happened to her before. The dreams always came in the darkest, loneliest hours of the night. She shivered and felt the first sharp claws of a panic attack steal her breath.

"I've had too much sun," she said out loud. "Or I'm getting sick." But neither of those explanations accurately described the way she felt. Something was drawing her toward the picnic house, a sense of mingled familiarity and fear. "I know this place."

But she didn't. Couldn't. She had never set foot

in Ohio, or anywhere within a hundred miles until yesterday. The police, Jamie's parents, Hugh. They all had retraced their flight from Boston using several different routes, hoping to find the spot where she'd given birth, where she'd left her baby behind. But Bartonsville, Ohio, had never been mentioned.

Whatever it was about this place couldn't be related to her past. She took heart from the thought and opened her eyes, brushing away the tears that had fallen on to her cheeks.

"Hey! Wait."

Beth looked around to see a male figure on a black dirt bike come racing down the slope toward her. He skidded to a stop, blocking her path. If he was some kind of a pervert, or country-style purse snatcher, she'd never be able to outrun him. Better to stand her ground and not show any fear.

"You don't want to go down there," he said, leaning his weight on the handlebars, breathing heavily. He was wearing a navy-blue ball cap and cutoffs that were so thin and well washed they might have been made of tissue paper. A faded red Bartonsville Patriots T-shirt stretched across his chest and flat stomach. His hair was red, not auburn, or chestnut, or ginger. Just red. He had freckles everywhere she could see, and warm brown eyes. She relaxed a little. He didn't look like a rapist. He looked as innocent as Beaver Cleaver. And he wasn't so intimidating after all, not with that grin. He was maybe five-seven or five-eight. Although, he did have broad shoulders for his height, and well-muscled thighs below the

cutoffs. She jerked her gaze upward. She didn't notice things like that about boys anymore.

"I want a drink of water." She tried to sound as
old, and as annoyed as she could manage. "Please
get out of my way so I can get to the pump."

"That's what I'm trying to tell you. If you go that
way you'll be up to your knees in mud. The town
fathers saw fit to build that cute little bridge over the
stream, but they didn't appropriate any money for
draining the path. It's like a swamp down there this
time of year. If you were from around here you'd
know that."

"You're right. I'm not from around here." She
sounded churlish and felt slightly ashamed. He
wasn't a rapist. He probably played halfback on the
Bartonsville high school team, or maybe he wrestled.
And now that she looked at where he was pointing,
she did see that he'd saved her from getting stuck in
the mud. He might not be quite the boy she'd first
thought him to be, either. Something about the way
he held his body, the directness of his gaze bespoke
a measure of maturity. "You're a man," she blurted
in one of those horrifying lapses of control that still
plagued her in stressful situations.

He laughed, a rich full-throated, masculine laugh
that made her add another two or three years to her
estimate of his age. "Last time I checked."

"I—I'm sorry. I m-m-meant to say I thought you
were just a kid when you came barreling down that
hill." The effort to keep her brain and tongue from
tying themselves in knots was causing her to break

out in a cold sweat. And the continued unsettling pull of the picnic shelter added to her distress.

"I know I look like a kid," he said without offense, pulling the ball cap off his head and wiping his forehead with the back of his forearm. "Makes my job hell some days. Look, it's too damn hot to stand out here. Come on, I'll show you the dry way to the pump. And don't worry. Faith Carson will vouch for me. I'm Kevin Sager. I teach science at Bartonsville Junior High. I just had my kids out there to see the butterfly house a week or so ago."

"How did you know I was staying at Faith's place?" Almost against her will, Beth turned her bike and followed him along the bank until they came to a narrow path leading down to the picnic shelter. She kept her eyes averted from the building. No matter how ordinary—even inviting—it looked, she would rather die than go inside.

"The Painted Lady decal on the back fender of your bike. I run across renters of hers biking here every once in a while."

"Oh." She hadn't noticed the butterfly decal before he pointed it out.

He dropped his bike in the grass beside the pump and started working the handle. Beth just stood where she was, staring at the sparkling flow of water. "Cup your hands," he said, after a few moments. "My good manners only last so long. I'm dying of thirst and I forgot my water bottle this morning."

"I—I—?" For a terrible moment her mind came up entirely blank, unable to grasp the concept of making a cup with her hands. She looked at him helplessly, blinking back tears. She hadn't had this kind of block for months and months.

"You must be a city girl," he said, laughing again, as though nothing were terribly wrong.

"I am." What had she expected him to say?

"Thought so. Do this." He placed his hands side by side, scooped up a palm full of water and brought it to his lips, slurping noisily. "Ahhh, the only thing that could beat that right now is an ice-cold beer. Come on, your turn." He went back to pumping.

Beth dropped the kickstand on the bike and balanced it carefully on the grass. Trembling she laid one hand over the other and stared down at her stiff fingers. Something wasn't right? But what? She felt panic nipping at the edges of her thoughts again and battled it back. She took a deep breath and closed her eyes, recalling the movements he'd made. He had nice hands, she thought, big and square with a dusting of hair on the knuckles. And his name was Kevin. She liked that name. Suddenly, the concept clicked into placed. She curled her fingers upward and stuck her hands under the falling water.

"It's cold," she said, bringing her hands to her mouth.

"Spring fed. So's the pond. Want to go skinny dipping?"

"I—I— No." He was flirting with her. He was treating her like a normal girl…woman…not an invalid, not a mental case. Not a mother who might have done something so terrible to her baby her mind refused to remember a single thing about her birth. She didn't know how to respond. She took a too hasty step back and he grabbed her wrist to keep her from tripping over her bike. He let go of her as soon as she was steady on her feet, but the warmth of his wet hand lingered on her skin.

The devilish grin he'd been wearing disappeared, sharpening the angle of his jaw, dispelling any notion that this was a boy and not a man. "I'm sorry. I was just teasing. Not good form when you don't even know the name of the person you're teasing. What is your name, by the way?"

"Beth Harden."

"From?"

"Houston. Houston, Texas."

"I know where Houston is."

She felt herself blushing.

"And I'm Kevin Sager, fourth generation citizen of good old Bartonsville, Ohio. There we are, properly introduced. The formalities are over, right?"

"Right."

"Okay, no more teasing. Now can I make a serious request? Beth Harden from Houston, Texas, do you want to go skinny-dipping with me?"

CHAPTER SEVEN

HUGH HADN'T REALIZED how worried he'd been about leaving Beth alone until he pulled the Blazer to a halt beside the cabin just before sundown and saw her peering at him through the old-fashioned screen door. She was wearing shorts and a halter top, something she never did in public.

"You look like you could use a cold beer," she said, holding open the door. "Too bad we don't have any here."

"We do now." He pulled two plastic bags of groceries and a twelve pack of beer out of the back of the Blazer. "I stopped to get a few essentials."

"Like taco chips and salsa?" Beth asked with a smile, taking one of the bags and peering inside. "And cheese spread in a squirt bottle?"

"Hey, I like the stuff."

"It's pure fat. It will clog your arteries while you sleep."

"I like living dangerously."

"You always have."

He changed the subject. "No neighbors for the night, I see."

"Nope. But a couple did stop to look at the place

for a week later in the fall. I wasn't eavesdropping. The guy must have been deaf. He talked so loudly I imagine Faith's ears were ringing for an hour after they left.'' Hugh watched her closely. She seemed relaxed and untroubled. Her speech was clear, her movements smooth and coordinated. If she'd had a bad day, he would be able to tell. And she wouldn't be wearing shorts. On bad days she layered on the clothes no matter what the weather was like, cocooning herself against the world like the butterflies that haunted her dreams.

He relaxed a fraction. It seemed whatever interaction she'd had with Faith Carson hadn't upset her. But what did that mean? Had Beth made no connection with the woman or child in her damaged brain whatsoever? Or was he was one-hundred percent wrong in his speculation that Caitlin Carson was Beth's lost child? He'd have to tread carefully in his attempt to find out which it was.

He'd taken the time to remedy one of the other glaring omissions he'd made. He pulled a cell phone out of his pocket. ''Here, I thought you might need this to keep in touch with the world.''

''I don't know about keeping in touch with the world. But I'm glad I can keep in touch with you. And the pizza place out by the highway delivers within a fifteen-mile radius. I hear they make a great veggie sub.''

''How do you know that?''

''I met a guy. He told me.''

''You met a guy? Where? Who? We're out in the

middle of nowhere and you don't have a car." It was the last thing he'd expected her to say. She hadn't shown any interest in dating since the accident. At first Hugh had figured it was because she'd focused all her energies on her recovery. But over the past few months he'd begun to worry that it was because she felt herself too damaged to enter any kind of a relationship. He'd been searching for a way to bring up the subject, but now it seemed events had overtaken him.

"I had a bike. Maybe I shouldn't tell you his name. You sound as if you're going to track him down and beat him up." The sparkle he saw too seldom in her blue eyes faded away.

"Sorry. Big brother protocols kicking in." He turned to put the beer in the small fridge, squatting on his heels to place each can in the door shelf while he talked.

"Tell me about him. Is he from town?"

A smile curved her lips. "Yes. His name's Kevin Sager. He teaches junior high science. This is just his second year, so you can't complain he's too old for me," she said, anticipating his next question. He popped the top on a can of beer and motioned for her to keep talking.

"I met him at the park down the hill that Faith told me about when she loaned me the bike. I was going to take a ride along the bike trail, but it was too hot by the time I got there, so I thought I'd stop for a drink of water. I was kind of...wound up...and the place gave me the creeps for some reason." She faltered for a moment. "I haven't the slightest idea why. It's just a nice little country park." The statement caught Hugh's attention but he didn't let his interest show. He'd learned early on in her recovery not to show worry for her, or she would clam up, unwilling to confide in him further if she thought he was upset by her anxiety or pain.

"Okay, so far so good. We've got an age-compatible, gainfully employed, single male here. He is single, isn't he?"

"He's single. At least he told me he was and I believe him. He told me to check with Faith if I wanted a character reference. He's had his class out here to study the butterflies. He...Kevin..." She threw up her hands and laughed. "He rode up like a knight in shining armor on his bike and stopped me from walking into a swampy place, and probably wrenching my knee. And then he asked me to go skinny-dipping with him."

"He what?" So much for the nonchalant approach. Hugh crumpled the empty beer can in his fist. He was hot and dirty and he needed a shower and another beer, but first he wanted to get the low-down on this character who was hitting on his sister.

Beth laughed again, and the sound went straight to his heart and settled there with a warm glow. "Don't get yourself worked up. I admit it was a terrible pickup line, but he was just kidding." She colored slightly, and Hugh guessed the guy probably damn well had wanted to go skinny-dipping with his sister. He wouldn't be human if he didn't. "He's a nice guy, really. We rode back here together. He's coming back tomorrow and we're going to ride the trail to the river. He says it's great at sunrise. What time is sunrise anyway?''

''About six this time of year.''

She wrinkled her nose. ''Oh, well, I guess I can struggle out of bed that early if I have to. Do you want me to fix you a salad or something?''

''No. I grabbed a burger and fries on the way out of the city.'' Hugh decided he would play it cool and not ask any more questions about the school teacher his sister had taken a fancy to. But that didn't mean he wasn't going to get some answers somewhere else. He hadn't been around to keep her from tragedy with Jamie Sheldon, but he wasn't going to stand idly by and let her get her heart broken a second time.

''Want to come sit outside with me and watch the sunset? The TV reception is lousy today.''

The remark hit another sore spot in his conscience. ''Beth, are you sure you're going to be okay out here? We can look for a place closer to the project. I'll rent you a car on the days I'm working. You can do some shopping....''

''I don't want to move into the city. But maybe I will take you up on the rental car. I think it will be easier to get comfortable driving again here in the country, instead of in freeway traffic, don't you?''

Her breezy tone didn't fool him. She wanted to stay here, and he should be glad. He wanted answers to all the questions that had eaten at him like acid since the moment the doctors had told him Beth had given birth, probably just hours before the accident.

He wanted to know what Faith Carson knew.

But there was something more than concern for his sister and her lost child driving him, something deep inside him that would not be denied.

God help him, he also wanted to learn all there was to know about Faith Carson for himself.

HE CAME TO HER in the moonlight, as she stood at the edge of the meadow. There was a slight breeze blowing from the west, ruffling the surface of the pond, keeping the mosquitoes at bay. The movement of the air cooled the nape of her neck, but it wasn't strong enough to ground the fireflies, or lightning bugs, as they were known in these parts. They danced and sparkled above the meadow flowers as thickly as stars in the sky.

"Hello, Faith," Hugh said, and the low, rough timbre of his voice caressed her skin like the wind.

"Good evening."

"Are you out stargazing?" he asked, resting one foot on the bottom rung of the rail fence that divided the lawn from the butterfly meadow. He was wearing cutoffs and a white T-shirt that stretched across his chest. She pulled her gaze upward, to his face. His expression was lost in the shadows, but she felt him watching her.

"Just enjoying the evening."

"It's just about perfect. Enough breeze to keep away the bugs and no clouds to block the view." He was looking up at the thin crescent moon. She leaned her elbows against the top rail of the fence and tipped her head back. The Big Dipper was directly overhead, and she concentrated on tracing its outline. She simply couldn't allow herself to be drawn in by the warmth of his low, rough voice. He was her enemy, not a man that she might find pleasure in conversing with on a moonlit night.

"Is Caitlin asleep?"

She jerked her head around. An ordinary question, but fraught with hidden meaning. Nothing about this meeting was ordinary, and they both knew it. Faith answered carefully. "She had a long and exciting day. She almost fell asleep in her SpaghettiOs." She slipped her hand into the oversize pocket of her sundress and touched the remote unit for the nursery monitor.

"My sister told me about it. Baby-sitting school, I believe she said."

"Yes, Caitlin loved it. She was the star pupil today. She can't wait for tomorrow. She'll be up with the sun."

"She's a sweet kid."

"She's my life," Faith said, unable to stop herself in time.

He didn't seem to notice, or ignored the opening she had given him to pounce. And pounce was the right word. He seemed as dangerous and predatory as a hunting cat.

She waited, tense and alert, but he changed the subject, throwing her off balance once more. "My sister had an exciting day, too,'' he said, resting his palms on the top rail. His arms were as well muscled as the rest of him. And once more she felt a flash of longing for those arms to be wrapped around her. ''She met a man.''

''A man? But where? I mean, she went to the park down the road, but she was back in an hour. I know because she brought the bicycle back to the barn.''

''She met him there. He was bicycling, too. He says he knows you. That you'd give a reference to his good character.''

''Me?'' The number of men in her life were few. There was Steve, and Reverend Kanine at church, Dr. Elliot at the hospital. ''What did he say his name was?''

''Kevin Sager. Is he the pillar of the community he says he is?''

''Kevin Sager? Yes, I know him slightly. He's the new science teacher at the junior high. His father's a county commissioner. Good family, as they say around here.''

''Thank you, I appreciate that. Beth hasn't had a lot to do with boys since her accident.''

''Kevin's not a boy. He's a man, although a young one. And your sister is a grown woman who probably won't appreciate you vetting her choice of friends.''

''But she's fragile as hell.'' He was protective of Beth. A man of honor and loyalty, as Mark had been. Faith knew that instinctively. But he was still her enemy. She could not forget that for a moment.

He had the power to destroy her.

And he would soon tire of this polite game and begin to question her in earnest, demanding answers she dare not give him. For a brief, wrenching second she wished she could lay the whole burden of her secret life on him, so they could work through it together, the way she and Mark had worked through their problems.

But that could never be. And she shouldn't succumb to such weak moments even in her fantasies.

"I really should be going inside. Even with the monitor on, I don't like to leave Caitlin alone in the house."

"Why is my sister afraid of the park?" Hugh asked. He moved to block her path to the house so quickly she gasped. His broad shoulders blocked out the moonlight and left her standing in darkness, alone and scared.

"I—I don't know what you're talking about."

"I think you do. Something about that little wayside park at the bottom of the hill upsets her. Why should that be? There's nothing out of the ordinary there. I've seen the place. Just a shelter, a pond, some swings for the kids."

"Yes. That's all it is. I walk Addy there often. There's a path from the backside of the meadow through the woods." Another incriminating bit of knowledge he might not have discovered for himself. His eyes gleamed in the moonlight, like the hunting cat she'd compared him to earlier, and she suppressed a shiver.

He let the silence drag on a few moments longer.

"I think you know why I'm asking, don't you, Faith?"

"On the contrary, I don't have any idea at all."

"Beth told you about her accident this morning."

"Yes. A little." She would stick to the truth as much as possible. She curled her hands around the top rail until the splintery wood bit painfully into her palms.

"Did she tell you about the child?"

"No." She had answered too quickly. She dared not let herself break eye contact, hopeful that the moonlight hid her expression at least as well as it did his. "She...she didn't mention a child. Not a word. What...what happened to it?" How much curiosity was normal? How much was too much, not enough?

He was silent, long enough for her to take two deep breaths to try to slow her racing heart. "She didn't have to tell you about what happened to the child, did she? You already know."

The accusation that had lain unspoken between them was finally in the open. She surged away from the fence, but he moved too quickly for her. He braced one long muscled arm on either side of her, keeping her captive where she stood.

"You know why being at the park upset her. She's been there before, hasn't she?"

"I don't have the slightest idea what you're talking about. Let me go." She didn't attempt to hide the panic in her voice. His actions, what he was saying were surely enough to panic any woman, not just one with secrets she didn't want him to learn.

"Is Caitlin truly your daughter, Faith?" There was no threat in his voice, only the implacable will to discover what she wanted no living soul to know.

His wording gave her an opening. "Yes, she's my daughter. Do you want to see her birth certificate?" She let her fear turn into rage. She would not be intimidated by him. "Although, I don't know why in hell I should show it to you. Now let me pass."

"No, I can't let you go. Not yet. Not until I've had my say."

"I can't help you." Dear Lord, that was the truth, and the conviction in her tone shook him momentarily, but only momentarily.

"I think you can. I'm not trying to frighten you, Faith."

"You *are* frightening me. You're not making any sense. And I don't like being threatened like this." That also was the truth. Did he mean to claim Caitlin here and now? Did he want to make her confess to Beth what had happened and hand over her child? But Beth wasn't blameless. She had abandoned the infant. The authorities wouldn't automatically take her from Faith and give her to his sister. Didn't he realize that Caitlin would be the biggest loser if he pressed the issue?

Hugh took a step back, but didn't let her go. "I've spent the last two and a half years trying to find my sister's child," he said. His voice was hard and intense. "A child she doesn't remember giving birth to."

"Amnesia." The word sifted past her stiff lips. It

was the only explanation. True amnesia was rare, but it did occur.

He nodded once. "She was badly injured in the accident. She lost a huge amount of blood. There was some brain damage. The doctors say she may never remember any more than she does now. But she has nightmares of blood on the snow and a baby crying."

"I'm sorry she has nightmares." Again, she could speak the truth.

He continued to watch her closely. "There are butterflies in her dreams."

Faith closed her eyes. She could not hold his searching gaze one second longer.

"So that's why you came here. Because of the butterflies?" She recalled as clearly as if the moment had just happened, Beth's pain-filled gaze fixed unblinkingly on her butterfly-covered sweatshirt. The image had somehow been retained by her damaged brain and translated into a recurring nightmare. Such a small detail to be of such importance to them all.

"Yes. That's the one clue that's been missing for all the other searchers. And there are other searchers out there, Faith. Did you know that?"

"Why should I?" Her throat closed and she swallowed hard. Did he realize that fact terrified her more than anything else he could have said? She had thought her days of looking over her shoulder, of being suspicious of every car that came up the lane, were over.

"The Indiana police searched for the baby for weeks, but found nothing. They checked birth records in Ohio and Kentucky, too. All babies born within seventy-two hours of the time the doctors estimated Beth's baby was born. That was the criteria they used.''

''No one ever questioned me. No one.''

''Probably because they didn't look at records this far east. And maybe because you didn't register Caitlin's birth until almost a week later. I checked.''

''I wasn't able to get to the courthouse before that time.'' Short sentences. Just bare facts. ''I was alone. All alone.'' She didn't have to fake the tremor in her voice, it was all too real. Then she betrayed herself. ''You said you weren't the only one looking for...for Beth's baby.''

''Her boyfriend's parents are looking, too. They have been all along. They have money. They hired private detectives, but by then the trail had grown cold. But they were concentrating on a much smaller area near the accident site. Jamie and Beth paid cash for everything they bought from the time they left Boston, so there was no paper trail. They were traveling east when the accident happened. Jamie's parents think it was because they'd given up on getting to me through my old firm in Texas, and were coming back to Boston. I think it was because they were coming back for their baby. Coming back to you. It was the butterflies that gave you away even though you didn't start operating the farm until the next year. What happened, Faith? Did you stumble across them in the park? Was Beth in labor? Did you deliver the baby?''

Too close. He was too close to the truth. Faith pushed at his arm but she might as well have been trying to push over one of the fence posts. "I don't have to stand here and listen to any more of your wild accusations."

"They're not wild accusations, Faith. They're facts. You have a child born on the same day as my sister's. You were alone when you gave birth. No witnesses. You raise butterflies."

"But you just said it yourself, I didn't start raising butterflies until after Caitlin was born."

"But you were interested in them. So was your husband. He died trying to get to the place in Mexico where monarchs winter over close to a year before you broke ground for the butterfly house."

"Who told you that?"

"It's common knowledge in town."

He was right. She had no reason to lie about Mark's death, or that she had been only slightly injured in the crash. The only lie she told about that day, was one of omission. That their baby had not died, too.

"Beth has nightmares of butterflies and snow and a baby crying. Why does she dream of them, Faith? Because you talked with her about butterflies as you delivered her baby?"

"I don't know why she dreams of butterflies," she said desperately. "I can guess why she dreams of a baby crying. I would have that dream, too, if I had lost my child." He didn't move. "Let me go. I need to be with Caitlin." This time she pushed against the wall of his chest with as much force as she could muster. The air rushed out of his lungs with a whoosh and he took an involuntary step backward. She surged past him, but he reached out and stopped her with a hand on her arm.

"Beth needs to learn her child's fate," Hugh said quietly. His grip on her wrist was loose. She could pull away from him easily. It was the force of his will, his conviction, that held her there. "I have to know the truth for her sake."

"I can't tell you anything. Nothing."

"Faith, you don't need to be frightened of me," he said quietly.

She pulled her hand loose and whirled on him. She laughed, a sound harsh with nerves and incipient panic. "Not be frightened of you? Of course I'm frightened of you. You came here under false pretenses. You have me investigated behind my back. You question my friends about me. You accuse me of—" She stopped herself before she said the betraying words aloud. "You believe my daughter is another woman's child. I'm crazy for not sending you packing yet tonight."

"You can't send me packing. If you do, it's the same as admitting I'm telling the truth."

"It is not! It's the only sane thing to do."

He covered the distance between them in an instant. Faith knew she had made a mistake by not running as fast and as hard as she could into the house and locking the door when she had the chance.

He gripped her arms with both hands and his touch was not gentle. His face was only inches from hers.

"I'm not here to threaten you, or to take your child away. I'm here to try to salvage my sister's happiness. Don't send us away, Faith. Beth needs to be here. I can see the difference in her in only two days. Regardless of what you think of me, don't turn her away. Please."

"What can I do for her?" He was so close she was seared by the heat of his body radiating toward her. She could see the glint of gold flecks in his eyes, feel the tension in the muscles of his arms. He could kiss her, or strangle her, before she could cry out for help. But she had lied when she said he frightened her. She wasn't afraid of what he could do to her physically. She held herself as stiffly as he did. God help her, it was the only way she could keep herself from closing the small distance between them.

"You can be her friend."

"She isn't going to remember anything about this place, or me." The words were a prayer as much as anything else.

"I'll accept that if I have to." His mouth hardened into a straight line.

What choice did she have? She couldn't go to the sheriff and accuse Hugh of anything.

He had said there were others searching for Caitlin, too. She dared not take the risk of stirring the calm surface of her life in Bartonsville for fear that all the secrets that were buried beneath would rise to the surface. She had to agree to what he asked, at least for now.

"You can stay. Now let me go."

He dropped his hands and stepped back. "Thank you, Faith." He didn't say anything more, didn't give her false assurances that she would not regret her decision. She already regretted it. She didn't for a moment think that Hugh Damon would give up his quest. She must be on her guard every moment of the day and night.

And she could never, never be this close to him again.

CHAPTER EIGHT

"WHAT ARE YOU planning for the rest of the day?" Beth asked, her good leg drawn up against her body as she painted her toenails on the hard, stiff-cushioned sofa in the main room of the cabin. It had been one of her goals in therapy to regain the dexterity to paint her toenails whatever damn color she pleased.

"Work," Hugh admitted.

Beth had been busy over the past week. Small vases of blue cornflowers, yellow mustard weed and Queen Anne's lace graced the table and windowsills. Kevin had taken her antiquing three days in a row and she'd brought home vintage crocheted throws, "afghans" she'd called them, to drape over the back of the sofa and arm chair. She'd even gotten Faith's permission to hang a picture or two. Paint-by-numbers renditions of country mills and barns that Beth assured him were the next rage in collectibles. Slowly but surely she was turning their temporary quarters into a home.

"You've been on site every day since I got here. It's Sunday. You need a day off."

"Things are finally getting on track. I need to stay ahead of the game."

Beth looked up, the nail polish brush poised above her shocking-pink toenail. "Kevin and I have something special planned for today."

"I figured as much. What is it? Antiquing? Driving into Cincy?"

She jumped in with her defense. "I need the practice. Most sixteen-year-olds have more driving time under their belts than I do."

"Especially nighttime driving hours." Hugh grinned back at her from the table where he was perusing schematics on his laptop.

She rose from the couch and padded across to him. She put her arms around his neck and rested her chin on the top of his head. Hugh went very still. She was rarely demonstrative. "We haven't been out that late. Only a little after midnight a couple of times. Poor old Hugh. You've been lonely."

He grunted in a noncommittal tone and shut down the laptop.

"I have been spending a lot of time with Kevin, haven't I?"

"Ten evenings in a row, but who's counting?"

"I never thought the time here would go so quickly."

Neither had he, but not for the same reasons as his sister. He had finally accepted what the doctors had said all along. Beth's memory would not return. She still had no recollection whatsoever of Faith Carson.

And Caitlin was just a cute little kid as far as she was concerned.

Hugh would have begun to doubt his own certainty of Caitlin's parentage, except for two things. Beth would not set foot in the butterfly house or go back to the little park. He'd even, God forgive him, driven her there himself, on the pretext of checking out the bike trail. She'd stayed in the Blazer, her face pale, her lower lip caught between her teeth in the nervous gesture she'd had since she was a child. He could feel her watching him as he explored the stone-and-wood shelter. Back inside the truck her uneasiness was palpable. That evening she'd turned down Kevin's suggestion of a swim in Faith's pond and went to her room, lying on the bed in the darkness, listening to her portable CD player.

Hugh felt like a jerk for days afterward and swore that he wouldn't try to force her memory anymore.

"Well, you're not going to work today," she said decisively. "We're having a cookout with hot dogs and hamburgers and potato salad and baked beans and s'mores. The whole nine yards."

He pushed the laptop to the middle of the table. "Where's this all-American cookout going to happen?"

"At Faith's. Kevin and I were discussing the idea this morning when I was helping out in the greenhouse. The plans were getting complicated, trying to decide whether to go to Wal-Mart and buy one of those little bitty charcoal grills, or borrow your Blazer to haul Kevin's dad's gas grill out here, and then haul it back to town. And, well, to make a long story short Faith said we could use her grill. And then I finally remembered my manners and insisted that she and Caitlin join us. You don't mind, do you?'' She swept right on past any objection he might have made. ''But Kevin started grousing about it being as much work to haul her grill up here to the cottage as it was his dad's. And—''

''And?''

She spread her arms. ''Kevin looked so put upon that now it's going to be a family affair out by the pond. Steve and Peg and the boys are coming, too.'' Beth leaned around him so that she could see more than his profile. ''You don't sound very enthusiastic about the cookout. Don't you want to spend some time with Kevin? I thought you liked him.'' She looked worried, and he could see her beginning to form all kinds of wild conjectures, like giving up the boy she was infatuated with to please her ogre of a big brother.

''I like Kevin.'' It was Faith he was reluctant to spend time with. He had promised her that he would stay out of her way and he'd done his best to keep his word. But living here meant he did run into her. And the more he and Beth did things with Faith and Caitlin the more he began to dream of what it would be like to be part of a family again. To have a woman…to have Faith to love and cherish and bear his children. He'd even caught himself fantasizing that there might be a way out of this tangled and dangerous mess he'd created. One that would bring a happy ending for all of them.

"Then it's settled. I know you like Faith so that's not a problem. But—" Beth laughed self-consciously "—I was afraid you thought I shouldn't be seeing Kevin."

He uncrossed her arms from around his neck and turned in his chair. "Why the hell would you think that?"

"I—I don't know. I guess because of all that's happened. My—my problems."

"Nothing that's happened to you should keep you from spending time with a great guy like Kevin." He lifted her chin so that she had to look him straight in the eye. "Do you hear me, Beth? Nothing."

"Do you think he's really that great?" she asked wistfully. "Do you think he won't look at me like I'm some kind of monster when I say, 'Oh, by the way. I not only got my boyfriend killed in a car accident. I had a baby that same day and I misplaced her? I haven't the slightest idea where she is or what happened to her?'" Tears glistened in her blue eyes and she blinked furiously to hold them back.

"No more of that talk, Beth," he said forcefully. "Listen to me. I don't think he'll look at you like you're a monster, because I think he's a bright, intelligent guy who cares for the woman you are now, not the scared, confused kid you were three years ago." He hoped to hell he was reading Sager's character right. If he wasn't and he hurt Beth, he would have to answer to Hugh, and the outcome wouldn't be pretty.

She sniffed and gave him a tentative smile. "Okay, big brother. I'll do it your way. I'll wait for just the right moment and then dump my sordid past in his lap. If he's got the right stuff I'll know it then, won't I?"

"Don't let him push you past the point you want to go, Beth." He'd begun to worry about the physical aspects of the relationship in the past few days.

She didn't pretend to misunderstand. "Don't worry about that. He's been a perfect gentleman. He hasn't even tried to get my bra off, even when we were parking in the moonlight." She sounded a little miffed.

"Good for him."

She gripped his hands with her much smaller ones. "Hugh, don't worry. I'm not going to make the same mistake I made with Jamie. I won't let him make love to me until everything's right between us—no matter how much I might want him to before then."

He knew Beth wouldn't make love just for the physical release. She was too emotionally scarred to be promiscuous. If she made love with Kevin Sager it would be because she had given him her heart. "Are you that serious about him?"

"I could be," she said softly, and smiled.

THERE WAS A DULL throbbing ache behind Faith's eyes but it wasn't caused by the fact that she'd forgotten her sunglasses, at least not entirely. The sun was well down on the horizon, almost ready to disappear. It was warm and muggy, and now and then a mosquito sang past her ear. Spring had turned into full summer, even though the official start to the season was still a couple of weeks away. The source of her discomfort was the usual one these days, the continued presence of Beth and Hugh.

Every hour that went by increased her guilt and remorse. Beth spent time each morning in the greenhouse, taking over bit by bit the chores Faith had saved for Steve's niece, Dana, who was busy with the American Legion traveling softball league on which she was the star first baseman.

Beth had waved off her objections that guests weren't supposed to act as unpaid laborers, and kept right on showing up to dust figurines in the gift shop, deadhead the butterfly bushes and the coneflowers and pinch back the pots of kitchen herbs.

And while they worked they talked, about all manner of things, from fashion to hair color, to books and music, to politics and world events. Beth was eager to learn, to catch up on the parts of her life she'd lost out on during her recovery and rehabilitation. But she also fell silent for long periods of time, and Faith stayed silent too because she still didn't know when a simple word or phrase, or glimmer of an idea might spark Beth's memory of the day Caitlin was born. Yet despite these sometimes awkward moments, Faith was certain Beth considered her a friend and that was another burden she had to bear because there was no way that Faith could feel the same.

And then there was Hugh. Always watchful, always in her thoughts, always a threat. But also a man of quiet strength and dignity, who appealed to her on so many levels, not all of them having to do with the workings of her mind.

She watched him now involved in the volleyball game with Steve and Kevin and Dana, who was spending the night with Peg and Steve. Beth was acting as linesman and referee and her laughter carried out over the still water of the pond and echoed along the tree line. Jack, Guy and Caitlin, Addy at their heels, were darting in and out between the player's legs. Every once in a while Hugh or Kevin or Steve went sprawling in the grass avoiding a little one. The game was spirited, but good-natured and not for the first time Faith found herself watching Hugh as he moved with the kind of effortless grace of a man completely at home in his body.

Perhaps she had let her gaze linger on him too long, because now Hugh glanced her way as he set up for an overhand serve. Their eyes caught and held for a fraction of a second before Faith looked away, as a now familiar shiver of awareness danced up and down her spine.

She poured herself a glass of iced tea from the thermos sitting on the tailgate of Steve's truck, and walked out onto the wooden decking that served as dock and diving platform. She sat down on one of the built-in benches and turned her back to the sunset, looking instead out over the rolling farmland.

She waited as Peg left her lawn chair on the sidelines of the game and came toward her. Faith scooted over so that there was room for her sister to sit beside her. "Can I beg a swallow of your tea?" she asked. "I left my glass by my chair and I'm too lazy to go back and get it."

Faith handed over her glass. "Are you sure you're okay? You barely touched your food." It wasn't the first meal Faith had noticed her sister not eating in the past week or so.

"Hey, that's my line, remember?" Peg countered. "You still look as if you're not getting enough sleep."

"We're not talking about me. I'm fine," Faith insisted.

"So am I. Or I will be in eight months or so." The sun had set but there was still plenty of light in the sky, so she easily saw Peg's lips curve into a smile.

"You're pregnant!"

Her sister's smile grew wider and she nodded. "Yes. But just barely. Only a few weeks. We haven't told the boys. It's a long time for them to wait for a new baby."

"Oh, Peg, I'm so happy for you." And so thankful that she'd resisted each and every temptation to break her promise to herself and tell Peg about Beth. Peg's boys had been strong, healthy babies, but her pregnancies had been difficult. There was no way that

Faith would add stress to this one if she could avoid it. She leaned over to wrap her sister in a hug just as the volleyball sailed over their heads and landed with a splash in the pond.

''Heads up, ladies.'' Running feet came pounding onto the deck. Faith and Peg broke apart with a gasp as Kevin made a shallow, running dive to retrieve the ball that sent a shower of cool spray over both of them.

''Man overboard!'' Guy hollered, executing a perfect cannonball that sent water cascading onto the deck, soaking his mother and aunt. His brother was only two seconds behind, and his splash was even bigger. The boys were wearing swim trunks and inflatable arm rings and had been in and out of the pond a half dozen times during the course of the afternoon.

''You monsters,'' Peg sputtered. ''And to think I was just congratulating myself on replicating the little beasts.''

Steve ambled onto the deck and Faith reached out to squeeze his big work-roughened hand between her own. ''Congratulations. Peg just told me the news.''

''Thanks,'' he said, resting his other hand on Peg's shoulder. ''You're the first to know. We haven't even told Mom and Dad yet.''

''I promise not to tell a soul. What do you want?'' she asked, low-voiced. ''Boy or girl?''

''A girl,'' Steve said without a moment's hesitation. ''Just like Caitlin.'' Faith's throat tightened at his simple declaration.

"But we'll take another boy." Peg gave her husband a peck on the cheek. "I probably won't have a choice. The Badens tend to breed a lot of boys."

Beth and Dana followed Steve onto the deck, with Hugh a couple of steps behind. The girls held Caitlin's hands as she hopped along between them. Faith was no longer nervous when Beth spent time with Caitlin. The little girl liked Beth, and Beth seemed to enjoy being with her daughter, but Faith detected no deeper attachment growing between them, and in the most private places in her heart she rejoiced at the knowledge. Caitlin clambered up onto the bench beside Faith and sat on her lap.

"I could use some help out here." Kevin came up sputtering, as the boys ganged up to try to shove him under.

Steve lifted his leg. "Sorry. Bad knee. Old basketball injury."

"I never swim before the middle of August. The water's too cold," Peg demurred with a shiver.

"And I have Caitlin to look after." Faith was glad the light was beginning to go. She was wearing a sundress with thin little straps and no bra. The bodice was lined, but she could feel her nipples contract as the wet fabric was cooled by the evening breeze.

"Hugh?"

"You're on your own, buddy." Hugh laughed and Faith warmed to the sound. What would it be like to be able to relax in his presence and enjoy his company with no reservations? She would never know and that realization hurt.

"Beth, you aren't going to let them drown me, are you?" Kevin was treading water, effortlessly, fending off the boys with one hand. He looked to be in no danger at all from his small attackers and Beth said so. She was wearing shorts and a football jersey with the Bartonsville Patriot mascot on the front and Sager emblazoned across the back above the number. The jersey was faded and frayed at the hem and sleeves. It was obvious it had been a gift from Kevin.

Jack and Guy hooted and hollered and dared Beth to come in so they could dunk her, too.

"You're bad boys," Caitlin said, and promptly snuggled closer to Faith.

Kevin swam over to the deck, shrieking little boys still clinging to his back, reached up and closed his hand around Beth's ankle. He tugged lightly, being careful not to pull her completely off balance. "Help me, Beth. The two of us can take these guys."

Beth had her hands braced on the deck railing. She was shaking her head, but was laughing at the same time. "I don't have a suit on."

"Neither do I," Kevin said. He'd jumped in wearing cutoffs and a T-shirt. "C'mon. You won't melt." He tugged once more and Beth threw up her hands. "Oh, why not."

She jumped lightly off the deck and disappeared in the dark water, surfacing with a squeal. "It's freezing," she shrieked.

"I told you it would be cold," Peg said. "No one listens to me."

"Get Beth," Jack yelled and both little boys attempted to swim away from Kevin in favor of their new victim.

"Oh, no, you don't." Kevin grabbed first one boy then the other and tossed them toward the shallow end of the pond. "Go let the bluegills nibble on your toes for a while."

"No!" Both were shrieking with laughter.

"They're not bluegills. They're piranhas," Jack said, menacingly.

"Your toes won't last too long," Kevin said with a diabolical laugh. "No one can save you now."

"Aghhh, they've got me," Guy screamed, arms and legs flailing as he splashed around in mock terror.

Kevin put his arms around Beth's waist and began towing her out into deeper water. "Now that I've provided a diversion for the man-eating bluegills we can have our moonlight swim without getting nibbled on ourselves."

"You think you're very clever, don't you," Beth said, but let him pull her toward the shadow of the willow tree that overhung the far bank.

"Jack. Guy," Steve called, leaning out over the deck railing. "It's almost dark. Time to get out of the water."

The boys began loud protests that ceased immediately when Dana announced that if they wanted to stay in the pond, she'd eat all the S'mores herself. She swung Caitlin onto her hip and marched off, initiating a mad dash for sneakers and towels.

"C'mon, Steve. You're the best marshmallow

toaster in the county.'' Peg and Steve went off arm in arm, leaving Faith and Hugh alone on the dock.

Faith looked up at the stars, remembering the last time they'd been alone like this. Hugh put his foot on the bench and leaned his forearm on his knee. ''The moon is brighter than it was the last time we were alone together.''

''It will be full in a few more days.''

He fell silent, watching Beth and Kevin as they floated beneath the willow's overhanging boughs. ''He's good for her,'' he said at last. ''He's brought her out of herself when I couldn't. Do you know this is the first time I've seen her wear shorts in public since her accident?''

''They do seem to be a good match.''

''Beth is almost ready to confide in him.'' Hugh's words stole the warmth from her blood.

''About...about the accident.'' She couldn't say *about the baby.*

''About everything.''

She had been dreading the day that Beth's feelings for Kevin overcame her fear of rejection. One more person who might put two and two together and come up with four. A man who hadn't suffered traumatic brain damage and who might think it was more than a coincidence that Caitlin and Beth's lost baby had the same birthday.

''Faith, I want her to be happy. I want the empty places in her mind and her heart to be filled. I want her to have what she has right now.''

Kevin had wrapped his hand around the trailing

willow branches to hold them in place, his other arm was around Beth's waist. They must think they were lost in the shadows of the big tree but a last glimmer of twilight outlined them and the kiss they were sharing.

Faith clasped her hands in front of her. She wanted those things, too, including a man who would make love to her under the trailing branches of a weeping willow tree.

"I want Beth to know the truth." Hugh's voice was pitched low so it wouldn't carry over the water to Beth and Kevin. "You have the key to that truth, Faith."

Faith rose and put her hand on his arm so that he turned to face her. "You're asking me to confess to a crime, a very serious crime," she said. "Do you realize that?" Another of her fears. One she'd thought banished to the darkest corner of her subconscious. She should hate him for being the catalyst to revive all her nightmares, but she could not. She had chosen this road, knowing it was one way only with no exits to happy-ever-after.

A frown furrowed his forehead. "What you tell me would never go further than the three of us. I mean you no harm, Faith."

She laughed in disbelief. "You're threatening everything I hold dear in this world. My very life, if anything should happen to Caitlin. And if you're right and Caitlin is not my daughter but Beth's, your sister might not be held blameless, you know. If your theory is right, she abandoned her baby in the middle of a terrible storm. More than likely the authorities would take Caitlin away from all of us. Is that what you want?''

He dropped his head to stare down at the dark water below the deck. The breeze had begun to ripple the surface of the pond. It stirred the thick layers of his hair and brushed against her cheek. ''Of course not. I want to—''

''You want to mend what can't be mended.'' She attempted to tug her hand free of his without success. She gave up the struggle. She wanted his touch, even though, at the same time, she longed to be somewhere safe and alone.

''You can trust me, Faith,'' Hugh said quietly so that the words wouldn't carry out over the water. Kevin and Beth had broken their embrace and were swimming lazily toward the deck.

''No,'' she said unable to filter out the regret she felt at the words. She did want to trust him. She had been fighting against that weakness for days and days. She looked down at their joined hands, willing him to set her free. He did, moving a step away.

She shivered. She couldn't confide her secret to any man, certainly not this one. Pain, greater than she should have felt, shot through her when she admitted the truth. She had never thought to love again, but if she did, Hugh Damon would be the kind of man to whom she could give her heart. If he had been anyone other than who he was. ''You're wrong. You're the last person on earth I can trust.''

Headlights sliced across the surface of the pond as a car turned into the lane.

"I wonder who that is?" Beth asked, climbing onto the dock. She was shivering and her teeth were chattering. Kevin came up behind her and grabbed a towel from the bench, wrapping it around her shoulders.

"It's probably the couple who've rented the cabin on your left," Faith said. She was still trembling from her conversation with Hugh, but she managed to keep the tremors from reaching her lips. "Excuse me, I need to go greet them."

She began walking toward the luxury sedan as it pulled to a halt before the greenhouse. The security light gave Faith a good view of the couple. He was of medium height, thin, with a full head of silver-gray hair, dressed in a casual open-necked shirt and khakis. The woman beside him was also thin, and almost as tall as her husband. She was wearing a sleeveless T-shirt and cream-colored pants with a matching jacket thrown over her shoulders. Her hair was shoulder length, and curved smoothly against her cheek. The color was hard to gauge in the security light's glare, but it seemed to be golden brown.

"Who is that?" Beth asked. Faith was already several yards along the path. She turned back, surprised to see Beth's face was chalk white.

"Their name is Templeton. They've booked a cabin for the rest of the week."

Beth's eyes were wide and fearful. She shook her

head. "No," she said. "Tell them they can't stay. Tell them to go away."

"I—I can't do that." She lifted her hand in a gesture of supplication. Beth's panic was infectious. Faith felt her heart rate speed up. "Hugh?"

He had his arms around Beth's shoulders and his face was expressionless, hard and cold. "Their name isn't Templeton. It's Sheldon. Harold and Lorraine Sheldon. They're Jamie's parents. And it looks as if they've finally tracked us down."

CHAPTER NINE

BETH PUT THE CAP on the toothpaste and set it back on the shelf of the white enamel medicine cabinet. She shut the door and stared at herself for a moment in the slightly wavy mirror. She didn't look too bad for six o'clock in the morning. She was getting used to being an early riser.

Especially these past few days, when it seemed the only time that she wouldn't encounter Jamie's mother or father. Beth hadn't believed for one moment that they'd only tracked her and Hugh down because they were worried about her, afraid that Lorraine's insistence on her seeing a hypnotherapist had caused her to run.

Avoiding the hypnotherapist had been why she'd left Houston, of course, but she wouldn't give Lorraine Sheldon satisfaction by admitting the fact. She may have run away from Texas, but she was glad Hugh's work had brought them to Painted Lady Farm. She liked Faith and Caitlin. And Kevin.

She might even be halfway to falling in love with Kevin.

She certainly hadn't planned to feel this way about him. But she didn't regret it.

Even more importantly, she was starting to know and like herself again. She hadn't had the butterfly dream since she'd arrived. Not once. She still didn't want to be around the insects, but they no longer frightened her.

And she was learning to be at peace with the things she couldn't change. She no longer tortured herself with endless hours of trying to remember something, anything, about her baby's birth and disappearance. That didn't mean she didn't want to know. She did, sometimes so much her heart ached with the wanting. But she had begun to accept that she might never be granted that knowledge. That she would have to go on with her life.

And she would start by telling Kevin what had happened to her three years ago. She wanted him to know, and not just because she had caught him talking to Harold and Lorraine more than once, and she was afraid they might give away her secret first. The desire to tell him everything had been growing steadily, almost from the first day they'd met.

She closed her eyes because for a moment the face reflected in the mirror had been her face a month before. Scared and uncertain.

No more. She was in control now.

She hurriedly rinsed her mouth and ran a comb through her hair. She needed to vacate the bathroom for her brother.

Something was bothering Hugh. Every night she heard him tossing and turning. Sometimes she would awake and see the glow of his laptop screen coming from the main room.

She was coming to the conclusion Faith Carson had a lot to do with her brother's condition. Sadly, he didn't seem to be making much headway with her. Beth didn't know what she could do about that, either, but she'd keep working at it. Heaven knew, she'd sung his praises to Faith until she was breathless. Unfortunately, Faith seemed as reluctant as Hugh to take their relationship any further.

It wasn't because the attraction wasn't there. They just weren't acting on it.

Maybe they needed a push in the right direction. Would Hugh ask Faith out if she offered to baby-sit for Caitlin—

Baby-sit for Caitlin. The thought brought Beth out of her matchmaking reverie. Was she ready to take on the responsibility for a child even for a few hours? For almost three years she'd barely been able to take care of herself.

She closed her eyes and looked inward, searching for that kernel of confusion and fear that always lurked inside her. She took a deep breath and exhaled slowly. If it was still there it was buried deeply. She felt good about herself. She felt good about the future—

She glanced at the clock. Not quite six-thirty. Hugh should have been up pounding on the bathroom door by now. She padded across the linoleum and knocked lightly on his door. "Rise and shine, brother dear," she sang out.

His only reply was a muffled groan. "Go away."

"Hugh. It's six-thirty."

"Damn, my alarm didn't go off."

A few moments later he appeared in front of her in a T-shirt and cutoffs.

He ran his hand over the stubble of beard on his face and wiped the shadows away. "I'll shave and jump in the shower and we can head into town for breakfast."

"Faith's expecting me at the greenhouse. Why don't you come down there? I'll treat you to a blueberry muffin."

The furrow between his dark brows returned, as it always seemed to do when she mentioned Faith. "You're not punching a time clock, are you? Let's give the blueberry muffin a pass. I've got a hankerin' for sausage biscuits and gravy."

The Sheldons usually didn't get up very early, but she didn't want to meet them at the greenhouse if they did. She'd do whatever it took to avoid them until she told Kevin the truth. Maybe that was cowardly, but she didn't care. She had too much at stake to take any chances with Jamie's parents. "Okay," she said. "I guess Faith can hold down the fort without me for an hour or so. The Golden Sheaf for breakfast it is. But no sausage gravy and biscuits. That's just a heart attack on a plate. Oatmeal and fruit, okay?" She brightened a little inside. "Maybe we'll even run into Kevin if we get a move on."

"MRS. SHELDON. Good morning." Faith was fixing the feeding trays in the greenhouse. She'd wakened at sunrise and had been unable to go back to sleep. Caitlin had heard her in the shower and was wide-awake and bouncing on her bed when Faith came out of the bathroom. Now she was sitting at her little table behind the counter with a bowl of Froot Loops, out of Lorraine Sheldon's view. She was surprised to see Jamie's mother up and around. It was by far the earliest either of the Sheldons had risen since they arrived.

"Good morning, Faith. I decided to come and see the butterflies before it gets any hotter. Is that convenient?"

"I'll be changing the feeding trays in a few minutes. I'll be happy to have you join me," she said as politely as she could manage.

"Thank you." Lorraine rubbed her hand up and down her arm, looking around at the figurines and potted plants that still remained for sale. Summer travel was in full swing and Faith had been kept busy with visitors to the butterfly house, so her contact with the Sheldons had been blessedly brief.

"Would you care for a cup of coffee? Or tea?" Faith took a step to her left, obscuring Caitlin from the other woman's view.

"Tea would be nice." Lorraine was wearing linen slacks and a silky sleeveless shell in shades of pistachio and cream. A finely woven straw hat protected her makeup from the strong morning sun. Her jewelry was gold and heavy, her manicure flawless. She looked as if she were ready for a day's shopping on

Fifth Avenue or Rodeo Drive. Faith wondered how she'd made it down the lane in her Italian leather sandals without twisting an ankle.

Faith wasn't certain where to place Lorraine's age. She supposed she must be in her midforties or older. After all, she would have had a son in his early twenties if Jamie had lived. One thing was certain. She was years younger than her husband. Harold Sheldon was pushing sixty. Had she been a trophy wife? Indulged by an older, wealthy husband, her only child the center of her existence? That would go a long way in explaining why she had tracked Beth and Hugh down at Painted Lady Farm.

"I'm afraid all I have are tea bags. But I do have English Breakfast."

"Oh." Lorraine made a little moue of disappointment. "In that case I'll just have juice."

"Orange or cranberry?"

"Cranberry." Faith stooped to get the bottle from the small refrigerator. "Thank you," Lorraine said when Faith handed her a glass. "I thought perhaps Beth would be here this morning."

"She does usually show up about this time."

Lorraine took a delicate sip, then fixed Faith with a practiced smile. "I've had so little time to talk to her. She's miffed with me, I'm afraid." She made a little face. "I hope you aren't, as well."

"I don't understand."

"I mean, because I booked our reservations under my maiden name—"

"It wasn't necessary to employ a ruse," Faith said

coolly. She would never have rented a cabin to the couple if she'd had any inkling they were Jamie's parents, of course, but she kept that damning detail to herself.

"I should have explained the whole situation to you the moment we arrived...." Lorraine's voice trailed off and she shrugged her thin shoulders. "It's all so very complicated."

"I know some of Beth's story," Faith said carefully. She felt as if she had walked to the edge of a crumbling cliff and was looking down into an abyss.

"She seems to be doing very well here."

"Painted Lady Farm is a wonderful place to heal, as I found when I moved here after my husband was killed."

"I'm sorry for your loss," Lorraine said. "I know how hard it is to deal with losing a loved one." There was genuine sorrow in her voice, and Faith thought back to the tall, good-looking boy she had met. Would he have grown up quickly enough to become a strong and loving man and face his responsibilities if he'd lived? Faith hoped that would have proved to be the case.

"Beth is making a future for herself. I think she'll do fine."

"I pray you're right. My husband and I are very fond of Beth. We were very, very worried about her when she disappeared from Houston that way without a word. I couldn't be at ease until we had tracked her down and seen for ourselves that she was all right."

"Why wouldn't she be?" Faith couldn't stop herself from asking, although she knew she should change the subject. "She's with Hugh and he seems to be very solicitous of her."

"I didn't mean to imply otherwise. But he's a man, and they have different priorities. I just don't think he realizes how—" She stopped talking and took another sip of her juice. "Beth seems to have made a friend since she's been here. Kevin Sager. My husband and I have met him at the cabins. He seems like a nice young man."

"He is. He grew up here and he teaches junior high science. I like him very much."

"I'm glad. I wouldn't want Beth to be taken advantage of."

As Jamie had taken advantage of her? Faith caught herself before speaking the words aloud. No wonder Beth was a nervous wreck when Lorraine was around. The woman was relentless in probing every aspect of her life. "If you're finished with your juice I'll take you into the habitat," she said to forestall any more questions.

"I'm ready." Lorraine placed her glass on the counter, peering over at Caitlin. She was still in her pajamas, her flyaway hair in pigtails. Addy stood protectively at her side, keeping watch for wolves and rustlers and the occasional dropped Froot Loops. "Your little girl is adorable.

"Thank you."

"I haven't seen her much since we came."

"She's been spending several hours a day with my

brother-in-law's niece and two of her friends. They have started a temporary play school for two- and three-year-olds for their 4-H projects.'' Faith felt her throat tightening. She didn't want Lorraine showing interest in Caitlin.

''I'm two,'' Caitlin said holding up two sticky fingers as she shoveled cereal into her mouth with the other hand. ''This is my dog. Her name's Addy.'' She gave Faith a sly look. ''Watch out. She sniffs your bottom.''

''I…I'll remember that.'' Lorraine didn't smile at Caitlin's favorite joke. Instead, a small frown appeared between her carefully arched brows. ''She's left-handed.''

''Yes. She's very definitely left-handed.'' Caitlin had had a decided preference for her left hand since she was very little.

Lorraine kept on staring at Caitlin. Then she moved around the counter and asked the question Faith had been dreading. ''You're two, are you? Do you know when your birthday is?''

The toddler shook her head. ''When it gets cold again.'' Caitlin changed the subject with lightning swiftness. ''I'm going swimming today.''

''You are? That's nice.''

''Would you care to see the butterflies now, Mrs. Sheldon?'' Faith interrupted. She didn't want the older woman to put the clues together. She picked up a plate of fruit and stepped toward the entry to the habitat. ''The less time the door is open the better,'' Faith prompted.

"What? Oh, yes. The butterflies."

"I come, too." Caitlin pushed back her chair.

"Why don't you stay here and finish your cereal, Kitty Cat?" She didn't usually leave Caitlin alone in the greenhouse—once or twice Faith had caught her leaving the building on her own to play on her swing set or look for a strayed Barbie—but it would only be for a minute or two. She would change the feeding plates and then leave Lorraine alone to wander among the butterflies.

"I come." Caitlin could be stubborn when she set her mind to it.

"All right, but you must be a good girl and leave the butterflies alone."

"I be good. Addy, stay here," Caitlin commanded. The sheltie whimpered and looked up at Faith.

"Stay, Addy." Addy dropped to her belly with the guilt-inducing look in her brown eyes that all shelties had perfected.

As consolation, Caitlin dribbled a spoonful of soggy cereal on the ground for Addy to eat. "Good dog," she pronounced and skipped over to the door. Pretty butterflies. One. Two. Three. Four. A. B. C. D," she began to sing the familiar ditty in a high, clear voice, hopping from foot to foot.

"She's very vocal for thirty months," Lorraine said. Her tone was conversational but her eyes were sharp and questioning.

"She is very quick. And so eager to learn. She'll be going to preschool three mornings a week in the fall." Faith left the feeding dishes sitting on the counter and picked Caitlin up.

"She said her birthday is when it gets cold again. So she'll be three before the end of the year?" Before Faith could object Lorraine reached out and brushed her fingertips over Caitlin's pigtails.

"Yes." Faith opened the habitat door and gestured Lorraine inside. She launched into her standard tour patter to avoid any more questions from the older woman. "On the left is the chrysalis room. I have about seventeen species of butterflies here. I have them shipped in from a breeder in New Jersey, although someday I hope to obtain the licenses I need to breed the tropical species here. But right now the habitat isn't winterized so that's not possible."

"Interesting." Lorraine smoothed her hair with both hands, barely glancing at the pupae hanging from their colored pins.

"All of the butterflies in the habitat are tropicals. But you can usually observe a number of local species along the meadow walk. And, of course, you probably noticed the monarchs in the walk-in cage in the greenhouse. We tag all the monarchs we find here in the meadow, although only the last generation to hatch each season actually migrates south to Mexico."

"How can you tag a butterfly?" Lorraine looked puzzled.

"You net them and then very carefully affix a tiny color-coded sticky dot to their wing. It doesn't hurt them if you do it correctly. You're welcome to come along and watch next time.''

''Perhaps I will if it's not too hot.''

Caitlin had gone to the waterfall the moment she was inside the habitat. She was sitting on the edge, dabbling her fingers in the small pool at the base. She looked up and smiled at Faith, pointing to a huge iridescent blue butterfly with a wingspan the size of a saucer. ''Blue morpho,'' she said in a stage whisper.

''Is that what it's called?'' Lorraine's attention was focused on Caitlin, not the butterfly.

''Yes. From Costa Rica. One of the most beautiful butterflies in the world.''

''How many more does she know?''

''Not many, really. Monarchs and painted ladies because of our logo. She recognizes the large moths and the zebras.''

''And she isn't even three. Such a pretty child. I had a son. He died in a car accident. Perhaps Beth told you of it?''

''I knew that Beth's boyfriend was killed in the accident that injured her. I didn't know he was your son until you arrived,'' Faith reminded her.

Lorraine ignored the reference to her duplicity. ''There's more to the story. I don't suppose Beth or her brother told you that part?''

''I don't think—'' Faith began but Lorraine went right on talking.

''Beth was pregnant when she persuaded Jamie to run away with her. I'm not blaming her,'' she said, but the tightening around her mouth told Faith she did hold Beth responsible for Jamie's death. "I—I made a mistake. I—I thought it would be better if Beth didn't have the baby. When I realized that was the wrong thing to ask of her, I made a second mistake. I tried to persuade her father and stepmother into pressuring her to give the baby up for adoption. Now Beth hates all of us."

"I don't think Beth is capable of hating anyone."

Lorraine didn't acknowledge Faith's reply. "I have a grandchild. A little girl," she said quietly. "Somewhere. When is Caitlin's birthday?"

"November," Faith responded, feeling panic slithering along the edges of her nerves. She fought it down. She could do this. She had lied to Hugh, to Beth, to the world. Lorraine Sheldon was no different than the others.

"When in November?" Lorraine wrapped her arms around herself as though she were standing in the middle of the ice storm that had greeted Caitlin's birth, instead of a tropical butterfly house.

"The eleventh."

Lorraine sucked in her breath. "My granddaughter was born on the eleventh. At least we believe she was. And Caitlin is left-handed, just like Jamie. He got his left-handedness from me. It's much less common in girls. You're not left-handed, are you?" She glanced sharply at Faith who met her gaze without hesitation.

"No, I'm not. But my husband was left-handed."

Dear Mark, another small detail of heredity that might save her.

"She has Beth's hair coloring and slight build—" Her voice dropped to a whisper. "And Jamie's eyes."

"No," Faith said firmly. "She has my eyes."

Lorraine made no indication that she had heard Faith's words. She looked blindly around her and sat down abruptly on one of the wooden benches lining the path through the habitat. "Oh, dear God. Why did Hugh Damon come here?" she asked abruptly.

"I—" Faith knew she had to get hold of herself. She was only giving Lorraine more reason to doubt every word she said each time she hesitated in her response. But panic had engulfed her. Her legs became too wobbly to hold her upright. She stiffened her spine. "He found Painted Lady Farm on the Bartonsville Chamber of Commerce Web site, exactly as you told me you did."

"His work is forty-five miles from here. We passed it on our drive in. That's hardly convenient."

"He feels it is."

"No. There's another reason he's here."

"If there is, I have no idea what it might be. I suggest you ask him for yourself," Faith said.

Lorraine's gaze was fixed on Caitlin with total concentration. "I know why he came here. He found some clue that our detectives missed. It's Caitlin, isn't it? That's why he's stayed here these past weeks. She's my Jamie's baby."

"You're wrong," Faith said evenly, no trace of

doubt or fear tinging her voice. "She's mine. No one else's. It's all just coincidence, nothing more."

It was all suddenly very clear. This woman was the embodiment of her nightmares. The faceless being who sat in judgment of her and came down from the shadows to take her baby away. Lorraine Sheldon was her enemy, not Hugh Damon.

Lorraine was convinced that Caitlin was her son's child. Faith wanted to sweep her daughter into her arms, and run until they were both so far away Lorraine Sheldon could never find them again, but she resisted the frantic urge.

Still, she was filled with fear because she was a mother, too. And she knew without doubt that Lorraine Sheldon would not change her mind. She would do whatever she must to prove Caitlin was Jamie's daughter.

CHAPTER TEN

HUGH SAW the Closed notice swinging beneath the Painted Lady Farm sign and Kevin Sager's beat-up old Buick parked in front of his cabin at the same time. The closed sign was unusual enough for a weekday afternoon, but the sight of Kevin sitting with his back against the front door was even odder.

"Hugh, I'm glad you're home." Kevin jumped up as Hugh got out of the Blazer. "Beth's been locked inside all day. She won't come out or let me in."

"What the hell happened?" Hugh glanced at the cottage where Harold and Lorraine had been staying. Their Lexus was gone. There had been a car with Indiana plates parked at the third unit when he left that morning, but it was gone, too.

"I don't know what happened, but it must have been bad. Faith was almost as upset as Beth."

"Is the door locked?"

Kevin nodded. "From the inside."

Hugh knocked on the dark green door. "Beth, it's Hugh. Let me in."

For a long moment there was only silence from the other side. Hugh considered kicking the door in.

It opened, and Beth stood before them, tearstained

and pale. The room was stifling. Beth hadn't bothered to turn on the never more than adequate air-conditioning unit. "Are you alone?" she asked, as she stepped back to let him in.

"I'm still here." Kevin entered before she could shut the door on him. Hugh followed him inside.

Beth dropped onto the couch and pulled her knees up to her chin, wrapping her arms around her legs. "Have you been sitting out there all this time?"

Kevin leaned over the back of the couch so that his face was close to hers. "I told you I was staying put until you let me in. I meant it. I always mean what I say, Beth."

She lifted her hand and touched the tip of his nose. "You're sunburned."

"It's damn hot out there."

"Beth, what happened?" When he saw that she was not physically ill, Hugh had gone to turn on the air conditioner and cool down the overheated room.

He needn't have bothered, the anguished look she gave him froze his heart. "Oh, Hugh. Why didn't you tell me what you believed about Caitlin? Why did you let Lorraine tell me?"

"Caitlin? What are you talking about, Beth?" Kevin sat down beside her and pulled her against him. She turned her face into his chest and started to weep.

"I wanted to tell you. I was going to tell you, but this— I—I j-j-just can't take it in. I c-c-can't remember."

The heartache in her voice cut through the shock

that had held Hugh motionless. He had waited too long to tell her what he believed to be the truth, and now he was going to pay the price of losing his sister's confidence once more. He'd known it was only a matter of time before Harold and Lorraine Sheldon figured things out, yet he hadn't done anything to prepare Beth.

And what of Faith—and Caitlin?

"Tell us what happened," Hugh prompted. For a moment he thought she would ignore his question, but finally she began to speak.

"After you dropped me off I w-w-went down to the greenhouse to help Faith like I always do. Faith came out of the greenhouse with Caitlin in her arms. She looked—I don't know—frightened, angry, both those things at once. Caitlin was crying and Addy was jumping up and down, barking like crazy. Lorraine was right behind them. She was crying, too. The way she always does when she's upset about Jamie. And—" she gave a harsh little laugh "—I should have known then." She looked at him once more, heartbreak in her eyes. "Oh, Hugh...you should have told me."

"What happened next?" He couldn't begin to make things right until he knew the extent of the damage Lorraine had caused.

"W-w-we all stood there staring at each other. Then Lorraine turned on me and said, 'My God, Beth, how could you not—'" She stopped abruptly and dropped her head in her hands. "I—I... can't—"

"Yes, you can. You can tell me, Beth," Kevin said, rocking her against him as though she were a child. Hugh stood where he was, silent and grieved, and for the moment completely shut out. It was Kevin Beth had turned to in her need, not him. He had failed her once more.

"You'll hate me," Beth whispered. "I hate myself."

Kevin lifted her chin and looked at her. "I won't hate you, Beth. I… Never mind that for now. Why does Jamie's mother upset you so?"

"I told you that Jamie died in the accident."

"I remember. But there was more you didn't tell me, wasn't there?"

"I w-w-was going to tell you. Soon. Today. Really I was." She started to cry again.

"I believe you. Go on."

Hugh snagged a box of tissues from the counter and handed them to Kevin. That was all he could do for her right now, all she would let him do. Beth sat up, took a tissue and blew her nose. As upset as she was, she was trying to pull herself together. Hugh's chest tightened with pride.

"Something happened before the accident, didn't it?" Kevin urged once more.

"I was pregnant. I had a baby. A little girl. I know that much from my diary. But when the accident happened she wasn't with us. She was gone." Her voice was low, a tremulous whisper tinged with an old horror brought to the surface. "There was no trace of her. The police searched. Hugh searched. Lorraine and Harold are still looking. But nothing for all this time. Every day I wake up wondering if she is alive...or dead. And then somehow...today... Lorraine got it into her head that Faith's little girl isn't Faith's child at all. She's mine.''

She started to cry once more. She seemed to remember Hugh for the first time in several minutes. ''Hugh, you don't think that, too. Do you?'' She turned to him but her hands were clasped firmly in Kevin's. ''It's impossible, isn't it? It's just a horrible coincidence that Caitlin was born on the same day as my baby, and that Faith delivered her here at Painted Lady Farm with no one to help her. We're miles and miles from where the accident happened. The police said they had no proof we'd ever even been in Ohio. It's just a coincidence we came here. The butterflies are a coincidence. The park—''

She stood up, pulling her hands free of Kevin's grasp. ''The p-p-park.''

''Is just a park, Beth,'' Hugh said. He had to pull her back from the nightmare that had nearly claimed her sanity after the accident. If he had to lie to her now to spare her more misery, he would. And he would go on lying. ''I admit it was the butterflies that first brought Faith to my attention. But she didn't open the butterfly farm until after Caitlin's birth. That Caitlin was born on the same day as your baby? Chance. Coincidence. Nothing more.'' He was lying to protect her—and Faith and Caitlin—from Lorraine Sheldon. She was the greatest threat now.

Beth stood and came toward him, walking a little uncertainly. Hugh took a long stride around the table and she came into his arms. "I'm sorry I jumped on you the way I did. It's j-j-just that I thought you weren't telling me the truth. You promised to always be straight with me, remember?"

"I remember." Her happiness and well-being meant everything to him. He folded her into his arms because he couldn't chance her reading the guilt he knew clouded his expression.

Beth sniffed and wiped her nose again. "I knew it. If Caitlin was my flesh and blood I'd feel something, wouldn't I? I don't. At least I didn't at first. Now she's like a little cousin to me. Or a friend's child. But not mine. Wouldn't I feel it if she were mine?"

The last of the fading hope Hugh had cherished of Beth recovering her memory died at those words. He had felt a connection, tenuous though it might have been, the moment he'd laid eyes on Caitlin. Lorraine Sheldon had felt it, too, and it was strong enough for her to have acted on it. But Beth felt nothing.

She was trembling harder than before, and he knew she was close to breaking down again. He tried to get her to think of something else. "Where are Lorraine and Harold?" Hugh asked, releasing her so that she could return to Kevin.

"They're gone. Faith insisted they leave." She almost smiled. "You should have seen her, Hugh. She stood there with steel in her eyes. Lorraine started crying again, but Faith wouldn't change her mind.

Harold tried to get me to open the door for a long time after I ran back here, but I wouldn't talk to him. I thought maybe they'd grab me and haul me off to the hypnotherapist. Or the cops. Finally they left when Faith threatened to call the sheriff. I heard it all from in here.'' Her voice cracked, then she gave a watery little laugh that twisted Hugh's heart. ''But I wouldn't let Faith inside, either. Or Kevin. I was a little crazy there for a while, I think.''

''Where are Faith and Caitlin now?''

''She's at her sister's,'' Kevin interrupted. ''She insisted on staying here in case Beth needed help, but Caitlin was getting hot and fussy. I suggested she close the butterfly house for the rest of the afternoon. She headed off about two hours ago.''

''She probably won't even let me near Caitlin again after that awful scene with Lorraine.'' Tears blurred Beth's eyes once more and she wiped them away with the back of her hand.

''Faith will understand,'' Hugh said, but he wasn't so sure it was true.

''I hope so. We'll work it all out later, right?'' Beth recited the words as though she had practiced them over and over again in her sessions with the therapist. She rubbed her temples. ''I...I have a terrible headache.''

''I don't doubt it. It's after seven,'' Kevin said. His voice was steady, his tone bracing. ''Have you eaten anything since breakfast?'' She looked puzzled for a moment, then shook her head. Kevin stood up. ''That's one thing we can put right. I'll take you to a little place I know that's got great food. It's far enough away that not too many people from Bartonsville go there. Do you want to wash your face and comb your hair first?''

Beth reached up and ran her fingers through her tangled hair. ''Yes, I must look like a madwoman.''

''You look like you're roasting in those clothes. And you look like you've been crying all day, but nothing worse than that. Don't dress up. It's an old-fashioned drive-in with carhops and trays that hook onto the car window. Burgers as big as plates. You'll love it.''

''I don't eat red meat. How many times do I have to tell you that?''

''A chicken sandwich, then.''

''How's the root beer?''

''The best I've ever tasted. Let's go, I'm starving.''

Beth took a shaky breath and managed a smile. She lifted her hand and touched Kevin on the cheek. ''You sat out there all day in the sun with nothing to eat?''

''Damn straight. And you know how I hate to miss a meal.''

''You did that for me?''

''I told you—''

''You'll always be there for me,'' she whispered.

''Yes. But I'd rather be there on a full stomach.''

She smiled and this time it was real. Hugh felt the tension inside him unknot slightly. Kevin would look after her. ''I'll be ready in ten minutes.'' She turned toward the bathroom then pivoted back to face Hugh. "Will you be—"

"Don't worry about me. I'm fine. You go with Kevin. Everything will look better when you've had something to eat."

She shook her head. "It won't look better, but maybe it won't look like the end of the world."

Kevin rested both hands on the back of the couch, but remained silent until the sound of running water from the bathroom covered his words. "I suspected there was more to Beth's story than just running away from home because she didn't get along with her dad and stepmom. But this?" He dropped his head and stared down at his hands. "It's a hell of a thing to have to live with."

"She wanted to tell you about the baby."

He nodded and looked up again. "I know that. But you took a hell of a risk bringing Beth here if you thought Faith Carson's little girl is really hers. You must have known there was a chance something like this would happen."

Hugh turned his back on Kevin, struggling to get his feelings under control. Anger flared and died within him. Kevin was right. It was his fault, his alone. He should have come clean the moment the Sheldons arrived. Now he'd have to face the consequences of his own inaction. He just hoped he didn't end up losing his sister's love along with her respect.

"Tell me exactly what's going on here," Kevin said. "I need to know for Beth's sake."

"Beth is my responsibility."

"For the time being." Kevin met Hugh's gaze with steady regard. "I intend to make her my responsibility if she'll have me."

"Beth isn't in any shape for a love affair."

"It isn't going to be an affair. And I know she's not ready for anything too serious right now. I'm just telling you it *is* serious on my part. I won't be shut out of her life because her big brother is trying to fix the major screwup he's gotten us all into."

Once more Kevin had cut straight to the heart of the matter. Hugh balled his hands into fists, but he was far madder at himself than at Kevin. Keeping her boyfriend in the dark wouldn't help Beth face the mess he'd made of everything. Kevin Sager had to be trusted with what he knew, and what he suspected.

"Beth started having nightmares about six months ago. She kept dreaming of a baby crying, butterflies changing to drops of blood on the snow. She'd wake up night after night, crying and terrified. I'd damn near given up trying to locate any new leads on the baby. But when the dreams started I gave it one more shot, added butterflies to the mix, widened the search area and came up with Faith Carson. Widow, nurse, mother of a daughter born the same day as the doctors said Beth's baby was born."

"And owner of a butterfly farm. Not your everyday occupation." Kevin nodded. "Okay, so far I see where you're coming from."

"It was just one too many matches to be coincidence. I signed on to the Cincy job when the structural engineer they'd hired died of a sudden heart attack. It was the perfect cover, but I would have come here anyway. I'd have found some excuse.''

''You could be right,'' Kevin said, leaning forward. ''Faith's made a lot of friends in town the past couple of years, but I'd be lying if I told you there wasn't talk when she first showed up on Main Street with a baby. I remember my mom and her friends discussing it. Not that anyone saw much of her those first few months after she moved here. But she didn't look pregnant, you know, and people remembered. And then to have the baby all alone in the middle of the biggest ice storm in twenty years. Well, it was sure something to talk about for a while.''

''And it will be again if the Sheldons start asking questions about Faith and Caitlin.''

''You don't think they're gone for good?''

''Lorraine will move mountains to find the truth now that she's convinced Caitlin is Beth and Jamie's child.''

''I think you're right to be worried about Lorraine Sheldon. She looks like the kind of woman who gets what she wants regardless of the consequences. Bartonsville's a good place to live, but people are only human. There are plenty who love a good scandal, and this would be a doozy.''

''I thought Beth might remember if I brought her here,'' Hugh admitted, feeling the discouragement seep into his very bones. ''She didn't, but I kept hoping, for her sake, that she would. Maybe that's why I let it go on so long.''

And because he wanted to be near Faith for his own reasons, an equally bad decision.

"So far it's your word against Faith Carson's."

"I have no proof but my own suspicions."

"Stalemate."

"Exactly, until Lorraine Sheldon arrived. I want Beth to have peace and happiness. But I don't want Faith Carson branded as a baby stealer. I've been feeling my way since the day Beth got here. I waited too long to tell her what I suspected. Instead of a miracle, I got the Sheldons breathing down our necks. Then it was too late to leave. Lorraine would have thought that was suspicious, too. And it would have put Faith into an untenable position." Which, of course, had happened anyway. He heard the water shut off in the bathroom. Beth would be back with them in a minute or two.

"What are you going to do now?" Kevin asked. "This could get really ugly if Mrs. Sheldon decides to keep poking and prodding. And I have a nasty suspicion she'll do just that. Faith could end up in jail. And Child Services would certainly take Caitlin."

"Don't you think I know that?" Hugh growled. "All I wanted was for Beth to be happy and whole."

"At the expense of Faith and her daughter?"

"No, damn it. Of course not."

The bathroom door opened. Beth came out, still red-eyed but composed. She'd traded the heavy sweatshirt for a tank top but she still wore her jeans.

Kevin glanced across the room, a smile on his lips for Beth, but the words he spoke, low enough that only Hugh could hear, were blunt. ''Then I suggest you figure out a way to do something about it.''

... near ... *... as* ...

CHAPTER ELEVEN

"No MORE SQUIRTING your brother in the face, Jack," Peg informed her older son in her I-mean-it-or-else voice that Faith remembered from her own childhood. "Dana will have to be in charge of the hose if you do it again." She settled back in the wooden swing that hung on the deck of her twenty-year-old brick rambler. She and Steve had bought the house when they'd become engaged a year ago from friends of his parents who were retiring to Arizona. Peg's decorating expertise had brought her quite a bit of business when prospective customers saw what she'd done with the interior.

Caitlin was sitting on top of the slide on the boy's swing set with Dana hovering protectively nearby, as she watched her cousins chase each other with the hose. The last of the afternoon's warmth was fading into a cool, June twilight.

"Dana's going to deserve a baby-sitting medal before the summer is out." Faith propped her elbow on the back of the swing and rested her cheek on the back of her hand.

A drumbeat of tension still beat behind her eyes, but it had faded to a dull ache and she ignored it. "I have to be getting back to the farm," she said. "I can't have it look as if I let the Sheldons run me off my own property. And I'm worried about Beth. I shouldn't have left her alone for so long."

"We've been over this. You said Kevin Sager was there."

"Sitting outside the cabin."

"He'll look after her. I'm more worried about you. Do you want Steve to follow you home, just to make sure those people are gone?" Her sister was stroking Addy's silky ears, and the little sheltie, worn out from following Peg's big yellow Labrador retriever around all afternoon, snuggled closer to Peg's thigh and began to snore gently.

"Of course not. I'm fine. But sneaking around behind Steve's back to lay my troubles on you is one more thing I have on my conscience."

Peg didn't pretend ignorance. She covered Faith's hand with her own. "I have a confession to make. I told him about Caitlin right after we were married. And I called him to tell him about what happened this morning when you were putting Caitlin down for her nap."

"He's known all this time?" Faith thought back over the time since the wedding. Not once had her rock-solid brother-in-law given her any inkling that he knew she was not Caitlin's birth mother.

"I know I promised I would keep your secret." They were in shadow on this side of the house but Faith had no trouble detecting the sheen of tears in her sister's eyes.

Faith leaned forward, took Peg's hands between her own. "I should never have asked that of you."

"At the time it seemed the most natural thing in the world. I never intended to become involved with another man. Ever. Thank goodness I can be easily swayed." Peg laughed, and the sound held such happiness that Faith felt a quick jab of longing for what Peg and Steve shared, and that she would never know again.

Peg rested her hand on her slightly rounded belly. "I didn't think second-time-around miracles like Steve happened to women like me."

"He's worthy of your love and your trust," Faith whispered.

"And your trust," Peg responded.

Faith closed her eyes against a sudden sting of tears. "I know." She remembered what Steve had said at the picnic by the pond the night the Sheldons arrived. "I hope we have a little girl like Caitlin." He had known then that Caitlin was not her flesh and blood and he had said it anyway.

"He thinks you should get a lawyer—"

"No." Faith wasn't ready for that step. "No. Not yet."

"Honey, we have to be prepared. Maybe not for what Hugh and Beth might do, but for what the Sheldons certainly will."

"Beth and Jamie drove away. They abandoned Caitlin to a stranger in the middle of a storm."

"I know, honey. Those kids weren't blameless. At least Jamie wasn't. But Beth must share some of the responsibility. Hugh probably realizes that and doesn't want to see his sister branded an unfit mother.''

· ''I agree with you. That's partly why I let him stay. I...I knew he couldn't make a claim on Caitlin without hurting Beth.'' Hugh. Loyal, devoted, his sister's champion. Could he be her champion, too? Somewhere deep inside her she kept hoping that they could forge some kind of alliance for Caitlin's sake. *For her sake.*

''But the Sheldons. They're something different, aren't they?'' Reality washed away her momentary fantasy.

''Lorraine Sheldon wants her grandchild. She doesn't care who she hurts achieving that goal.''

Peg had been pushing the swing with her foot. She stopped, and planted both feet on the deck, her hands braced on her knees. ''I hope you're exaggerating. Surely she can be made to see it's Caitlin who would be hurt most if she's taken away from you.''

''Don't ever say that out loud again,'' Faith begged. ''Don't you know how often I've awakened in the middle of the night imagining that very thing?''

''I'm sorry,'' Peg said, leaning across Addy to give Faith a reassuring hug. ''We're both on edge.'' She sighed. ''I should have known. I should have recognized Beth—''

''How could you? Why should you have even thought twice about her? She and Caitlin don't re-semble each other that closely. Until this morning she had no idea that Caitlin might be her missing child. I'm convinced of that.'' Poor Beth. She had been stricken dumb by the scene she'd walked into.

"No. But I should have picked up on things. There was her name. The accident she was in. How upset you've been since she came. And here I thought it was because you had the hots for her brother—'' Peg stopped talking abruptly. She whipped her head around, her eyes raking Faith's face. "You look as if you've been hit by a two-by-four. You do have feelings for Hugh Damon. I knew it. I told Steve so after the picnic.''

"I do not. How could I? He's done this to me.''

Her sister wasn't impressed by her protest. "He's also your best ally against the Sheldons.''

Hugh had said they were allies that night in the moonlight.

"He's only interested in his sister's welfare.''

"And I'm interested in yours and Caitlin's. Steve and I will always be here for you. We'll help you any way we can, you know that.''

"I've never doubted it for a moment. And I can't fault Hugh for wanting to know what happened to Beth's baby. If the situations were reversed you would have done the same thing for me.''

"Yeah, he's a knight in shining armor, all right.'' Peg leaned over once more to enfold Faith in a hug. "I'm just sorry my little sister is the one who gets stuck fighting off the dragons. Why don't you leave Caitlin here for the night just in case the Sheldons decide to stage a repeat performance? She and the boys can have an indoor camp-out. Dana's staying, anyway, since Steve and I both have to be up and gone at the crack of dawn tomorrow.''

Faith looked out at her laughing, bright-eyed daughter. She hadn't seemed unduly alarmed by the morning's events, but Faith dreaded the possibility of Caitlin encountering the Sheldons again. ''Thanks, Peg.''

''We love having her.''

Steve walked out of the barn, and the sisters watched in silence as he crossed the yard and came to stand beside them, resting his arms on the top rail of the deck. ''From the look on your faces, I guess Peg 'fessed up to what she's told me.''

''Yes, she has.''

''Good. I don't like keeping secrets from family. I want you to know Peg and I will stand by you,'' he said. ''I think you made the right decision for Caitlin. She would have gone into the system if you'd turned her over to the authorities. There's no guarantee she would have been given back to Beth when they were finished investigating. The law might not agree with me, but as far as I'm concerned, she's yours. She's one of the brightest and happiest little girls I know. I meant it when I said I hope we have a daughter just like her.''

Faith swallowed the lump of tears his words had brought into her throat. Peg squeezed her hand, hard, and Faith squeezed back.

''Thank you, Steve.''

''I'd better be getting the boys dried off and settled

down, or we'll be up until midnight.'' His voice had
roughened around the edges, telling Faith her
brother-in-law was more emotional than he wanted
to admit. He turned away and jogged off to join the
melee around the swing set.

''Where do you think the Sheldons are tonight?''
Peg asked after a moment.

''Not far away, I imagine.''

''There's nothing fancy enough for the likes of her
within fifty miles of here.''

''I think she'd set up housekeeping in a barn if
she thought it would get her what she wants.''

Her sister's next words sent an icy tremor down
Faith's spine. ''And what she wants is Caitlin.''

THE SUNSET WAS incredible, red and orange below,
streams of mauve and purple above. The twilight was
long, lingering well into the evening, now that the
first day of summer was near. This was beautiful
country, Hugh had come to realize. The kind of place
where people watched the cloud patterns in the sky,
and the leaves change color on the trees. A man
could settle down here, grow old and die in peace
and prosperity. For a man who had spent close to a
dozen years building dams and bridges on every con-
tinent on earth, it suddenly didn't seem like such a
bad way to go.

The sound of a car engine approaching ended his
reverie. Hugh watched Faith drive slowly past the
cemetery as he rubbed a last bit of polish onto the
hood of his long-neglected Blazer. He'd had a lot of

nervous energy to burn off after Kevin and Beth left. He'd needed something to do with his hands, something that would let him think as he worked. He'd settled on washing and waxing the Blazer, but always one small part of his brain had been listening for Faith, watching for her to come home.

She slowed, but didn't stop at the ornate wrought-iron gate that marked the entrance to the cemetery. In life Mark Carson had loved her and cherished her; in death he had given Caitlin a name. But a dead man's memory couldn't help her now. She must face the future alone.

Unless she faced it with him.

He didn't know when the idea had come to him, that standing together they would be better able to protect Beth and Caitlin from the Sheldons' interference. It would be a partnership, legal and binding. A marriage of convenience, it used to be called. Would she agree to it?

He wondered if he could bring it off. Have her be his, but not his. The thought of being married to Faith Carson heated his blood and filled his head with images that would send her running if she could read his mind.

Except for Addy, ears pricked as she sat in the seat beside Faith, she was alone in the minivan, Hugh noticed. She must have left Caitlin with her sister for the night. She stopped the car, slipping out to take the Closed sign from the hooks where it was hanging. Regardless of what had happened that morning, it was obvious, tomorrow Faith intended to return her life to normal. But she was more upset than she let on, he surmised, or she would have her daughter at her side.

Addy sniffed around the base of the sign then looked in his direction, barking a greeting, but waiting at Faith's side. She saw him watching her and came toward the Blazer. Her arms were folded beneath her breasts, emphasizing their soft roundness. He kept his gaze on his work, but the sheen on the hood of the Blazer reflected her image like a dusky mirror.

"Is Beth okay?" she asked, as soon as she moved into earshot.

He wadded the old T-shirt he'd been using as a polishing rag into a ball and threw it into the bucket that had been hanging beneath the outside spigot on the side of the cabin.

"She's doing all right. Kevin took her to get something to eat a couple of hours ago."

"I knew she was in good hands with him. That's the only reason I left her."

"How are you?" he asked, moving around the front of the Blazer to stand beside her.

A hawk cried out overhead and in the distance a dog barked, causing Addy to give a quick yip in reply and warning.

"I'm fine."

"I don't believe you," he said quietly. There were dark circles under her eyes and faint stress lines bracketed her mouth.

"I'm still shaking inside," she said bluntly. "For

the second time in two weeks someone has accused me of taking another woman's child as my own.'' She met his eyes with proud defiance, but he saw the terror beneath. ''Did Beth believe Lorraine?''

He shoved his hands in the pockets of his jeans and leaned back against the fender to keep himself from taking her in his arms.

''No.''

''Did you tell her *you* believe that Caitlin is her child?'' She emphasized the pronoun very slightly.

''No.''

''Why not? It's the truth, isn't it? You're just as certain Caitlin is Beth's daughter as Lorraine is.''

''Faith, we don't have to be on opposite sides here.''

She gave a startled little laugh of disbelief, then her eyes narrowed. ''You denied it, didn't you? You didn't tell Beth why you brought her here.'' She backed away. ''Why?''

''Because I have no proof. I thought—'' He dropped his head back, staring at the darkening sky, searching for words that wouldn't come. He had thought they could work it out, he and Faith, come to some understanding, some arrangement that would give all of them what they wanted. Beth, her peace of mind, Faith, her child. And him? What did he want? A wife, a lover, a mother for his children?

''She trusts you,'' Faith said. ''How long can you lie to her about what you believe before she begins to suspect?''

She had touched a nerve rubbed raw by his own restless thoughts. "As long as it takes."

"As long as it takes for what? For me to confess what you want to hear? That won't happen until the sun falls from the sky." She whirled away as though to leave.

Hugh's hands came out of his pockets and fastened around her shoulders. "Don't go. We have to talk this through." He wanted to pull her closer. He wanted her tight against him, but he loosened his grip, holding his breath that she wouldn't turn and walk away.

"We have nothing to discuss," she said wearily, wrapping her arms around her waist, as though to ward off a chill. "Caitlin is my daughter."

"And she needs our protection. So does my sister. Don't you see what I'm asking, Faith?"

"No, I don't."

"We need to form an alliance, a partnership." He raked his hands through his hair. "Hell, maybe even a marriage."

Her eyes grew round, and darkened to the same color as the pond water beneath the willow. "What are you talking about?"

"Together we can keep Harold and Lorraine from ever learning the truth about Caitlin."

"No." She shook her head, rejecting his idea, rejecting him. "They would see it as a threat. A—a declaration of war. They'd suspect there was an ulterior motive and they would be more determined than ever to find out what happened the day Beth's baby was born.''

He drove home his point, trying to overcome her objection. ''Together we double our strength, our resources. Our ability to protect your daughter and my sister from the Sheldons.''

''No.'' Her voice had risen slightly. She closed her eyes refusing to look at him again. ''There has to be some other way. I—I can't marry you. I—I don't love you.''

He reached out then and gathered her into his arms without thinking. He cradled the back of her head with one hand, holding her gently, but firmly so that she couldn't run away. ''Does love have to be part of the equation?'' he asked, searching her face for some sign that she would soften. He found none, but he refused to accept that. Hugh lowered his head and kissed her. He felt her stiffen and her hands came up to push against his chest. He gentled his mouth on hers, willing her to open for him.

And then with a small sigh of surrender she did. Her mouth opened beneath his. She tasted of honey and mint and she smelled of sunflowers and summer grass. She wrapped her arms around his neck and let his lips skim over her eyelids, her cheeks, the curve of her ear.

When his lips returned to hers she leaned her full weight against him. She was soft and round in all the right places, and holding her in his arms was just as glorious as he had imagined it would be. He wanted to sink down onto the soft green grass and take her then and there, but he held back. When the kiss ended he didn't attempt another. He let her rest her cheek against his shoulder as she caught her breath, then let her step backward until only the tips of his fingers connected her to him.

"Together we could take on the world," he said.

"Not as husband and wife, no matter how important the cause. There has to be some other way. I can't marry without love. And you're not in love with me." Tears glistened on her lashes.

He lifted her chin with the tip of his finger. "Maybe not." He let the words hang in the air for a long time. "But I don't think that would be such an impossible thing to do."

She turned and fled, her dog at her heels.

HUGH FOLDED HIS HANDS across his bare chest and leaned one shoulder against the door frame. He looked out over the starlit fields, watching the mist swirl in the hollows. It was after three. The moon had set hours ago. Beth and Kevin had not returned and he couldn't sleep.

He couldn't sleep not only because he was worried about his sister, but because he couldn't get the memory of holding Faith out of his mind.

God, he'd screwed up big time tonight. He'd meant to present his proposal of an alliance in a no-nonsense, businesslike way. Instead he'd taken her into his arms and all but admitted he was more than halfway to falling in love with her.

She'd run from him as though he were a madman.

And to her way of thinking he probably was. She saw him as less of a threat than the Sheldons only because she trusted him not to do anything to hurt Beth. But now she would believe she couldn't trust him even the little amount she once had, because he'd shown her his attraction.

He wanted to protect them all, Beth and Caitlin and Faith. But he had blown his best chance of doing that. From now on Faith would do everything to keep him at arm's length—and set herself to face the challenge of Lorraine and Harold Sheldon alone.

CHAPTER TWELVE

HE SNORED. Not loudly, but she supposed she could get used to it. And his beard was a much darker red than his hair. She reached out and touched his chin, very lightly. Kevin frowned in his sleep and brushed at her hand as though she were a fly.

Beth stretched gingerly. Sleeping in the back seat of a twenty-year-old Buick was not like spending a night in a suite at a fancy hotel. She was stiff all over, and she had at least a half dozen mosquito bites in places she wasn't sure she could reach to scratch. Still, she wouldn't have traded the past twelve hours for anything in the world.

They hadn't made love. She had wanted to, but Kevin had held back. "Not tonight, Beth," he had told her. "When we make love the first time, it's not going to be because you want to forget all the pain you've got bottled up inside. And it's not going to be in the back seat of this damn car."

He had held her and comforted her, kissed her and stroked her hair, but he had gone no further. And he hadn't said he loved her. But he did. She knew because she was falling in love with him, too. But she wouldn't say it aloud, either. Not until she had come to terms with what happened yesterday.

She needed time, and Kevin knew that, too. He would wait for her to make sense of the jumble of emotions inside her. Was Lorraine right? Was Caitlin her child? Her lost and longed for baby? If she was, then all the feelings she thought she would have if they were ever reunited, were not the ones she was feeling right now.

She liked Caitlin. She was a sweet little girl, pretty and smart. But she didn't feel like Beth's child. Like the baby she'd dreamed of holding in her arms every night and day for almost three years.

She was Faith's child.

And Beth couldn't imagine what she could do to change that perception in Caitlin's mind—and in her heart. And did she even want to?

Kevin woke up with a little grunt and his arms tightened around her. "Good morning."

"Good morning," she said back. She kissed him lightly on the tip of his nose, then buried her face in his shoulder. They had spent the night together, but that was a long way from being comfortable waking up beside a man, when you had morning breath and tousled hair and no makeup.

"How did you sleep?" Kevin asked, sitting up with a groan and pulling her up beside him.

Beth thought back over the night just past. "I...I slept all right. No bad dreams."

"Good. I'd better get you home. Your brother's

probably waiting by the door with a baseball bat right now.''

''I'll protect you. But we should get home. I don't want Hugh to go off to work worrying about where we are.''

''Or what we've been doing.'' Kevin wriggled his eyebrows and she laughed.

''Or what we've been doing.''

But she did need to know what Hugh really believed. Was it all just coincidence as he had assured her yesterday? Or *was* he convinced that Caitlin was her baby?

If he did believe that, then he'd been lying to her for weeks. And Hugh had never lied to her before.

Kevin opened the car door and climbed out. The sun was up and the birds were singing, although it was still very early. They had spent the night on the riverbank at the end of a rutted and overgrown lane that Kevin had had no trouble finding, although it was almost invisible to Beth. She had a good idea why he knew it so well. It was a perfect make-out spot, but she didn't ask how many other girls he'd brought here in the past. ''C'mon. I'll take you home, unless you want to pee in the bushes.''

''No, I don't.'' Beth laughed. That was one of the things she liked about Kevin. He didn't treat her as if she were made of glass. Even after yesterday. ''And I do have to pee so step on it.''

''I will after we get back on the road. Otherwise I'll bounce us around so much it will be too late by the time we get back to the cabins.''

"Do you have to work today?" she asked, as he maneuvered the car in the narrow space and headed back up the lane.

"No. I'm yours. You can decide what you want to do while I go home to shower and shave." Kevin worked several part-time jobs in the summer. He lived with his parents and was saving for a house of his own. She liked that about him, too. He wasn't ashamed to say he lived with his parents. Family was important to him.

"Good. I..." She took a deep breath and slowed down a little. She wasn't going to stutter, or forget the words, or lose track of what she was going to say. Her mind was clear as a bell. "I need to talk to Faith sometime today."

"What are you going to say to her?"

She turned her head toward him. "I don't know," she said simply and truthfully. "But I do know one thing. I think it's time for me to see what the butterfly house is like inside."

FAITH OVERSLEPT the next morning. Caitlin was reluctant to leave the boys and Dana, so it had taken an extra twenty minutes to finish her toast and cereal and round up the toys she'd taken with her to Peg's. They barely made it back to the farm before a bus tour of thirty senior citizens arrived. It was the middle of the morning before Faith could take the time to clean the Sheldons' vacated cabin, and to leave fresh linen for Beth and Hugh.

She assumed Beth was all right because she had

seen Kevin Sager's car parked in front of the cabin beside Hugh's Blazer as she went to fetch Caitlin. When she returned, the vehicles were gone. Hugh had gone to work, as usual. She was doing her best to pretend everything was the same as it had been yesterday, too, but she couldn't maintain the illusion when she thought of what had passed between them last night.

A partnership. A loveless marriage to a man whose loyalty was divided between two women? Was she willing to go so far to protect her secret?

Faith pulled herself up short. Once again her longing to turn to Hugh had nearly betrayed her. She could not count him as an ally, as a partner, certainly as a husband, because she could not confide in him. She was as alone as she had been on the day of Caitlin's birth. She must never forget that, not for a moment. She would never have a man like Hugh to stand beside her.

"Look, Mommy. I made a house." Caitlin was busy playing in a turtle-shaped sandbox that Hugh had brought home in the back of his Blazer one day and set up in a corner of the greenhouse. Beth had found it "for a steal" at a Bartonsville yard sale and Caitlin had been so delighted with the gift that Faith would have seemed churlish refusing it. She had thanked Hugh and Beth, and felt another small weight added to the guilt in her heart. "I make a big house." Caitlin upended another bucket of damp sand and began patting it into a more interesting shape.

"It's time to go clean the cabins, Kitty Cat. Do you want to help me?" Faith asked and knew immediately she'd made a mistake. You never, ever, gave a two-year-old a choice. They would pick the one you didn't want them to every time.

"Stay here," Caitlin said, not looking up.

"We'll take the wagon," Faith tempted. "I'll pull you up and we'll coast back down the hill if you're a good girl."

Caitlin's face lit up. "Okay." Sand, toys and pigtails flying, she scrambled out of the sandbox. "Let's go."

"Just as soon as I load the linens and cleaning supplies into the wagon. And you go potty and wash your hands."

"Don't have to potty," Caitlin announced. "But I'll wash my hands. I'm a good girl, aren't I, Mommy?" *Mommy.* She loved this child so much. How could she face life without her? She would do whatever she must to keep her as innocent and happy as she was this very moment. Even give herself to a man who loved his sister, but didn't love her?

Unwilling to explore those thoughts any further, Faith swept Caitlin up in her arms and whirled her around until she squealed with joy. "You're the bestest little girl in the whole, wide world."

It was hot inside the cabin where Harold and Lorraine had been staying. Faith opened the windows and both doors. A nice breeze was blowing, keeping the day from being too hot. The cabin wouldn't take long to clean. It was the smallest of the three, one bedroom, a minuscule bathroom and a main room with a small kitchenette.

There was no sign of the Sheldons except for the dirty towels in the bathroom and the unmade bed. She stripped the linens and cleaned the bathroom while Caitlin played on the small patio at the back of the cabin with two of her Barbies and a stuffed kitten that she'd insisted on bringing along for the promised coast back down the hill.

Faith had just taken the clean linen into the bedroom when she heard a car drive up and a door open and close. Faith brushed her hair behind her ears and walked to the screen door, aware that it might be the Sheldons returning. Instead she came face-to-face with Beth. Kevin lifted his hand from the steering wheel in a wave, then drove off, leaving the two women alone.

Beth's expression was strained, but she tried to smile. She was wearing shorts and a Baylor T-shirt, and she'd pulled her hair into a little ponytail on top of her head. She looked about sixteen and scared. ''Hi, Faith. I'm glad you're back. I sent Kevin away. I...I—'' Faith waited as she took a deep breath and gained control of herself. ''May I come in? I think we need to talk.''

Faith opened the screen door. Beth stepped inside, blinking to adjust to the change in light. She scanned the cleaning supplies Faith had laid out on the kitchen table, and the clean linen piled beside it. ''I guess I needed to see for myself that they're really gone.''

"I doubt they've gone very far."

Beth looked around the little cabin, as though re-assuring herself her eyes weren't playing tricks on her. "No, they won't have gone far. And they'll be back. Lorraine wants to know what happened to my baby more than anything. Now that she thinks she's found her, she won't give up. I'm sorry." She lifted her hand and let it fall back to her side. "I'm sorry about yesterday. I didn't know what to do, or to say to make it better."

"It was as difficult for you as it was for me." Faith chose her words carefully as she always did with Beth. The problem was that she liked Hugh's sister. She wanted her to be happy and successful. She just wanted her to do it without ever knowing that Caitlin was her daughter.

"Where is Caitlin? Did you send her away?"

"She's out on the patio." Faith motioned toward the open back door of the cabin.

"Is she all right?" Beth walked around the bistro table that sat in the middle of the room and looked out at Caitlin playing on the paving stones. "I mean, is she all traumatized, or anything? Did Lorraine's crying and calling her Jamie's darling and wanting to hold her frighten her?"

"A little," Faith admitted.

Beth turned her back on the door. "It frightened me, too. She's like that. Really excitable. I can't re-member if she was like that before, but she probably was, or why would we have been so hell-bent to get away from her?" She shrugged. "Or maybe it has something to do with her age? You know, hormones and menopause and all that. She's almost fifty, you know.'' Faith hid a smile. Beth was so young, really. Being fifty was as impossible to imagine as being two hundred was. ''She ties me up in knots. I feel like I'm back in the hospital and can't even remember how to say my own name. It's as though she can't really believe I don't remember what happened that day. If she just asks me often enough, or finds someone else to ask me often enough, I'll be able to tell her where I left my baby. Doesn't she know I'd give my life to be able to remember what happened to her? Doesn't she think I would feel something, some extra special connection to Caitlin, if she really was my child?''

Faith felt her heart hammer against her chest. Beth did not feel a connection to Caitlin. She had said it clearly and emphatically. She was *right* to keep her silence. ''She loved Jamie very much. She's a mother, too. She's desperate to find the part of him that remains.''

''Yeah, that's something I can understand about her. The wanting. Jamie was an only child. He wasn't spoiled, though. At least not too much. He was cool and rich but he never treated me like I wasn't as good as he was. At least that's what I wrote in my diary. I don't remember him at all. Maybe he got the good genes from his dad? Harold isn't such a bad guy. I can talk to him when Lorraine's not around. But he thought I should give my baby up for adoption, too. He thought we were way too young to raise a child.''

"You probably were," Faith said quietly.

Beth smoothed a wrinkle from the pillowcase on top of the pile of linen. "I wanted someone to love, who loved me, too."

"I think that's a common emotion for teenage mothers."

"I know it is. I've had enough therapy, and read enough to figure that out. And I've also figured out I'm in charge of the rest of my life, so you don't have to give me the standard riff."

Faith chuckled, she couldn't help herself. "Oh, dear, was I so obvious?"

Beth smiled, too, the same mischievous grin that Caitlin had. It was the first Faith had noticed it. She wished she hadn't because now she knew Harold and Lorraine could also see the similarities between the two.

"No. I don't think there are too many other ways you can say it. Poor Hugh, he wants to make everything right again, and there's no way he can. We both know it, but he keeps on trying. He's that kind of guy. Never give up. Never say die. Maybe if Hugh told me he thought Caitlin was my baby I'd start to believe, too. But he says it's all a coincidence. And if I can't believe Hugh, than I can't believe anything or anyone else." She gave the pillowcase another pat, then picked up the stack of linen. "I'll help you make the bed."

"Thank you." Faith could barely get the words past the constriction in her throat. Dear God, what had Hugh done in trying to protect Beth with his well-intentioned lie?

Faith unfolded the bottom sheet and flipped it over the mattress. Beth continued talking as they worked. "Hugh explained to me last night why he came here in the first place. It was the dreams. My…my dream about the butterflies." Her voice was slightly muffled. She had a pillow tucked under her chin to anchor it while she placed it in the pillowcase.

It was the first she had stuttered in some time. Faith watched her closely. Her hands were trembling slightly, but she seemed to be in control. She had been right when she'd told Lorraine Sheldon the day before that Beth had come a long way in her healing. "He told me that, too."

"But he doesn't believe Caitlin is my baby. I want you to know that."

Faith tucked the pillows beneath the chenille bedspread, grateful for something to do with her hands as they talked. "Caitlin is my daughter, Beth."

"Please don't blame Hugh for the Sheldons coming here. It's all coincidence—the date of her birth and the butterflies and…and everything—" She seemed to want to say more, but stopped. "Just coincidence."

"You can accept that?"

"Yes." She lifted her shoulders in a sad little shrug. "I have to, don't I? Faith, would you tell me something?"

"If I can."

"You're a mother. You'd never not recognize your child, no matter what had happened—"

"Mommy! Mommy!" Caitlin's shrill cry was a full-blown scream by the time she'd come to the last drawn-out syllable. Addy began to bark in sympathy, adding to the din.

The color drained from Beth's face and her eyes grew huge, terror filled. "Caitlin, my God. What happened to her?"

Faith dropped the pillow she was holding and skirted the bed but Beth was already at the back door. She dropped stiffly to her knees and pulled Caitlin close against her. "What's wrong, Kitty Cat? Are you hurt?"

It didn't take more than a glance at the handful of blossoms scattered at Caitlin's feet, and the red swelling on the back of her hand she had cradled against her chest, to conclude she'd been stung by a bee while picking flowers from the beds bordering the patio.

"Kitty Cat, tell me what's wrong," Beth begged.

"Owie! Owie! Mommy!" Caitlin held out her arms and reached for Faith, crying all the harder. "Nasty old flower bit me."

Faith ignored the pain of seeing her daughter held and comforted in her birth mother's arms. She sat down on one of the red metal chairs, warm from the sun and took Caitlin onto her lap. "Let me see your owie." Beth rose stiffly, using the other chair to help her stand.

"Is she okay? What happened?"

"It's a bee sting." Faith held the dirty little hand cupped in her own and pointed to the "owie," raising her voice just enough to be heard over the wails. "See. There's the stinger. Mommy will make it better." Faith smoothed her thumb over the stinger, which showed up as a dark center to the welt. Caitlin sobbed harder, her eyes screwed shut, anticipating more pain. "There," Faith said. "All gone."

Caitlin opened her eyes and looked down at her hand. "Nasty gone?"

"All gone," Faith assured her.

"It still hurts. Need med'cine."

"Beth, could you do me a favor?"

"Yes. What do you need?" Her blue eyes were still wide and dark with anxiety but color had come back into her cheeks and she no longer looked on the verge of panic.

"There's a box of baking soda in the door of the fridge. Mix a spoonful with a little water in a glass to make a paste. It's the best *med'cine* there is for a bee sting."

"Baking soda?" Beth looked momentarily blank. "Baking soda. I don't—"

"Yes, you do. It's a white powder in an orange box," Faith said patiently.

"Orange box?" Her anxious expression cleared a little. "I remember. Baking soda. Brush your teeth. Make cookies."

"Now you've got it." Faith used the same soothing tone for Beth as she had for Caitlin.

"Make a paste. In a glass or a dish?"

"Either will do." Faith smiled. "And a cold compress. There are clean cloths with the cleaning supplies on the table."

"Cold compress. That, I remember."

Five minutes later Caitlin's cries had dwindled away to a few hiccuping sobs. Her hand was smeared with baking soda paste and wrapped with a cool, wet cloth. She was leaning against Faith's shoulder as she rocked in the red chair, Addy on guard at her feet. Beth sat beside them, looking out over the meadow toward the house.

"I think she's falling asleep," she whispered.

Faith nodded. "She's had a very busy week. She's behind on her sleep."

"I thought she must have fallen and broken both her arms and legs the way she was crying," Beth confessed.

"She has very good lungs." Faith kept a straight face with difficulty.

"You acted as if it were all just so ordinary."

This time Faith did let her smile break through. "She's two and a half, Beth. Bee stings and bumps and owies are all in a day's work for mommies."

Beth relaxed against the back of the chair. "You're right. I don't remember being around little kids very much. I haven't had any contact with them since my accident. I haven't trusted myself to be alone with anyone else's child since my baby disappeared."

Faith felt tears sting the back of her throat. So much guilt for Beth to carry, but Faith could do nothing to alleviate the pain without betraying herself. "You did very well with Caitlin today."

"Once I got my brain working again, maybe. But not at first. At first I panicked."

"Only for a moment."

"We both know that's long enough for something terrible to happen," Beth said quietly. Faith was aware she wasn't thinking only of Caitlin's bee sting. She didn't respond. There was nothing she could say.

Caitlin sat up. "Go home. My owie still hurts."

"Let's go watch a video and have something cool to drink," Faith said. She knew better than to suggest a nap. "We'll come back to finish the cabin when it's cooler."

"Let me clean it for you," Beth said quickly, forestalling Faith's automatic protest. "I need something to keep me busy. Kevin won't be back for a while. We're going through the butterfly house later. It's time to get over this butterfly phobia of mine. I'll probably never know where it came from, but I'm going to try to figure it out by bearding the little monsters in their lair." She laughed, trying to make a joke of what was obviously going to be an ordeal.

"If you like, I'll go with you and Kevin, and give you the grand tour."

"Lend some moral support?" Beth stood up smiling and entered the cabin.

Faith felt small and low. "Yes, exactly. And perhaps it won't seem so much of an ordeal with others about."

Beth held open the screen door for Faith to carry Caitlin inside. "I like that idea. It's a deal."

The sound of cars turning into the lane caught their attention at the same time. The Sheldons' green Lexus rolled past the cabins.

"Oh, no." The smile disappeared from Beth's lips. "They're back."

A second car followed, a county sheriff's cruiser. Faith's throat closed, and she fought a sudden wave of nausea as the blood rushed from her head to pool in her stomach.

"What is the sheriff doing here?" Beth stepped back into the main room of the cabin so that she couldn't be seen by the cars' occupants.

"I don't know." Faith saw her own fear mirrored in the younger woman's eyes. For a moment she felt exactly as Beth must feel when words or concepts refused to come to mind when she required them. It was like treading water in a vast sea in the middle of a starless night. "I'd better go see."

"No, don't go," Beth pleaded.

"I have to. I have nothing to hide from Lorraine Sheldon or the sheriff," Faith lied.

Tears welled up in Beth's blue eyes and spilled onto her cheek. She shook her head, looking miserable and torn. "If I go with you they'll start asking me questions about the baby again."

"Stay here. You don't have to talk to them if you don't want to."

Beth was shaking like a leaf, but Faith had no other comfort to give her. She needed it all for herself. It was no coincidence that a sheriff's deputy had accompanied the Sheldons to her home. Lorraine had taken her suspicions to the authorities, and they were here to learn if there was any truth to her accusations.

If Faith couldn't convince them otherwise, her worst nightmare would come true. Her secret would be revealed to the world, and Caitlin would be taken from her.

HUGH WAS ALREADY three-quarters of the way back to Painted Lady Farm when he got Beth's call. Her voice was shaking, and her stutter had returned, but he had no trouble understanding what she was trying to say. The Sheldons were back, and damn them, they'd brought the law. How many strings had Harold and Lorraine pulled to get the sheriff to listen to their story?

Maybe not as many as he'd thought they'd need. The case of Beth's missing baby was still an open one. The authorities would be interested in any new lead that came to their attention.

He could hear the struggle in her voice as she battled to hold back tears. "When can you come back?"

"I should be there in twenty minutes." Or less, he told himself.

"Thank God, but how did you know I needed you here?"

"I didn't know. We had to shut down early today. A city utility crew broke through a water main and flooded the entrance to the access road. Just hang in there. I'll be as quick as I can."

He heard her take a deep breath. "I ran back here when Faith went to meet the Sheldons, but I can't let Faith face them alone. Maybe I should go down to the farm. I—I can tell the deputy he's got the wrong little girl. Caitlin isn't my baby. You were right. It's all just a bunch of weird coincidences. I'd know if she was mine. I'd feel it in my heart even if my brain's forgotten, you know that as well as I do. My baby is still lost."

"Beth. Beth, wait." She'd broken the connection. He pulled the cell phone away from his ear and glared at it as if sheer force of will could get her back on the line. "Damn." Two miles to his exit, then another ten to Faith's farm. Fifteen minutes. Long enough for Lorraine Sheldon to wreak havoc. He tossed the phone onto the passenger seat and stomped his foot down on the gas pedal.

He had set this whole mess in motion and now he had damn well better be able to do something to put it right. Something that wasn't going to break Beth's heart.

And Faith's.

CHAPTER THIRTEEN

FAITH WISHED she and Caitlin didn't look quite so bedraggled. She walked across the parking lot, pulling her daughter in her red wagon and feeling hot and sweaty. Caitlin was still tear-streaked, pouting because she couldn't coast down the hill. Addy had decided to play watchdog and was growling at both the Sheldons and the sober-faced sheriff's deputy standing beside his patrol car.

"Addy, quiet," Faith ordered sharply. The sheltie quit growling but stayed beside the wagon. She bent to brush Caitlin's hair from her eyes, knowing the others had noticed both the makeshift bandage on her hand, and the mulish look on her little face. "Go play on your swing, Kitty Cat. Momma has to talk to these people and then I'll come swing you."

"No," she said folding her arms in front of her and sticking out her lower lip. "Stay here." She glared up at the sun. "I hot."

Faith pulled the wagon farther under the huge maple that shaded most of the backyard. "Does this feel better? It's cooler here." Caitlin rested her elbows on her knees and continued to scowl at all and sundry.

"She's hurt," Lorraine said, pointing to the bandage. She took a step toward Caitlin, but her husband put his hand on her arm and she remained where she was.

"A bee sting, that's all," Faith said. She turned to face the deputy. She held out her hand. "I'm Faith Carson. I'm sorry to keep you waiting. How may I help you?"

"Chief Deputy Gibson, ma'am," he said, touching the brim of his hat with the tip of his finger before shaking her hand. "Mr. and Mrs. Sheldon have come to us with some serious accusations."

Faith was shaking so hard inside she wanted to wrap her arms around herself to hold in the tremors, but she kept her hands at her sides. "And those accusations would be?"

"That you are not the mother of this child." He glanced at Caitlin. "Would you prefer we do this without the child present?"

"I am a widow, Deputy Gibson. My daughter is only two, too young to be left alone in her room. She is tired and hot, and probably frightened by the three of you. What do you suggest I do with her?" She had no intention of inviting the Sheldons, or the deputy, into her home.

The deputy reddened slightly. "I see your point."

"Where's Beth?" Lorraine interrupted once more. "She should be questioned as well."

"I don't know where Beth is at the moment," Faith said, selecting her words carefully. "I was cleaning one of my rental units when I saw your cars turn into the lane. I came as soon as I could."

"Beth is off somewhere with that boy she's been seeing, isn't she? It doesn't matter. She will only claim she can't remember anything."

"Lorraine, you're not being fair. You've seen the doctors' reports. Beth isn't faking her amnesia." Faith was somewhat surprised that Harold Sheldon had contradicted his wife so publicly. In the short time Faith had known them he'd mostly remained silent.

"It was you who was hysterical yesterday, Mrs. Sheldon," Faith couldn't stop herself from saying, "not Beth."

Deputy Gibson cut in. "Beth is Beth Harden, the missing baby's mother?"

"Miss Harden has been staying in one of the cabins with her brother for several weeks. He's an engineer working on a project north of the city. Mrs. Sheldon and her husband arrived several days ago. She told me she found Painted Lady Farm on the Bartonsville Chamber of Commerce Web site, just as Mr. Damon did. I had no idea there was a connection between them until that time. Mrs. Sheldon believes that Beth Harden is my daughter's real mother. When she made her belief known to me I was very upset, as you can understand. I asked her and Mr. Sheldon to vacate their cabin and leave my property."

"Can't say as I blame you," the deputy said under his breath. He was a sandy-haired, whipcord-thin man about her own age. "But enough of what Mrs.

Sheldon claims checks out that my boss asked me to come out here and talk to you.''

''Am I under arrest?'' Faith asked.

He hooked his thumbs in his gun belt and looked down at Faith from under the brim of his hat. ''Did I say that?'' he asked.

''No. I'm sorry, Deputy. This is all very upsetting, surely you must see that.''

''I admit it's one hell of a story.'' He leaned his hip against the fender of his car and turned to Lorraine and Harold. ''Why don't you start at the beginning so I can get this all straight. What makes you think that the little girl is your grandchild?''

''So many things,'' Lorraine said.

Harold spoke up. He and Lorraine were standing in a pool of hot, yellow sunlight while Faith and the deputy were in the shade. He squinted against the sun. He wasn't wearing a hat and perspiration began to bead on his forehead. ''Caitlin was born the same day as our son died. We have searched the country over for the past two and a half years. We had no idea Beth's brother was still searching for the child, too.''

''Something led him to this place and this woman and child,'' Lorraine broke in. She, too, was looking flushed. She held out her hand as though to implore the deputy to see her reasoning. ''It's not just coincidence that Hugh Damon brought Beth to a place where a woman with no husband gave birth to a baby without a single witness on the same day our grandchild was born. He knows something more, I'm convinced of that.''

While Lorraine had been talking the sound of a car engine approaching underscored her passionate words. Faith felt the knot of nerves in her stomach tighten still further. She didn't want to deal with a carload of tourists wanting to tour the butterfly house. She didn't want friends or neighbors to see her being interrogated by the police.

Or, perhaps it was Peg. Dear, loyal Peg, who would stand by her side and compromise herself still more to keep Faith's world intact.

But it was neither tourists nor her sister who pulled into the parking lot. It was Hugh's black Blazer. And he wasn't alone, Beth was with him. Faith hadn't expected him to return for several hours. Even if Beth had called him as soon as she got back to their cabin, there was no way he could have made it back to Painted Lady Farm so soon. He'd obviously returned for some other reason and found Beth, who'd told him everything. Hugh parked beside the deputy's cruiser and walked around the truck to help Beth out of the vehicle.

Faith searched his face for some clue to his thoughts as he held out his hand to the deputy and introduced himself and Beth. His expression gave nothing away. Faith had no idea what he would say. Since she had dismissed his offer would he add his accusations to the Sheldons' and strengthen their claim?

"We have a pretty good idea of why you're here," Hugh said to the deputy without preamble.

Deputy Gibson was equally blunt. "Your sister is the mother of the missing baby?"

"I am." Beth looked pale but composed. She kept her gaze averted from Harold and Lorraine and stood close to Hugh.

"This is a very unusual case. You all understand why the sheriff wanted me to check it out."

"We understand," Hugh said. "We all want to believe we'll find Beth's baby someday. But Mrs. Carson's daughter is not my sister's child." Faith fought to keep her relief from flooding her face and giving her away. He was only trying to protect Beth, she warned herself. He had not had a change of heart.

"Can you prove that?" the deputy asked. He spoke to Hugh but he looked at Beth. She stayed silent. It was Lorraine who spoke.

"If she's not Beth and Jamie's baby, why did you come here in the first place? Why did you bring Beth?" she demanded, crossing the sun-dappled space between them.

"I came because of my work." Hugh stepped forward, blocking Lorraine's path to his sister.

"You came because something drew you. What was it, Hugh? I don't know what clue led you here but I intend to find out."

Hugh's voice was as steady as his tone was unyielding. "There's no clue, Lorraine. I admit there are coincidences. Caitlin's birth date is the most obvious."

"Mrs. Carson, your daughter was born at home and not in the hospital, am I correct?" Deputy Gibson asked. He had taken a black spiral notebook from his shirt pocket and flipped it open.

"Yes." She was on familiar ground here, she didn't falter. "My husband had died six months earlier. I was alone. I went into labor early, in the middle of that terrible ice storm we had three years ago in November. The phone was out. I couldn't drive myself to the hospital because the roads were so bad."

"You also didn't seek any prenatal care from any doctor in the area, is that correct?"

The question caught her off guard. No one had asked it before. She supposed it was because most people assumed she had been seeing a doctor. They were always more interested in the story of the delivery. "That is correct. I—I wasn't thinking very clearly after my husband died, but my pregnancy was uneventful and thankfully Caitlin was born healthy." She never embellished her lies.

But as she spoke a frightening new possibility had entered her mind. Was it possible the authorities, or the Sheldons—or Hugh—would now try to track down the doctor in the remote Mexican village they'd taken her to after the accident, and prove she had never carried her baby to term?

"You registered your daughter's birth at the county records office six days after she was born."

"Yes, that was the first day I felt safe enough, and strong enough to leave the house."

''I still can't believe this state doesn't demand more concrete proof of maternity than just turning up with a baby in your arms,'' Lorraine said scathingly.

''You'll have to take that up with the state legislature, ma'am,'' the deputy said dryly.

''She's not my baby, Deputy.'' Beth blinked back tears and her voice rose a little even as she struggled visibly to control it. ''No one will believe me. I don't remember anything about this place. I don't remember ever seeing Faith until my brother brought me here.''

''If you'd only allow the hypno—''

''No! I won't. I'm not going to remember what happened that day, no matter how many therapists you try to bully me into talking to, don't you understand that?''

''I only understand my son is dead because of you and the one thing that would give me comfort, my grandchild, might be dead because of you, too.'' For the second time Faith saw Lorraine Sheldon shaken out of her polished calm, her face was contorted with grief and frustration.

''Shh, Lorraine. Don't say anymore. You'll regret it later, you know you always do.'' Harold put his arm around her shoulders and drew her against his chest. Every day of his sixty-some years was visible on his face. The sorrow in his expression was of a man who knew he might never see his only grandchild before he died.

Hugh had his hands on Beth's shoulders, steadying her, comforting her. Only Faith stood alone. She knew it was the way it had to be, but she longed for someone to stand beside her.

The longing surged into her veins. Longing not for Mark, the man who had once held that place in her heart, but for Hugh, the one man she could never have.

She felt a tug on the hem of her shorts. "Mommy. I'm hot. I want a drink."

She looked down. Caitlin had climbed out of her wagon and stood looking up at her, tear streaks dried on her face. "Don't like them," Caitlin said, pointing her finger at Lorraine and Harold. "Go away," she said loudly. "You're bad."

The pronouncement had the effect of drying Lorraine's tears. "Don't be angry, Kitty Cat," she whispered cajolingly. Faith wanted to scream at her not to call Caitlin by the name Faith had given her when she was only hours old and had made little mewling sounds as she tried valiantly to suckle from the makeshift nipple. "I like you very much."

"Don't like you. Go away," Caitlin repeated.

"Yes, please. Go away," Faith said. "I don't want my daughter upset any more than she already has been. Deputy Gibson, isn't it plain Mrs. Sheldon's grief is causing her to labor under a false assumption?"

Lorraine tore her eyes away from Caitlin and fixed them on the deputy with a desperate intensity. "No, wait. I demand some kind of action. Surely, you can order Mrs. Carson to have blood tests, or DNA tests, or something. All you have is her word against mine.

Caitlin is my granddaughter. I know it. I feel it in my heart and soul.''

"I will do no such thing." Faith no longer had to fight to keep the tremor from her voice. She was suddenly forged of rock and steel. She could never allow that to happen.

Lorraine's eyes narrowed. "Why should you object if you've nothing to fear?"

"I refuse to discuss your unfounded accusations any further. I want you off my property. At once.'' Rock and steel. She clung to the image to keep her inner terror at bay.

"Deputy—" Lorraine's voice had grown shrill once more.

"I don't have the authority, ma'am," Deputy Gibson responded patiently. "All I can do is report back to the sheriff, and he'll contact the Indiana state police. If they see any reason to reactivate the case they'll let us know.''

"That's all?" Lorraine was incredulous. "Why, by tomorrow morning Mrs. Carson could be on her way out of the country with the child.''

Deputy Gibson looked around at the flower beds, the greenhouse, the well-tended lawn and garden. "I don't think that's likely, ma'am. I suggest you and your husband do as Mrs. Carson asks and leave. We don't want this to get unfriendly.''

"I'll do no such thing. Not until I get some satisfaction. I'll find someone with the authority to make Mrs. Carson comply. My husband is a very wealthy man, Deputy. We have friends in very high places. They know how I've suffered these past months. They'll see to it we get the answers we need.''

''You do what you think you have to, ma'am. I don't have any jurisdiction in a civil case, and until I receive an order from someone who does, I'm going to be on my way. Go back to your motel. Get out of the sun and get some rest.'' It was an order, politely stated. He touched his finger to his hat brim once more. ''I'll be in touch.''

He got in his cruiser and drove away leaving the others standing as though they'd been rooted in place. Lorraine was still crying, and now Caitlin was sniffling. ''I'm thirsty,'' she whimpered.

Faith picked her up and cradled her in her arms. ''Please go. All of you.''

''I meant what I said,'' Lorraine repeated as her husband put his hand under her elbow, urging her toward their car. ''I won't rest until I have absolute proof that Caitlin is not my grandchild.''

''Is that a threat?''

''If you chose to interpret it that way. We can do it the hard way, lawyers and lawsuits and more visits by the likes of Deputy Gibson. Or we can settle the question in a matter of days. I'm willing to pay for any tests necessary for you to prove to me that Caitlin is your child.''

''Don't do it, Faith,'' Beth said. Her voice was tight with strain, but steady and her speech was clear. ''You don't have to prove anything to her.''

Lorraine waited for a full minute while Faith

searched her brain frantically for some way out of the trap she'd fallen into. She couldn't say yes to the tests and silence would condemn her, just as surely.

Triumph was evident in the older woman's eyes. "Our lawyers will be in touch. That is unless the sheriff decides to take matters into his own hands first."

"We're staying at the Lebanon Inn in Carrington," Harold said. Carrington was the county seat, about twenty miles north of Bartonsville. "If you want to discuss this further we'll be there." He looked as if he wanted to say more, but did not. He took Lorraine's arm and helped her into the passenger seat of the Lexus, then got behind the wheel.

A minute later they were gone. Faith was shaking so hard she thought her legs might give way and she would find herself sitting on the ground. She didn't look at Hugh and Beth. She couldn't. She walked to the pump and set Caitlin on her feet. She began working the handle.

What was going to happen to her and Caitlin now? How long could she fight off Lorraine and Harold Sheldon?

She dropped to her knees to offer the ladle of cold, spring water to Caitlin. She took a big drink, water dribbling down her chin. She wiped it away with her bandaged hand and gave Faith a big, wet smile. "Good, Mommy. But I still need a cookie."

Caitlin. Her love. Her reason for living. Tears pricked behind her eyelids and she blinked them away. She felt Hugh's presence behind her, warm and strong and solid. She no longer considered him her enemy, but could she trust him enough to make him her ally? Her husband? If she told him her secret could they somehow find a solution that would allow her to keep her daughter? Or would she only be giving him the weapon he needed to take Caitlin away?

CHAPTER FOURTEEN

FOR THE NEXT FEW DAYS Faith waited for something, anything, to happen. But she heard nothing from Harold and Lorraine Sheldon, or Deputy Gibson. Hugh, also, had taken pains not to be alone with her, although there had been times, even amid the noise and crowds of Bartonsville's Fourth of July celebration they all attended, that he could have taken her aside. Did he regret the kisses they had shared? The offer of a partnership, a marriage, that he had made? She thanked God for the reprieve from the Sheldons, but could not bring herself to feel the same relief about Hugh.

One thing had changed over the holiday weekend. Beth had come into the butterfly house. It wasn't Kevin, or Hugh, who accompanied her, but Caitlin.

Faith looked up at the sound of the air lock opening and saw her daughter leading Beth by the hand. It was late in the afternoon, and the butterflies were everywhere, darting and flitting among the plants, sunning on the rocks of the waterfall, sipping delicately at the feeders.

"See. Pretty," Caitlin said, tugging Beth toward a

trio of black-and-gold Australian skippers congregated on a purple African milkweed flower.

"I thought you were swimming with Jack, Guy and Kevin?" Faith said summoning a smile that she hoped showed none of her inner turmoil. Both Caitlin and Beth were wearing Patriot T-shirts over their bathing suits, and matching hot-pink flip-flops that Beth had found at the Volunteer Fireman's flea market booth the day before.

"She was missing you, so I brought her here to find you." Beth's smile looked as strained as Faith's felt.

"Don't touch the butterflies," Caitlin cautioned shaking a grubby finger.

"Don't worry," Beth said with a quivering laugh. "I won't touch."

"Are you all right?" Faith was torn between pride in Beth's courage and the ever-present trepidation that each step forward she took could trigger her memory.

"Caitlin doesn't understand phobias. She insisted I see all the pretty butterflies." Her voice was bright, but her eyes were large and apprehensive.

"You can leave her with me," Faith said. "You don't have to stay."

"No. I want to. I told Kevin it was long past time for me to face this." She let Caitlin tug her along the path to the big waterfall then sat down beside her on the rock ledge bordering the pool. "It is pretty."

"I think so." Faith sat on the bench across the path and waited. She'd turned on the fans to move the warm air and it stirred Beth's silvery hair. She pushed it back off her cheek. Her hair had grown longer since she'd arrived at Painted Lady Farm. It was almost the same length as Caitlin's now.

Caitlin slipped off her sandals and dabbled a toe in the water, watching for Faith's reaction from the corner of her eye. Her daughter hadn't asked permission, but Faith let the infraction pass unremarked. It was very warm, after all. Now both feet were in the water. "No splashing," Caitlin said, to show she knew the rules even when she was bending one of them. "'Flies don't like to get their wings wet.''

Beth watched an orange-and-black giant African swallowtail float majestically by. She looked down at the top of Caitlin's shining head, then shifted her gaze to Faith. "Nothing," she said. "Nothing but butterflies. I thought...I thought maybe something would come back.''

"Do you still have the dream?" Faith asked softly. She was on dangerous ground when she talked with Beth about the past, more so since Deputy Gibson's visit.

"No. No more butterflies and blood on the snow. But...I dream of her.'' She dropped her eyes to her hands. "I hear a baby crying and I keep looking but I don't find her.''

Water flew from the pool to cover them both. Caitlin's dabbling had grown more energetic as they'd talked and finally her feet had broken the surface of the water. "Caitlin!"

Beth jumped to her feet, the back of her shirt soaking wet. "Yikes," she said shaking her head to get rid of the droplets in her hair. "That's cold."

"And that's a no-no," Faith said, scooping Caitlin into her arms, relieved that the conversation had been interrupted.

"Sorry," Caitlin said, but she didn't look sorry. Butterflies were on the move throughout the habitat. All those sunning on the waterfall had flown to safety, disturbing others at their rest, causing traffic jams on the feeding trays. Caitlin flapped her arms. "I fly, too."

"You're flying inside for a nap," Faith said.

"I'll stay out here and watch the greenhouse until she's settled."

"You don't have to do that."

"Yes, I do. I have a lot to think about," Beth said, watching a quartet of elegant and sophisticated-looking black-and-white tree nymphs as they glided by in formation.

Faith's throat was tight. What if she told Beth the truth? Between them could they come to some arrangement that would allow her to keep Caitlin? It seemed as the days passed the little girl brought them closer together, but she also kept them apart. Perhaps she would have found the courage if the Sheldons had not brought with them the danger of the authorities reopening the investigation into the baby's disappearance. With that threat hanging over her head, Faith could not vanquish her own fears and tell Beth the truth.

"I don't think we'll be very busy this evening,"

Faith said. "There's the chicken barbeque in town, and the fireworks coming up. Everyone else is down by the pond. Why don't you go join them? If a car turns in the lane we can see it from there."

A huge, ghostly cecropia moth brushed her forearm as it whispered past and Beth shivered. "Maybe you're right."

"I'm not sleepy," Caitlin insisted, hanging heavily on Faith's arms because she wanted to be let down to walk.

If she put Caitlin down for a nap now she would be able to stay awake for Bartonsville's fireworks display, the finale of the weekend-long community celebration, which was scheduled for dusk. "I want down," she repeated stubbornly, and Faith relented. When her daughter was in this mood she fought sleep like a ninja warrior.

"Okay, back to the pond." Maybe if she sat with her in the covered glider Caitlin would fall asleep on her own. The three of them left the habitat and walked through the greenhouse into the late afternoon. Kevin was coming toward them.

"I've been looking for you," he said, his brown eyes searching Beth's face. He had known where she was and was concerned about the outcome.

"I went to see the butterflies," Beth told him, and linked her arm through his.

"DO YOU THINK they're sleeping together?" Peg asked an hour later as she followed Faith along the meadow path on the regular monitoring walk for the

Ohio Department of Natural Resources. Once a week she followed the same path through her meadow and counted all the butterflies she saw within eight feet on either side. The sun was getting low in the sky and the butterflies were beginning to find their way to favorite nighttime resting places so she was getting a good count. They had left Steve fishing for blue-gills in the pond while Kevin and Beth played catch with Jack and Guy under the trees. Caitlin had fallen asleep in the glider on the dock, as Faith had thought she might, and Hugh had promised to keep an eye on her.

"I suppose they could be." Faith pointed out five bright-yellow common sulfurs feeding on a stand of purple clover. Peg penciled the sighting into the log. "If it's gone that far I hope she doesn't get hurt any more than she's already been."

"I think it's more likely Kevin who'll be hurt when she and Hugh go back to Texas."

Faith had been thinking of that day, too. When would it come? How would she feel?

And she would be alone again.

"At least the Sheldons haven't been around the past few days."

"It's like waiting for the other shoe to drop," Faith admitted.

Peg gave an exaggerated shiver. "I know what you mean. She's up to something, I can feel it in my bones."

"She's searching for her grandchild. I don't think there is any more determined creature on earth,"

Faith didn't want to think about Lorraine Sheldon anymore that day. "Look, there's a pair of painted ladies. And the red admiral I've been seeing the past couple of weeks."

"Where?"

Faith pointed out the black-and-orange-red butterfly swaying gently on a tall milkweed pod. "They're territorial. That's his favorite perch."

"Except for the monarchs and the painted ladies they all look alike to me." Peg lifted her hand and shielded her eyes from the sun. "Is it just me or are the kids being awfully quiet all of a sudden? I think I should go see if the boys have Kevin and Beth hog-tied to a tree. It's too quiet over there."

The boys didn't have Beth and Kevin hog-tied to a tree. In fact, the entire group was gathered around something on the coarse sand at the shallow end of the pond, including the two men.

Hugh held Caitlin, still sleeping, cradled against his shoulder. He looked at Faith and smiled, and her heart flipped. He had promised Faith he wouldn't leave her daughter's side, and he'd kept that promise, even though he was now standing no more than ten yards from where she had been sleeping. The boys and Kevin were hunkered down on the balls of their feet engaged in an animated discussion.

"What did you find?" Peg called out.

"A turtle," Jack hollered back, as if they were standing in the middle of the cornfield instead of fifty feet away.

The sound of his voice woke Caitlin and she lifted

her head from Hugh's shoulders and gave him one of her glorious smiles.

"What's that?" she asked, instantly wide-awake. She wound her arms around his neck and looked down at the ground. The simple trusting gesture sent heat through Faith, making her intensely aware of how strong and solid and loving Hugh Damon could be.

"Come see," Guy said, hunkered down on the balls of his feet like Kevin.

"If it's a snapping turtle I don't want to see it," Peg informed them.

"Hey, do you think I'd be in this position if it was a snapping turtle," Kevin asked. Beth laughed and the sound was so infectious that Peg and Faith laughed, too.

"It's a box turtle, but a big one," Steve said. "No wonder Hugh and I keep getting the worms stolen off our hooks when we're fishing."

Peg and Faith came close enough to look down at the big turtle, seemingly unperturbed by all the attention as it attempted to amble back into the water. Caitlin had wriggled out of Hugh's arms, but she didn't come directly to Faith, instead she moved cautiously closer to get a better look. Beth reached out and laid her hands on Caitlin's shoulders. The sun shone like spun gold in their hair.

It seemed to Faith that Caitlin and Beth grew more alike physically as each day passed. Or was it only that she was finally admitting to herself how similar they were?

"Stinky," Caitlin pronounced, wrinkling her snub nose. "Take it away."

"I think I will go put it in the creek," Kevin said. "Let him hunt for frogs and minnows like a real turtle. He's getting too big and fat stealing night-crawlers off our hooks in the pond."

"We'll go, too." The boys were already jumping up and down in anticipation of a trek through the meadow to the creek.

"I'm staying here," Beth said. She smiled at Kevin. "It's hot. I'll fix lemonade for you so it's cold when you get back."

"Thanks. I could kiss you for that."

"Later."

Kevin picked up the turtle, which immediately withdrew head and feet into its shell, and headed off to the creek with his noisy minions in tow.

"I'm going to make use of the glider now that Caitlin's not using it for her nap," Peg announced, handing Faith her monitoring log.

"C'mon, Hugh," Steve urged. "Our competition for the bluegills is out of the picture. Let's see if we can hook a couple."

"Sounds like a good idea." Hugh grinned.

"Cookie time," Caitlin said pointedly.

"You just had—" Faith paused as a familiar car pulled into the parking area by the greenhouse.

Peg groaned. "I spoke too soon. It's that devil woman back again." It was indeed Lorraine Sheldon who got out of the car. She was alone and Faith knew with cold certainty that whatever it was the woman had to say she didn't want to hear.

"Who?" Caitlin craned her neck to see who Peg was talking about. "Bad lady."

"Oh, dear," Peg said, pursing her lips to stop a smile from forming. "Where did she pick that up?"

"Hello, Caitlin," Lorraine said, dropping to her knees, heedless of her pale linen slacks. "How are you? Have you been swimming in the pond?"

"Yes," Caitlin said, not looking directly at Lorraine.

"I have a very big pool at my house. It's far away but maybe some day you could come there and visit and we could swim in it."

Caitlin shook her head. "Bad lady. Don't like you."

"Steve, I think we should take Caitlin inside for her snack," Peg interrupted.

"Yes, please," Faith said. Blessed Peg, always there when she needed her. Steve lifted Caitlin into his arms and without another word they left.

Lorraine rose to her feet. "You've turned her against me."

"No," Faith said. "I don't want her upset by you. You're a stranger to her, and a frightening one at the moment."

"And you intend to keep it that way."

"There's no reason she should encourage a friendship between you and her daughter," Beth said. She'd lost all the sparkle she'd had moments before.

Hugh said nothing but took a step closer to his

sister, laying his big hands on her shoulders. The underlying implication was not lost on Jamie's mother. Her defiance left her for a moment. Her lips trembled and she held out a shaking hand. "Beth, don't you want to know what happened to your baby?" she asked. She looked older, less polished, less assured. It was hard for Faith to keep all her barriers in place when twinges of empathy kept sneaking up on her. Lorraine Sheldon was a mother who had lost her son. And her grandchild. She was in pain.

Pain that Faith held the key to alleviating, but dared not use.

"You know the answer to that question. How many times must I repeat it? What did you really come for, Lorraine?" Beth's voice was tremulous, but she didn't falter. It seemed as though she was gaining courage as Faith was losing hers.

"I wanted to give you one last chance to cooperate. For Caitlin's sake. For all your sakes."

"No," Faith said. "I will not give in to your threats. I will not submit myself or my daughter to medical tests, or any other notion that comes into your head."

Lorraine took a deep breath. Her nostrils flared a little as she exhaled. "Very well. You leave me no alternative. I'm going to contact the appropriate authorities in both Ohio and Indiana and ask them to reopen Beth's case. I'm also filing suit in civil court to force you to prove beyond any reasonable doubt that Caitlin is not my grandchild."

"No." Beth's denial was instant and torn from her heart. "You can't. Where's Harold? Does he know you're doing this?"

"My husband had to fly back to Boston on a business matter. But I don't need his permission to do this, Beth. I have means and resources of my own. Friends in high places who know that finding my grandchild is the most important thing in the world to me. They have agreed to help get your case re-opened and then you'll have to cooperate."

She looked at Faith and her eyes were hard. "All of you."

THEY ATTENDED the fireworks display at the town park for the boys' sake. Caitlin had fallen asleep in Faith's arms on the way home and was now tucked away in bed. Peg and Steve and the boys had gone home. Hugh had said good-night and returned to the cabin, Beth and Kevin had gone off together. The holiday was over. Fast-gathering clouds had moved in to block the moon and the smell of rain was heavy on the air. Faith hoped it wouldn't rain too much. Steve had wheat to combine in the coming days, and any delays now would damage the quality of the crop.

She slipped the baby monitor inside the pocket of her dress and stepped out under the trees. She heard footsteps on the gravel and moved deeper into the shadows of the big maple, her heart beating just a little too fast. There was little crime around Bartonsville, but she didn't want to encounter a stranger wandering in her yard in the middle of the night.

"It's me, Faith." Hugh's low voice came to her ears a moment before he stepped into the beam of the security light. "Beth left her CD player here this afternoon. She just called on her cell phone and asked if I would pick it up for her."

Was he having as much trouble falling asleep as she had? Is that why he was awake to answer the phone so late at night? "I saw it earlier on the picnic table. I put it in the greenhouse for safekeeping. I'll go get it."

"It can wait until morning if it's in a dry spot."

"It's not a problem. It will only take a moment to fetch it."

"I didn't mean to startle you."

"You didn't startle me. I just stepped outside for a breath of fresh air before I went to bed." She'd been out in the fresh air all day, and he knew it. Tonight the air was heavy with rain and the scent of new mown grass, making it hard to breathe.

"I'll come with you." He moved to her side as she walked toward the greenhouse, waited as she fumbled with the key and opened the lock. He leaned forward, his arm brushing hers, and pulled open the heavy door panel for her.

"Thank you."

She walked into the semidarkness. "Here it is," she said finding the small, flat oval of the CD player and headphones by touch more than sight.

"Thanks." He seemed to find conversation as difficult as she did. She wished he had never offered her a proposal that had started a chain reaction of impossible wants and wishes inside her. ''I'll let you get to bed.''

Bed. She would never share a bed with a man again. With this man. The thought saddened her.

''Would you like to see the butterfly house by moonlight?'' she asked, because she couldn't just let him walk away into the night.

''The moon isn't shining. In fact I think it's starting to rain,'' he said. She could barely see the smile that curved the corner of his mouth, but she could hear it in his voice.

''The security light performs the same service as the moon. It's just not as…romantic.'' There was no other word to finish the sentence. She hurried on. ''You've never seen my night-blooming flowers. Peg calls it my moon garden.''

He laid the CD player back down on the counter. ''Show me your moon garden, Faith.''

The air inside the butterfly house was warmer and heavier than outside, although not by many degrees. The scents of night-blooming jasmine and the pale, saucer-size globes of moonflowers perfumed the air. Chopin played softly in the background. She had forgotten to turn off the sound system when she'd closed up, it seemed. The gentle puff of air from the door stirred tendrils of her hair that had escaped from her combs.

One of the huge cecropia moths she'd raised sailed by in the dimness. Smaller moths, lunas and sphinx moths fluttered about the white blossoms enjoying the night.

They moved farther into the habitat, as silent as the winged occupants and stood beside the waterfall. The sound of moving water and the Chopin was counterpointed by the patter of raindrops on the glass roof.

"It's very different in here at night."

Faith nodded although she wasn't certain he could see the movement. "I come here sometimes when Caitlin's asleep just to sit and watch—" And dream a little, she'd almost said aloud.

"Beth told me she came inside with Caitlin before Lorraine Sheldon showed up this afternoon."

"Yes, but she didn't remember anything more." She wished she had been able to hold her tongue but the words had come spilling out.

"I didn't mention it to try to pry information from you, Faith."

She pushed her hands into the pockets of her dress to still their sudden trembling. "I haven't any to give you." She sighed. She couldn't help it. It would always be this way between them. United in silence, but for different reasons. "You're asking because you want to protect Beth."

"I want to protect all of you." He moved a step closer. Faith could feel the heat of his hard, sleek body through the thin fabric of her sundress. Was he going to kiss her again?

She wondered what it would be like to lift her hair from the nape of her neck and have Hugh lower the zipper of her dress. To let the straps slide from her shoulders, to turn and be held in his arms, taken into his bed. She knew, now, that the touch of his lips was as warm and firm as she'd imagined it to be.

"I've found you a lawyer, Faith. She's a friend of a friend. An expert in family law and custody battles. I want you to contact her first thing tomorrow morning."

She blinked in surprise. It was not what she had expected to hear him say. "A lawyer?" She hadn't taken that step herself, although Steve and Peg had urged her to do so. She knew she was hiding her head in the sand, but she couldn't help herself. It was like tempting fate to seek legal representation before she needed to. But, of course, after Lorraine's visit that afternoon she knew she could procrastinate no longer. "I...thank you. I'll consider it."

"Not consider it, Faith," he said exasperation edging his words. "You'll do it."

Her chin came up. "I will make my own decision on the matter." She couldn't give in to the powerful longing to let herself be protected by this man.

"You need to do it for Caitlin's sake."

"It's not in Beth's best interest for you to offer me a lawyer whose services you might need for yourself and your sister."

"Your having expert representation is in all our interests." He reached out and put his hand on her shoulder. "Take my advice on this, Faith, if that's the only thing you let me offer you."

"That's all I *can* accept from you."

He was silent for a moment and then he let his breath out in a low whistle. "Still, I'm going to ask for one thing more," he said. He was so near that if she leaned forward her breasts would brush against his chest.

"I...I have nothing else to give," she whispered. She could not give him her heart. She couldn't accept trust and give only silence in return. But the effort to hold herself aloof left her shaking inside and out.

"All I ask is this." He lowered his head, blocking out the moths, the raindrops drumming on the roof, the light filtering through the tree fern beside the waterfall.

She closed her eyes and waited for what she both dreaded and craved. She opened her mouth beneath the pressure of his. She wound her arms around his neck, let the small distance between them dissolve away. She remembered, after so many days and nights of feeling nothing at all, what it was to be a woman loved. The sudden hardening of her nipples beneath the thin lace of her bra, the slow, hot pooling of sensation deep inside her, the sudden overwhelming need for more.

He made a low, rough sound deep in his throat and smoothed his hands down her back, pressing to bring their lower bodies together. She felt his arousal against her belly, hard and insistent. Faith was dizzy. Would it be so wrong to let him make love to her amid the heavy warmth and heady scents of the butterfly house? They could give each other pleasure and comfort and for a little while, at least, forget the problems that awaited them beyond the glass walls.

Hugh lifted his head and broke the kiss so suddenly Faith felt as though her soul had been wrenched from her body.

"Hugh?"

He rested his forehead against hers. "This is going to get out of hand in another minute."

"I don't care," she whispered, obeying age-old feminine urging, not her brain. She swayed toward him once again.

The muscles in his arms knotted but he tightened his grip only fractionally. "You do care."

He was right, of course. God help them; their situation was complicated enough without adding unprotected sex to the equation. "I'm sorry," she whispered. Sorry for so many things, she meant to say, but not for the kiss. But she hesitated too long and the moment passed.

Hugh touched her swollen lips with the tip of his finger. He looked at her for a long, long moment and then said, "I'm falling in love with you, Faith. I have been, in bits and pieces, since we first met, I think."

She shook her head and the words she spoke seemed sharp and jagged to her ears, as sharp and jagged as the pain they caused her. "Don't you see that's why it will never work out between us, Hugh? Because that's all we can offer each other. Just bits and pieces of our hearts."

CHAPTER FIFTEEN

"IF YOU'RE A GOOD GIRL and stay right here on your swing, I promise Kevin and I will take you for ice cream at the Dairy Barn after you eat your dinner, okay?"

"Okay." Caitlin didn't look as if she planned to stay on her swing for very long, though. Even in the few weeks that she and Hugh had been living at Painted Lady Farm, Beth had noticed changes in Caitlin's behavior. She was growing more independent each day. Just a couple of mornings ago Faith had left her sleeping in her bed while she opened the screened panels on the butterfly house, a job that took maybe five minutes at most. But when she came back to the house Caitlin had awakened and come downstairs to fix herself breakfast. It had taken Faith and Beth—and Addy—fifteen minutes to clean up the spilled milk and cereal. Faith had said she didn't know whether to be angry or scared or proud that Caitlin could get the cereal out of the cupboard, a bowl and spoon from the dishwasher, and the milk out of the refrigerator all by herself. Beth suspected she was mostly proud, even if it was an awful mess to mop up.

Beth counted six cars in the parking lot by the barn. There were two or three women looking over the merchandise in the greenhouse, and a couple of bored-looking, middle-aged men watching as Steve Baden maneuvered a big, dual-wheeled, tractor out of the barn and down the lane to one of the fields that bordered the creek. She gave him a big wave as he rolled by, and he returned it with a wave and a friendly smile of his own. She wondered if he was going to bale hay today. Kevin helped some of the farmers around Bartonsville do that when he wasn't working his summer construction job.

She gave Caitlin one more push on her swing. "I'd better go see if I can help your mommy in the greenhouse," she told the little girl who was leaning precariously far back in the swing, watching the pattern of light and shadow in the leaves overhead. "You stay right here with Addy until Dana or I come back, okay?"

"Okay," Caitlin said, looking at her upside down from the swing.

Steve had dropped Dana off at the greenhouse just as Beth was setting out to walk down the lane from the cabin. Beth liked the teenager. She was bright and quick, and her smile was the friendliest Beth had ever encountered. She was a real help to Faith. Beth hoped she was, too, even if she didn't enter the butterfly house any more often than she had to.

The women who had been shopping in the gift aisle joined the two men outside, showing off their purchases. They all climbed into a big car and drove slowly up the lane to the road. Faith came to the doorway of the greenhouse and Beth waved.

"I'll be back in a minute, Kitty Cat," she repeated over her shoulder. "Stay right where you are."

"It's going to be a scorcher this morning," Faith said, fanning herself with her hand.

"Ninety degrees every day this week with a chance of thunderstorms in the afternoons."

Faith laughed, a warm rich sound that Beth loved to hear, but seldom did these days. "You're turning into a real country girl, listening to the weather report first thing every morning."

"I know. Who'd a' thunk it?" Beth laughed, too. "I'll water the herbs," she offered. "That way I can help keep an eye on Caitlin and you and Dana can do the tours of the butterfly house."

"Thanks, Beth," Faith said. She smiled but it didn't reach her eyes. They were sad and guarded. Beth would have blamed it all on the threats Lorraine Sheldon had made the week before, except Hugh wore the same expression these days. She wished Faith and her brother could find the same kind of happiness she was experiencing with Kevin, but so far it hadn't happened, and that made Beth sad, too.

"Glad to do it." And she was. She liked working with the plants, if not yet with the butterflies. She'd always figured she'd live in the city all her life. Now she wasn't so sure. Now she wanted a house with a garden and a yard where she could grow her own flowers and vegetables and herbs.

Maybe even a house in the country. In a little farming town. In Ohio...

Beth realized she'd been standing in the sun, staring at nothing in particular, for longer than a natural break in the conversation would warrant.

But it didn't matter because Faith was staring at something, too, and from the look on her face it didn't involve daydreams of houses and gardens and red-headed husbands to take care of them. The sound of a car approaching registered at the same time Beth saw dismay, and a flash of stark terror, sweep across Faith's expressive face.

Beth turned as quickly as she could manage, expecting to see Lorraine Sheldon's Lexus. But it was a county sheriff's cruiser coming down the lane. Thirty seconds later the patrol car pulled to a halt beside them and Deputy Gibson climbed from behind the wheel, an ominous and official-looking envelope in his hand.

"Good morning, Mrs. Carson," he said politely. "Miss Harden." He wasn't smiling and his expression was solemn.

"Good morning, Deputy." Faith's tone was even and equally polite, but she was rubbing her palm up and down her arm as though the steamy July morning had suddenly turned cold.

"I'm sorry to do this but I have the duty to serve you with this summons to civil court." He proffered the envelope, and Faith took it, breaking the seal with a fingernail. Her hand was shaking but that was the only sign of the inner turmoil she must be experiencing.

She scanned the pages and looked at Beth. "Lorraine and Harold are suing me to gain custody of Caitlin on their late son's behalf. The suit claims that Caitlin is their grandchild."

She should have been expecting this. She knew that Hugh had given Faith the name of a lawyer, but she didn't know if Faith had made an appointment to see the woman yet. She'd told herself it wasn't any of her business, but of course, it was and she should have asked Faith about it.

"What about me?" Beth heard herself ask the deputy in a voice that was almost as calm as Faith's, although inside she was shaking. She looked down at his empty hands. "Are they suing me, too?"

"I have no knowledge of that," the deputy said.

"Beth," Faith said gently. "Harold and Lorraine are claiming that you are Caitlin's mother. But that you are physically and emotionally unable to seek custody of her for yourself."

"That's not true." Beth couldn't help herself, the words came out high and breathless, making her sound just as weak and unstable as Lorraine and Harold claimed.

"That's for the court to decide, ma'am. I'll be going now. I'm sorry as I can be about all this, Mrs. Carson."

"You're only doing your job, Deputy."

From the corner of her eyes Beth saw another car turn down the lane. She shouldn't be surprised. It was July. People all over the country were on vacation. It was Faith's busiest season, but she wished the new visitors would turn around and drive away again. That everyone here today would go away and leave them alone to deal with this.

"I can give you some good news, Mrs. Carson." Deputy Gibson's expression softened a little around the edges. "The Indiana State Police informed our office yesterday that they see no grounds to reopen the case of Miss Harden's baby's disappearance with only the Sheldons' claims to go on. In light of that finding, our office has declined to look into the matter any further. I'm on my way to deliver that news to the Sheldons."

"Thank you." There was no relief in Faith's tone.

Beth didn't feel any, either, although she supposed she should. What good did it do to have one sword removed from over your head, when there was another one there?

"Good day." He got back into the car and left.

A couple of Faith's customers eyed the departing cruiser curiously but soon went back to perusing the shelves in the shop.

"I hope to God we never see that man again," Faith said in a voice so low that only Beth could hear. She straightened her spine just a little and smiled at the middle-aged couple and three small children, obviously their grandchildren, who got out of the car. "Hello," she said as brightly as though nothing at all in the world was wrong. "Welcome to Painted Lady Farm."

The rest of the afternoon passed by in kind of a blur for Beth. She watered plants, restocked shelves, ate lunch with Dana and Caitlin chattering away about what rides they were going to go on and what food they were going to eat at the upcoming county fair.

Beth did her best to enter into the spirit of their conversation, stoutly defending her choice of funnel cake over cinnamon candy apples as the very best food there was.

Storm clouds gathered on the horizon. Caitlin grew hot and fussy, begging to go swimming in the pond and becoming weepy when she lost her beloved Barbie for the third time that day. As the clouds thickened the butterflies grew less active, coming to rest on leaves and ledges, content to wait until morning for the sun to shine again.

The last customers pulled away as thunder rumbled low in the distance. Beth came out of the greenhouse after a fruitless search for Caitlin's lost doll, just as Steve drove into the barnyard on the tractor. He parked it in the barn and walked over to where Faith and Dana and Caitlin had joined Beth. He traded observations on the state of the weather, both he and Faith agreeing it would be just garden variety summer thunderstorms brewing, quick to blow through, but welcome, before he and Dana drove off in his pickup.

"Steve's going to hang up the Closed sign," Faith said, rubbing the back of her neck with her hand. Caitlin was holding on to her hand, her face tear-streaked. ''And I'm going to take Caitlin in for a short nap.''

''No nap,'' Caitlin whined. ''I'm not sleepy. I want Barbie to go swimming with me.''

''No swimming. It's going to rain,'' Faith said. She sounded tired. She looked frayed and distracted suddenly, and Beth realized what an effort it must have taken for her to appear upbeat and welcoming all afternoon long.

''Why don't you lie down with her?'' Beth suggested. ''I can lock up the cash drawer and close the screen panels before I go back to the cabin.''

''You don't have to do that.'' The words were automatic, good manners, nothing more.

''I know I don't have to. I want to. Please, Faith. Let me help you.''

She nodded, as though her mind were on other matters, and Beth knew what those matters were. The summons was sitting on the counter in Faith's kitchen. Beth had seen it when she took Caitlin inside to get a drink of juice a couple of hours ago. She'd been tempted to read it, to see her name spelled out in black and white, as a woman who was so fragile and unstable she couldn't be trusted with custody of her own child—if that child turned out to be Caitlin.

It was all so complicated. She wished Hugh were here to help her work through it. She wished Kevin were with her for the same reason.

Faith picked Caitlin up, holding her close as she walked slowly into the house without looking back.

As the door swung shut behind her, a van pulled

into the yard. Four adults and three children piled
out. "We've been driving around for half an hour
looking for this place," a large, red-faced man informed Beth. "We're on our way back to Michigan.
We came to see the butterflies."

"I'm sorry, we're closed," Beth said. Another low
rumble of thunder off in the west underscored her
words. "Butterflies don't fly much when it's
cloudy."

"We really would like to see them," the older of
the two women replied. A family group on vacation
Beth guessed, parents, kids, and grandma and
grandpa.

At that moment the sun broke from the clouds and
a large patch of blue sky grew with it. "Look," one
of the children said, pointing up. "The sun's shining
now."

Beth added up the admission charge for seven people and made her decision. There might as well be
some extra money in the cash drawer to make this
awful day a little less awful. And she had nothing
else to do until Hugh or Kevin came home except
fuss about what the Sheldons were trying to do to
Faith. "All right," she said. "None of our interpre-
tive guides are here right now, but I can let you go
through the butterfly house on your own if you are
careful to follow our rules."

It was over an hour later before the van and its
occupants left. Beth was hot and sticky and sorry
she'd given in to their demands. Not that they'd been
loud, or obnoxious or misbehaved, but the humidity

had been climbing steadily the whole time they were inside until the building felt like a sauna.

Beth locked the cash drawer and hid it between the two bags of mulch the way Faith had showed her, closed the screen panels and locked the greenhouse door. It was after five, the storm clouds had regrouped, and thunder sounded all around her.

She trudged across the yard and started up the lane, her leg aching more with each step. The barometer was falling in advance of the storm and she felt it in her bones. Oddly enough the ache now made her realize that it hadn't bothered her for days. She was getting stronger here at Painted Lady Farm. In body and in spirit. Lorraine and Harold Sheldon would learn that to their dismay, once she talked to Hugh and figured out how they would be able to help Faith fight the suit.

She did intend to help Faith. Caitlin was not her baby. She would know that, she repeated over and over in her mind, with each step she took. A mother would know her own child.

She caught a glimpse of Hugh's Blazer turning onto the road that ran along the edge of the farm before it disappeared down the rise. If she quickened her pace she'd arrive at the cabin just about the same time he did.

"Beth!" She spun on her heel. The note of anxiety in Faith's voice was impossible to ignore. "Beth, are you still here?"

"A vanload of people wanted to see the butterflies. I let them in...."

Faith brushed aside her explanation. "Is Caitlin with you?" she asked hopefully, hurrying across the front yard.

Beth shook her head. "No." Her throat closed and she couldn't say more. The terrified look on Faith's face was frightening her.

"Oh, God. I woke up and she was gone. I can't find her."

Beth felt goose bumps rise on her skin. Faith's eyes were big and dark with fear. "She's not in the house. I looked everywhere. I had such a headache. I lay down beside her and fell asleep. She must have gotten outside somehow."

"I didn't see her when I was in the greenhouse." Beth was looking, too, scanning the yard and the fields while she spoke, just as Faith was. The corn was high now, almost as tall as she was. If Caitlin had wandered into the cornfield it would be hard to find her. It might be impossible. Beth shuddered, refusing to imagine anything more.

Addy came around the side of the house and stood whimpering at Faith's heels, sensing her mistress's distress. "The pond," she said in a terrified whisper. "She wanted to go swimming. Oh, dear Lord, what if she's fallen in the pond?"

Hugh's Blazer pulled to a halt in front of the cabin. Beth was torn between following Faith as she ran toward the pond, Addy barking frantically beside her, or running toward the cabin to enlist her brother's help.

Her faith and trust in her brother won over the urge

to follow Faith. "Hugh! Hugh!" she called, jogging as quickly as she dared over the rough ground. He lifted one long arm in a wave and disappeared from view. Surely, he didn't think she was running and yelling for him in ninety-degree weather because she had nothing better to do? "Hugh, it's Caitlin."

She stopped a moment to catch her breath. She could see Faith running toward the deck that jutted out over the deepest part of the pond.

She looked as lost and frightened as Beth herself had for so many days and weeks. She needed a friend to comfort her, to help her in her frantic search. Once more Beth turned back toward the cabin. And what she saw made tears of relief fill her eyes.

Hugh was walking toward her, Caitlin balanced high on his shoulders, laughing, her little fingers clutched tight in his hair.

"Faith! Faith!" Beth hollered into the wind. She began jogging toward the pond, forgetting the heat and fatigue. "Faith! Look!" This time Faith heard her above the rising wind and the thunder. "It's Caitlin. Hugh found her."

Faith put her hand to her mouth as though to hold back a sob. Then she took two steps forward and sank to the ground.

HER LEGS SIMPLY refused to carry her any farther. Faith dropped to her knees and struggled to hold back tears. The surge of relief left her weak and trembling. Caitlin was safe. She wasn't going to find her floating facedown in the pond. Addy jumped onto her lap and licked her face. She closed her arms around the little dog and held her close, letting the panic drain from her.

Beth was talking animatedly to her brother. He bent slightly, nodding once or twice as she talked. Faith knew she was telling him of the day's events, of Caitlin going missing. Was it only five minutes ago? It seemed like five hours. She had never known such a hollow, empty feeling, not even when Mark had died. Not even when she'd lost the child they had made together.

That baby had been just a promise. Caitlin was flesh and blood.

"Caitlin." She held out her arms. She still didn't trust her wobbly legs to hold her weight.

Hugh swung Caitlin down from his broad shoulders and set her on the ground. Her daughter flew into her arms. "I went for a walk," she said proudly. "You were asleep."

"You shouldn't have done that, Kitty Cat," Faith scolded, but her heart wasn't in it. Later, when she wasn't so emotional they would discuss leaving the house on her own. Not now. Now she just wanted to hold her daughter and reassure herself she was safe and sound.

"Hugh find Barbie," Caitlin insisted. "I went to get Hugh."

He dropped to one knee beside Faith. It was the closest they had been in days. Faith took a breath and filled her nostrils with the spice of his aftershave and the scent of his skin. "I'll help you look for

Barbie, but you mustn't frighten your mommy that way any more. Promise.''

Caitlin narrowed her eyes and tilted her head, gauging the seriousness of his words. Hugh didn't blink, look for look. After a moment she nodded. ''Okay. I come with Mommy next time.''

Hugh shifted his gaze and his eyes held Faith's for a moment. They both knew she wouldn't be coming to the cabin, with or without Caitlin. It was Faith who looked away first.

Hugh stood up and reached down. ''C'mon, Kitty Cat. We'd better get inside and look for Barbie. It's going to come down in buckets in a few more minutes.''

Caitlin giggled. ''Like my sand bucket?''

''Even bigger,'' Hugh said, nodding solemnly.

''It doesn't rain buckets.''

''You're right,'' he said, lifting her high over his head so that she squealed with delight. ''My mistake. It's going to rain cats and dogs.''

Caitlin laughed even harder. Hugh settled her in the crook of his arm and reached down to offer Faith his hand. She steeled herself and let him help her stand. He let go of her hand immediately and Faith wished he hadn't. ''I can't believe she walked all the way to the cabins by herself,'' she said to hide the awkwardness of the moment.

''She was sitting on the step waiting for me. She said she came looking for me to help her find her lost Barbie.''

''She couldn't have been there more than a minute

or two,'' Beth said. Faith felt the shaking begin again. Even a minute or two was long enough for her to wander out onto the road, or into the pond. The new spurt of fear must have shown on her face. ''She's fine, Faith,'' Beth said, as though their positions were reversed, and for the moment they were. ''Put it out of your mind.'' There was a world of experience contained in the words.

''I'll try.''

So that was what Beth had been living with these past thirty months. The utter terror of not knowing where her child was. What had happened to her. When, or if, she would ever see her again. Faith's taste of that darkness had been mercifully brief. She hoped and prayed she'd never feel it again.

But she also knew she was going to have to tell Beth the truth about Caitlin's birth. That realization had come to her with blinding certainty when she saw Hugh walking toward her with her daughter safely perched on his broad shoulders. She had it in her power to ease some of the heartache that Beth felt.

Telling Beth everything that had happened that icy November day was the right thing to do. Hugh had known that from the beginning, had done his best to make her see it.

But where was she going to find the courage to speak the words aloud?

CHAPTER SIXTEEN

"HUGH LOOKED so right with Caitlin in his arms," Beth said. They were sitting outside the Golden Sheaf, waiting for the rainstorm to pass. The rain was coming down in buckets as her brother had told Caitlin it would, but according to Kevin, it wouldn't last long. "He loves her. I could see it in his eyes. He loves Faith, too. But I don't think she's in love with him."

"How can you tell?" Kevin had his knee propped against the steering wheel. His eyes were closed, his head resting against the back of the seat. Only their hands were touching, but that was enough contact to make Beth feel all warm inside.

"I don't know." She thought about it some more. "Maybe I'm wrong. Maybe it's not that she doesn't love him. It's that she can't let herself love him."

Kevin's hand tightened a little on hers. He opened his eyes and turned his head toward her. "Do you have a theory as to why?"

Beth sighed. "Caitlin, of course. She's afraid to love anyone who might take Caitlin away from her. Not that Hugh ever would. He doesn't think Caitlin is my daughter. He told me that and I believe him."

Her brain may have short-circuited the connection that would let her recognize her child on some instinctive level when she found her. But Hugh had had no such injury. If Caitlin was of his blood he would have told her so.

"Would you take Caitlin away from Faith?"

She looked out the rain-streaked car window. She wished she hadn't started this conversation. Her mouth was suddenly dry, and her heart had begun to race, not from passion, but from fear. Kevin had been so wonderful to her these past weeks. But she knew he wanted to take their relationship to another level. And not just a sexual one. Kevin wasn't that kind of guy.

"I think Caitlin's the sweetest little girl in the world."

"But…?"

"But I don't feel anything more special than that for her. I don't feel in my heart that she's mine." She'd told him everything else, but she couldn't tell him that she was afraid to let herself believe Caitlin was hers. Because if she did, circumstances might combine to give Caitlin to her. And she couldn't trust herself to raise a child on her own. Tears pricked behind her eyelids. She couldn't stop them. "The rain's letting up," she said hurriedly. The heavy downpour had given them the illusion of privacy. Now the sky was starting to clear, reminding her that the outside world would reappear at any moment. "Let's go inside and order. I promised we'd bring food back for supper. I'm starving. I'll bet you are, too.'' Hugh and Faith hadn't been thrilled by her offer when Kevin showed up a few minutes after Hugh had brought Caitlin back from her wanderings, but she'd made it anyway. Maybe if they spent a little time together things would be better between them.

Kevin made no move to exit the car. ''We need to talk, Beth. I need to know where you stand on this lawsuit the Sheldons are bringing against Faith.'' She had told him about Deputy Gibson's visit on the drive into town.

''I want Jamie's parents gone from my life. From Faith's life,'' she said, pulling her hand free from his. ''I'm not so damn fragile and unstable that I—''

''Couldn't take care of a child of your own?'' He reached out and tugged her hand back into his. Lightning flashed overhead, but it was nothing compared with the jolt of yearning that exploded inside Beth. Red-headed boys like Kevin, a little girl who looked like her to love and cherish. A dream she didn't deserve? Or her future?

''Kevin, please. Don't go there.''

''I need to go there,'' he said softly, but firmly. ''I want kids, someday, Beth. A whole houseful of kids.'' He lifted her hand to his mouth and brushed his lips across her knuckles, mindful of the diners in the Golden Sheaf who could see into the car. ''I want to make those kids and raise those kids with you. I love you, Beth. I want to marry you.''

''THE RAIN'S starting to let up,'' Faith said. She was standing in the breakfast alcove in her kitchen, watching as the fast-moving summer storm raced off across the fields. "Beth and Kevin will be back soon with the food. I'd better set the table. Would you like to eat in the dining room?"

She didn't turn to look at him as she spoke. Hugh had never been in her dining room. He hadn't even been inside her house since the first days after he'd arrived at Painted Lady Farm. "This is fine," he said, indicating the breakfast nook where he knew Faith and Caitlin ate most of their meals.

Caitlin was already seated at her little table, eating Froot Loops and jelly toast, with the faithful Addy standing watch at her side. Her long walk to the cabins had left her too hungry to wait for Beth and Kevin to return, she'd insisted. And from the way she was devouring cereal and toast Hugh had to believe she was telling the truth.

The silence lengthened. If he didn't do something soon, the distance between them would be too wide to ever breach. He took a step toward her, but she sensed his movement and turned, putting the table and chairs between them.

The large envelope containing the Sheldons' suit lay on the table. He touched it with the tip of his finger. "Did you take my advice and see the lawyer I recommended?" It wasn't what he wanted to say, or do. He wanted to take her in his arms and hold her close against his heart.

"She's on vacation. I have an appointment on

Thursday. It's the first day she'll be back in the office.''

"She's very good, Faith. She'll fight for you."

"Then perhaps you should retain her for yourself. To protect Beth's interests."

"I'll protect Beth," he said hearing the gruffness in his own voice. Could he protect his sister? Not from the legalities, but from all the lies that were piling up on each other? His uncertainty must have shown briefly on his face.

"How will you protect her from the pain of learning you've lied to her?" A last flicker of lightning on the horizon punctuated her words. The thunder that followed was low and far away, felt more than heard.

"She never needs to know."

Faith shook her head. She glanced at Caitlin, head bent over her cereal, absorbed in separating all the pink Froot Loops into one part of the bowl. "I can't let you do that. You'll hate yourself for it," she said very quietly. "She needs to know. I'm going to tell her."

"Faith—" He didn't know what to say next. He didn't want to say anything. He just wanted to comfort her.

"When Caitlin was lost…" She swallowed hard and pressed her fingers to her lips to still their trembling. "When I couldn't find her and I didn't know if she'd wandered off into a cornfield, or drowned in the pond, or been taken away by someone who had come to see the butterflies, I realized that I might never see her alive again. Before today, I thought I knew what sorrow was. But this was something more. Something much worse. I realized it's not knowing that withers your soul and leaves you only half alive. I care for Beth. I want her to be free of that terrible weight.''

Hugh had to swallow hard before he could speak. She was trusting him with her most closely guarded secret. "You're telling me that Caitlin is Beth's child.''

She nodded. Her hands clamped around the top of one of the high-backed kitchen chairs, until the knuckles whitened. ''Yes. I delivered her in the shelter in the park. Jamie panicked and drove away with Beth, leaving the baby in my arms. I read about the accident later. I'd thought they'd both died. I thought God had given me a miracle. I kept her for my own.'' Two tears ran down her cheeks. He couldn't stand it anymore. He moved to take her in his arms, but she held him off. ''No, Hugh. Don't, please.''

''I love you, Faith.'' He had promised not to speak of love again, but he couldn't help himself.

''I know. And I love you.'' She smiled and the pain beneath it tore at his heart. ''You said you'd fallen in love with me in bits and pieces. That's the way it was for me, too. And the last piece fell into place today when you came walking toward me with Caitlin on your shoulders.'' Once more he moved to take her in his arms, but she stepped out of his reach. ''I love you, Hugh. But you'll never hear me say it again.''

"Why?"

"Because after today, after I tell Beth the truth, your commitment will be to her. As mine will be to Caitlin. No love can survive that kind of conflicted loyalty."

The kitchen chair between them was the kind of tangible barrier he could deal with. He sidestepped it so quickly she couldn't move farther away and took her in his arms. "My loyalty isn't divided. It's to you, to all of you. We'll stand together against the Sheldons. I told you that before."

She swayed toward him for an instant, and in those few heartbeats he rejoiced because he thought he had won. But then she stiffened and pushed lightly against his chest with both hands. "You don't know what Beth will say or do when I tell her the truth. You can't promise me you'll never regret the words you've just spoken, or that I'll regret what I've confided to you."

"I—"

She touched her fingertip to his lips. "And I won't let you lie again."

The familiar sound of Kevin's rattletrap pulling into the yard came through the open screen door. Caitlin's head popped up. "Beth's back," she announced loudly, bouncing to her feet. "She's going to bring ice cream."

Faith dashed away the residue of her tears with the back of her hand. "Please, Hugh. Let me do this my own way. I want the timing to be right. I... It may take me a day or two to get up my courage."

He nodded, there was nothing else he could do.

"I need a moment to get myself together. Beth knows where everything is."

"We'll manage."

"Thanks." She left the room still wearing that sad little smile that tore at his heart.

"Hi, Beth." Caitlin pounced the moment Beth opened the screen. "Where's my ice cream?" she asked. Beth was standing just inside the door, empty-handed. And alone.

"I'm sorry, Kitty Cat. I forgot it." She looked down at her empty hands. She raised stricken eyes to his. "And your supper. I forgot that, too."

"I want ice cream," Caitlin pouted. "I'm telling my mommy. I want ice cream." She bounded away to find Faith.

"Oh, dear, now she's mad at me, too."

Hugh realized he had heard Kevin's Buick turn around and drive away as he talked to Faith. He looked closely at Beth's face. Were those raindrops or tears on her cheeks? She had gone to get food for all of them and returned empty-handed. Kevin had driven off as though the devil were on his tail. "What's wrong, Beth? Did you and Kevin have a fight?"

She gave a harsh little laugh, her mouth twisted into a mocking grin. "Worse than a fight. He asked me to marry him."

"You don't look like a newly engaged woman."

"I'm not engaged. I told him I couldn't marry him."

She looked so young and so lost standing there. But even though she was young in years, she was old in disappointment and heartache. He loved her so, and Faith was right. He had only made her pain worse by telling her he didn't believe Caitlin was her child. "Do you love Kevin?" he asked.

"Yes, but that's not enough." Her tone was tear-filled, but firm.

"Why? He knows about the baby. He obviously loves you enough that it makes no difference to him."

"It makes a difference to me. Don't you see, Hugh? Kevin wants a family someday. He loves kids. He's good with them. And I—I can't trust myself. I can't take the risk of having a baby until I know what happened to my little girl." Tears were running freely down her cheeks now, and she did nothing to wipe them away.

Hugh hated seeing her in such pain. He would do anything to take the pain away. But only Faith could do that.

"I can't marry Kevin until I know that I did no harm to my child." She wrapped her arms around her stomach, swaying a little, holding in her misery. "I can't remember." Her eyes flickered past him to the doorway where Faith stood, a still-pouting Caitlin in her arms.

Hugh sought her gaze. "It's time, Faith," he said.

She searched his face for a long, long moment, then closed her eyes, nodding slowly.

"It's time." Involuntarily her arms tightened

around the little girl. Tears glistened in her eyes but she blinked hard, holding them back. She looked past him to Beth. "You don't have to wonder what happened that day any more, Beth. I can tell you everything you want to know. You see, Beth, my daughter is your daughter, too."

SOMETIMES when you're given what you thought you wanted most, it turned out not to be the best thing after all. Beth laid a small bouquet of cornflowers, Queen Anne's lace and little yellow wildflowers whose name she didn't know, in front of Mark Carson's stone.

Caitlin had been told this man was her father. She pointed to his picture on the mantel in Faith's living room and called him Daddy. But what of Jamie, whose grave was in a Boston cemetery that Beth had never visited? Should Caitlin be told of him someday?

"And what about me?" Beth closed her mouth with a snap. She was talking out loud to herself again, something she hadn't done in a while. *What should Faith tell her about me?*

Faith had answered one question for her three nights ago, but in answering one, she had created so many more.

And knowing that Caitlin was her baby, alive and safe and happy, hadn't made everything right for Faith and Hugh. They tiptoed around each other as though they were walking on eggshells.

Hugh tiptoed around her, too, because she had

taken her frustration and unhappiness out on him when they were alone. He had lied to her about Caitlin, she had stormed in the privacy of their cabin. He had never done that before. Maybe she wouldn't have been so blindsided by Faith's confession if he had told her what he'd really believed.

It had been so overwhelming. She had not let herself believe that Caitlin was her daughter, because she'd never felt a mother's love for the little girl.

Faith hadn't changed the way she acted toward Beth. She didn't forbid Caitlin to spend time with her. But everything was different. In those first sweet moments she'd indulged her most private fantasy of sweeping her lost child into her arms and never letting her go. She hadn't acted on that fantasy, but Faith had read it in her eyes.

Until last night. Beth had been playing a matching game of shapes and colors with Caitlin on the picnic table as Faith closed up the butterfly house. Hugh was jogging. He wouldn't come back until dark, she knew, and then he would go straight to his room, avoiding being alone with her.

Caitlin was ready for bed. Beth had given her her bath for the first time. Her fine, silvery hair was in pigtails. She was wearing a sleeveless, petal-pink nightgown with ducklings and bunnies sprinkled over it, and her little bare feet peeked out from under the hem. Beth thought to herself, *Now I can go shopping for Caitlin and buy frilly pink nightgowns and even fuzzy bunny slipper to match if I want to. I'm her mother.*

Caitlin was jabbering away a mile a minute about how Addy was going to be in real trouble if she didn't quit chasing skunks. "Skunks," Caitlin informed her knowledgeably, "smell the worstest of anything in the whole world." She clamped her hand over her nose and squinched up her eyes. "P U," she said, fanning the air in front of her face.

"Caitlin, it's time for bed," Faith said coming through the gate. She didn't betray any of the pain she was surely feeling at the sight of Caitlin almost sitting in Beth's lap.

"Nope," Caitlin said, picking up a yellow square and placing it on the matching shape on the game board. "I stay with Beth."

"It's late, Kitty Cat. You'll be sleepy in the morning if you don't come to bed now." Faith sidestepped the child's demand. She didn't look directly at Beth anymore. It was as if she couldn't bear to see the same love she felt for Caitlin in Beth's eyes.

"Then sleep over with Beth." Caitlin hopped up and threw her arms around Beth's neck. It was so spontaneous, so right feeling that Beth had hugged her back, never wanting to let her go.

"It's all right. I'll take her to the cabin for a while."

"Sleep over," Caitlin insisted.

Caitlin slept over at Peg's house. She'd even stayed all night with Dana once or twice. Surely, it would be all right for her to stay at the cabin only a couple of hundred yards away. "Would it be all right if she stayed with me?" Beth asked. Faith's gaze

settled on a spot just past her left ear, or so it seemed.
She looked fragile, as though the sadness was growing so heavy within her that she could barely stand
up under its weight any longer. Beth wanted to reassure Faith, but the expression "little pitchers have
big ears" wasn't just some old-fashioned saying anymore. Caitlin was so quick and smart. She had already picked up on some of the tension swirling between the three grown-ups. Beth didn't want her to
become aware of any more.

"All right, but you must put your game away and
go potty." Faith's voice broke a little on the words.
Beth wanted to put her arm around Faith and tell her
everything would be all right. And it would be, but
for the moment, just this one night, she had wanted
to savor the wonder of her child sleeping in her arms.

Hugh was back from his run when they walked
into the cabin. He had frowned when she told him
with false brightness that Caitlin was going to sleep
over. "She's not used to being away from her
mother," he'd said carefully.

"I'm her mother," she'd shot back. Couldn't he
let her live out this one small dream?

"I know you are." He'd turned away and gone to
sit on the back stoop, looking out over the fields as
the lights came on in Faith's house.

She had taken Caitlin into her bedroom and let her
bounce on the bed, play with the stuffed animals
she'd picked up at the Fourth of July flea market,
and then curl up beside her and fall asleep.

Lying there beside her sleeping child she had tried

to come up with a way to solve this mess. But she was so distracted by the sound of Caitlin's breathing, the sweetness of her skin, she couldn't make her mind work. She gathered Caitlin's little body into her arms, snuggled close and closed her eyes.

When she woke it was full dark. Hugh was standing in the doorway, silhouetted against the light from the main room. He was still fully dressed, and Beth suspected he hadn't been able to sleep. Caitlin was sitting up in bed beside her, rubbing her eyes, sobbing.

"I heard her crying," he said quietly.

"What's wrong, Kitty Cat?" Beth asked hugging her close. "Did you have a bad dream?"

Caitlin snuggled against her, but didn't stop crying. "Bad lady got me. I'm scared. I want my mommy."

"I'm your mommy," Beth whispered, but the words were almost inaudible. She knew why she couldn't speak more loudly, or more convincingly. Because it was no longer the truth. She looked up and saw Hugh watching her. She swung her legs over the side of the bed and stood up, lifting Caitlin into her arms, walking carefully so that her weak leg didn't betray her.

Beth knew what she must do. It might not have been the decision she would have made three years ago, if Jamie had not forced her to do something else. But it was the right one to make now. "She had a bad dream and she wants her mommy." Her voice threatened to crack but she willed it firm. "If you loan me the keys to the Blazer I'll take her back to Faith."

CHAPTER SEVENTEEN

TEARS STILL welled in her eyes when Beth thought back to the moment she'd returned her child to the woman who'd raised her.

She'd made her decision, and she'd made her plans. Caitlin's nightmare about the "bad lady" reminded her that Lorraine and Harold must still be dealt with. But above all else she needed to talk to Kevin. He had told her when she realized she was strong enough to handle being his wife and the mother of his children he would be waiting.

She was strong enough. She had proven that to herself when she'd strapped Caitlin into the passenger seat of the Blazer and driven her back to the only mother she had ever known.

She needed to make things right with Kevin.

And her brother. For the past couple of minutes she had watched Hugh climb the hill toward her. He hadn't gone to the site today because he was worried about her, she knew. She had left the cabin before he was awake, not because she was still angry with him for lying to her, but because she needed time to make her plans.

That planning was done now and she was almost

as anxious to make amends with Hugh as she was Kevin.

"You've been up here a long time," he said, as he came toward her, hands in the back pocket of his jeans. "I thought I'd check and see if you were okay." He stayed a step or two away, uncertain of his welcome.

"I'm fine." She patted the stone bench she sat on. It was marble like the oldest headstones, rough with lichen and cool to the touch even though it was a warm afternoon. "I've had a lot to think about."

Hugh took her invitation as the peace offering she intended it to be and sat down beside her. He took off his sunglasses, blinking a little at the brightness. "Including what happened last night?"

She nodded. "I did the right thing," she said softly but with all the conviction she felt.

Hugh rested his forearms on his knees and let his sunglasses dangle from his fingertips. "I know you did." He was silent a moment. "I'm sorry I didn't tell you my suspicions about Caitlin from the beginning. I don't have any excuse except I love you and I didn't want to see you hurt again."

"I think what made me so angry is that you didn't think I could handle it." She blinked back tears. "You've always had faith in me, Hugh. Every day since I woke up after the accident, every step of the way."

"I won't underestimate you again." He reached over and covered her hand with his. "I promise, Beth. Never again."

She launched herself into his arms. "I love you, Hugh."

"I love you, Beth."

She let herself relax against his chest for a minute, then pushed herself upright, wiping away a tear that had somehow sneaked past her resolve not to cry.

"You're going to be fine," Hugh said quietly.

She smiled again. "I know. And I'm going to make it right for all of us."

"How do you intend to do that?"

She'd gone over and over it in her mind so the words just tumbled out. "I'm going back to the cabin to make some calls. Then I'm going to track down Kevin…and make my peace with him. If everything turns out the way I want it to I'll have Lorraine and Harold Sheldon back here in a couple of hours."

"What are you going to do then?"

"What's best for Caitlin. What's best for me." She hoped it was what would be best for Faith and Hugh, also. "I don't have time to explain the whole thing right now. But will you go down to the farm and warn Faith they'll be coming?" He frowned slightly but she didn't let his reluctance to be alone with Faith sway her from doing what she knew she had to. "I—I really want to find Kevin." She reached out and squeezed his hand. "Trust me, Hugh?"

"I trust you." His gaze was direct and unwavering. He reached in the pocket of his jeans and pulled out the keys to the Blazer. "I'm right behind you no matter what it is you have to do."

SHE TURNED into the junior high school just as summer school classes were letting out. She'd been so caught up in her own affairs, she'd forgotten Kevin was substituting for one of the other teachers this week. She'd driven past Peg and Steve's farm to see if he was baling hay, his parents' house, the contractor's where he helped out, looking for his car, before she remembered what he'd told her.

She drove the Blazer up behind Kevin's car and let the engine idle. She tapped her fingers on the steering wheel in cadence with her pounding heart. Now that she was here she was getting nervous. What if he'd changed his mind in the days they'd been apart? What if he'd realized he was taking on way more than he was comfortable carrying? What if—

"Hi, Beth."

She hadn't realized she'd closed her eyes until she heard his voice at her elbow. He was standing at the open window, wearing a green shirt that looked terrific on him.

"I've come back," she said quietly. "I...I've got my head on straight."

He skirted the hood of the truck and opened the door, climbing in beside her. "I've been waiting. And it's been the longest three days of my life."

She rushed into her speech before he could say anything else. "I...I don't know if I'm ready for marriage just yet. Maybe in a year or two. I want to get my degree—"

He smiled and held up a restraining hand. "I can wait. But I have to tell you we can't move in to-

gether. It's in my contract. No living in sin for Bartonsville Junior High science teachers.'' She knew
he wasn't serious, but it was a reminder they would
be living in a small town where everybody knew
each other's business.

She leaned over and gave him a quick peck on the
cheek. ''But we can have great sex in the back of
your car.''

He sucked in his breath and pulled her into his
arms. ''I love you, Beth.''

''I love you. And that's why I'm asking you not
to follow me home.''

He kissed her quick and hard and then settled back
against the passenger door, putting some distance between them. There were still students coming and
going from the school building, and they would be
quick to note the two of them sitting in the Blazer.

''Why not? I'm not sure, but I think we just got
engaged, or almost anyway. Aren't I supposed to ask
your brother's permission or something?''

''I think you're supposed to ask him first.''

He grinned, that sexy, wonderful grin she remembered from the very first time she met him. ''Better
late than never.''

''Kevin, there's something I have to tell you.''

''That Caitlin is your daughter.''

She supposed it should have surprised her that he
knew, but it didn't. ''You guessed, too?''

''She looks just like you. At least to me.''

She wasn't going to cry. She had made her decision. "She was born in the little park. Faith came along and delivered her. Then Jamie panicked and drove away leaving her behind with Faith."

"That's why that place bothers you so."

"Some unjumbled part of my brain remembered it, I guess." She sat quietly for a moment. No other memories came to her, and she realized they probably never would. She could live with the blank spots though, now that she knew what had happened. "I've made up my mind what I want to do about Caitlin's future, Kevin."

"Tell me." No long, drawn-out speeches or cautions from Kevin. She hadn't thought it was possible to love him more than she had a few minutes ago, but she did.

"I called the Sheldons. I told them to be at Painted Lady Farm in an hour. I don't want any more hard feelings. I want Lorraine to be at peace, too. She's not a bad woman, really. But if this doesn't work, if Lorraine and Harold don't agree to what I'm proposing, then I don't—"

"You don't want me to be involved. Is that it? Beth, I'm going to be your husband. And in less than a couple years, too. I want to be involved."

The certainty in his voice sent a thrill through her, but she did her best to ignore it. They had the rest of their lives to spend together. For the moment she had to stay focused. "I don't want to risk it. The Sheldons are already suing Faith. After today they'll probably sue me. Or worse, call in the police again. You might have to testify. You—"

"Might be tempted to lie under oath? I'll take the risk. We're a couple now. A team. And what involves you and Caitlin involves me."

He would be Caitlin's stepfather, a wonderful stepfather, if she claimed her daughter. But she wasn't going to claim Caitlin, and he deserved to be there when she told the others.

"I just wanted you to be safe if my plan doesn't work out." Her voice trembled in spite of her best efforts to keep it under control.

His smile was back and she felt as if the sun had come out from behind a dark cloud. "Don't worry. I don't think I'll ever have to contemplate perjury. My money's on you to KO the Sheldons in the first round. I wouldn't miss this fight for anything."

IF SHE COULD HAVE her dearest wish come true it would be for her life to stay as it was at this moment, Faith thought. The day was perfect. Warm, but not too hot. The sky was filled with clouds as white and puffy as the cotton candy the vendors would be selling at the county fair next week.

Caitlin was sitting at her little table behind the counter in the greenhouse, coloring a picture of a roly-poly puppy a bright magenta, chatting away to faithful Addy and two of her nearly naked Barbies. Occasionally she asked Hugh's opinion of a good color for the puppy's tail or dish.

He leaned his hip against the counter and pretended to study his choices.

Faith knew that there was something important he

wanted to tell her, otherwise he wouldn't have come to the greenhouse, but for the moment she didn't care what it was. She only wanted to see him with her daughter, and wonder for a moment what might have happened between them if she had never met Jamie and Beth.

She had just finished showing a vanload of seniors through the habitat and they were taking their time leaving the greenhouse. The ladies of the group looked through the gifts on display, cooed at Caitlin and petted Addy. It was almost twenty minutes later before the van pulled out of the driveway.

"Is there something you wanted to see me about?" she asked coming to stand by him at the counter. There were no more cars in the parking lot or pulling into the lane. Business had been steady all day and she was a little surprised by the sudden lull.

"There is," Hugh said quietly, dropping to the balls of his feet to add a couple of dancing butterflies to Caitlin's picture with a few deft strokes.

"Pretty," Caitlin said, holding up the coloring book for Faith to see. "Thanks, Hugh."

"You're welcome, Kitty Cat." He stood up. "I put the Closed sign out before I came down here."

"Why?" Faith felt her pulse begin to race.

"Beth asked me to."

She looked around. "Is she back? I've been worried about her. She's been gone all day."

"She's fine. She's the reason I'm here. She's contacting Harold and Lorraine, Faith. She wants them to meet us here. That's why I put the Closed sign out. I don't think we'll want customers around.''

''What is she going to tell them?'' She was going to side with Jamie's parents. She wanted Caitlin for herself. Faith felt the color drain from her face. She had feared this would happen ever since she'd told Beth the truth. For a few hours last night, after Beth had brought Caitlin home to her the fear had lessened, but now it was back full strength.

''It's going to be all—'' Hugh never had a chance to finish what he had been going to say. The Blazer turned into the lane and directly behind it was the Sheldons' Lexus.

''They're here. I—''

''Damn, they must have come the moment Beth called them. We didn't expect them for another hour or so.''

''I don't want to talk to them.'' She wasn't ready for another confrontation. She wasn't even scheduled to meet with the lawyer until the next day.

''Beth wants this all out in the open and settled.''

''I'm not ready for this.'' She tried to keep her voice level, ordinary for Caitlin's sake. She looked down. Caitlin was still absorbed in her coloring, her fair head bent over the page.

''Trust me, Faith. Trust Beth. She's made all the right choices the past few days.'' Hugh's voice was ordinary too, but when she looked into his eyes she saw the love he held for her.

Trust me. Faith closed her eyes against the surge of longing that almost sent her into his arms. Not now. Not yet, she told herself. She let the meaning of his words sink into her mind and her heart, let them comfort her. What he said was true. "She has come far since the day you brought her here, hasn't she?" She took a deep breath, let it out with a little whoosh. "I trust her. I trust you." It was the closest she could let herself come to telling him she loved him.

"I'll be there for both of you."

Faith turned to the doorway of the greenhouse as the Sheldons and Beth and Kevin entered. "Hello," she said, to Lorraine and Harold. "I believe Beth has brought us all here to tell us something important."

"I have," she said, looking pale but composed.

Caitlin had raised her head, checking out the group. She frowned at Harold and Lorraine but favored Kevin with one of her huge smiles. "Hi, Kevin."

"Hi, yourself," Kevin said. "I haven't seen the butterflies for a long time. Will you show me around?"

Faith gave Kevin a grateful smile. She didn't want Caitlin to witness what was about to be said. Caitlin took Kevin's hand and went into the habitat. The door closed behind them leaving the five adults standing in charged silence.

Beth folded her hands in front of her. Her knuckles were white beneath the skin, but she showed no other outward sign of nerves. She gave Faith a quick, encouraging nod. "I suppose I should start at the beginning.'' She turned to Harold and Lorraine. ''Caitlin is my baby.''

Lorraine gasped and dropped her face into her hands. ''I knew it,'' she said. ''I knew it.'' Harold put his arms around her shoulders, a smile on his face, but his eyes somber and watchful.

''I was in labor and we were lost. We stopped at that little park down the road from here. It was icy and cold, and I was scared to death. So was Jamie. I know all this because Faith told me. She delivered my baby.''

''And then she kept her!'' Lorraine burst out.

Faith wanted to cry out and defend herself. Hugh rested his hand, very lightly, on her hip. It was a simple gesture, but as meaningful as if he had taken her into his arms. She felt his strength and she stayed silent, allowing Beth to handle the situation in her own way.

''Yes, and I thank God she did. If she hadn't kept her, Caitlin would have died in that accident. We had no safety seat, nothing to protect her.''

''This is the proof we need to have her prosecuted. To get Caitlin back for you,'' Lorraine whispered.

''No,'' Beth said emphatically. ''That's only part of the story. I didn't give Caitlin to Faith. Faith kept her because Jamie panicked and drove away without her.''

''No.'' Lorraine lifted her face to Harold. ''That's not true. Our Jamie wouldn't do that.'' She turned beseeching eyes to Beth. ''You don't remember. You have only this woman's word for what happened that day, and the last thing she wants is for you to claim Caitlin as your own.''

"I may not remember," Beth said softly, but firmly. "But I know that's what happened. Jamie thought it would be faster if we traveled alone. He put me in the car and then he…" She faltered for a moment and lifted her hand to her mouth to stop her lips from trembling.

Faith stiffened. She wanted to go to Beth and comfort her. She remembered the look of anguish on her face that day, would never forget it. She hadn't wanted to leave her child behind. She had had no choice. Behind her she felt Hugh's hand tighten slightly. He knew what her impulse had been, was urging her not to act on it. Beth needed to handle this on her own.

"He asked Faith to keep her until we could come back for her and then…he drove away and left Faith standing in the storm holding our baby. That's why I don't like the park. That's why I never want to go there."

"It was November. There was ice and a storm, why do you dream of butterflies?" Harold asked.

"I was wearing a sweatshirt decorated with butterflies," Faith explained. "Beth focused on it so intently while she was delivering Caitlin that the images must have been so deeply imprinted that even the trauma she suffered couldn't entirely destroy them."

"So when Hugh learned about the butterflies he

started looking for the baby again. That's how he found you?''

''Yes.'' Faith looked at Harold and saw the sorrow of a lost child tempered by the realization that his grandchild was alive and well.

''No wonder the investigator we hired kept coming up blank. He didn't have the key to the puzzle.''

''We'll hire lawyers for you.'' Lorraine's expression showed no such bittersweet happiness, only a single-minded determination to prevail at any cost. She wiped away her tears with a manicured hand, heedless of what it was doing to her makeup. ''You must fight for custody.''

Beth took a deep breath. ''*We* won't hire a lawyer, Lorraine. *I* won't, either, unless you force me to. Faith has a lawyer. A very good lawyer.'' She tilted her head and gave Faith and Hugh a faint smile. Faith smiled back. They were united where Caitlin's future was concerned. Beth stood a little taller, lifted her chin as though ready to do battle for her child. ''She'll advise her on the best way to make everything legal. You see, I won't be seeking custody of Caitlin.'' She didn't falter. ''I gave birth to Caitlin, but I'm not her mother. Faith is.''

''You must fight for custody. Caitlin is all we have left.'' Lorraine looked from Beth to Faith, then frantically to her husband. ''She won't let us see her. You know in Ohio grandparents have no visitation rights. We must find some way—''

''That's enough, Lorraine.'' Harold gave her a gentle shake. ''We are not going to do anything more, do you understand? We will abide by whatever decision Beth and Faith make. I have lost my son. I may never hear that adorable child call me Grandpa, but by God, I will not live the rest of my days referred to as the husband of the Bad Lady.''

He took a step toward Beth and held out his hand. ''My wife and I would like very much to have some part in Caitlin's life. You have my word that there will be no more talk of police investigation or custody battles.''

Beth ignored his outstretched hand, instead she rose on tiptoe and gave him a kiss on the cheek. ''Jamie was trying to bring me back to Faith and the baby when he died. I believe that with all my heart. He was afraid. That's why he drove away. But we were coming back.''

''I know you were.'' His voice broke and he cleared his throat. ''I know.''

The air lock door opened and Caitlin bounced through two steps ahead of Kevin. She spun in a half circle, presenting her backside. ''No butterflies,'' she said proudly. ''Kevin hasn't got any on him, either.''

He went to Beth and took her in his arms. ''Are you okay?''

''I'm fine,'' she said, ''just fine.'' There were tears in her eyes but she was smiling.

''Mommy.'' Caitlin wrapped herself around Faith's legs and sent her a beseeching look. ''I'm starving,'' she moaned, eyes shut as though in abject misery. ''Cookie. I need a cookie.'' She was bent so far backward that her hair brushed the ground. Faith detached her clinging hands and held her so that she didn't topple over. Caitlin opened her eyes and stared at Lorraine. "Bad Lady, go away. Don't like you."

Lorraine's tears dried instantly. She dabbed at her eyes with Harold's handkerchief. "I'm not a bad lady, Caitlin."

"You make my mommy cry."

"She won't do it again," Harold said, going stiffly to one knee to be closer to Caitlin's height. She straightened up and turned around, her hands still in Faith's. "Are you a bad man?"

"No." Harold's eyes glistened but his voice was composed and friendly. "I'm a good man and so is my wife."

"Her?" Caitlin looked skeptical.

"Yes, her."

Caitlin looked him over from head to foot. "Do you have cookies?" she asked.

"Do you know something? I do have cookies. In my car. I hoped we might share them. Would you like to have some with me?"

He looked to Faith for permission. Once more she felt the pressure of Hugh's hand on her hip. Caitlin looked up at her. "Okay, Mommy?"

"Okay."

Harold dropped his head for a moment. "Thank you," he said when he'd composed himself.

Caitlin held out her hand as Harold rose stiffly to his feet. "My mommy says it's okay. What kind of cookies?"

"They're Oreos. My favorite."

"Me, too."

"I knew a little boy once who loved Oreo cookies."

"Boys stink," Caitlin said succinctly. She walked over to Lorraine, hand and hand with Harold. Faith had let her child go to Jamie's father without a single qualm because Hugh had been right. She could share Caitlin's love. Hugh had shown her that about herself as well. She turned to him, and he smiled, once more reading her mind.

"It's the right thing for all of us," he said very softly, for her ears alone.

"I know." She didn't add *I love you*. She didn't have to. He knew that as well.

Caitlin stopped in front of Lorraine and eyed her up and down. "She's not bad?"

Harold looked at his wife, reached up to wipe a tear from her cheek. "No, she's not bad at all."

Caitlin held out her hand. "Then you can have a cookie, too."

EPILOGUE

"HI THERE, beautiful ladies. Want a ride?" Hugh pulled the Blazer alongside Faith and Caitlin. She was pulling her daughter in her wagon down the gentle slope of the lane. Addy danced around her feet barking, but when Hugh spoke she stopped and wagged her tail. Caitlin was wearing a hooded purple jacket, and her nose was pink.

"No thanks, we'll walk." Faith's nose was pink, too, she suspected. It was unseasonably cold for the middle of October, and according to the weatherman there was no warm up in sight.

"I'm cold," Caitlin muttered. "Want to ride with Hugh."

"It's only a little farther. We'll have cookies and hot cocoa later to warm you up."

"Okay." Caitlin perked up at little at the promise of her favorite snack.

"What's going on at the cabin?" Hugh asked.

"Beth and Kevin are arguing over drapes," Faith informed him, rolling her eyes heavenward. "Beth found these fiberglass drapes at the church rummage sale. They're covered with ferns and cabbage roses. Vintage fifties. Truly awful. She's wild about them and insists Kevin hang them in his bedroom. Caitlin and I left them to argue by themselves.'' Kevin had become Faith's tenant the week before. The cabin was winterized and with the addition of two new baseboard heaters it would be comfortable in even the coldest weather. Kevin and Beth could have their privacy, but still maintain the proprieties until their wedding, now tentatively set for late spring. But Faith suspected that if Kevin had his way it would be much sooner.

Beth was enrolling in Wright State University in Dayton, a forty-five minute drive north on the interstate. She was considering a major in psychology, saying she'd undergone enough therapy in the past three years to qualify her for a degree already. Attending a few classes during the winter quarter would ease her back into academic life.

She had even reestablished contact with her father and stepmother in Boston, at least through e-mail. Trace Harden deserved to be told his granddaughter was alive, Beth told Faith, but a timetable for introducing him into Caitlin's life hadn't been set.

Hugh parked the Blazer behind Faith's van and met them in front of the greenhouse, now closed for the season. Steve and Hugh had helped drain the waterfalls and move the big tree ferns and other tropical plants into the chrysalis room where it would be easier to keep them alive over the winter.

She was back at work at the hospital. The news of her marriage to Hugh the second week in August was no longer the main topic of conversation around the nurses' desk, and she was glad for that. She smiled to herself. She had the feeling that something else about her life would soon take its place.

Hugh had met some of her friends and co-workers, who thought him wonderful. He'd gone to church with her and Caitlin, and to the Bartonsville football homecoming game with Steve. They'd been invited to Sunday dinner with Kevin's parents. He seemed to like life in small-town Ohio and had decided to stay on with the Cincinnati engineering firm. His next assignment was rebuilding a hundred-year-old bridge over the Ohio River, a project far more to his liking than constructing a shopping mall.

She had everything she had ever wanted from life, and more. She placed her hand on her still-flat stomach. She wasn't certain, hadn't taken a test or gone to the doctor. But she was sure she was pregnant. She felt her color rise and hoped the chill in the air would hide her blush.

Another love. Another child. Miracles both.

Caitlin climbed out of the wagon and ran to Hugh. "I need my Barbie," she said breathlessly as he lifted her high above his head. "She's in the greenhouse."

"I don't think so, Kitty Cat," Faith said. "You haven't played there in days."

"She has so many dolls I'm surprised she even notices when one is missing." Hugh rubbed noses with Caitlin to show he was only teasing.

"Believe me, she notices." Tonight when they were alone in her bed—their bed—she would tell

him about the baby. She wondered what he would
say. Would he think it was too soon? She watched
her husband, Caitlin secure in his arms, as he carried
her to the greenhouse, and her worries dissipated like
mist in the sunlight.

No, he would not think it too soon to add to their
family. Because they were a family. An unorthodox
one to be sure. Beth and Kevin would always be part
of Caitlin's life. Faith accepted that. Their children
would grow up side by side.

The lawyers were still deciding on the best course
of action to legitimize Faith's custody of Caitlin. It
was an unusual case they all agreed, each step must
be carefully evaluated before being taken. But in the
end they had no doubt Caitlin would be Faith's legally and forever.

And there was also Harold and Lorraine to deal
with. They had returned to Boston at the beginning
of October, but planned to be in Ohio for Thanksgiving.

"We might as well invite them to Thanksgiving
dinner," Peg had said upon hearing the news. She'd
been wearing an old sweatshirt of Steve's stretched
over her belly. "They are Caitlin's grandparents, after all. And every kid deserves grandparents. Especially rich grandparents." She grinned at Faith.

"I hadn't thought of that," she said.

"Well, I have."

So the invitation had gone out, with Beth's approval, and Kevin had volunteered to winterize one
of the smaller cabins for them to stay in.

Hugh had the door to the greenhouse open. He stepped inside and put Caitlin down so she could search her table and sandbox for the lost doll. Faith and Addy followed them inside.

He was standing before the monarch cage, watching something. Caitlin had found her Barbie beneath a sand bucket and was busy cleaning her up with a piece of paper towel she'd pulled off the role Faith kept under the counter. She moved to Hugh's side, and he reached out to put his arm around her waist. "What are you looking at?"

He pointed to the back of the cage. Two monarchs were perched on a wilting milkweed plant, slowing fanning their wings. "I didn't think you planned on hatching any more this year."

"I didn't. Obviously I overlooked a couple of chrysalides when we turned the last batch free." Monarchs were a migratory species. The last generation hatched each summer carried the instinct to make the long, dangerous journey to their winter breeding grounds in Mexico. Faith had released her butterflies a week before the current cold snap.

"These guys won't have a chance if you turn them loose now. It's supposed to get below freezing for the next three nights," Hugh said.

"I know. It's a shame. They'll feel the pull to fly south, but instead they'll have to live out their lives here." She could provide them with nectar substitute and the greenhouse would stay warm enough to keep them from freezing. Still, it was too bad they couldn't join the others on their journey.

Hugh turned her to face him. "What if we took them someplace warm and let them go? Aren't monarchs able to find their way back to where they came from no matter where you turn them loose?"

"We'd have to drive a couple of hundred miles to do that." Instinct would lead the butterflies unerringly back to their breeding ground, and their offspring would return to Bartonsville to begin the cycle again next spring.

"Actually, I was thinking of more than a couple of hundred miles." He was watching her closely, and as it always did, his nearness and the intensity of his eyes short-circuited her thought processes. It took a moment for the meaning behind his words to register. "How about a quick honeymoon in Texas? I need to get rid of my stuff. Besides, we've been married almost two months. It's time we had a few days to ourselves, damn it."

"Uh-oh. Bad word, Hugh." Caitlin's clear voice came from behind them.

Hugh's eyes widened in surprise. "Caught again," he said.

"She has ears like a bat," Faith said.

"I'll try to remember."

She looked over her shoulder at the two orange-and-black butterflies. Mark had loved them so. She did, too. Raising them was part of her life now. And she did want some time alone with her new husband. The house was big, Beth's room was at the other end of the hall, but still— "I'm not scheduled to work again until next week. I suppose I can ask Peg to watch Caitlin and Addy.''

''She doesn't need another dog and a not quite three-year-old underfoot. We could ask Beth to keep Caitlin.''

She swiveled her head to meet his eyes once more. He was waiting for her to answer, waiting to see if she was really at peace with Beth's involvement in Caitlin's life.

She smiled. ''I think that would be okay. She's so much stronger. And she has Kevin to back her up. I think they'll do fine.''

He pulled her close for a quick hard kiss. ''Turning these fellows loose where they have a chance to make it home is my way of saying thanks for their bringing me here to fall in love with you.''

''And I with you.''

Her heart felt as light and free as the butterflies they would be sending to find their home beneath the warm Mexican sun. She tightened her arms around his neck and kissed him back.

0208/25/MB129

— *Queens of Romance* —

An outstanding collection by international bestselling authors

1st February 2008   7th March 2008   4th April 2008

2nd May 2008   6th June 2008

One book published every month from February to November

Collect all 10 superb books!

www.millsandboon.co.uk

M&B

Queens of Romance

Ethan's Temptress Bride

Millionaire businessman Ethan Hayes thought Eve was
a spoilt little rich girl hell-bent on bringing men to their
knees but, after rescuing her one night, he found himself
posing as her fiancé, with her 24/7 and tempted
beyond even his control…

The Salvatore Marriage

For the sake of their tiny niece, Shannon Gilbraith is
reunited with Luca Salvatore, but she isn't prepared for the
searing attraction that reignites between them. Given all
the intense passion, anger and emotions they feel, how
can their marriage of convenience survive?

Available 4th April 2008

Collect all 10 superb books in the collection!

As the Battle of Britain rages over the Essex coast, two teenagers fall in love…

On the bleak family farm on the Essex marshlands, Annie Cross slaves all day for her cruel father. The one thing that keeps her going is her secret meetings with Tom Featherstone.

But war steals Tom from her when he joins the RAF. Annie would love to do her bit but, stuck on the farm, she lives for Tom's letters – until they stop coming.

When, against the odds, her beloved Tom returns, he finds a different, stronger Annie to the one he left behind. But he also finds the girl he loved is carrying another man's child…

Available from 21st March 2008

MIRA

MILLS & BOON
Romance

On sale 7th March 2008

Join Mills & Boon® Romance in the fairytale mountains of Europe, on the shimmering Italian coast, at a grand Australian estate and don't be late for an engagement in the boardroom!

A ROYAL MARRIAGE OF CONVENIENCE
by Marion Lennox

Duty must always come first for Prince Nikolai. But Australian country vet Rose, his convenient wife-to-be, is not quite what he was expecting...

THE ITALIAN TYCOON AND THE NANNY
by Rebecca Winters

In the first of this emotional **Mediterranean Dads** duet, Julie feels out of place in Massimo's palatial villa, but her biggest challenge is ignoring her attraction to the brooding tycoon...

PROMOTED: TO WIFE AND MOTHER *by Jessica Hart*

Career-girl Perdita's a whiz in the boardroom. But when she meets executive Ed, she wonders whether being a wife and mother would suit her better!

FALLING FOR THE REBEL HEIR *by Ally Blake*

Everyone says that opposites attract. Kendall likes safe and secure – and Hudson's got danger written all over him, but when he proposes a deal, Kendall's tempted to accept...

MILLS & BOON
Desire 2-in-1

On sale 15th February 2008

Thirty Day Affair *by Maureen Child*

Rich and gorgeous Nathan Barrister may have to stay in this town to fulfil the terms of a will, but that didn't mean he had to spend those thirty days alone…

The Prince's Mistress *by Day Leclaire*

When the soon-to-be king struck a deal to save his country, he wasn't prepared to fall for his mistress of convenience!

Expecting a Fortune *by Jan Colley*

This Fortune heiress must face the New Zealand millionaire she slept with months ago…and reveal he's about to be a father.

Fortune's Forbidden Woman *by Heidi Betts*

Can Creed Fortune risk his family's honour to fulfil his unrequited passion with the one woman he's forbidden to have? Can he control their dangerous attraction?

Mini-series – The Fortunes

The Millionaire's Seductive Revenge *by Maxine Sullivan*

When the boss, Brant Matthews, and his secretary, Kia Benton, are together will the chemistry between them be too strong to ignore?

The Tycoon's Hidden Heir *by Yvonne Lindsay*

Helena thought her secret was safe from the world. Then the father of her son stormed back into her life and stirred her deepest passions.